THE REDEEMABLE

HELL'S REDEMPTION: BOOK 1

GRACE MCGINTY

ALSO BY GRACE MCGINTY

Hell's Redemption Series

The Redeemable

The Unrepentant

The Fallen

The Azar Trilogy

Smoke and Smolder

Burn and Blaze

Rage and Ruin

Dark River Days Series

Newly Undead In Dark River

Stand Alone Novels and Novellas

Bright Lights From a Hurricane

The Last Note

The Castle of Carnal Desires

Treasure

Hunting Isla (Coming Soon)

ISBN:
Cover artwork by Natasha Williams
Cover by Everly Yours Covers

For my Mother.
I want to be you when I grow up.

THE REDEEMABLE

PART I

CHAPTER ONE

Today was a brittle day. My body felt like it would fall to pieces at any second, leaving me a gory mess of plasma and regrets on the pavement.

Almost home now, just hold your shit together, Ace said. Ace was complicated. Complicated in that she was merely a voice in my head. My calm voice of reason crossed with the attitude of the angst ridden preteen I'd been when I'd first heard her. Like an imaginary friend who bitched a lot, but had my back. The psych's said I'd developed her to cope with the traumas of my childhood and the combined blows of my parents' death. But despite the cocktails of drugs and therapy, she persisted, and deep down I was glad.

I pushed my way through the turnstiles and down the stairs to my subway platform. Groaning, I pressed my hands to my temples as I took in the scene. A fight had broken out, and the crowd had formed a circle around the dueling businessmen. This was New York, so fighting stockbrokers wasn't the weirdest thing I'd ever seen, but it was unusual enough to draw an audience.

I pushed my way around the crowd, desperate to make my train. The musty smell of the tunnel was gusting from the darkness, the silent harbinger of my train's imminent arrival. I edged way too close to the safety line, but there was no other way around the ring of spectators. People behind me jostled and shoved, and I plowed into the back of a man standing in front of me.

Despite the force of my meagre weight pushing into his back, the man didn't shift an inch. He didn't even turn, so I could politely ask him to move. Dammit.

He was huge and muscular, not someone I wanted to annoy, but he was in my way.

"Excuse me," I yelled over the shouts of the fight.

This time the man turned, and I took an unconscious step back. I took in his tense jaw, not-so-straight nose, and his flinty grey eyes. Small scars littered his face. His hair was shaved so close it may as well have been a five o'clock shadow to match his beard. It all added together to make him look rough and cruel. Plus, he was a behemoth, must have easily been six and a half feet. Those gray eyes stared down at me with an intensity that made my sluggish heart beat faster.

"What?" he said, the words soft, at odds with his hard expression. I pulled together the shreds of my dignity and tried to stop staring.

"Excuse me. This is my train and I can't get past you. Could you please move?" I gave him a polite smile as my headache began to thump.

"You have to be fucking kidding me. You?" He

looked over my head, towards the crowd watching the fight. "Ri, get the hell over here."

He still hadn't moved, and his eyes were back on my face.

"I'm sorry? Do I know you?" I was very sure I didn't. He wasn't someone you'd forget.

An equally large man joined him, but this one had caramel colored skin inked in dark black patterns from his neck down. Dark brown curls were cut close to his head and his eyes were the color of whiskey.

"Lux, what's up man? The fight was just getting good. One guy just hit the other with his briefcase." His voice was smooth and deep and his grin was guaranteed to melt the panties of any straight woman under a hundred.

"It's her," the behemoth said, and the new guy's face lost every trace of mirth as he looked down at me with the same intense expression as his friend.

"Are you sure?"

The behemoth placed a warm, gentle hand on my cheek, and I found it oddly comforting.

"Holy shit," the new guy muttered.

Snap the hell out of it, Arcadia. Random strangers are touching you in the subway. Do you not remember any of those after school specials we had to watch as a kid? This is not normal. Ace was beginning to sound very un-calm.

I moved my face away from the behemoth's outstretched hand as the whistle of the train echoed down the tunnel.

"That's my train. I really gotta go." I edged around the behemoth, but that just put me in front of the new guy, the one called Ri. The train blew its horn again and I could see its lights coming out of the tunnel over his shoulder as he moved to do the same thing as his friend. He reached up and put a hand on my cheek, his full pink lips parted as he just stared down at me, mute.

From what I can piece together, several things then happened at once. My heart began to thunder in my chest until the edges of my vision began to blur, and I could hear Ace yelling in my head to stay upright until I was on the train, but her yelling was only making my head thump more. Simultaneously to this small problem, the fight had shifted closer to me, and I turned at the last moment to see a briefcase connect with a face in a spray of blood, and the overly soft body of an office worker lurched toward me. As the office worker connected with me and my body toppled sideways towards the track, I remember thinking only one thing as the darkness replaced the bright lights of the train. There were worse ways to die.

I WOKE up on a leather couch that wasn't my own, a set of light blue eyes staring down at me from a chair placed beside it. My brain was foggy, but Ace was loud and clear.

You've been abducted. How the hell did we end up here? She sounded worried, but I just couldn't summon the energy to care.

"I need my meds." My voice was rough. The man beside me held up my pill bottle and a glass of water, helping me to ease into a sitting position. I realized there were more people in the room with us. Five more men to be exact.

Shit. You are about to become a late night repeat of America's Worst Crimes.

I scooted away from the man, and perched on the edge of the couch. I shook out a couple of pills from the bottle and dry swallowed them. They could've put anything in the water.

"What am I doing here? Where am I?"

"You passed out in the subway. If Lux hadn't grabbed you when he did, you'd probably be dead. When they realized you wouldn't wake up, they brought you back here to me. I'm Dr Elias August. These guys call me Eli."

I finally noticed the stethoscope around his neck as he pulled it on and placed the end on my back. I took a deep breath out of reflex.

Great, a doctor. At least the cops will be able to appreciate the mark of a professional when they find your dismembered body in a dumpster.

"I'm Arcadia. Everyone calls me Cady. Who are those guys?" My voice was barely a squeak. So far the other people in the space had just been standing quietly at the edges of the room, staring at me with an intensity that was both confusing and a little scary.

"We'll get to them in a second. Don't worry, they are completely harmless to you." He placed the stethoscope on my chest. "Any pain?"

"No more than normal."

"Diagnosis?"

"Severe dilated cardiomyopathy."

"You're on the transplant list?"

I shook my head sadly. No matter how many times I repeated this bit, it was never any less of a blow to my soul.

"I'm in remission for Hodgkin's Lymphoma. The transplant board said no."

Eli placed his hands on his thighs, his fingers curling under and flexing hard. He had nice thighs.

A totally inappropriate thought to be having right now, in this situation, Ace groused.

"So you are dying?" Eli sounded stoic and professional, but someone else in the room sucked in a breath as if they'd been sucker punched.

"Essentially, yes. But hey, at least it wasn't today!"

"You can't be any more than eighteen." Eli shook his head.

"Twenty actually. I have a baby face." I gave him a tight smile and stood. "I better be heading home. Thank you for doctoring me," I said to Eli, and turned to find behemoth, or Lux I guess his name was. "Thanks for saving me." He was even better looking in this moment, his face less harsh now he wasn't under the fluorescent lights of the subway. I gave myself a few seconds to really drink him in.

"Didn't really save you, did I?" His voice was still a scary low growl though.

I shrugged. I knew the look he was giving me all too well. I'd seen it far too many times in my life. Frustrated hopelessness.

"You can't save them all, right?" I walked around

Eli's chair towards the door. "Can someone point me to the nearest bus stop?"

Lux said something to Eli in a language I didn't understand and had never even heard before. "What language is that?"

"Latin," a voice said from somewhere in the room. I peeked around the couch to find another guy lying on the ground behind the backrest, like a lost dollar. He had a full red beard, long hair that was tied in a messy bun on top of his head, and a red checkered shirt. He looked like a sexy lumberjack. His hands were linked behind his head and he was grinning at me without the intensity of the rest of the room's occupants.

I raised an eyebrow. "Who speaks latin, anyway?"

"Rich private school kids and those two. Definitely not me. I barely speak English with any kind of fluency. I'm Oz by the way."

"Cady."

"You're cute. Kinda like a pixie."

"Uh, you too?"

Eli and Lux finished arguing in latin, and Eli turned toward me. "Lux will drive you home. Is there someone there to take care of you? Parents? A boyfriend? A roommate?"

"Uh, no. My parents are both dead. But my friend calls me every day to check on me. She'll know if I'm missing."

Great save, Arcadia. Smooth. Let's not tell them that she's actually working in Somalia right now, nursing orphans or some shit.

Lux smothered a smirk, and Oz openly laughed from his spot on the floor.

"I understand, but I'm worried that if you have another episode like the last one, you may fall and hurt yourself. Would you perhaps think of staying here until you are well? We have a big house and I promise you'll be completely safe. We would be overjoyed to have you."

Fuck no.

My automatic response was no too. They were strangers, and I was being reassured that they are good people by another stranger. Besides, I would never be well again. No was the right answer.

The only answer!

But I looked around and instead of feeling scared to be in a room of guys, I felt a level of comfort that was just bizarre. Earnest reassurance came off them in waves, and I I really wanted to say yes. I had two years left in my life, did I really want to spend them home alone watching HBO? Maybe I wanted to take this chance?

Have you gone mental? How are you even contemplating this? You might only have two years, but the wrong choice could make chemo seem like a resort spa. Haven't you ever seen the Saw movies? Ace was outraged in my mind, but lucky for me she was just a voice.

Seeing me so obviously vacillating, Eli came to my rescue.

"You don't have to make your decision now. Stay for dinner, Valery is a three hat chef. He's making something extravagant, I'm sure. No one else is allowed in the kitchen." He turned to look at a man who was leaning against the doorjamb. He was shorter than the other men in the room, but still inches taller than me. He had floppy blonde hair and a smile that made his eyes crinkle at the corners.

"Unfortunately, I was only making mac and cheese," he replied. His voice had a slight accent that I couldn't place.

Oz scoffed. "Mac and cheese with blue cheese and some other fancy shit. Not like you poured it out of a box, Val."

Valery smiled wider, dimples creasing his cheeks. He was very cute. Actually, they were all kind of hot. So weird.

I smiled back at him. "I'd love to stay for dinner. Thank you." They did save my life. It would be rude to turn down their dinner invitation.

How have you even survived this long?

Valery looked like all his Christmases had come at once. "Excellent. I shall be in the kitchen," he said and left, muttering to himself about bread and maybe pick-les? His accent made him sound like he was saying 'keeshun' and it was adorable. Maybe French?

I took a better look around the room. There was a massive flat screen TV in the center of one wall, and the leather sectional sofa was positioned around it. A glass bookcase held a small collection of books, some very old judging by the cracked leather spines. Everything tastefully minimalist in muted tones of silver and navy. It was definitely a bachelor pad. There wasn't a throw pillow in the place.

"Please, sit. Everyone can stop loitering around

now," Eli said, and everyone converged toward to the sofa. "Oz, put on some music please." I leaned over the back of the couch to see Oz hadn't moved from his comfortable position.

"You aren't coming up here?" There was something about Oz that made me want to tease him.

"Nope, but you can always come and join me down here." He gave me a wink and I blushed. It didn't help that I could see a small strip of his flat stomach where his shirt had ridden up. "Mini-Oz, play 'Pretty Girl Dinner Party' playlist," he yelled at nothing, but sure enough, the sound of Frank Sinatra started to pour softly into the room from hidden speakers.

"That is seriously amazing."

"Voice controlled home management system. The pinnacle of technological laziness." He grinned widely at me and I grinned back.

"Well, I'm impressed."

"You shouldn't encourage him," a soft voice said from beside me. I whipped around to see the most beautiful man I'd ever laid eyes on sitting mere inches away on the couch beside me. He must have been hiding in a dark corner or something, because I definitely would have been dumbstruck before now. Thankfully the guy ignored my unhinged jaw and continued. "He's hidden the remotes, so now the channel can only change on the TV if he says so. It's super annoying."

I could only nod as I took in the man's midnight blue eyes, high cheek bones and ash blonde hair. He looked like a Scandinavian super model.

"I'm Sam," he held out one huge hand. I took it,

and tried not to sigh contentedly as its strong, soft warmth enveloped by own.

"Cady, nice to meet you."

"The pleasure is all mine. I wanted to introduce myself before I had to head out to take Ri to work." He nodded toward the pretty guy from the subway station with the golden skin and the tattoos. And the voice like raw sex.

I gave Ri a little wave, and he smirked back. "Nice to see you with some color in your cheeks, Beautiful Girl. You scared the hell out of me back there."

"I'm sorry," I said, meaning it.

He gave me a sad smile. "Me too."

He picked up a leather jacket from the back of the couch and threw it over a black jeans and tight grey shirt combo that sculpted his body like a liquid. My mouth physically watered.

"Well, I better get to work, I'm already late. But if I turn up with the great Sam Sigurdsson, they'll forgive me once the pictures start hitting Instagram and Twitter. Free press."

Sam Sigurdsson. The name rang a bell. Hang on. "Oh my goodness. You're the Calvin Klein model from the side of the bus."

They all laughed, and someone muttered something about five foot junk.

"Hopefully you're still here when we get home. But if not, I hope to see you again soon. Take good care of yourself." Sam took my hand in his and kissed it. I forgot to breathe. Ri winked as he followed Sam out the door.

Now Sam had left, I could see the person sitting on

the couch beside him. My mouth swung open again. "You're the Armani suit guy from the Times Square billboard. What the hell is this place? Mecca for models?"

Oz man-giggled from behind the couch.

The Armani model slid his perfectly proportioned body up the couch toward me. His face showed signs of a mixed heritage, but I couldn't guess what. He had beautiful golden skin, not quite as dark as Ri, a smooth square jaw and almond shaped eyes.

"Tolliver. Nice to finally meet you."

Odd choice of words, but then he smiled and I was distracted by the shiny white perfection of his teeth.

"Hi," I squeaked. "Aren't there any trolls amongst you at all?"

"Comparisons have been made between Oz and Bigfoot." Tolliver sounded amused, but he didn't crack a smile. "Would you like a tour of the mansion?"

"Wait, mansion?

CHAPTER TWO

Apparently, I was being invited to live in SoHo, on my own floor of an apartment building owned by these guys. These seriously mouthwatering guys.

I'm pretty sure you are dead and this is just your version of heaven.

Somewhere around the gilded marble bathroom the size of my apartment, Ace had gotten over her general distrust of the guys and was enthusiastically in favor of moving into this place. Well actually, I'd be moving into the pool house, which was basically a full apartment on the floor below the rooftop pool.

From what I could gather, they were all friends, though they were sketchy about how they met. Whatever. Maybe they all met at Hooters.

They left me to explore the pool house, and I discovered it has a galley kitchen, a walk in wardrobe, a flat screen TV and a king size bed. And that bathroom! It was bigger than the kitchen and living room combined in my current apartment. I walked up the stairs that were just outside the front door, and onto the rooftop.

The rooftop had been professionally landscaped, and there was a full herb garden and patio sized lemon and lime trees. A wide deck hugged the edges of the lap pool. I smoothed down the back of my dress and sat on the edge. I dipped my toes into the cool water, watching the summer sun set over the city.

Would it be crazy to live here? To live with strangers?

Yes, but I was probably going to do it anyway. The door locked and my medical bills were crippling. I was eating ramen noodles and was three months behind on my rent in my apartment. When I'd asked Tolliver how much the rent here would be, he'd made a slightly disgusted noise and insisted there would be no need to pay rent. They were all loaded. Eli was an elite neuro-surgeon. Tolliver and Sam were both highly paid models who flew all over the world together. Lux was a champion UFC fighter and Valery owned a famous restaurant in Brooklyn. I wasn't sure what Oz did except fill out his Levi's like a boss.

Someone cleared their throat and I turned. Lux stood behind me, wearing loose sweats that hung so low on his hips that I was literally praying he'd step on the hems and I'd get an eyeful. His T-shirt had the name of some martial arts Dojo in the Bronx. I couldn't tear my eyes away from his chesticles.

You need to get laid. Ace wasn't wrong.

"Val said dinner is ready if you'd like to join us? We try and all sit down together at night, whoever in the house that is. Sometimes there's no one here except Oz, depending on our schedules."

It was the most I'd ever heard him talk, and I was again shocked by how gentle his voice was, although it was rough. It felt like I've water over heated skin. Delicious but shocking. He spoke quietly and with a kind of hesitancy that made me think he was worried I'd spook and hightail it out of here.

Ha, no chance. At this rate they'd have to pry me out of here with a crowbar.

"I'd love to." I stood a little too fast and wobbled dizzily. Lux grabbed for my arm, steadying me again.

"Sorry. Dizziness is a side effect of pretty much everything." Lux still hadn't let go of my arm, and the aura of comfort I'd felt back at on the subway platform enveloped me again. I stared up into his luminescent grey eyes, and held my breath.

Lux shook his head and stepped back, letting me walk past him toward the door to the lower floor. Although he didn't touch me again, I could feel the warmth of his hand hovering just above the flesh of my lower back, ready to catch me again if I needed it.

We rode down to first floor, which was apparently Valery's apartment. The couch I'd woken up on had been in Eli's apartment on the fourth floor.

The smell of cheese and butter met me in the doorway and I followed the delicious smell into the kitchen. And then I stopped dead.

It wasn't just a kitchen. It was the kitchen of my dreams. An industrial oven and cook top. Double-door Smeg fridge with built in touch screen. Stainless steel benches with copper bottom pots hanging from the pot rack above the island bench.

"I think Cady just had a big O, and it was Val's kitchen that got the honor," Oz laughed from where he was setting the table in the formal dining room.

Lux whacked him over the back of the head. "Be respectful."

Oz just smirked at me, completely unrepentant. My face was flaming.

Lux pulled out a chair for me in the middle of the table, and I sat down. The table was a long farmhouse style. A small vase of daisies sat in the center. It was shabby chic in the middle of upper-class SoHo. I was interested to see who sat at the head of the table in this household of large men with, from what I'd seen so far, large egos.

Oz plopped in the chair to my left and Tolliver sat directly opposite me. I was unsurprised when Eli and Lux took either end of the table. That left a spot for Valery, who was carrying in a huge casserole dish of mac and cheese. He placed it on the table in front of me, then returned with a bowl of steamed greens and chicken mignon's piled high on a serving plate.

"Sorry it isn't anything too fancy. Next time I will plan better," Val apologized, and I had the urge to lean over the delicious food and hug him for his thoughtfulness.

"This looks amazing. Seriously, I was going to go home and eat cheerios out of the box for dinner."

Valery clicked his tongue against his teeth disapprovingly. "No more. From now on you eat with us, no?" His eyes twinkled as he passed the bread rolls to Tolliver.

"Arcadia hasn't chosen to live here with us yet, Val. No pressuring her," Eli admonished, but there was a hopefulness in his eyes that I didn't really understand. It was almost as if they wanted me to live here with them.

Oz broke the silence before it got awkward. "Oops, forgot dinner music. Mini-Oz, play 'Dinner party music to impress a pretty girl' playlist."

I laughed as light piano music played in the room.

"Do you have a playlist for every occasion?"

"Almost every occasion, I think." He passed me the greens. "I'm still working on one for the apocalypse."

Finally my plate was loaded and I was staring down at my food like it was sent from the heavens. I couldn't even remember when I ate anything that even smelled as good as this did. With rent and medical bills, I didn't have a lot of money left for non-essentials like food, so I ate mostly grilled cheese sandwiches and cereal. I once experimented with combining the two for variety, but it wasn't a good outcome.

Unusually, both Valery and Oz ate with single minded focus, ignoring the table conversation and their fellow diners. I could understand it. My first bite of Valery's mac and cheese was basically a biblical experience. Luckily, my other three dinner companions were happy to pick up the conversational slack.

"What kind of work do you do?" Eli asked as he sipped his wine.

"I work for a temp agency, mostly administration stuff. It isn't overly exciting but it pays the bills. Well, most of them anyway. I'm not anyone's idea of a perfect employee candidate." I cleared my throat awkwardly. "So Lux, when is your next match? Game? Fight thing?"

A small smile curled his lips, and there was something about his hooded eyes and that sexy ass smirk that went straight to my ovaries. "It's called a fight. The next event is in twelve days. You should come. A couple of the guys always come to watch, I'm sure they'd be happy to bring you along?"

He looked at Tolliver.

"Unfortunately, Sam and I are in London for Fashion Week." He actually sounded regretful to be flying to the other side of the world to attend glamorous parties and wear beautiful clothes in lieu of watching two grown shirtless men beat the hell out of each other. I surreptitiously perved on Lux out of the corner of my eye. Yeah, it'd be a tough choice for me too.

"I'll bring her," Oz said through a mouthful of food. Tolliver's brows rose high, and even Eli looked surprised.

"You never go to these things," Valery said, and I couldn't work out if it was a statement or an accusation.

Oz gave me the weirdest look before taking another mouthful and answering. "What can I say, I'm feeling more energized."

"Have you been sick?" He looked healthy as any six and a half foot man with full ginger beard and shoulders the size of a Mack truck could look.

"You could say that, I guess. But nothing for you to stress about." He hooked an arm around my shoulders and gave me a quick side hug that felt way too nice and was over way too quickly.

I needed to go home so I could separate my hormones from my sense of rationality, though apparently my rationality had abandoned me in my hour of need. What was the point of an imaginary voice in your head if she let you do crazy things because of a few hot guys and a pretty house?

Seven hot guys, Arcadia. And there is a rooftop hot tub by the pool. A hot tub! Ace was beginning to sound a little unhinged, which was never a good sign.

We finished off the main, and I helped Valery clear off the plates, much to everyone's protests. But I stubbornly persisted. I'd been raised right, for the most part anyway.

Your parents would die all over again if they knew you were considering moving in with seven men who are almost complete strangers.

I cringed and ignored Ace. She wasn't wrong though. They would be horrified.

Carrying the dirty plates into Valery's kitchen, I rinsed them and placed them in the state of the art dishwasher.

"I have some serious kitchen envy right now."

Val laughed, "You are welcome to come down and use it at any time. The pantry is always fully stocked," he said, pulling a tray of ramekins from the oven. Each one contained the perfect chocolate soufflé.

He transferred the dishes to a tray quickly. "Grab the chocolate sauce from the warming rack and the clotted cream from the fridge." I hustled to do as he said, though my eyes never left those light chocolate creations.

Ever since I was a kid, I loved food. I guess it was probably because my parents were a little older and very well off when they had me, and they basically treated me like a third adult. We went to fancy restaurants and the opera and other places that don't typically see a lot of four year olds. That slowed of course when I got cancer at twelve and stopped altogether when my parents died when I was sixteen.

But those years eating in the finest dining establishments had given me a lifelong love of good food.

"We should tell her. We don't have much time," Tolliver whisper-shouted, as I rounded the corner into the dining room.

"Tell me what?"

Ah dammit, I knew it was too good to be true! Ace pouted.

When I was met with only silence, I asked again. "Tell me what?"

Predictably it was Eli that answered. I was beginning to sense he was unofficial leader of this strange collective. "There are some small details you should know about us, but I'd prefer not to say until Sam and Ri get back. Lux is texting them now."

I edged toward the door. "Shit, Ace was right about this. You guys are serial killers or something."

"Ace?" He was on his feet, walking slowly towards me.

Argh, I was getting frazzled and everything was starting to slip. "Never mind. I'd like to go home now." Although I did throw one last longing look at the soufflé. Until we meet again, Soufflé.

"Of course, Lux will drive you home, if that's what you wish. But I beg you to stay until we can explain everything. I swear on my Hippocratic oath that we would never do anything to harm you in any way." Eli seemed so earnest and sincere, I found myself wavering and he could see it. "After the other guys get here and we tell you our story, if you still want to go home, we will put you in a cab and you will never have to see any of us again."

I bit my lip hard, torn and confused by his sincerity. So I did something I hadn't done in years. I asked Ace for advice.

Oh she talked to me a lot over the years, handing out unsolicited advice and opinions like candy on Halloween, but I hadn't spoken back to her since I was eighteen and onto my fifth psychiatrist.

Do you think I can trust these guys? I asked, and I could sense Ace's shock and surprise. Or was it my shock and surprise? See, this is why I stopped talking to the voice in my head.

I think so. There is something about them that feels, I don't know, like home? Familiar even. They haven't done anything untoward except feed you and offer you a place to live, which sounds suss but may be completely altruistic. If they wanted to do anything awful, just Lux could have tied you up and killed you by now, burying your body in a drum in the basement and who would ever know?

I screwed up my nose. *Thanks for the visual, Ace.*

I tuned back into the room to see Eli looking at me like I was an enigma he couldn't quite figure out. Welcome to the club, buddy.

"Fine. I'll wait and hear you out. But I want to go home after that."

"Done." Eli placed a hand on my elbow and led me back to the table. "Please sit."

Valery placed a ramekin on a small plate in front of me. He held the chocolate sauce above the plate, pouring it from the jug in a long steady stream of chocolatey goodness.

If they murder me, I hope someone put on my headstone, 'Died for the world's most perfect soufflé.'

Ace snorted. *Consider it done.*

We ate in silence, just the sound of Oz's playlist and the tinkling of cutlery echoing around the room. I was just scraping the chocolate from the bottom of my bowl when the door opened and Sam and Ri walked in.

Ri gave me a big smile, his dimples and white straight teeth practically blinding in their perfection. It was enough to make my broken heart stutter.

"I'm so happy you are still here, Beautiful Girl. I was worried this lot had blown it all."

I swallowed hard and consciously tried to calm my heartbeat. Sam looked nervous, and for some reason that was amping up my own anxiety.

"Everyone's here. Get to it."

Lux, who'd been suspiciously quiet until now, looked me straight in the eye.

"We are all dead."

CHAPTER THREE

I blinked. My mouth opened and closed, but I had nothing to say to that. Ri rubbed his hand over his face.

"Fucking hell, Lux. This is why we let Eli do the talking."

"Do you guys mean metaphorically or something? Are you a doomsday cult?"

Oz laughed and Eli shook his head. "No, we aren't a cult. Valery, get the book."

Valery stood from the table, walking with heavy feet to the living room. He picked up a heavily gilded tome from the bookshelf and brought it over. It was a beautiful leather-bound book that I instantly wanted to stroke. The title was in French. He flicked to a page in the center and handed it to me.

Staring up at me from the pages of a book that had to be at least a hundred years old was Valery, dressed in a powdered wig with rouged lips. Underneath, in beautiful looping script were the words 'Marquis de Roux, 1788'.

Valery looks good in that shade of lipstick. I wonder if he'd share.

I looked at Valery. "Is this an ancestor of yours?" I asked hopefully, ignoring Ace again.

"No, that is me," Valery said.

"Wow, you look good for 220 odd years old there, Val." I sounded like a bitch but I hated that they were making a fool out of me. "Look, this is ridiculous. If you don't want to tell me, just take me home."

Valery sat back down on his chair with a great sigh. "It is the truth. My name was Valery de Lyon, the last Marquis de Roux. I died during the French Revolution, guillotined in the streets of Paris because I ate sumptuous feasts every night while the people of my fiefdom starved to death in the fields. A portrait I commissioned hangs in the Louvre. I was rich and hedonistic and I died horribly for it." He sounded sincere but he couldn't possibly be telling the truth.

"Yet here you sit, your head completely attached. Eli must be one hell of a surgeon."

"I am, but I died a hundred years before Valery was even born."

I was beginning to think that this whole day had been a prank, an elaborate scheme for someone to post on YouTube for hits. If that was the case, they better cut me in on the money they made at my expense

I pressed my fingers into my temples. "Okay. What about you? When did you supposedly die?" I asked Lux.

"Around 70 BC by the Julian calendar."

"You are all insane. I mean I thought I was nuts with the voices and all, but you guys are certifiable."

"Voices?" Eli asked, instantly in doctor mode but I ignored him.

"Let's put aside reality for a second and pretend you are all super old, yet literally look like models-"

"I only died in the seventies. Just sayin'," Oz interrupted.

I gave him a hard look and he mimed zipping his lips.

"As I was saying, you all look pretty youthful to me. And alive. So what are you? Immortals? Vampires?"

Tolliver physically winced, and Sam shook his head.

"This is going to sound crazy no matter how gently you break it to her. Maybe Lux had it right, just put it all out there and rip the Band-Aid off," Ri suggested. "I'll get the brandy."

He disappeared into Val's kitchen and returned with a bottle of brandy and eight glasses. Not that I was going to get drunk around these guys. I still wasn't convinced they weren't some kind of cult going to lock me in their basement as a way to reproduce come the Zombie Apocalypse. Though they totally chose the wrong girl if that's why they were going to all this effort.

Lux took a deep breath. "Just try to think outside the box, okay?" I shrugged and he continued. "We are the physical embodiment of the seven deadly sins given a redemptive second chance at life because the big guy is not so bad."

"The big guy? You mean God?"

"No, the Devil. Who we were in our former lives meant we were relegated to his domain," Sam explained.

"The Devil is the good guy? This isn't thinking outside the box, Lux, this is thinking outside the stratosphere." I was beginning to understand how Alice felt in Wonderland; I was definitely tripping my way down a rabbit hole right about now.

Oz had moved away from the table and laid on Valery's couch. "I wouldn't say that he was a good guy. He's still the Devil. He's just a lot more forgiving of humanity's foibles than the other guy. But he isn't someone I'd trust in a bar fight, you know?"

Uh, no. I didn't know. I'd never been in a bar fight or met the Devil. There was literally nothing in that statement I could relate to.

"Just a quick recap guys, just to make sure I've got this all. You are all dead, as in formerly alive people."

Lux nodded.

"You all went to hell and met the Devil."

This time Eli nodded too.

"And now you are zombies back in the world to atone for your sins, so you decide to become models and UFC fighters?"

Tolliver laughed mirthlessly and shrugged.

I sighed and stood up from the table, walking over to the couch where Oz was lying. I was tired, mentally and physically. Today had just been too much. I could hear the scrape of chairs as everyone stood to follow me. I eyed the only sofa and Oz moved to sit up, offering me his spot. It was kind of sweet. I sat down where his feet had been, tucking my own feet under me.

"Other than some musty old books, can you prove what you are saying?"

Eli sat down on the armchair opposite me. "Well, yes and no. Normally, if we went out amongst the humans, we would instill part of our sin in them, causing them to act a certain way."

I frowned.

Say what, now?

Oh, good. I wasn't the only one who was confused as hell about this.

"I'm not explaining this well. Think of our sin as contagious. We infect those around us with it." He pointed to Ri. "Take Orion for example-"

"Wait, Ri is short for Orion? That's... a pretty nice name," I quelled my enthusiasm a little.

The man in question gave me a lopsided smile. "Thanks, Beautiful Girl." His eyes looked at me as if he wanted to devour every inch of my body with his tongue, and my body was a very willing victim right now.

Oz gently took my feet out from under me and placed them on his lap and I turned so I was more comfortable as he began massaging. No sane woman turned down foot massage, especially when it felt so good. I bit my lip to hold in a sigh of pleasure. Zombies gave great foot massages apparently.

Eli cleared his throat. "As I was saying, Orion was

sentenced to hell for the sin of Lust. Now, if he goes into a crowd of humans alone, people will stop what they are doing and immediately start fornicating with each other, despite their mental consent. Or if there is no crowd, they will try to have relations with Ri himself. If one of us goes out with him, the results of two Sins together seems to dampen the effects of either one. So while the human would still feel lustful, they wouldn't be inclined to act on the sensation against their will. "

Okay. Ri was Lust in the Seven Deadly Sins. My body's willingness to jump on him and ride him to Timbuktu kinda made sense now.

I stared at Ri, who stood there and let me peruse his body with smug grin. His body was broad and strong, with thick muscular thighs, and an ass that would make grown women weep, strong arms and biceps wrapped in swirling tribal tattoos and that face. Strong jaw, dimples, and eyes that promised your every naughty fantasy would be fulfilled.

Yep, I could see how he would be the sin of Lust. He certainly set my libido on fire.

"I can see that."

Ri grinned so wide I thought his face was going to crack. I was drawn to him like a moth to a neon sign.

"Ah, you see, that's where you come into this."

I turned back to Eli, pinning him with my gaze. This was the part I needed to know. The rest of this story had been cuckoo, but I had no idea what it had to do with me.

"The redemptive part of our deal with the Devil states that we have to find the One, the Redeemer, and that she will help us find our redemption and be our salvation. We will know her because she will be immune to our sins."

I could feel the eyes of every one of them burning against my skin, but I needed a minute just to wrap my head around this madness. Oz had stopped rubbing my feet, but was still clutching them tight like a life buoy.

"What makes you think it's me? I mean, I seriously want to jump Ri's bones, so I can't be immune to his Lust juju or whatever it is."

Orion smirked again.

Lux made a strangled noise from where he was sitting on the ground beside the couch. "I knew it was you because you were polite to me in the subway. I confirmed it when I touched your face and you didn't try and take my eyes out. I am Wrath."

I studied him, his warrior body and gentle voice, his face marked with old silver scars. Wrath. Vengeance. Such negative emotions in such a beautiful package.

"So you think I'm the Redeemer, because I have good manners?"

"Coupled with the fact you didn't press yourself into Orion like a cat in heat when he touched you. That confirmed it. What you feel for him now is just ordinary attraction. It has nothing to do with his sin."

That explains the smirk. Ace sounded smug.

That's all you have to say to this whole thing? This doesn't sound crazy to you?

Ace snorted.

Okay, wrong choice of words.

Look, Arcadia. There had to be a reason I was saddled with you, and maybe this explains it. Maybe you are this 'Redeemer' character who is meant to help them find… whatever it is they have to find, and maybe you aren't. But, girl, you're already a dead woman walking. What do you have to lose?

She was right. I could just be a temp worker until I eventually dropped dead from heart failure, or I could help these guys and go out with a bang.

Hopefully literally and figuratively with a bang, Ace purred. My unholy attraction to them all was a problem for another time.

I mentally scrabbled for any knowledge I had on the Seven Deadly Sins. Lust, Wrath, Sloth… Bashful? No, that was one of the Seven Dwarfs.

A small giggle escaped my lips and turned into a full blown belly laugh as I imagined them each as a dwarf.

"I think you guys broke her," Oz/Dopey said.

I took a deep breath in through my nose and out through my mouth, trying to get the giggles to subside.

"Sorry, sorry. I was just trying to remember all the deadly sins and thought of something funny." I pointed to Ri and Lux respectively. "So you're Lust and you're Wrath."

I pointed to Eli.

"Pride," he said.

Hmm, made sense.

"Valery?"

"Gluttony, of course." He gave me a self-deprecating smile. There was a quiet brokenness to Valery, his eyes permanently sad even when he smiled. I wanted to fix him. But later.

I pointed to Sam and Tolliver, who were being super quiet, letting the whole thing play out.

"One of you guys has to be Envy, but you are both ridiculously beautiful I can't tell which one."

Sam laughed. "I'm not sure if I should be flattered or insulted. I'm Envy, Tolli is Greed."

Tolliver shrugged and stared at me in the eyes, daring me to judge him for it, hurt and anger simmering beneath his outwardly beautiful exterior. I wanted to hug him, but I'd sooth his hurts another day. I looked at Oz.

"I can't remember the seventh sin."

"It's Sloth. I am Sloth." There was an anxiety in his face, a fear of rejection. I pulled my feet away and watched his face fall but I quickly swiveled so my head was lying on his lap instead. "I think better when some-one's playing with my hair."

He smiled down at me through his ginger beard, his green eyes sparkling with an emotion I couldn't name. But he obligingly started running his fingers through my short hair. It was still growing back from my chemo, so his nails gently scraped against my scalp. I resisted the urge to purr.

I stared at the ceiling, sorting through everything I'd learned.

"Okay."

"Okay?" Tolliver echoed with disbelief.

"Okay, I will help you guys. But I'm not sure how you think this will work."

Oz pulled me up into his arms like I weighed nothing and held me tight against his body. "We'll take care of you too. You'll never feel lonely again." I pulled back and looked into his face. He was surprisingly perceptive for the joker of the group. I gave him a smile and let myself succumb to the insane urge to snuggle into his chest. Just for a little while.

"I think I'm ready for that brandy now."

CHAPTER FOUR

I'd never been good at math but apparently if you get seven buff guys and tell them to empty an apartment, they can do it in two hours, including spackling the holes where my paintings had hung.

After they'd dropped me home last night, I'd fallen into a deep dreamless sleep, the best sleep I'd had in a decade. Then I was up at dawn, more resolute than I'd been the night before.

I couldn't explain it, but it was like I knew these guys, that we were all part of a matching set, except I'd been the missing piece up until now. I knew things about them instinctively; their hurts and their hopes, although their stories were still a mystery. It was the feeling of completeness I had around them, the magnetic draw that I felt to each one, which had convinced me to abandon caution and commit to their offer. Like the whole thing was fated.

I'd given notice to my landlord, who'd grunted his assent and handed me paperwork to fill out before slamming his door in my face. I'd packed up all my worldly belongings, which equated to six boxes, three of which were just books, and left my old life behind before lunchtime.

Although they hinted that I could quit my job and they would take care of me, I refused. I would take a sabbatical from accepting any temp jobs for a couple of weeks, but I was going to stay on their books because I wasn't an idiot. I'd made up some lame excuse about traveling Europe and my boss was excited for me. I only felt a minor guilt for lying. She would never believe the truth, or even the watered down version of 'seven rich hot guys I met yesterday asked me to live with them and they'd bankroll me out of the goodness of their hearts'.

I called Clary and told her voicemail that I was moving, and gave her my new address.

And that was that. My old life was stored away in less than twelve hours.

I was putting my books onto my new bookcase, in alphabetical order, when there was a knock at my door. When I pulled it open, Oz was standing there, his shirt untucked and his hair in messy waves to his shoulders. He held a cardboard box in his hands.

"I brought you your own home management system. You can use it to access any technological features of the apartment." I ushered him into my apartment and he pulled the little round machine from the box and placed it on my hall table.

"The guys have all given permission for you to have complete access to their apartments, too. You just have to say 'Mini-Oz, let me into user: Oz's apartment' and it'll unlock the door. No one has the permissions for your apartment though, I promise. It's also programmed with everyone's phone numbers, control over the TV and lights, and I gave you permission to my entire iTunes collection. I just need to program your speech patterns." He pressed some buttons. "Okay, now say 'the quick brown fox jumped over the lazy dog'."

I repeated the sentence into the speaker of the sphere.

"Now say, 'chicken soup'."

"Chicken soup."

"Now say 'Oz is the hottest, most amazing person I've ever met'."

I laughed. "Dude, have you seen Sam? That guy is basically a wet dream made real." Oz pouted. "But you are definitely the sweetest, hot guy I have ever met, and you are definitely amazing."

An automated voice came over the surround sound. "User: Arcadia has been identified."

This was so exciting. "That's some pretty sophisti-cated tech you have there."

Oz fiddled with the buttons to finish calibrating my machine. "Thanks, I wrote the code for it myself."

"Is that your job? Computer programming?"

He gave me a wan look. "Sweetheart, my sin is Sloth. I don't have a job, per se. I make my money by creating YouTube vlogs of me playing video games. Twitch TV on occasion as well."

"People pay to watch you play video games? Are you naked?"

A giant laugh burst from his body like a sonic boom.

"No. You can't see me, just the screen I'm playing on. God, you are so damn cute. Okay, all set up here." He took a step back from the bench. "Give it a whirl."

"Mini-Oz, turn on the TV." The TV turned on. "Mini-Oz, turn off the lights in the living room." The lights went off. "It's like something out of a sci-fi movie."

Oz just shrugged one shoulder self-consciously. "Someone else made the tech, I just built on it. I've programmed it so if you say the word 'Help' twice, it will send an alert to everyone. You don't need to say 'Mini-Oz' just 'Help'. This is the only time we'll be given permission to enter the apartment without your say-so. Mini-Oz text the guys to tell them I'm running a test."

"Text sent," came from the speakers.

Oz walked out, and I watched the tight muscles of his back move as he left. The door shut and I heard a muffled "give it a try!" from the other side.

"Uh, help! Help!"

Nothing happened, but I could hear Oz's phone ringing and the lock on the door clicked open. He strolled back in, a pleased smile on his face. "Worked perfectly." He reached back into the box and pulled out a bright pink wristband. He looked... nervous.

"Are you gonna propose or something with that thing?"

He laughed and went down on one knee. "Not a bad idea. Cady, will you wear this wristband which monitors your heart rate and blood pressure, so death don't us part?"

"Why?"

"It's connected to Mini-Oz and will send the help

signal and your GPS coordinates to us if your heart stops or your vitals seem like you are in distress, no matter where you are. If I sync it with your phone, it'll work wherever you have phone reception."

I chewed on my lip as I looked down at him on his knees. I could understand the concept of it, but did I want them to be able to track me all the time?

It was the earnestness on his face that sold me. He was doing this because he genuinely cared, and didn't want me to drop dead tomorrow. Besides, if I didn't want to be tracked, I could always take it off.

I put my hand out and he strapped it on. "It's water-proof and shockproof. You shouldn't need to take it off unless you want to."

I pulled him to his feet. "Did you just have this lying around the house?"

"Nah, I picked it up this morning on my way to your apartment."

Sloth, my ass. He was going above and beyond for me. I closed the distance between us and wrapped my arms around his chest. "If you are Sloth, how are you so damn buff?"

I could feel his chuckle vibrate through my cheek, and his arms came around my back, holding me close.

"If I go to the gym with Sam and Eli, enough of their sins rubs off on me to get me lifting weights for about half an hour or so a day. Wrath needs a sparring partner who doesn't need a pretty face to make money, so that's either me or Ri. Val keeps me on a calorie controlled diet and voila, this couch potato remains a red hot spud."

I groaned at his bad pun. I looked up into his eyes, and felt the warmth of his body against mine and suddenly I desperately want him to kiss me. Maybe more.

He leaned down, brushing his lips lightly against mine, his beard tickling my chin. Then he pulled back.

"You just got here. As much as I want to kiss you right now, then lift your beautiful body onto the bench and make love to you like you deserve, it wouldn't be right."

I pouted, but I knew he was probably correct. Still…

"Mini-Oz, play 'songs for sex' playlist," I called out to the room.

"Did you mean 'songs for sex with a pretty girl' playlist?"

I raised my eyebrows at Oz. "Is there a 'songs for sex with an ugly girl' playlist?"

"Access denied. This playlist does not apply to user: Arcadia," the automated voice replied.

Laughter bubbled up and Oz looked amused.

"Even your AI has great pickup lines!"

The moment passed, and I took a small step back but still kept an arm around Oz's waist. I didn't know what it was about Oz, maybe it was because he was born in modern times, but I felt the most comfortable around him. Like we could be besties. I missed having a bestie around since Clary took her post overseas last year. I hadn't ever been able to keep close friends. I missed a lot of school as a teen, so I never had a chance to make that lifelong friendship group. Besides which, it took a certain kind of person to befriend someone who was inevitably going to die and break your heart. Same with boyfriends. I hadn't ever had a boyfriend that lasted more than six weeks. They ran as far and as fast as they could when they learned I was dying.

I hadn't even told Clary the full extent of my myocardiopathy, because I was petrified deep down that it would just be too much. I didn't want to die alone.

I looked over at Oz, who'd moved over to unpack my dinnerware into the small kitchen. He'd promised I would never be alone, and I trusted that he meant it. I would break his heart, but he didn't care.

"Mini-Oz, give Oz permission to enter my apartment at any time." He looked at me and gave me the most radiant smile I'd ever seen and my heart swelled with an affection I didn't know could happen so fast.

Trust went both ways.

DINNER THAT NIGHT was a more subdued affair. Valery had left a coq au vin in Sam's oven, as he had to be at his restaurant 'Epicurean' for the dinner service, and Oz was his designated pair. Ri and Lux had training and then Lux had to go with Ri to work in order to dampen the effects of his Lust juju. I discovered they rarely went anywhere alone, except Eli. Apparently neurosurgeons all had god complexes anyway, so the effects of his sin didn't register too much amongst his peers. He had also negotiated little to no bedside contact with his patients.

That just left Tolliver, Sam and I to drink way too much red wine and eat dinner in Sam's beautifully designer apartment. His Nordic genes really shone through, with white and a pale grey being the primary color scheme, from the walls to the carpet. His cabinets and his table were a pale Norwegian wood. It was like stepping into an interior design magazine. I was petrified I was going to spill red wine on something.

Every time either one of them smiled at me, or flirted (which Sam did a lot, he was an incorrigible flirt) my heart raced and I lost concentration. It was inevitable that I was going to spill something in the plush white carpet.

They made great dinner companions, telling me all the gossip of about the New York Fashion scene, of which there was a lot. I now knew who was suffering from an eating disorder, who got blacklisted from all high end fashion magazines for sleeping with an editor's husband, and who got told they were too fat to be a Victoria's Secret Angel. The fashion scene was a battlefield that I was glad I didn't have to play on.

What really struck me was that Sam and Tolliver seemed so close, like the flip sides of the same coin. They finished each other's sentences, laughed at the same jokes. I wondered if they were a couple.

We all retired to Sam's living room after dinner, and I was so full my belly bloated into a little food baby. They sat either side of me on the couch, the bottle of wine close by on the coffee table.

What I wouldn't give to be the meat in that man sandwich. Ace had been quiet for most of the day, but apparently this was too much. I blushed, and Tolliver quirked a brow. I hoped one of their superpowers wasn't reading minds.

"So tell us about your family? I know your parents are deceased, but there is no one else? " Sam asked, sipping his third glass of wine. His lips were perfect. Full and shaped like Cupid's bow. They looked soft and almost feminine in a face that was all male.

"My parents died in a road accident when I was sixteen, and the lawyers tried to find some living relatives, but either there were none or they didn't want to be found and be saddled with a chronically ill teenager. So I petitioned to become an emancipated minor and my trust funds were released. I've been on my own ever since."

"My condolences," Tolliver said, and I was beginning to think that his accent was part Brazilian, with his golden skin and square cut jaw. But his almond eyes, dark straight brows and dark black hair hinted at Japanese too. Whatever the combination, he was the epitome of male beauty.

I realized they were waiting for me to say something and instead I was staring like a goofball.

"Thanks. It was a long time ago now."

Tolliver bit his full lower lip, and I physically had to drag my eyes away.

"And you've been alone ever since?"

I shook my head. "I decided to move to New York to be closer to all my specialists. I answered a 'roommate wanted' ad for a tiny apartment, the other occupant being the youngest child of a huge Irish family from Boston, who'd run away to become a singer at eighteen. Her name was Clary Mulligan and after twelve failed auditions, and sitting with me through round after round of chemo, she decided to put herself through school and become a nurse instead. Now she's a nurse for Doctors Without Borders." I couldn't help but smile anytime I thought about eighteen year old Clary. She was something else. She didn't take shit from anybody, which is why she would have hated the entertainment industry but loves being a nurse. When the chemo was bad, she'd sat beside me while I hugged the toilet bowl, gagging every time I puked but refusing to leave me without any support. She's the best. "I would have been lost without her in those first couple of years."

They were both giving me soft looks of polite pity. "Well, she has our eternal gratitude," Tolliver said in his usual stuffy tone. There was something haughty and autocratic about him that made me desperately want to know what his previous life was like, but I held my tongue. They'd tell me when they were ready.

"You should remember that, because she is going to have a shit-fit when she finds out I've moved in with seven hot guys who were basically strangers. Not to mention the fact that you guys are all basically zombies."

Sam laughed and Tolliver looked indignant.

"I am not a zombie!"

Sam launched himself at me, making chomping motions at my faces. "Brainnnsssss!"

I squealed and scooted back onto Tolliver's lap to escape. Sam squashed me between them, miming snacking on my forehead. I couldn't breathe from laughing. Maybe the wine had gone to my head, but it was nice just playing around.

"Don't worry, I'll save you," Tolliver whispered against my ear, his lips brushing against the sensitive skin.

I shivered. I wasn't laughing anymore, but I definitely didn't want to move. I looked up at Sam, and saw the heat I felt mirrored in his eyes. He knelt on the floor between my knees. The buzz of excitement ran through my body as Sam lowered his mouth to mine.

"May I?" his voice was just a low rumble, and it went straight to my lady parts.

"Yes," I breathed back. What was it about these men that sent my hormones into overdrive?

"And me?" Tolliver asked, sweeping my hair from my nape and placing a lips there.

"Yes."

Then Sam lowered his mouth to mine and kissed me, softly at first, sipping at my lips. Then harder, his tongue running along my lower lip before plunging into my mouth.

I don't think they're gay.

Pleasure blocked out Ace. We'd always had an agreement that she mostly stuck to. She stayed the hell out of my head during sex. It was like having someone watching me otherwise. Not another participant, but a commentator. It was not fun. So we'd come to an agreement after I'd chucked a hissy fit.

The force of Sam's body pressed me back into the hard torso of Tolliver, who was trailing kisses from my ear down the curve of my shoulder. A hand crept up under my shirt and I held my breath as gentle fingers ran up over my ribs to tease the edge of my breasts.

Sam pushed his long lean body between my thighs and I could feel the evidence of his attraction pressing against my leg.

There were hands and lips all over my body, and Tolliver was whispering something to me in another language that I couldn't understand but set my body on fire anyway. Someone was moving my t-shirt up over my stomach, higher until Sam moved his mouth away from mine and trailed his lips down to the swell of my breasts. I felt light headed, my breaths coming in pants.

Sam's front door banged open and we flew apart like guilty teenagers. I jerked away quickly and banged the back of my head into Tolliver's chin, and he let out a yelp of pain.

Oz and Valery stood there, worry etched on their faces. As they took in the scene before them, Oz's expression morphed into amusement.

"Your health alarm went off. I thought you were about to have a heart attack. I think we are going to have to recalibrate your wristband. I better cancel the alert before the rest of the cavalry arrives."

Sam swore. "Too late."

I looked behind Valery and Oz to see a stormy looking Lux. Uh oh.

CHAPTER FIVE

"What were you two assholes thinking? Hey, it's our only chance at redemption's first night in our place, how about we get her naked and have a threesome, I'm sure her weak heart will be fine? Are you completely stupid?"

Lux had been walking back and forth in front of the couch for ten minutes chewing out Sam and Tolliver, only stopping every so often to unconsciously run a hand over my head, as if he needed to reassure himself again and again that I was okay. Then he'd start up again.

"I had to leave Ri alone at the club and it's probably turned into a massive orgy that'll get the place shut down or at least create a scene that could get us noticed. All because you guys couldn't keep your hands or your dicks to yourselves."

"Don't be such a prick, Lux. I've seen how you look at her, you want her just as much as we do. It's like a physical ache that I can't get rid of," Tolliver argued and I whipped my head towards him. They felt the pull too?

"Of course I want to make love to her, she's beautiful and sweet and brave and her soul calls to mine in a way that can only be preordained. But I have something called restraint, maybe you guys should try it sometime? It's not that damn hard!"

Oz laughed, "I bet something is damn hard."

Lux gave him nasty look and he just smirked back. No fear of Wrath in that one.

I studied Lux's face, searching for the truth. He couldn't know that I was any of those things in the time we'd known each other, and I wasn't actually very sweet, or beautiful or even brave. But he'd sounded so sure.

"You guys really feel that way? I mean, I am hopelessly attracted to you as well, but I just thought it was my hormones and the fact I haven't gotten laid since I moved to New York. To be honest, I was feeling a little guilty that I was so ready to jump into bed earlier with Oz, and now with Sam and Tolliver. It's not like me. I don't do that kinda thing! This feeling has to be something else, something to do with your Sins."

Lux swung a dark look at Oz, who put up his hands in a placating gesture. "It was just a little kiss. I didn't think it was a good idea to put moves on her the first day she was here."

Sam groaned. "Thanks, man."

Tolliver rolled his eyes at the guys in the room. He wrapped an arm around my shoulders and pulled me tight against his body. "Never feel guilty for your desires. They let you know you're alive. Especially not your desire for us. We feel the same need you do, probably worse. Lux is right, we should have had better control. But I'm not sorry about what happened." He leaned in close and whispered, "I can't wait to get you naked and under me. Or over me." He pressed a small kiss to the corner of my mouth. "Soon, when the Doc gives his approval, though between you and me, he isn't all that unbiased either. Not that I think he'd risk your health or anything."

I leaned back against the couch and looked at the men in the room. My gaze stopped on Valery, who'd been quiet since he got back.

"You too?"

He nodded slowly. "Very much so." Hunger warred with the sadness in his eyes.

What a quandary. You have seven hot guys lusting after your body, who want to turn your life into the porn version of Snow White and the Seven Buff Dwarfs. My heart bleeds for you. Ace could bludgeon you to death with her sarcasm sometimes.

I let out a little frustrated huff. *But what if they don't want me, it's just their response to me being the Redeemer or whatever? Some predestined attraction that would happen even if I looked like a swamp troll.*

Ace let out a sigh so heavy, it was a wonder the guys couldn't hear it. *Who the fuck cares? You like them, you think they are hot, they are all nice guys. They seem to like you, if the bulge in Tolliver's pants is anything to go by. So why the hell not, already? And if you die getting banged against the wall by some ancient fucking warrior, all the better. Geez, you can be such a damn over-thinker sometimes.*

I hated it when Ace was right; it made her smug and completely unbearable for a week.

The door to Sam's apartment opened once more, and Ri walked in. He took one look at our faces and cocked his head to the side.

"Did I miss something good?"

"We walked in on Tolli and Sam getting it on with Cady, Lux chewed them out for their poor timing and bad manners. Then Cady found out we are all attracted to her," Oz summarized, taking a seat on the couch.

"Hell yeah we are attracted to her. I've been walking with a hard on like a steel bar since I touched her cheek on the subway. I've tried to make myself scarce so I don't overwhelm her too early though. I find it hard not to touch her."

Lux pointed a hand at Ri and glared at Sam and Tolliver. "See, restraint." He turned back to Ri. "How was the rest of your shift?"

"I don't envy the clean-up guys. Get a black light in there and the whole place would light up like a messed up Rorschach inkblot. But it was no worse than Saturday nights, so I think it'll be fine"

"Saturday nights are S&M night at the club," Tolliver informed me.

Ri looked at me, his eyes hooded and a slow smile curling his face. "You should come one Saturday. I'll take you. It'll be lots of fun."

He made fun sound like the dirtiest word in the world and my eyes got even wider.

Lux clapped his hands together so loudly, I jumped in my seat.

"That's enough. I'm escorting Arcadia to bed before you all give her a heart attack. Breakfast meeting in the morning with Eli so we can talk this out like adults instead of horny teenagers."

Oz snapped a salute, and Sam gave him the finger.

Valery came over and gave me a light kiss on the cheek. "*Bonne nuit*, Cady. Sweet dreams."

I don't know how those simple words managed to sound like the promise of pleasure, but they did.

Lux gave a frustrated grunt, took my hand in his and pulled me towards the door, muttering obscenities under his breath. We rode the lift up to my floor in silence, though Lux still held my hand in his. When the elevator groaned to a stop, he walked me to the door.

"Mini-Oz, unlock User: Arcadia's door," he said loudly.

"Access denied. You do not have permission to unlock this door."

Lux grunted. "Good. Those horny bastards won't be able to sneak in here in the middle of the night."

"Are you really worried that would happen?" I asked, manually unlocking the door with my key. Old habits.

"No, but it makes me feel better anyway."

I stood in my doorway and looked at Lux in the dim light of the hallway.

"Did you mean what you said or were you just making a point? About wanting me? Do you want Arcadia or the Redeemer?"

He reached out and grabbed my arms, pulling me

gently against his chest. He stared down at me, his eyes molten silver with heat.

"It was the truth. I feel an attraction to you as the Redeemer, I'm sure, but you are irresistible to me as Arcadia. It's taking everything in me not to lift you against the wall and worship your body one inch at a time." His voice was soft, but I could hear the gravelly need in it.

"What if I want that too?"

A groan tore from him and in one swoop, he had his hands under my ass and pressed my back against the wall. I wrapped my legs around his waist instinctively and gasped at his hardness pressed against my core.

Then he kissed me, gently but with so much feverish passion that I was breathless. He sucked on my lower lip, biting it gently before flicking his tongue over the tiny hurt. I moaned, my body desperately trying to push closer to his.

He drew away, panting hard. He buried his face in the curve of my neck and I ran my head over the soft spikes of his hair.

"Soon." He lowered me to the ground and left without another word.

THE MORNING WAS BEAUTIFUL, the warm sun biting into the skin that was exposed along my shoulders, my pretty blue sundress not hiding much of them from the sun. We sat at a large glass table on the deck near the pool. A plunger of some kind of fancy coffee sitting in the center of the table, along with pastries from a local bakery and an array of fresh sliced fruit. I felt like I was living the life of a movie star.

Lux and Eli were swimming laps, and I was watching them like a hungry piranha. They were swimming while we waited for Oz to arrive.

Finally, Oz dragged himself up the stairs to the roof, wearing nothing but faded tartan pajama pants that were one stiff gust of wind away from falling around his thighs. He scratched his beard and rubbed his eyes with his forearm. His chest had a dusting of strawberry blonde hair that glinted in the sun, trailing down over abs and thickening just above the waistband of his pajamas.

My brain melted. He walked over and kissed the top of my head.

"Mornin' Cady." Then he reached for my coffee cup and emptied half of it in one swallow.

"Hey!" I punched his abs, which only resulted in me hurting my hand and him laughing.

"I'll make you a fresh one." He leaned past me and grabbed the pot, and I was momentarily transfixed by the two dimples that sat on his lower back, just above his ass.

He stuck the mug back under my nose, smug satisfaction on every feature when he busted me perving.

"Get over it. You know I think you're hot."

He laughed and sat down beside me. Lux pulled himself out of the pool, and Eli followed suit.

Jesus. I was gonna go blind.

They sat down at the table and grabbed a pastry.

"How are you settling in, Cady? Your first night

sounded... eventful." Eli sounded far more amused than Lux had. Though he hadn't walked on me about to get busy.

"I'm almost all unpacked. The apartment is beautiful. I can't thank you guys enough for letting me stay here. Are you sure I can't pay you guys rent, or help out in some way?"

Valery returned holding a small silver dish and handed it to me. I lifted it to my nose and breathed in the smell of dark, rich melted chocolate. He passed me a plate of fruit and pastries. "For dipping," he said with a smile, sitting down the end beside Eli. If Valery kept feeding me this way, I'd be the size of a house by Christmas.

Sam laughed. "You are saving our immortal souls. Pretty sure that's payment enough."

Lux grunted his agreement.

Eli nodded. "Quite. That brings up my next point. I'm not entirely sure how exactly you are meant to redeem us. Lucifer was a little vague on the details. I assume we have to make amends for the sins of our former lives, but how we are meant to do that and where you come into the equation I do not know.

"All we know for certain is that you are immune to our influence and mute their power over us completely when you are in our vicinity, which has been a blessed relief. I am fairly certain that you would nullify them completely if you are touching one of us when in a crowd of humans. I think that is the cause of this insatiable need to be with you, in the biblical sense. It is nature's way of telling us that we need to touch you."

I screwed up my nose. "So you guys don't really like me, it's just your nature's telling you that I am what you need." I wasn't sure I liked the idea. It made me feel used.

"No, don't look at it like that. All attraction is nature's way of showing us that, 'hey, this person has what you need to make a good mate and reproductive partner'." He looked at me, three little lines creasing his forehead. "Love is a different force altogether. That is something greater. But all love usually starts with attraction."

I leaned back in my chair and thought about what he was saying. Did they have something I needed too?

I chewed my Danish, and let the silence settle.

"So what's the plan? Tolli and I fly off to London tomorrow and I'd like to have this settled before we leave."

"We'll have to play it by ear. We have to assume that now that Cady is here, fate or divine intervention will lead us down the correct path."

"And her health? I don't know about you guys, but I'm not going to just sit with my thumb up my ass waiting for her to die," Tolliver said.

I just gaped. Of all of them, Tolliver struck me as the prim one, even when his hands were doing naughty things. Hearing him cuss just seemed weird.

He must have noticed my surprise. "This has been the first time since I died, maybe even before, that I've been entirely at ease. I mean, I wanted to *share* you with Sam. That's huge. I'm Greed. I don't share anything. And yeah, I want to have sex with you without wondering if I'm going to give you a heart attack. Even if it is just to prevent another lecture from Lux."

Lux gave him a flat look, and Eli had his doctor face on.

"If it's acceptable to Cady, I'd like to get some of my associates to take a look at her and run some tests as a favor to me. Maybe we can see if we can't appeal the transplant board's decision. But I don't think she should be exerting herself too vigorously until I run some tests to see the exact function levels of her heart."

Tolliver nodded. "Spare no expense, I'll pay. Bribe them if you need to."

Only an idiot or a rich person turned down free medical care. I was neither. "Sure, I'd appreciate some second opinions. As for the other thing, I'm pretty good at knowing my limits, so, uh, it should be fine."

I was the focus of every set of eyes on the rooftop, and they all looked hungry. I was beginning to understand how a gazelle felt.

"Be that as it may, you've only been here a day and known us for two. It may not be wise to rush anything." Eli was gentle but firm.

Tolliver sighed and shared a look with Sam. "Fine, but we want Cady time before we leave. If we can't impress her with our bedroom performance, then we are going to have to woo her with the next best thing," Sam said, and he looked at Tolliver who had a smirk on his face that I didn't quite trust.

"Oh yeah."

"Makeover day," they said in unison.

Everyone turned towards Oz. He had a milk

mustache on his ginger beard and his man bun had shifted to the side in a serious case of bed hair. He looked up and brushed the pastry flakes off his beard self-consciously.

"What?"

Oh, this was going to be fun!

CHAPTER SIX

O z was a red herring. Oh sure, they groomed him to within an inch of his immortal life. They'd trimmed his beard and cut his hair, although they kept it long at both mine and Oz's insistence. Now it sat to his shoulders in long, lazy waves. He looked practically edible now but let's face it, he was hardly a lost cause to start with.

Oh, the real lost cause was me apparently. The guys had gone all out, buying me spa treatment after spa treatment until I walked out of the day spa on wobbly legs. I was totally relaxed and I'd been buffed until I shone like a lighthouse in the sun. They then chauffeured me to a salon, in Tolliver's brand new Range Rover. The guy had some serious cash. The underground parking at the apartment building was filled with luxury cars, bikes, and speedboats.

"Did you make all your money modeling?" I asked. He shook his head.

"No, I made all my money by flipping companies.

The modeling I do because Sam needs a pair, and it was easier if we were both in the same industry. Plus, I own the agency we are signed to, and we have quite a few top models on the books. Big names. Not that anyone knows that. It's all run under my umbrella corporation."

I wondered how he ended up in hell, and then here, forever immortalized as Greed personified. I was burning with curiosity, but other than Valery, none of the guys had been very forthcoming about their life before the redemption deal. I didn't really want to ask. On a scale of one to ten in awkwardness, asking someone how they got damned to hell was probably a twelve.

We pulled up to a warehouse, its windows tinted, a roller door padlocked shut. In all honesty, it looked like a chop shop for stolen cars.

"Is this the part where you guys kidnap me and sell me to the Yugoslavian mob, because this doesn't look like a salon?"

Oz patted my hand from the seat beside me. "I wouldn't let them sell you to the Yugoslavians. The Russians pay better."

Sam rolled his eyes and turned in his seat. "Seriously, Oz. That's not reassuring. This is a pop up salon. Only those on The List get coordinates. It's a hipster thing. But the stylists are some of the best in the city."

"Is this really necessary? I'm happy with the spa treatments. You guys have spent enough."

Tolliver got out and walked around to open my door.

"If you get in there and don't want anything more

than a manicure, that is okay with us. You are beautiful without all this stuff. If you get in there and decide you want to walk out looking like Jessica Rabbit, we can do that too. We didn't end up in hell by being shining examples of human generosity, so please let us show our affection in the best way we know how."

How could a man, who knew some of the most gorgeous women on the planet, think I was beautiful? Compared to their peers, I was a gnome. I was having such a hard time reconciling the fact that not only did they think I was beautiful, but they wanted me on a deeper, physical level and I found it intimidating.

I mean, I wasn't an ugly duckling, I guess. My clothes came from a thrift shop, but my slight hourglass figure meant most styles sat well on me. My eyes were a little too big for my face, and my short blonde hair made me look like a little like an elf, something that was exasperated by my short stature. The overall package was waifish, but not unattractive. Well, that's what Clary says anyway, but her style is somewhere between Janis Joplin and Charlie Chaplin.

I could see myself with Oz, or even Lux, because they were perfectly imperfect. I'd be still batting way above my average, but it wouldn't make people stop and stare in the street like it did when I walked to the car between Sam and Tolliver. Even Eli, Valery and Orion were way out of my league, but it would still be within the realms of possibility. But Sam and Tolliver? Strap me in a space suit because they were so far out of my league we weren't even in the same solar system any more.

Sam walked around to stand beside Tolliver.

"Hmm." He nudged Tolliver out of the way, lifted me out of one car like I weighed nothing, shut the door and pressed me against it.

Then he kissed me. Holy crap, did he kiss me.

One arm around my waist holding me hard against his body, the other tangled tightly in my hair as his tongue stroked mine. The kiss deepened as his hips nudged against mine, his hand sliding down my side until he wrapped a hand around my thigh and lifted me up so I could hook a leg around his hips. He sucked hard at my lower lip until it felt swollen. When I was sure I was going to suffocate from a combination of desire and lack of oxygen, he pulled back.

"I didn't like the look of self-doubt on your face. You have a lot to worry about, but don't ever worry that I don't think you are as sexy as sin." He pressed his hips against my core, and I let out a little moan at the rigid length pressed against my aching center. "Tolliver's better with words. I'm more of an action kind of guy."

"So we all see," Tolliver said dryly. "Now if you're done with the PDAs, we have an appointment to keep. Anyone would think he's Orion," he muttered at Oz.

"Since Cady has arrived, I've come to feel a little more sympathy for Ri's plight, that's for sure," Oz said, shifting his jeans. "This was totally the wrong day to wear skinny jeans."

Tolliver took my hand and tugged me to his side. "Don't let them fool you, those two are more alike than you think. Absolutely no manners and they think that chivalry is a type of whiskey." He tucked my hand in the crook of his elbow. "Let me show you how you're meant to treat a queen."

He escorted me to a bright red door and knocked twice. A young girl with long platinum blond hair opened the door. Seemingly bored, she stared down at her clipboard.

"Name?"

"Tolliver Matteo."

Well, that made her look up. She stared at Tolliver, then Sam who was looming behind us, with Oz at his side. Her mouth swung open with an audible click. I knew the feeling.

The girl finally looked at me, and noticed my hand tucked in Tolliver's elbow and Sam's possessive hand on my hip. She looked between the four of us, as if trying to work out which one I was banging and then appraised me as if she could discover my secret to getting three hot guys.

Sorry lady, you're going to have to find your own hell spawn. I gave Ace a mental high-five. Too right.

"Sure, come on in Mr. Matteo, Mr. Sigurdsson. I'm a huge fan of your work."

"And his package," Oz said and the girl blushed bright red.

"No, I mean yes. I mean, I like your Calvin ad, Mr. Sigurdsson."

Sam nodded politely, but showed no further interest in the girl.

Fortunately, Tolliver helped the girl out. "This is Cady. Tell Anna-Maurice that she gets what she wants, no matter what it is."

"Sure thing, Mr. Matteo."

"We'll head over to wardrobe," Tolliver said, and strode away like he owned the place.

The girl let out a breath. "So hot. But so intense. I feel like my ovaries are going to explode just being in the same room."

"Preach, sister. Preach," I muttered as she led me through a curtain to my doom.

I STOOD in front of the door where Akoko, the blonde door girl, said wardrobe was. That was her name, though not the one she'd been born with I'd be willing to bet.

She sounds like French poodle.

No shit.

I'd been in the torture chamber with Anne-Maurice for four hours. Long enough to discover that Anne-Maurice wasn't a single person, but a duo of stylists that in turn, lead a whole team of other stylists. I'd been preened, plucked and perfected until I was basically unrecognizable. But I was also smoking damn hot. Like, I could light a crotch fire from a hundred paces. Now for the reveal.

I pushed open the door, and stepped inside. Oz looked up, then back at his phone, before his head snapped back up with a near comical look of surprise on his face.

"You look… you're so… holy hotness, Batman!"

I smiled so big at his shock that I probably blinded him with my freshly whitened teeth.

Sam turned from where he was looking at a rack of dresses.

"You look smokin' hot," he moved toward me for a kiss. I held up a hand. "No kissing off my makeup until Tolli gets to see it."

As if he'd heard his name, Tolliver strode through the door with a tall blonde man. He stopped short, and his eyes perused every inch of my face.

"Stunning. You always look beautiful, but right now you're a work of art."

The tall blonde man stopped in front of me. "Oh my, la swoon! I see Anne-Maurice did a beautiful job like always. My name is Pierre, and I am your wardrobe consultant. Let's see if we can't find a bow to put on that pretty package, shall we?" He walked me to the rack that was jammed with clothes. "No. No. Yes. Tolliver, sweetheart, come here and hold these dresses for our beautiful Cady. No. Yes. Hmm. No. Who chose this dress? Were they blind?" Pierre went on like that down the whole rack, occasionally holding a dress in front of my body before either discarding it back on the rack or handing it to Tolliver, who was rapidly getting lost under the mountain of clothes.

Sam came over and pulled a dress from the end of the rack, putting it on top of the pile.

"This one." It was the same dark blue of Sam's eyes, and covered in sequins. Well what there was of it. It was a romper suit. Like the kind you wear when you are four and prone to exposing your butt to the postman every day. But this one had a neckline that plunged almost to my navel.

"Oh yes. *Oui*. This is the one. Tolliver drop that pile, we won't need them anymore. Cady, you must go put this on immediately. I have just the pair of Louboutins," he swanned out of the room

I looked around desperately for a change room or a curtain and found nothing.

"Need a hand?" Sam grinned.

"Maybe two?" Tolliver's lopsided grin melted my heart. But not enough that I was going to get undressed in front of them. I didn't have that kind of self-confidence. I looked over at Oz, but he just waggled his eyebrows.

"Out, the lot of you. And if you see Pierre, hold him out there too. I'll call you when I'm dressed."

Sam pouted like a little boy who got his favorite toy taken away, but he left when Tolliver pushed him out the door.

I slipped off the straps of my dress letting it fall to the floor. Holding up the sparkling concoction, I had to admit it was pretty. It had long, gauzy embroidered sleeves, the blouse section was billowy and light, and although the shorts lived up to the very definition of the word, they flared out to create a kind of skirt effect.

I stepped into it, thankful that I could pull it up rather than mess my new hairstyle. I shucked my bra and appreciated my small boobs for the first time ever. There was no room for a bra, or modesty, with this outfit.

I looked in the mirror, what the room lacked in changing facilities it more than made up for in mirrors, and gaped.

The girl in the mirror wasn't the one I was used to seeing.

You look like Tinkerbell decided to ditch Disney and do porn.

I laughed, because she was kinda right. Anna-Maurice had given me this messy pixie cut, keeping close to my natural golden yellow but added highlights and lowlights. Their makeup artists had given me what they called a 'natural' look, but involved contouring my face until I was transformed. They'd widened my eyes and artfully applied liner to make my lashes look thicker than they really were.

In short, they were magicians. I'd never be able to recreate any of this.

The only thing marring the perfection of my outfit was the long surgical scar running down my sternum. I'd come to terms with the puckered scar that was still pink even after all these years. I'd even become accustomed to the occasional stares I inevitably got when I wore low cut tops. I wanted to wear this amazing outfit, scars be damned. The guys would love them or hate them, but they were a part of me.

"Okay, you can come in now." I took a deep breath and stood tall. The only person who entered was Pierre, a shoebox cradled in his arms.

"You cannot do a grand reveal without the shoes. Especially not without these shoes. Normally I would suggest a classic pair in nude, because every girl needs a pair of those, but for this outfit, we needed something with a little more attitude." He lifted the lid and revealed a sky high pair of bootie heels the color of my dress, but heavily studded with spikes. "These will add a little spice to your sugar, if you know what I mean." He sat me on a chair and knelt before me, sliding my foot into the Louboutin like I was Cinderella. I kind of related to Cindy right now.

"Now you may come in," Pierre shouted as he helped me to my feet. I wobbled a little unsteadily as I got my balance on the heels, and prayed they came with reinforced ankle support.

They all walked in and Sam whistled long and low, and Oz's gaze fell to my cleavage and stayed glued there. I could tell by the heat in his eyes that it was definitely my boobs that had him so intrigued, not my scar.

"How do you feel?" Tolliver asked, his heated gaze running a slow perusal up my body that I could almost feel.

"Surreal. And a bit like a princess."

Tolliver walked towards me and leaned in, kissing me gently. "You look like a goddess."

Oz murmured his agreement, and Sam came over, wrapped an arm around me and dipped me backwards, kissing me hard on the lips.

"Irresistible."

Oz smiled and came over, pulling me away and kissing my temple.

"I think she is beautiful. But this is just window dressing."

My face flamed with embarrassment, but I couldn't deny that their praise made me feel hopelessly pleased with myself.

There was a great sigh from the other side of the room.

"Wow," Pierre moaned as he looked between my men.

My men, is it? You jumped on the polyamory bandwagon awfully quickly.

I ignored Ace and concentrated on the look of wanting on Pierre's face. "Are you sure one of them isn't gay?"

He sounded so hopeful I couldn't help but laugh. They could be anything their hearts desired, as long as I made them mine.

CHAPTER SEVEN

They hustled me out the door before I could even consider changing back into my sundress. Which was lucky, because by the time we left the warehouse it was well past dusk, and the sky was a deep purple color.

"Okay, one more stop, and then Tolli and I have to catch the red eye out to London," Sam said, helping me into the back of the SUV while Oz and Tolliver put countless bags into the cargo hold. I had no idea what was in the bags, and I was pretty sure that I wouldn't even get a peek inside them until Sam and Tolliver had left the country and I couldn't insist that everything be returned. Devious bastards.

Sam pushed me over to the center seat and climbed in next to me. Tolliver climbed in the other side so I was sandwiched between them.

"Good evening, everyone. I'll be your chauffeur for tonight," came Oz's sarcastic voice from the driver's seat. "Actually, I'm a little excited. Tolliver never lets me drive his cars. He never lets anyone drive his cars. Buckle yourself in boys and girl, this is going to be fun."

He peeled out of the lot on a squeal of tires. He took the next corner too fast, and I slid into Tolliver's side.

"I regret my decision already," Tolliver said, wrapping his arms around my shoulders, his fingers lightly playing with my collarbone. I shivered as the butterflies amped up in my stomach. "Well, maybe not too much regret." I was pretty sure that if he looked down my top right about now, he could see to my belly button. He smelled like a woody musk, and vanilla.

Oz took the next left so fast the rear tires slid out and Tolliver allowed me to slide back into Sam's side.

"Slow down. We aren't in Grand Theft fucking Auto."

"We'll be stuck in traffic soon enough, so Hakuna your Tatas," Oz said with a massive shit-eating grin on his face.

Sam reached over and wrapped a strong hand around my thigh. "Maybe I just need something to hold on to." His hand slid upwards until his fingertips lightly drummed the sensitive flesh of my inner thigh. He brushed beneath my shorts, his hand running along the edges of my underwear. Actually, my underwear was one of the reasons I made them leave so I could change clothes. My practical, adult underwear had a picture of a panda wearing sunglasses on the ass. When they illustrated the dictionary, there would be a picture of me in my white panda panties next to the definition of unsexy.

I sucked in a breath and held it as he slipped a finger under the elastic.

"Do you want this? All you have to do is say no and I'll stop. We'll stop. No harm done," Sam said quietly, studying my face.

Tolliver murmured his agreement.

The problem wasn't that I didn't want to do it. Because, boy did I want to. It was a burning ball of need in my gut that refused to die down and only got worse whenever I was close to any of them. The only thing that held me back from throwing myself headlong into the moment was the conditioned shame that I knew I should feel. I mean, I was about to get off in the back seat of a Range Rover, pressed between two hot guys while another one drove in the peak hour traffic. Logically, I knew that I should probably feel ashamed of my thoughts and actions, but I didn't. All I felt was this overwhelming need, a need that grew every hour I was close to them. I didn't know if this wantonness was something that had always been a part of me but had been dormant until I met the guys, or if it was the weird ass situation that I now found myself in or even something more... magical. I didn't care. I wanted, I needed and I was going to take.

Fuck shame.

"Yes. Please."

Tolliver laughed. "Always so polite, even when you are asking us to fuck you. You are the sexiest, most adorable woman I have ever met."

He kissed me as Sam slipped his fingers beneath my panties, pushing them to the side and finding my clit like it was magnetized. I moaned and pressed against his hand.

Tolliver turned so he could kiss me hard, his tongue plundering my mouth. His hand moved beneath the neckline of my playsuit, finding my nipple and rolling it between his fingers. I made a tiny mewling noise as I arched into his grasp as white hot sensation ran through my body. Sam's fingers circled rhythmically, building the desperate heat in my body, his eyes watching my face even as my own eyes closed against the pleasure. He slid one finger inside of me, stroking slowly, and my body moved against his hand, wanting so much more.

Tolliver moved down my body, pushing aside the neckline of my playsuit a couple of inches and taking the aching bud of my nipple into his mouth.

"Oh." I twined my fingers in the inky, soft darkness of his hair, holding him close as he sucked and lapped at my breasts, the steady pull sending heat straight to my core.

He lifted his head. "I am buying you a hundred of these suits, just for the ease of access to your beautiful breasts."

"Speak for yourself. All I want is to taste her, but she's trapped in these things until I can get her naked," Sam groaned. With that, he plunged a second finger inside me, and I moaned.

"If you guys don't quit talking and fucking make her cum already, I'm going to pull this car over and do it myself. Those noises she's making are driving me crazy. I'm going to crash the damn car," Oz whined from the front.

Tolliver dragged his teeth along my nipple and Sam started pounding into me, stretching me until I thought my heart was going to thump out of my chest. Sam leaned forward and kissed me, before trailing kisses and taking my other breast in his mouth.

I looked down at the top of their heads through pleasure hazed eyes, one dark and one light and both completely focused on my pleasure. They both sucked hard, and Sam pulled out his fingers out of me and flicked my clit before thrusting them hard back in me. It was too much and perfectly enough. The sounds of my orgasm echoed around the car. Wave after wave of pleasure left me, and the guys didn't lift their heads or remove their hands until I lay limp in their arms.

The car swerved hard to the left and someone honked. Oz groaned. "I definitely chose the wrong day to wear skinny jeans."

IT TURNED out that the guys were taking me to Epicurean for dinner with the rest of the Sins. Although a stranger wouldn't be able to tell what had happened in the back of that SUV in peak hour traffic, the rest of the guys around the table knew instantly.

Lux's eyes appraised me, from head to toe, lingering on the small love bite I had on the side of my left breast from Tolliver's over-enthusiasm. "Are you okay?" he asked, his voice quiet enough that only I could hear it over the hum of the restaurant.

"I'm great, Lux. Don't worry. I know what I am doing."

"Do you?" he asked softly.

I couldn't tell if he was chastising me or if it was an

actual question. I decided I'd pretend I couldn't hear him.

Valery came to the table, dressed in his chef's jacket and a pair of tight grey jeans that hugged his thighs. He even had one of those tall hats.

"Good evening, Cady. *Tu es belle.* You are beautiful."

I blushed. "Thank you, Valery. Your restaurant is wonderful."

"All the more so now that you are here. Tonight, I have assembled some of my best dishes for you, rather than the table scraps I normally feed these heathens when they come into my restaurant. I have developed a nine course tasting menu just for you. They say that the way to a man's heart is through his stomach, but I think the way to woo a woman is not so different." He poured me a glass of white wine. "I must go before the kitchen burns down without me. I will send out the first course momentarily." He kissed my cheek and hustled back through the swinging doors to the kitchen.

I hadn't spent as much time with Ri and Valery, except on that first night, and I felt a little embarrassed that they knew I'd gone to second base with two of their friends. Hell, I was even at first base with Lux and Oz. How awkward. But I couldn't help but feel drawn to them anyway. It was definitely something 'other' sitting inside me, reaching out for them whenever they were near, and just wanting to ride them into the sunset.

Don't blame me. I think they are cute and all, but the pretty boys aren't my type. I like them darker, more damaged, Ace mused.

It was odd to think the voice in my head had a type

other than my own. Maybe I should talk to Eli about Ace.

As if he could read thoughts, Eli turned to me. "I have gotten you an appointment with two of my colleagues. The best oncologist in the US, Dr Martha Yan, and a cardiovascular surgeon, Alrich Herchstein. They have agreed to a conference about your condition next week. I have taken the liberty of booking you in for tests at my hospital. Is that fine with you?"

I thought about my complete lack of insurance. "I don't think my insurance will cover that."

Tolliver gave me a look. "We've covered that. I will pay for anything you need done. I will have them bioengineer you a heart if that is what it takes. Don't think about the cost. Think about getting well."

I nodded and gave them both a small smile. My life was like a weird dream/fantasy right now. Like everything my teenage self had ever hoped for. The fleeting worry that I was rushing into everything and making a huge mistake washed over me. I wasn't the kind of person who rushed into things. My life was a measured in tiny steps, not monumental leaps. But I shrugged it off. I wasn't going to live my dying days in fear of making a mistake. It wasn't like I'd have to live with those mistakes for long, anyhow. Silver lining.

Nine courses later, including two dessert courses and coffee, I felt less like a svelte goddess in my playsuit and more like fat Elvis before his death. I was a little worried the bulge of my drum tight belly was poking out of the plunging V of my outfit.

"I'm never going to eat again," I groaned. The guys

just laughed. I swear, they just inhaled each beautifully presented, tiny work of art that came before them. I wanted to take a picture of each dish before I took a bite.

"I could go a burrito," Oz said, and Sam agreed. My eyes bugged out. Where the hell did they put it all?

Valery returned for coffee and sat down at the empty seat beside me.

"How was your meal?"

"Epic. Possibly even biblical," I gushed. Because words could not describe the frothy little dessert the melted on my tongue as if it was made from air.

"I am glad you enjoyed it. These swine would not know good food if I slapped them in the face with a fresh Icelandic trout."

The guys joked, and Oz teased and I wondered what my earlier worry was about. Somehow I fit with these guys, like they each held a little piece of my soul and now I was home.

CHAPTER EIGHT

I kissed Sam and Tolliver goodbye on the footpath in front Epicurean, the flash of waiting paparazzi dazzling me.

"Don't worry, my scarf means that none of their photos will be usable," Sam said, kissing me one more time. I'd wondered about the odd shimmery texture and pattern of his scarf, but I had just thought it was some odd fashion statement. I still didn't know anything about fashion, even after today's makeover.

The valet brought around the SUV, and Oz, Sam and Tolliver climbed in. Tolliver was back in the driver's seat, unsurprisingly. Oz was going with them to bring the car back to the apartment; Tolliver didn't trust other people with his precious cars.

I stood between Ri and Lux, having said goodbye to Eli, who was on call for the ER again tonight, and was going to nap in Valery's office. Valery still had three more hours of the dinner service before he could go home.

"Where's your car?" I asked the guys.

Ri grinned and took my hand, leading me around to a side alley behind the restaurant. Sitting under a street light were two mean looking Harley Davidson motorbikes.

I looked down at my outfit, and smoothed a hand over my tousled hair. I could do this. I'd always wanted to ride a motorbike.

Lux grabbed my other hand. "She rides with me."

Ri smirked, and held up his hands. "No problems. As long as I get the first dance."

"Dance?"

"We are going to Dante's." His grin got wider.

"But it's not Saturday."

Ri chuckled. "Holding out for S&M night, were you? Don't worry, Beautiful Girl. We can go tomorrow too, if you want. I'll take you any night you like." He winked and threw a leg over his bike, pulling a black helmet down over his head. I appreciated his muscled thighs and the way his leather jacket pulled tight across his shoulders. That guy was just pure sex. There was no way I could ever null his lust abilities.

He revved the bike and sped out of the alley, the steady vibration of the motor's purr thrumming in my chest.

"Ugh, he is so ridiculously hot it's not fair. I feel like he should come with a warning label. Warning: will have incendiary effect on your panties."

Lux just grunted and handed me a helmet. "I'll take your word for it." He shrugged out of his leather jacket. "Take this too."

I slipped my arms into the sleeves, appreciating the lingering warmth of Lux's body, and the smell of leather and man. It was a heady mixture that spoke straight to my libido.

He hopped on to the bike and patted the seat behind him. Thank goodness my Louboutin's were bootie style. The spikes actually look a little badass biker-esque.

"Where's your helmet?" I asked, running my fingers over his scalp. I felt the tiny ridges of old scars running in a criss cross pattern across his skull.

"Don't need one."

"Are you guy's immortal?"

I had wondered this one and off for a while. Could they die? If I redeemed them, would they die again? Just fall to the ground in a pile of ash? I needed answers to these questions before we worked out how I was going to help them. I didn't think I could become so invested in them, only to watch them die at the end.

Huh, I wonder if that's how people thought about me?

"Yeah. We can't die by most mortal means."

"What if I strapped C4 to your chest and detonated it?"

"I don't think any being can come back from that." He sounded amused. "Is there a chance you might do that?"

"Well, no. But it's nice to know where the line is."

"Just get on the bike," he grinned, and I couldn't help but smile back. I threw a leg over the bike and kind of half shimmied, half dragged myself onto the back. It's not as easy as it looks in the movies, especially when you are as short as I am. Even with the fuck-me heels.

I wrapped my arms around his waist and pressed my torso tight against his. When he turned on the bike, the rumbling sensation went straight between my thighs.

"Hoo boy. Why don't more women ride bikes?"

"Hang on." With that, he revved the bike twice and tore out of alley, my arms becoming steel bands around his waist. I could feel every hard nuance of his abdominals, the strength of his back and the wetness between my thighs. Woah.

We tore through the traffic, weaving in and out of cars, going so fast that the lights blurred in my peripheral vision. I couldn't hear anything over the roar of the engine, even when we had to stop at the lights. I loved it.

We rolled past Dante's, the line to get in snaking around the block. The sign was lit up in blood red neon, flames licking around its edges. The club was apparently called 'Dante's Seven Circles' but everyone just shortened it to Dante's. We pulled into the staff parking lot around the back. Ri was there, leaning up against his bike, looking as sexy as… well sin.

"How was your ride?" he asked, double entendre fully intended.

"Invigorating," I smiled coyly back, and he laughed.

"Welcome to Dante's, Beautiful Girl. Let your corruption begin."

We pushed through a back fire exit and into a long dark hallway jammed with people lining up for the bathrooms. Ri led the way and Lux was at my back, a hand on my hip.

When we finally got to the main room of the club, the place was packed, probably past capacity. There was hardly any room to move without rubbing up against a stranger, and the dance floor was a writhing mass of bodies.

From what I could see over the heads of super-models on teetering heels and gym jocks with shoulders as wide as a VW, the club was set in circles. In the center of the room was a round bar, a dozen leather clad bartenders behind there. The women wore tight bustiers and leather mini skirts, and the men wore tight leather pants and no shirts. Not one of them had an ounce of fat on them and they definitely looked sinful.

Around the bar was standing room, people talking, flirting, and in one spot doing a drug deal in a rather obvious manner. Beyond that was the dance floor, a slightly sunken circle of smoke, flashing lights and grinding people. Above us was a balcony that circled the room in curving arches, and more people were jammed up there.

"We'll go up. That's the VIP area. We've got a table," Orion yelled over the heavy bass of the music.

We climbed a curving set of stairs, and Ri led us to the back corner of the VIP section, where three plush black sofas sat in a U shaped on a raised dais, a long glass coffee table in its center. Lux guided me to the couch that was up against the wall, and sat down next to me. We looked down over the rest of the VIP like over-lords on their fiefdom.

"Um, isn't this a little over the top? We aren't royalty. Why isn't anyone else sitting here? I'm pretty sure that kid over there made like seventy million dollars last year and had six number one songs? And isn't that the guy from the superhero movie? You know the one with the really awesome arms? Shouldn't the club put a big name here, rather than just... well us? A bartender, a fighter and a nobody."

Ri let out a huge, booming laugh then and even Lux cracked a grin. "What made you think I was just a bartender? Tolliver owns this club, and he is co-owner of Epicurean and a bunch of other businesses around the world. The guy is seriously loaded. This is the owner's table. We definitely get to feel like King Shit up here. If we aren't using it, which is most of the time, we let some of the more elite clientele up here. But tonight it's reserved for our Queen."

People were naturally giving us the side eye, and I wasn't very comfortable being the center of so much attention.

"Would you like to dance, or maybe a drink?" Ri asked, motioning to a waitress in tight black pants and a torn white tank that barely covered the underside of her boobs.

I was even less comfortable on the dance floor sober. "Tequila and lemonade, please."

The waitress nodded at me. "Sure thing." Her eyes skimmed over Lux's body. "How about you, Lux? What can I get you?" The invitation in her voice was pure sex; she may as well have just asked if he wanted to fuck right there on the couch.

"Grey Goose. Bring the bottle." He placed his hand

on my thigh and I resisted the urge to punch the air in victory. Take that super-hot waitress with perfect boobs.

She looked at his hand, and Ri's arm still around my shoulder, and curled her lip ever so slightly. Apparently, I had been found wanting.

She left with the orders, and I sank back onto the couch between their bodies. "People are going to think I am sleeping with you two."

"So?" Orion whispered in my ear, and I shivered.

"That waitress thought I was a slut. A slut completely unworthy of your attention at that."

"I don't give a shit what other people think. Yours is the only opinion I care about," he licked the outer shell of my ear and I nearly came right there on the couch.

"You are dangerous, Orion... uh? What's your last name? Actually, I don't know your last name either, Lux. I can't believe I've thought about having sex with you, but don't know your last names. The waitress was totally right."

"Pfft. Raquel just thinks she's the shit. Want me to fire her?" Orion asked, in complete seriousness.

I wasn't that petty. Okay, I had to seriously think about it, but in the end my morality won out.

"No. It's fine. It's something I'll have to get used to if we are going to do...this."

"This?" He asked as he kissed his way down my neck.

"Helping you and the other sins find your redemption, or whatever," I looked down at my feet and mumbled, "and the sex."

"What was that, Beautiful Girl?" I could tell by his smirk he knew exactly what I said. I raised my chin and looked him dead in the eye.

"I said if the eight of us are going to be fucking, then I will need to get used to the slut shaming. I mean, I probably am, by definition, but I don't care."

Lux grabbed my chin and turned me to face him. "You will not speak about yourself in such a derogatory sense. You are a beautiful, sexual woman and we fully intend on worshipping in the way you deserve to be worshipped. Yes?"

God, I drowned in those eyes every time the focused on me. There was something arresting about them that drew me in and kept me trapped until he chose to release me.

"Yes." It was a breathy whisper.

Unfortunately, Raquel returned at that moment, placing the tray of drinks on the table with a hard crack. She unloaded them slowly, her ass toward Orion and her breasts towards Lux. If I wasn't so annoyed, I'd be impressed by her ability to twist like that and still look natural.

"Is there anything else I can get you? Anything at all?" Wow. She couldn't take a hint

Ri went to reply, but I cut in. "No thanks, Rebecca, we're good here. Really good." I gave Lux a smoldering glance, my tongue darting out to lick my lower lip. His pupils dilated as he watched the movement, and Raquel was all but forgotten.

Orion chuckled and dismissed the waitress.

"Well now, the little lamb has teeth," Ri chuckled. I shrugged and my cheeks tingled as I blushed. "If we are going to do this, I want monogamy from you guys. I don't share well. I was an only child." I stared into Orion's amber colored eyes, just so he knew I was serious. He was the Sin of Lust. If anyone was going to have trouble with my terms, it was him.

His brows drew together, and I knew this was an important moment. If he could agree to this, it might mean that I could help him, help them all.

"I will try and help you find your redemption regardless of your answer, but I can't sleep with you, share something so intimate with you, if you are sharing that same intimacy with every other woman who breathes."

"And men," Lux whispered.

My eyebrows shot up. Why would lust be confined to some cookie cutter version of western social ideals? But the same rules applied. "No men either. Just me."

Orion nodded, but he didn't agree or disagree. He stood and I tried to quell my disappointed. Six out of seven wasn't bad.

"Would you like to dance?" he asked instead, and I gave him a tight smile.

"Sure." I downed my drink quickly and stood, straightening my outfit so I didn't accidentally have a nip-slip. Tolliver had shifted the fashion tape that was holding it all together earlier, so it wasn't as secure as it could be.

Lux said he would wait at their table, so Ri took my

hand and led me past the VIP tables, teeming with rich kids and rappers. One table was full of rich kids who looked like Abercrombie models and were generally treating their waitress like crap.

Ri stopped beside her. "Tell Raquel I said to swap tables with you," he said, and she looked grateful. I didn't think Raquel would feel quite so positive about the move.

He led me slowly down the stairs and we flowed with the crowd onto the dance floor. We moved through the crowd, closer to the DJ booth that seemed to be suspended halfway between the two floors. There was a definite energy on the floor, and electricity that flowed through all the bodies swaying and grinding, and in the case of one couple to our left, fucking.

My hips began to sway to the beat as the music consumed me. Ri stood close, our bodies moving together as he slipped his thigh between my legs and put his hands on my hips. It was a fast beat and we moved with a frenetic energy as songs changed seamlessly. He turned me and we danced, my back to his front, our movements so provocative that my mother would have locked me in my room until I was forty if she'd been alive and had seen the spectacle. But I was caught up in the music and the scene and the hard feel of Ri's body swaying into mine. And boy, the guy could dance. His movements were like liquid, and the press and swirl of the whole thing just made me think of sex. Hot, sweaty, dirty sex.

Another song came on, and everyone began to jump around.

I got jostled away from Ri, who was turned toward the DJ booth like everyone else. I got dragged backwards, further and further away by a set of hands. I called to Ri, but he couldn't hear me over the music or see me in the press of bodies. I turned, trying to see the person pulling at me, but I had to concentrate on not losing my footing. Eventually, we stopped, still on the dance floor and two bodies pressed into me. I recognized two of the guys from the Abercrombie Jerks table.

"Come dance with us. We can see you like two dicks at once and we are so fucking down with that," said the one in front, although his words were slurred and his breath smelled like stale beer.

"No, thanks. I'd like to get back to my boyfriend now."

"Don't you mean boyfriends? You are a dirty little whore, aren't you?" said the one behind me, holding tight as I tried to wiggle away,

My heart started to thud wildly, unevenly, and sweat began to run down my spine as I realized that even though we were surrounded by people, no one here was going to save me.

Stink breath in front of me ran a finger down the V of my top, between my breasts and I squirmed away, but that only seemed to excite the guy behind me.

"Calm down, we just want to dance," Stink Breath said, pushing his body into mine so tightly that I could hardly breathe let alone move. Panic started to choke me. I couldn't move my arms or raise a knee to pulverize some balls. A hand slid up under my shorts and I tried to squirm away futilely.

"We are going to have so much fun." The guy behind me grabbed my jaw, squeezing it tightly until extreme pain made me open my mouth. I tried to scream as Stink Breath forced a pill into my mouth, the sealed it shut with his hand, and the other guy behind me moved his hand from my jaw to my nose, pinching it tight so I couldn't breathe and was forced to swallow. As it slid down my throat, terror settled like a lead weight in my chest.

"I'm going to-"

Stink Breath didn't get to finish his sentence as a scarred fist wrenched him away by his hair. The same fist grazed past my face and into the nose of the guy behind me in bizarrely slow motion. His head snapped back in a deafening crunch, and then his arms were gone and I was frozen as I watched Lux fall onto the guy who was behind me, pounding his face in a sickening barrage of violence. Stink Breath was on his feet and trying to escape through the crowd, but Lux roared a sound that made a primal part of me want to run in fear. He was on his feet and he dove at Stink Breath, pushing him forward until the other man landed on his face. Lux was on his back, straddling his waist in an instant.

He grabbed the back of Stink Breaths hair and smashed his face repeatedly into the floor until the other guys face was an unrecognizable mess.

My head began to spin, my legs and hands going numb. The drugs were starting to kick in.

"Lux." My voice was strangled because my tongue felt fat. "Help."

His head snapped around, his hands still holding the guy's head, although Stink Breath's face was mangled and blood dripped in a river onto the dance floor.

I wondered if he was dead, if the thing that looked like Lux, but with flat dead eyes, had killed him.

CHAPTER NINE

L ux's face had been the last thing I remembered
about last night. When I opened my eyes the
next day, it was to see Eli hovering over me.
The anxiety coiled in my body instantly relaxed.

"We gotta stop meeting like this Doc." I smiled, and
then groaned as the pounding in my head made me
instantly regret my mirth.

"I wholeheartedly agree. Despite popular opinion, I
don't enjoy having you unconscious on my couch." He
shined a tiny light in my eyes, and then checked my
pulse, his warm, strong fingers pressed against the delicate skin of my wrist. I realized I wanted to know what
those fingers felt like in other places. I wanted Eli to kiss
me. When had he gone from reassuring doctor to poten-
tial sex partner in my brain? It didn't matter, because I
was having all sorts of torrid doctor/patient fantasies
now.

My pulse must have jumped a little, because he
looked away from the clock on the wall and back at my

face, his concerned look melting away when he saw the heat burning in my eyes.

He leaned forward and gently brushed a kiss across my lips. It was a promise of something more. But not right now.

"I don't think you've suffered any lasting effects of the rohypnol. I'll give you something for the headache."

He stood and I sat up on the couch. I expected the room to be full like last time, but none of the other guys were there.

"Where is everyone?"

Eli handed me to paracetamol and a glass of water. "They are… out."

The hesitation wasn't lost on me. "And Lux?" I held my breath, having a vivid flashback to the dance floor and his cold, dead eyes. What if he was in prison?

"Lux is in his apartment. He asked not to be disturbed."

Oh really? We'd see about that. I stood from the couch. I was still in my playsuit, but the Hollywood tape had lost all integrity hours ago. My left breast slipped out, and Eli's gaze shot to my chest with naked hunger that he didn't have time to squash before I saw it.

I stepped toward him, into his arms and his hands pressed me against his body. He leaned forward, kissing me with gentle persuasion, his fingers skimming up over my hip, then my ribs, before he cupped my wandering breast in his hand. His thumb scraped over my nipple and I moaned into his deepening kiss. He plucked at it and I gasped, pressing myself closer.

I wanted nothing more than to succumb to the sensation of Eli, but I had to fix Lux first.

I groaned as I gently broke the kiss, and Eli let me. His hands slid back down to my hips, but he didn't let go.

"We'll have our moment, I swear. But Lux needs me right now."

"I look forward to that moment." He leaned in and kissed my forehead. "Go take care of my brother. He will be feeling this very deeply."

I hesitated at his door. "What happened to those guys? The ones who…"

Eli shook his head, his face completely closed down. "I do not know." I looked at the neutrality of his face and knew he was lying, or at least not telling me the whole truth.

I walked out his door and into the elevator, going straight to Lux's floor.

Ace, are you there?

Silence. Panic gripped me. What if the drugs had burned her away? Ace and I had our differences, but I needed her. She was a part of me.

Aww, Cady, I didn't know you cared.

I'd never been so relieved to hear that snarky voice.

Yeah you did. We've got each other's backs. I love you.

A long silence again, before Ace spoke.

Love you too, Kid. Her voice was husky and rough.

Do you know what happened last night, after my blackout? I asked.

Yes. Her tone was the coldest I'd ever heard. *We owe Lux a debt.*

And those men, what happened to them?

That cold flat voice again. *They got what they deserved.*

A feeling of dread washed over me.

Are they dead? Silence. *Ace?*

She didn't answer.

Giving up on interrogating Ace, I lightly knocked on Lux's door but no one answered. I knocked louder, but still no answer.

"Mini-Oz, unlock user: Lux's door."

The lock slid across with a snick. I turned the handle and walked into the apartment. I'd never been into Lux's space, and the heavy curtains shut against the early morning light shrouded the place in pockets of darkness.

But I could still see Lux. He was hunched over on his couch, the only piece of furniture in the room, with a bottle of vodka dangling loosely from his fingers.

"Lux?" I called, but he didn't look up. I moved in front of him, but he still wouldn't look at me. I knelt on the ground at his feet, forcing him to see me.

His eyes lazily took in my face.

"You don't kneel in front of me, Arcadia. Never." He wrapped strong hands around my ribs and pulled me up onto his lap. I curled into the strength of his body, enveloping myself in the warmth of him.

"What happened, Lux?" I asked gently, my hand reaching up to stroke the lines of his face.

"I happened. Wrath. Revenge. You may null our abilities, but we are still the same people who got sent to hell for our sins. I'm still the person who slaughtered whole villages."

My eyes bugged out in shock. "That may be so, but I don't think the man who did those things in your former life felt such remorse." He shook his head, and buried his face in my neck. "Will you tell me about it? Your life before?"

He shook his head. "I was a Spartan soldier. One of the army's most brutal. That is all you need to know. The rest isn't... pretty."

I could see it then, in the hard edges of his face. I could imagine him in the armor, the helmet, holding a sword. My warrior.

I pulled his chin towards me. "I will save you, Lux. I will be your redemption, if you'll let me. But I think it's fairly logical that you can't murder anyone else, okay?"

One corner of his mouth curled slightly. "I didn't kill those kids at the club. They walked out of there alive."

I sensed more to that story, but I let it go. I would find out the details later.

Such pain on his face that it hurt to see. I needed to replace it with something else.

I turned so I was straddling his lap, our chests pressed together. "Lux, will you take me to bed?"

Heat roared from his body and strong arms wrapped around me. "Yes." It was a sigh, a chant, a proclamation, and without hesitation.

His mouth came down onto mine, hard. He kissed me with a desperation that bit into my soul; that called to me to sooth his hurts and forgive his errors.

I obliged, kissing him back with my own desperation.

He stood, his hands under my ass, lifting me with

ease. I wrapped my legs around his waist as he walked me towards what I assumed was the bedroom.

I broke the kiss. "Shower first." He was still speckled with blood and I wanted to erase any trace of those guys from the club.

He nodded, recapturing my mouth in another searing kiss.

We walked into the dark marble bathroom, and he placed me on my feet.

He reached into the huge shower stall and ran the water before turning back to me. His eyes devoured my body as he hooked to fingers around the top of my suit, and achingly slowly pulled it down, exposing my skin to the cool air inch by inch. My nipples pebbled instantly under his gaze, and he sucked a small breath through his teeth. Stooping a little, he pushed the rest of the suit down my legs until they pooled at my feet. I turned, stepping out of the fabric.

He knelt in front of me, then he grinned.

The smile was such a huge contrast I was momentarily shocked.

"There's a panda on your panties. It's wearing sunglasses."

I groaned. Dammit, the unsexy panda panties. But they were worth the embarrassment to see that smile.

I whacked him lightly on the shoulder. "Don't judge my panda underwear."

He pushed them down over my ass, his fingers tracing their path. "Never. I love them," he said, though his eyes were focused on other things. He traced his hands back up my legs, over my hips before coming around to grab my butt with a groan.

He stood and moved me toward the shower stall.

I stepped hesitantly into the shower stream, testing the water with the tips of my fingers. Of course it was perfect. The emotional part of me knew that despite tonight's show of violence, Lux would never do anything to hurt me, even have the shower water too hot.

I stepped under the steady pound of the water coming from a shower head as big as a dinner plate. Lux stepped in behind, his clothes gone, and the hard muscles of his naked body pressed tightly into my back.

I went to turn, I wanted to see, but he stopped me with gentle hands on my shoulders.

"Wait."

He moved me out of the water and grabbed body wash from the little alcove in the shower wall, popping open the lid. The smell of Lux filled the stall and I inhaled deeply. Squirting a good amount into his hands, he put the bottle back.

His slippery hands went back to my shoulders, and he slid them down my arms, washing me. His fingers were firm as they slid down my arms to my fingertips and then back up the sensitive underside, moving over my shoulders and then working in lazy circles down my chest. He leaned forward and trailed small wet kisses down my neck.

His hands finally reached my soapy breasts and I sucked in a gasp as he kneaded them, tugging my nipples between his fingers, each tug pulling at my core.

Those rough, strong hands slid even lower, down over my ribs and in big looping circles over my stomach, his finger dipping into my naval, making me suck in a quick breath. Lower, closer to the aching part of me that was desperate for attention.

His hands skimmed over my hips and down to the tops of my thighs, sliding inwards and brushing ever so close.

Instead of giving me what I wanted, he turned me, and I got my first look at Lux naked. He was beauty. Smooth, unforgiving muscle chiseled his body. Sitting hard and proud against his abdominal muscles was the biggest cock I'd ever seen. I swallowed hard in both fear and anticipation.

"Holy shit."

He chuckled as he fell to his knees in front of me, working the suds from my ankles upwards, building the tension all over again. His fingers skimmed the sensitive part behind my knees and he worked my thighs in long, hard strokes. Finally, he was back where I wanted him. He pulled me into the warm rush of water, rinsing off the rest of the body wash.

His fingers grazed over the folds of my pussy, giving my clit a quick flick, making me buck towards him on a moan.

"You're going to want to lean back for this," he said and lifted my left leg, hooking it over his shoulder. I took his advice and leaned back against the cool, black tiles. I couldn't breathe as he looked at me, staring at my pussy like it was a work of art. Then he leaned in and licked my seam in one long stroke.

The breath I'd been holding hissed out of me as he buried his face between my thighs, lapping and sucking like a starving man. My knees wobbled and he reached up, grabbing my other leg and placing it over his other shoulder until he was supporting my entire weight against the wall, two hands under my ass, kneading. And then he feasted.

Orgasm after orgasm hit me until I was just a screaming mess.

My body was jello by the time he stood, flicking off the water. He grabbed me up in his arms and carried me to the bedroom, both of us still dripping wet.

"Our first time won't be in a shower. I want to make love to you right," he whisper-growled at me.

He placed me on the bed, his body immediately coming over mine. He traced his tongue up the scar on my sternum, before drifting to suck my nipple into his mouth, making me writhe. I was panting by the time he switched to the other breast.

"I can't wait any longer," his soft voice was a plea.

"Don't. I need you inside me, Lux."

He growled, his cock at my entrance in seconds. He pushed the massive head into me, slowly, my gentle barbarian. The stretch was deliciously painful, but I was wet and ready for him.

With one powerful thrust, he was seated all the way in me and I'd never felt so full or so right in my life. This was perfection. He began to move, and coherent thought left me as we became a wave of movement and sensation, building and building. I chanted his name on every exhale until the pleasure built so high that I exploded, screaming, and my dodgy heart thundering in an out-of-time staccato.

Lux kept pumping, his rhythm getting ragged as he reached his own climax on a roar. Everything went black but I came around in seconds. Thankfully, Lux hadn't noticed my temporary lack of consciousness, or he might never give me such a mind blowing orgasm again.

His body lay along mine, a comforting weight, and I wrapped my arms around his chest, my nails tracing light patterns up and down his back. "That was…" There were no words.

"Yes," he groaned back, pulling out and rolling off me but taking me with him until I was lying on top of him. Stickiness dripped down my thighs.

"I will clean you in a minute. I just want to hold you while I catch my breath." His soft, rough voice did something to my heart.

"I don't mind. It means we can shower again later. I really like your shower, with you in it." I punctuated the words with a kiss to his chest. Fuck, he was amazing. I desperately wanted to lick every inch of him, but I was exhausted.

"Sleep, Sweet One. There will be time for more later. Rest."

His eyes closed, though his fingers traced light lines up and down my back, lulling me into sleep.

CHAPTER TEN

I flicked through the clothes in my wardrobe. When I'd finally returned to my apartment the other day, after hours of making love to Lux and sleeping in his arms, it was to a sea of shopping bags in my living room.

Unfortunately, I hadn't had time to go through them right then, I had an appointment to keep with Elias for tests, so I'd thrown on the first casual thing I could find, a halter neck rockabilly dress with a little red cherries pattern and a pair of black ballet flats.

When I'd returned, I'd been so exhausted after a day of tests that I had fallen into bed that night and hadn't woken up until noon. It'd been a long week on an emotional rollercoaster ride and my body had been wrung out.

I'd put away all my new things with my old thrift store finds. I appreciated my closet, full of clothes still with their tags. I hadn't had one of those since my parents had died.

Now, Monday had rolled around again, and for the first time in years I wouldn't have to go to work to make sure I could pay my medical bills and rent for the month.

I fingered a soft, pink sweater. It felt like a cloud on my skin. I would have to call Tolliver and Sam, and thank them again. I missed them now that they weren't here. How could you miss people you'd known less than a week? But I did. I missed Tolliver's serious face and dry wit. I missed Sam's laid-back nature and teasing sensuality. Only seven more days until they were home.

The black jeans with the grey tee, Ace weighed in on my outfit choices.

I had to agree; I'd tried those jeans on and they made my ass look like a peach.

Ace had also flourished since I moved in with the guys. Maybe I was just more accepting of her, or myself, because a voice in my head was no longer the craziest thing about my life. She liked the guys, though they still didn't know about her. Nothing came up in my brain scans when Eli ran them the other day, so she wasn't due to a brain tumor. I decided to keep it to myself for a little while longer. Eventually I'd let it slip, then I'd explain. Well I'd try. I didn't even know how to explain it to myself.

Ace is the badass bitch I wish I could be, Ace mimicked my voice almost to perfection, although it sounded a little whinier than I did.

"You got the bitch part right anyway," I teased back. I always spoke out loud to her in private. It was just too much pressure in my brain otherwise. I could put up with the pain if necessary, but only for a few minutes. It was like my brain was going to war with itself and it always gave me a pounding headache.

I shimmied into my 7 For All Mankind jeans, giggling at the irony, and the soft grey t-shirt. I was going to find Oz. He promised to teach me to play Call of Duty today. Whatever that was. It just sounded like a great excuse to sit on his lap.

Give the girl a little lovin' and she turns into a brazen hussy. Gotta say, I'm kinda proud right now.

"Jealous much?"

A scoffing laugh. *Hardly. Though, your boy Lux is packing some serious meat in his lunchbox.*

I laughed, enjoying our new camaraderie. There was a knock at the door. I glanced at my pink wristband that thankfully doubled as a watch. Oz was early. Eager much?

I didn't bother with shoes, but stuffed my phone in my pocket.

I was smiling as I pulled open the door.

"You're earl…"

But Oz wasn't at my front door. It was a stranger. A fucking scary stranger.

I couldn't pinpoint why I thought he was scary, though. He had dark black hair and dark eyes, a beautiful face with a sparkling white smile. He had on a Black Sabbath shirt and black jeans that were torn at the knees. He looked boringly average, if not a tad more handsome than the average Joe. But still a cold shot of fear ran down my spine.

I stepped back towards the Mini-Oz sphere on the

hall table. "Help, help," I said, praying it was loud enough.

"You must be Arcadia. It's a pleasure to finally meet you." The man stepped forward into my apartment.

I mentally willed the guys to hurry. My heart was beating too fast and I could hardly breathe. Something was wrong. I willed myself not to give into the darkness again.

"Don't worry about the fear response. It's just the primordial part of your brain trying to tell your nervous system to protect itself. I mean you no harm. My name is Luc. You might know me as Lucifer Morningstar. Or…" he grimaced, "The Devil."

Ace let out a piercing scream in my brain, the sound sending a spearing pain around my skull and making blood pour out my nose. Blackness swamped into my vision and the last thing I saw was the face of the Devil staring at me.

PART II

W hen I opened my eyes, the Devil was sitting on my couch drinking a beer. Not a devil; the Devil. Big D.

Well, I've only just got my memories back, but from what I remember you're right. He has a really big D...

I screwed my eyes closed again and let out a frustrated scream that could only be heard inside my head.

What the fuck was that, Ace? You nearly gave me a goddamn aneurysm and you knocked me out, in front of the fucking Devil. That scream... I shuddered. *And now you are making dick jokes?*

I sounded screechy even inside my own head but I was equal parts pissed off and scared.

Excuse me if I was finally remembering all my past lives at once, including my immortal soul being ripped from its vessel and placed into yours. I'm not sure if you are aware of this, Arcadia, but that shit hurts. A lot.

She sounded choked up and I felt momentarily bad that I yelled at her.

If you are done with your little shit-fit, I feel compelled to tell you that he can hear inside your head and knows everything we are saying. She sounded smug.

My eyes shot open again, and the Devil was still there, saluting me with his beer bottle, a slight grin on his face.

I sat upright so fast my head spun, and I clutched at it against the residual headache. Two strong arms came around me and pulled me onto a lap. I didn't fight it; I'd know Lux's scent anywhere.

"Not so fast. You're okay. I've got you," he whispered to me in his gentle voice, as he pressed me back against his chest. "You are the scariest person I've ever met, Arcadia Jones."

I twisted so I could see his face and raised both eyebrows. "How can you say that when we are sitting across from He Who Shall Not Be Named?"

"Hey, I resent the Voldemort comparison. That guy was seriously evil," the Devil said as he took another sip of beer. "Please, call me Luc. I insist."

Well, if the Devil insisted.

He can hear you, remember? You have to call him Luc in your mind as well, Ace said and I wanted to scream again. There were already two people in my head. Three was definitely a crowd.

Lux gave a little disgruntled huff. "Lucifer doesn't faint all the time, worrying me he might never wake up!"

I looked up into Lux's face, slightly pale despite the natural gold of his tan. His jaw was tight and two adorable worry lines fought for dominance amongst the scars. He looked scared. For me.

"I'm sorry. It doesn't usually happen this often but it has been a bit of a crazy week. You can blame Ace for that last one though."

"Who's Ace?" Another voice asked, and I looked over to see Eli was in my apartment too. Actually, all the guys were here, except Tolliver and Sam obviously, who were at Fashion Week. Oz was pacing near the kitchen. I'd never seen Oz pace. Ri was in the corner, his face as strained as Lux's. I gave him a little finger wave and a smile.

"I'm with Lux, Beautiful Girl. You are one scary mama," he croaked out as he shook his head.

Valery was drinking wine from the bottle in my kitchen, although last time I checked, I didn't have any wine lying around. Actually, he was most of the way through the bottle and his cheeks were a ruddy pink. He placed the bottle on the counter and came over to me. He bent down and said something stern in French, placing a palm on both of my cheeks and kissing me solidly on the mouth. His lips were soft and tasted like a fruity red.

As far as first kisses went, it was delicious if slightly unexpected.

He walked away, still muttering in French, but whatever he was saying made the Devil, I mean Luc, smile.

"Who is Ace?" Eli repeated, and I sighed.

This should be interesting, Ace said, back to her usual nonchalant self.

INDEED.

I flew to my feet as the Devil's - I mean Luc's- voice boomed in my skull.

"No, no, no get the hell out of my brain. Two is already a crowd and you are so loud. You just doubled my headache." Arcadia Jones, chastising the Devil and failing survival instincts since 1998.

APOLOGIES ARCADIA. I AM NOT SHOUTING. WE ARE JUST ON DIFFERENT FREQUENCIES I AM AFRAID. UNFORTUNATELY, YOU ARE THE ONLY CONDUIT I CAN USE TO SPEAK TO MY BELOVED ACEREZEAL.

Ugh, I hate that name. It sounds so angel-ish, Ace whined.

"Arcadia…" Eli was beginning to sound worried.

The urge to scream was beginning to build again. I huffed and sat back down on Lux's lap.

"Fine. Ace is the voice in my head who has been with me since I was sixteen and she's not a brain tumor but I don't know what she is other than the fact she swears like a pirate and is right about most things and that she loves me and protects me if I need it." It all ran out in one long, peevish sentence, and Eli remained silent. He just blinked at me slowly. Then he turned to Lucifer.

"Is this your doing? I checked her brain scans literally yesterday. There is nothing to support her having auditory hallucinations. She has no family history of psychosis or schizophrenia."

Luc drained his beer, and another appeared in its place. Guess I now knew where Valery's wine came from.

"Well, yes and no. Acerezeal, or Ace as Arcadia knows her, was one of the fallen, like me. She is my consort and her immortal soul lives inside the body of your Arcadia."

Lux pulled me closer to his chest, every inch of his body poised protectively around mine.

"Relax, I'm not about to commandeer your new toy, Lux. I would like Ace back where she belongs, in her own body."

I felt like I'd been sucker punched. For so long, I'd assumed that Ace was some long buried part of me that I needed to cope with my life. She was everything I wanted to be; calm, intelligent and a complete badass.

But she wasn't part of me at all. She was an angel stuffed into my body. It felt like I was losing something, my best friend. A piece of my soul.

Hey now, I'm not going anywhere yet. You're stuck with me being a parasite in your body for a lot longer. Even when I'm not... with you, I'll always have your back. Always.

She was preparing me. But for what?

"What aren't you telling us?" I narrowed my eyes at Luc, and he laughed.

"You are much more of a badass than you believe, Arcadia." He sighed and shifted in his seat. "You must remember that my life has been endless. The perpetual flow of time around me an imperishable object. And not just for me, for the other guy too."

I just stared. The other guy?

"Keanu Reeves?" Oz asked from where he rested against the wall. At least he'd stopped pacing. I resisted the urge to go to him and wrap him in my arms.

Lucifer grinned. "No, not Keanu. He goes by many

names, like me, but we are obviously speaking of God. Big G," he laughed and winked at me.

"I am the first to admit that I probably broke the old man's heart when I fell, though in my opinion he massively overreacted, but I made my peace with that and I quite like my new role. There's something to be said for the freedom to live how you wish. But Big G, well, he's seen a decline in numbers, while I gotta tell you, my domain is brimming. You should see the line to the eternal punishment chamber. Hell, I'm beginning to think that waiting in the perpetually unmoving line is punishment enough."

You're getting off track, Ace interrupted.

YOU ARE CORRECT, THANK YOU, MY HEART.

I grimaced. Painful and weird. Great.

"But I digress. Upon our last game of chess in Central Park in 1982, I remarked upon my current over-crowding problem. You see, he was having the opposite problem. There were so few without sin these days. He will forgive most things, but indulging in one of his ordained deadly sins, the very ones he cast his favorite son out of heaven for? Those he could not forgive and forget. And he is a stubborn old ass when he wants to be. I informed him that there were millions of souls in my domain that were truly repentant and would happily atone for their sins, without reward. He didn't believe that a soul, once judged, could change so much. So we had a wager. And here you guys are. The first of my Redeemable souls. And my secret weapon, the Redeemer."

There was silence around the room, every one of us

grasping at the tiniest glimmer of hope, and looking for a flash of deceit.

"And if we succeed?" Valery's voice sounded hoarse.

"If you succeed, people will be able to work their way up from hell and past the pearly gates. You guys get a free pass to heaven. Win-win for humanity."

"And what do you win, personally?" I raised both brows. Altruism isn't a trait usually associated with the Devil.

"If I win, Ace gets her body back. Her immortal soul was torn out by Azriel, on the Father's say so. I kept it in a vessel until the bet was decided and then I placed her inside you as you emerged from your mother's womb. Such a strong spirit already, I knew that Ace would not overcome you. I apologize. I am sure it must have been difficult, but there is little I wouldn't do for the woman I love."

Pfft, don't let the sweet talk fool you. He just likes this thing I do with my wings when we are in bed. I reach them around an-

"La la la la!" I plugged my fingers in my ears, and Luc laughed. A full, deep belly laugh that sent a thrill of pleasure through me. It made me happy to see him laugh. Or maybe it made Ace happy. Semantics.

YOU KNOW THAT IS NOT TRUE, ACEREZEAL. I WANT YOU BACK FOR YOUR HELLISHLY AMAZING TITS, Luc teased and Ace snorted, but it was a happy sound. Geez, it was sickeningly sweet inside my head right now.

Eli tapped a finger along the sharp line of his jaw rhythmically. "So you have been concealing a voice in your head all this time?" He sounded... hurt. I should have known that he wouldn't let it drop after Lucifer's explanation. Not my good doctor.

"Deep down I didn't think it was related to my illness. And I wasn't hiding it, really. I just didn't think there was a good time to bring it up? I mean, when is a good time to bring up the fact you hear voices in your head?"

Ri scoffed, one eyebrow quirking. "Probably at the same time we told you that we were returned souls from hell. I mean after that, voices that tell you to burn things are quite mundane."

He had a point, and I stuck my tongue out at him.

"I'm sorry guys. But hey, at least we don't have to worry it's a brain tumor now, right?"

Eli was still frowning. "But it could have been."

I shifted from Lux's lap, giving my butt a little wiggle for thrills, and was rewarded with a small smack.

"Tease," Lux growled. Heat pooled in my stomach as I had a brief flashback to the other night. He growled all sorts of dirty things in my ear as his body conquered mine. Heat flew to my cheeks. I was still a little way from being a sex kitten, but boy, I was really ready to ditch this room and get him naked again.

I swung my eyes back to Eli. I wouldn't mind getting him naked either. Three little lines ran across Eli's forehead, but his eyes looked disappointed. I knelt down in front of him.

"I'm sorry. I promise no more secrets. Trust me, I don't have any left. Unless you count that time I stole a chocolate bar from the grocery store when I was ten." I placed my hands on his strong thighs, pressing the tips of my fingers into the hard muscles because I just couldn't resist, and leaned in close. "I didn't even take it back. I ate it in secret behind my house in case anyone was trying to track me down."

Eli's lips twitched into a small smile. "I'll add klepto-mania to your list of symptoms."

I couldn't help myself. I leaned forward and pressed a light kiss to his full lower lip, sliding my hands up his thighs to his waist. He nipped my lower lip.

"Soon."

Lucifer cleared his throat and stood. "I guess that is my cue to leave. Places to be, people to poke in the ass with a pitchfork."

"Really?"

"No, Sweet Cady. How could you have a hellcat like Ace live inside you all these years and yet still be so unbelievably innocent? You seven need to fix that." He waggled at a finger at them. "But if you hurt her, I will personally assign you to the very lowest level of hell and you will beg for reprieve for eternity and there will be none." The temperature in the room dropped to frigid levels. "There are millions of you in my realm, you can be replaced easily, but Arcadia is special. Best you remember that."

A cold shiver ran down my spine at his words, and I resisted the urge to do what my brain was screaming at me to do and run away.

Lux stood, stepping toward me. "Received loud and clear."

Lucifer gave a curt nod, and then his normal

pleasant demeanour was back. Note to self, do not fuck with the Devil.

"Arcadia, could you walk me to the door please?" I stood from where I was on the floor and walked him out. I brushed against Ri on the way to the door, his fingers lightly running against my stomach. My eyes went to his, expecting his hooded gaze to shine with the lust that was always there, but all I saw was a show of support. Ri had my back. I gave him a half grin.

But I was pretty sure I was safe with the Lucifer. Safer than I'd ever been in my life. The guy had literally made a bargain with God to save the soul inside me. While ever I held Ace with me, I was safe.

You will be safe regardless of whether I am inside you or next to you, Arcadia. You know this.

INDEED, YOU HAVE MY DEEPEST GRATITUDE. BUT YOU MIGHT WANT TO BLOCK YOUR MENTAL EARS RIGHT NOW.

How the hell did someone do that? I decided to sing Jingle Bells on repeat in my brain, but it didn't block it all out.

YOU WILL BE BACK IN MY ARMS SOON, ACEREZEAL. THEN I WILL MAKE LOVE TO YOU LIKE THAT TIME IN THAT ITALIAN VILLAGE. DO YOU REMEMBER, WHERE THE DANCING SICKNESS TOOK THE WHOLE VILLAGE AND WE MADE LOVE IN THE CENTER OF THE TOWN SQUARE AS THE BODIES FELL AROUND US FROM EXHAUSTION?

Eesh. I couldn't hear Ace's response, she was much

more in tune with my mental frequencies, but I could imagine.

Out loud, Lucifer chuckled. "I bid you farewell, Arcadia. I will return soon."

"Wait. I need to ask. If I succeed redeeming one of the guys, what happens next? Do they just poof up to the pearly gates? Turn to dust? Because, I'm sorry, but I can't help if it means that I just have to watch them die. I have feelings for them already, I just can't."

Luc patted the top of my head and gave another booming laugh. "Oh, I chose well with you. Do not worry. The terms of the bargain states that if they are redeemed, they will be able to live out the remainder of their natural human lives here on earth. They all died quite young, and they have good hearts. It is why I chose them. Given more time on the earthly plane, I am sure they would have repented naturally. But they have to continue to live well once redeemed if they want to get up there, otherwise it's back to me downstairs. But there is a time limit, Cady. Any who aren't redeemed in that time will be back in my realm. There are no third chances."

"What is the time frame?"

Lucifer shook his head. "I do not know. The other guy decided that one."

Panic made my heart race. "What if it's a week? What if it's tomorrow?"

Lucifer shrugged. "You'll just have to have faith."

With that, he disappeared.

"Huh. I thought there would be smoke or flames or something," I said to the now empty corridor.

He's known to be a little theatrical when he wants to make an impressive exit.

I stared at the ornate cornice on the wall and tried to process everything that just happened. And failed. What had become of my boring, sedate life?

My door opened and Oz poked his head out. "Is he gone?"

I'd barely finished nodding when the door was flung open and I was in Oz's arms. "I was so fucking worried. Mini Oz sent out a help alert and I was the first one here and you were unconscious on the couch with Luc standing over you and I didn't know what to do, and then Lux was the next in and I thought he was going to try to kill the Devil. It was a mess. God, I'm so glad you are okay." He pulled back and put his hands on my cheeks, peppering my face with kisses.

I laughed. "It's okay, Oz. I'm okay, you're okay. We'll all be okay."

He picked me up, and I wrapped my arms and legs around him as he walked me back into my apartment. I pressed my face into his neck, appreciating the woodsy smell of him.

He walked me to the small breakfast bar and plopped me on top.

He stepped away and I was once again the focus of everyone in the room.

"Well, at least life isn't boring around here."

"It was until you came along, *mon chere.*" Valery ran a hand over my short hair, smoothing down the spiky tufts.

Oz slapped a hand to his forehead and pulled the phone from his pocket.

"Ah shit. I forgot to cancel the help call once we'd worked out you were in no danger."

Lux grunted. "She was dealing with the Devil. I wouldn't say that's safe."

Oz rolled his eyes. "You know what I mean." He scrolled through the notices on his phone. "Oh well, too late now."

Valery handed me a cup of tea he'd pulled from somewhere. I definitely didn't own these delicate little fine China tea cups. I was beginning to think Valery was some kind of magician too.

"Too late for what?"

"Sam and Tolliver are on their way home."

Oops. "But what about fashion week?"

"You are more important than fashion week. When they didn't hear from anyone, they dropped their engagements and took Tolliver's private plane home. They should be here in a few hours."

I should feel bad that I'd caused such an upheaval, but I wasn't. Maybe that made me a bad person, or selfish at the very least, but instead I was excited.

Tolliver and Sam were coming home early.

CHAPTER TWELVE

I bounced on the balls of my feet, desperate to see over the heads of the crowd. There was a Boy Scout troop amassing in the foyer of the airport, and I may have been silently cursing them.

"Can you see them?" I asked Oz for the hundredth time, wishing I had his over six feet height advantage.

"I keep telling you, you'll know when they arrive."

"How? We don't even have a little placard."

With that, there was a cacophony of shouts. I studied the Boy Scouts, convinced someone must have fallen and broken their neck given the yelling. But then I saw the flashes of light. Paparazzi.

"Why did you leave fashion week, Sam? Was it a pay dispute?"

"Sam, are you worried that Lance Caulfield will steal your crown as the most sought after male model of the 21st century?"

"Who's the mystery woman? Is she pregnant?"

As they finally made it to me, a woman's voice called out,

"Tolliver, what do you say to the speculation that you are gay?"

I scoffed internally at that one. Unlikely. Tolliver looked offended. He reached out, wrapped an arm around my back and kissed me like we were in an old school romance film, dipping me over his arm as he plundered my mouth. The kiss went on as the flashes blinded me like fireworks. I felt thoroughly possessed.

"I guess not," the woman's voice sounded amused.

He lifted his head and grinned down at me, and I couldn't help but smile back.

"I missed you guys," I whispered to him.

"We missed you too, Sweetheart. I'm glad you came out of your meeting with Luc in one piece. Doesn't happen as often as he'd have you believe." He slung an arm around my shoulders and led me out of the airport terminal, the flashes still blinding as the paparazzi followed along.

"Are you guys really three paparazzi famous? I mean, I knew you were hot commodities, and most people would recognize you on the street, but I didn't think people would be all that interested in your daily lives."

"Sam got drunk and did some heiress in the back seat of her Rolls, much to the delight of a Pap that happened to be hanging around hoping for that exact scenario, and it blew up. Now they follow us around hoping he'll be that dumb again. He's not allowed to go out drunk and alone anymore."

"Hey, the publicity was good for business eventually. People like a well-hung bad boy with great glutes." He leaned forward until he whispered in my ear. "Besides, the only person I like doing in the back of a car now is you."

Heat rushed to my cheeks and I bit my lip. More flashes. That was going to end up as the fifth run story on TMZ. Sam Sigurdsson trying to steal best friend's girl.

The truth is much more interesting, Ace chuckled. *Sam Sigurdsson wants to double team a girl with his best friend, despite the fact the girl is their only ticket into heaven. They could run it right next to the Elvis Spotted in Hoboken and Woman Probed By Aliens story.*

We pulled up to the spot where Oz had parked the car in a No Parking Zone, and I was actually a little surprised to see it still there. Money talked apparently.

The guys threw their suitcases in the back, and Tolliver slid into the driver's seat.

"No way am I letting that lunatic drive when you are in the car again. No wonder he died young."

Sam laughed, but Oz's face was contorted into complete devastation. It was gone in seconds, but I saw. I didn't even factor in that they might have died in terrible ways, I was too worried about their past crimes. But they were all dead. Obviously they must have died somehow, and given how young they were, it probably wasn't peacefully in their sleep.

I reached over and wrapped my arms around his torso. "I'm sorry."

"Thanks Cady-Lady. It was a long time ago." He

kissed the top of my head. "Let's go home. I owe you a Call of Duty lesson." His smile was back, but his eyes still held the bruises of past hurts.

I slid into the back with Sam, and almost instantly I was in his arms and he was kissing me like a starving man. He pulled me onto his lap, his arms wrapping around my waist to cup my ass.

"We gotta stop meeting like this or we are going to christen every one of Tolliver's back seats."

"I'm okay with that," I purred back. God, but he was pretty. It literally knocked the breath out me every time. It should be illegal.

"Cady needs her own seat, and seatbelt," Tolliver groused.

Sam sighed against my mouth, his perfect cupid's bow lips brushing over mine one last time. "One day soon, I am going to get you into my bed without interruptions. Then you will sing my name in moans, Baby."

With that, he slid me into the seat beside him, buckling me in. As Tolliver finally pulled out into the flow of cars, I snuggled into Sam's side.

"How was fashion week?"

Tolliver snorted. "Catty as usual. Pressure is high, stress is high and envy is rampant. Sam was in his element."

"The parties were endless. I would much rather have been at home with you. I'm kind of glad that Luc decided to turn up and send everyone into turmoil. Meant I got to skip the black and white ball where rich old socialites with too much plastic surgery, grope me and try to slip me their room numbers. Male model is not synonymous with gigolo," Sam sighed. "I just want to stay home and binge watch reality television with you. Toddlers and Tiaras. Dance Moms. Rupaul's Drag Race."

I rested my head against his shoulder. "Consider it a date."

We rolled straight into peak hour traffic and stopped.

Oz cleared his throat. "So, Arcadia currently possesses the soul of Lucifer's long lost lover in her body, and she manifests as a discombobulated voice in her head."

Huh, so there is an easy way to explain that. Bravo, Oz. If I could just get a peek at his trouser snake I think he might just push Lux out of first place for my favorite Sin, Ace mused.

I rolled my eyes. *No playing favorites. And no looking at their junk!* I protested.

Sure I won't. She didn't even try to sound sincere, the crazy pervert.

"See, that's what she's doing when she pulls that face. I thought she was having episodes, but she's talking to Ace. That's the demoness' name."

Please tell him that I am a fallen angel. NOT a demoness hussy. They are basically all boobs, no personality. I could kick their asses half way across Elysium before they'd unsheathed those ugly damn claws.

Touch a nerve, much? I teased. Oh man, it was nice when the shoe was on the other foot.

"Ace said she is a fallen angel, and would like to ensure that you never refer to her as a demoness. Considering her sugar daddy is the Devil himself, you probably don't want to piss her off. She's got permanent PMS naturally."

I could see the rapid blinking of Tolliver's eyes in the rear view mirror and Sam just frowned.

I punched Oz in the arm. "You could have waited until we got home. It's lucky we are in traffic or Tolliver would have crashed." I turned to the guys. "It's not as crazy as it sounds." And then I repeated everything that Lucifer had told me.

Sam knocked on my head. "Fuck. So there's a whole other person in there, just chatting away? Does she like one of us better than the others?"

Envy, thy name is Sam.

Better not tell him that he isn't even in the running for my favorite. Not even in the top three. Way too pretty for me.

"Nope, she doesn't have a favorite."

Lying will get you sent to hell, you know, she chastised gently. I couldn't even tell if she was joking.

The traffic was moving again, even if it was at a snail's pace. I turned to Sam. "So I've decided that you and Tolliver will be my first redemptions."

More silence in the car.

"Whoa, have you been taking lessons from Lux in dropping bombs?" Oz asked. "Why them?"

I leaned forward and ran my hand through his deep brown hair. He'd left it out today, and it fell in messy waves that felt like silk. I don't know what conditioner he used, but I made a note to raid his bathroom for the brand.

"Because they are the easiest. Greed and Envy. I've got a plan all figured out."

Tolliver quirked a brow. "Care to share this master plan?"

"It's simple really. We are going to spend all Tolliver's money. And Sam is going to quit being a model to help us do it."

The car swerved into the other lane, and the driver behind us leaned on his horn with an angry yell.

"All of it?"

"Most of it. Keep enough that the family can live comfortably, but the rest should go in trust to the foundation."

"A family? Is that what we are?" Oz laughed.

Maybe that wasn't the right word, but I still didn't know the correct terminology. "Polyamorous partners? Harem? Brother-Husbands? I don't know." Heat flooded my cheeks again, and Sam laughed, kissing my head.

"Lovers. Worshipers at the temple of Arcadia." His kisses slid from my cheek to the corner of my mouth, then softly to my lips. I sighed against them. No guy should look like that and be able to kiss like this. It was unfair. Against the natural order of things.

"I'm pretty sure that's heresy. We're trying to get you back to heaven, remember?" I chastised gently.

"You just wait until you are screaming 'oh god' in my bed later," he said against my ear, giving it a light nip and sending wet heat between my thighs.

"Keep it in your pants, Fabio. We are almost home," Tolliver said, his frown marring his perfectly ageless face. Maybe he wasn't such a fan of the plan. But I figured that the personality shifts would have to be pretty major to earn your way back to up top. Giving money to the bum who sat on the stairs of the subway wasn't going to cut it.

Sam, however, seemed perfectly at ease. Actually, I rarely saw Sam looking concerned about anything.

"Aren't you worried about giving up the modelling? You won't be plastered across billboards anymore. No Milan or London or New York fashion weeks."

"Not really. The whole thing was getting a bit tedious. The high maintenance designers, the psycho heads of fashion houses, the sleazy benefactors. Besides, I'm looking forward to spending Scrooge's money."

It was probably a shame. I was definitely going to get hate mail from the women of the world. He was perfection. Maybe this would be too easy for him. Because let's face it, you could walk past him in the street, and women would want to bang him on the sidewalk and men would envy him.

I was going to have to think on this more.

We rolled into the garage, and parked the Escalade between the Bugatti and the Range Rover. I knew where we could start.

But first I wanted to sit in a room with all the guys and just appreciate how fortunate I was.

CHAPTER THIRTEEN

"Left, no watch the sniper on the roof. Left. No your other left. Why are you looking at the sky?"

Oz let out an exasperated sigh. I was not going to be competing in the Call of Duty World Championships any time soon.

Surprisingly, other than Oz, it was Valery who was the best video game player. We all sat around Oz's living room, which looked exactly how I imagined it. Big comfy couches in front of a massive television, a computer set up that would make grown gamers weep, and a sink that was stacked high with dishes.

We'd all piled into Oz's apartment, except Eli who was at work, and Lux and Ri who were training and then heading to Dante's. Even Valery had the night off. None of them looked askance at the pair of Oz's jeans that had been flung over the light shade or the balled socks on the couch. Apparently they were used to Oz's less than stellar cleaning job. Well, I guess he was Sloth.

We ordered pizza from the nicest pizza place in Soho and just chilled out. It was the best. Like all the slumber parties I missed growing up.

Tolliver and Sam had only lasted until the last slice of pizza was gone before jet lag caught up with them and they headed off to bed, but not before giving me panty-melting kisses goodnight.

As my avatar died for the fifteenth time that night, I threw down the controller and huffed.

"Let's play Mario Kart. I bet I could kick your butt in Mario Kart."

Oz looked almost offended. "I do not own Mario Kart!"

"Dance, Dance Revolution?"

"That's it, get out of my apartment," he joked as he pulled me tighter into his arms. I turned in his lap so I could press my face into his chest. I tried to stifle a yawn, but couldn't. It had been a rather messed up day.

"You're tired *mon chere*, I shall wish you *bonne nuit*," Valery said, coming over to lift me from Oz's lap and into his arms. "I feel like I just can't get enough time with you. You are this ray of light just out of my grasp. But I would like to remedy this, if I could."

"I'd like that too." And I would. Beside Eli, and probably Ri, Valery worked the most of any of my Sins. I was worried about how I would redeem him if I never saw him.

"Tomorrow, come to my kitchen and cook with me? Around ten?" I could feel the warm press of his solid body, and briefly thought it was unnatural that the Sin of Gluttony wasn't pudgy. While Valery wasn't ripped like Lux, his body was firm and hard.

"Sounds perfect. It's a date."

I tilted my head up for a kiss, and Valery happily supplied the gentlest, most tender kiss I'd ever received. If a kiss could promise you that you were going to be worshipped, it was that one.

"Sweet dreams, *mon chere*."

He left, stepping over one of Oz's discarded boots and giving us a little wave as he closed the door.

"Then there were two," Oz said, and I sat back down on his lap. Sure there was a couch, but it wasn't warm, hard and full of promise.

"Cady?"

"Mm?"

"Do you want to stay with me tonight?"

I looked up at him, really looked at him. I looked past the bushy red beard that hadn't had a trim since my makeover day, and the long straight nose, and even past the pine green colour of his eyes. I looked deep into their depths and saw the vulnerability, his self-consciousness.

"I couldn't think of anywhere else I'd rather be right now." He gave me that huge white smile, the one that made my chest feel full. He shifted me from his lap and stood.

He wrapped an arm under my legs and the other around my shoulders, and carried me towards the bedroom.

"You guys realize I have two functioning legs, right? Everyone seems to want to carry me everywhere," I mock chastised. In reality, it kind of made me feel like a princess.

"I like holding you in my arms." He moved further into the apartment, down a short hallway.

I'd prepared myself for Oz's bedroom to be filthy, but I'd been so wrong. His room was immaculate. His bed was made and dozens of candles were burning in colored glass jars.

"Wow, Oz. This is beautiful. Have these been burning this whole time?"

He reached into the jar closest to us and pulled out a flickering LED tea light candle.

"I wouldn't jeopardize you safety. I don't mess around with fire."

"I love it."

The room glowed with a soft warm light, and I could see elements of Oz in the room. His alarm clock was Mickey Mouse. His lamp was Darth Vader holding a lightsaber. Several signed posters were framed on the walls. On his mahogany drawers sat a framed newspaper article, two photos blurred by the lack of light. I went over to read it, but Oz's hand stopped me.

"Not tonight. I'll explain that tomorrow. But tonight I just want it to be us, not our pasts. Is that okay?" His face was scrunched in a frown, and his voice trembled a little at the end.

I nodded. Although I was now desperate to know what the newspaper said, I could respect Oz's wishes for tonight.

We stood slightly apart, and Oz pulled his shirt over his head. His broad chest was covered in soft, dark hair that trailed tantalizingly down in a thin line towhere his jeans hung low on his hips.

I pulled my tank top over my head and stood in front of him, topless. I had forgone a bra for the night. Yay for small breasts.

Oz's eyes dropped to my boobs. And stayed there. "Fuck."

And that was all the warning I got before he slammed me to him, his arms going around my body, and mashing our chests together as his lips covered mine with a hunger that was like a red hot fever.

I stood on my tiptoes, kissing him back with just as much passion. He groaned, putting his large hands under my ass and lifting me. I wrapped my arms around his neck, twining my fingers in his hair so I could plunder his mouth. His groans rumbled against my nipples and he walked me back towards the bed. He placed me down gently, and just stood there looking, his eyes full of hunger. He removed his jeans slowly, popping the button and then slowly sliding down the zip of his Levi's. He pushed them down his hips, his thumbs catching under his boxer briefs on the way down.

They fell past his knees to the floor, but my eyes were glued on his cock.

Holy fuck.

Holy fuck is right. Someone call the zoo. There's been an escape from the python enclosure. Did he roll that bad boy up to fit it in his Levi's? Move over Lux, we have a new reigning champion, Ace crowed.

Out of my head. Now. I could feel her amusement but she was blissfully quiet.

I realized Oz was giving me a strange look.

"Uh, Ace says hi. And wow. I mean I'm saying wow. Well, she said wow too. I'm just going to be quiet now."

Oz's cheeks turned the most adorable shade of pink. I didn't know big strong lumberjack looking guys could blush, but it was cute as hell. He gave me a lopsided grin.

"Will she be joining us?"

"No!" Well, not really. I wasn't completely confident she wasn't voyeuristically watching in there. She probably had a scorecard system.

Oz knelt on the end of the bed between my knees, reaching up to run his fingers over my collarbone and down my surgical scar. My skin prickled at his feather-light touch as his fingers kept whispering down, over my navel and the slight swell of my stomach, to the waistband of my own jeans. He ran his fingers from one hip bone to the other. He flicked the button with one hand, his other hand slipping under my lower back to lift me up. He peeled my skinny jeans down, until I was just there in my panties. White lace this time. No pandas in sight. I'm pretty sure my panda panties were still in Lux's bedside table.

He leaned forward and caught the edge of the lace between his teeth, and I lifted my butt so he could drag them down over my hips with the help of his thumbs. I could feel his hot breath cooling the wetness of my panties, and I was beginning to squirm.

"Oz…"

His fingers hooked them and pulled them down my thighs and off my feet. Then he palmed my knees apart and kissed the insides of my thighs, first one and then the other. I buried my hands in the soft strands of his hair, gently urging him to where I wanted his mouth. Okay, not so gently. He let a deep chuckle, and took my clit between his lips. And he sucked hard. I bucked off the bed. Then he moved his mouth back to the tops of my thighs, nipping them gently.

My gentle Oz was being wicked.

He leaned on his elbows, parting my thighs a little more with his shoulders. He placed his hands under my ass and squeezed, before lifting my pussy to his mouth, and running the full length of his tongue along my slit like I was his favorite triple scoop.

"Oh my…" Words failed as he gave it another long lick, his tongue flicking on my clit at the end. He did that over and over, just lapping at me, until I had one hand wrapped in his hair and the other anchoring me to his duvet.

"Please, Oz, please," I begged. My body was hot and restless. I was so close to something big. I just needed a little more.

He stiffened his tongue, and buried it in my pussy, stroking and swirling, as his nose brushed my clit. I was moaning so loud it was almost a scream. With one last hard thrust, I came, coating Oz's face in my juices. He swirled his tongue around my clit one last time as I rode out my orgasm. Damn.

I pulled him up to me, letting his hard body cover mine.

"Where did you learn to do that?"

"YouTube."

I laughed. "Really?"

He kissed me, and I could taste myself on his lips. He kissed my jaw, then the hollow beneath my ear.

"Hell yeah. You can learn anything on YouTube."

I ran my hands down his back, over the hard ropes of his muscles as he rested above me. He had a great ass. I just wanted to dig my nails into it.

Oz's hand came up and cupped my breast, his thumb rolling against my nipple. Like I was toggle on his Xbox controller. Well, at least all that gaming had made his thumbs dexterous. His mouth moved down to my nipple, and he flicked his tongue over it before sucking it gently between his lips. He steadily pulled on them, sending lighting right down to my core.

He rolled off and laid beside me, spooning my smaller body into his. I felt the long hardness of him pressed along my ass.

"We'll take this slow, okay? Just tell me if you need me to stop," he said against my ear, then slid his lips to kiss the back of my neck. I felt the head of his cock parting me, sliding into my soaking wet core, hitting every hot point on the way in. He let out a long groan, whispering my name on each breath. He lifted my thigh, spreading me wider to take him deeper.

"Oh. Oh. Oh."

I was consumed by sensation, every inch of him stretching me. With one last grunt, he thrust himself to the hilt, bumping my cervix.

"Oz. Oh fuck. Oh fuck." I'd never felt this before, this sensation of being so full that it almost hurt in a weird pleasure pain.

"Are you okay?"

I nodded, and hoped he caught it. He slid back and moved again. My vision went spotty, as my breathing got ragged.

"You think this is what they mean when people say 'fuck me sideways?'"

"What?" I tried to turn but he just slid out and slid into me harder. What was the question? Once more and I was coming again, wave after wave of pleasure sinking me in bliss. But he wasn't done.

He stilled, giving me a minute to catch my breath. How he stayed so still, buried balls deep inside me, was a marvel. Someone should give him sainthood just for that.

Too soon, and not soon enough, he was moving in me again, harder this time, slamming himself into me until his movements were a ragged mess. Our bodies were a slick with sweat and cum and the only sounds in the room were our combined moans and the slapping of our bodies.

He reached around, one hand sliding up to cup my breast and the other one circling my clit, and that was it. I came again. I screamed his name, and it echoed around the room, probably around the whole apartment. Oz came on a yell.

"Cady!"

A few more thrusts and he stilled, his breathing coming out in heavy pants between my shoulder blades. My heart beat erratically.

"Wow," he whispered. "That was definitely worth waiting a decade."

"You haven't had sex in a decade?" I gasped out.

"I haven't had sex since Luc brought us back."

"You guys have been here ten years?"

"Mm," he murmured into my hair.

"Weren't you lonely?"

He rolled me in his arms, so we were nose to nose. "Desperately. But not anymore." He kissed me gently on the lips. "Sleep, Arcadia. We won't be alone again."

Except I was dying.

I was going to break Oz's heart, and just the thought made my own heart crack in two.

CHAPTER FOURTEEN

I woke to some killer beard rash between my thighs and chest hair itching my back. It was the best feeling ever. I snuggled back further into the warmth of Oz's body, and his arm tightened across my stomach.

I could really get used to this.

Ace sniffed. I *bet you could. Hot bod, and packing some serious heat in those tighty whiteys.*

"Good morning, Beautiful," Oz's voice was scratchy with sleep. I turned in his arms and kissed his cheek. We'd made love twice more last night, and I was pleasantly sore. I was going to need to put an ice pack on it or something.

"Hey." I was so content, that I could have happily laid in bed with him forever. Except I had to pee. "I'll be right back."

The apartments were all pretty much set out the same, which made finding the bathroom easy. I did my business, checked what kind of conditioner he used because seriously his hair was super soft, and was back in his doorway in a flash.

I moved back towards the bed, but my eyes snagged on the framed newspaper article. I hesitated. I desperately wanted to know, but didn't want to ruin the good vibes we had going.

"Grab it, Cady. You aren't going to be able to rest until you know." He was right, but I still didn't want to ruin the moment.

My curiosity won out in the end. I picked up the frame and read the article heading.

12 Die in Apartment Fire.

The article was dated December 26th, 1973.

"Bring it back to bed. I'd rather tell this story with my arms wrapped around you."

The frame felt impossibly heavy as I slid back into bed and laid down in the crook of Oz's arm. I ran my eyes over the print. The pictures that were too blurry last night were the pictures of two kids, a boy and a girl about ten, their smiles wide.

"The twins, Elise and Robert. They lived in the apartment next to mine. Their mother worked nights and their grandmother babysat. She was a holocaust survivor. She survived Auschwitz, just to die in an apartment fire. The twin's mother lost her whole remaining family that night."

I hadn't noticed the smaller photos that lined the bottom of the article. Ten more pictures. He pointed to an older woman, her hair in a thick white bun. "That's Greta, their grandmother." He pointed to two smiling twentysomethings.

"Samantha and Tony only got married and moved in a month before. They were the apartment opposite mine. No smoke alarms in the building so by the time Tony woke, Samantha had succumbed to smoke inhalation. He tried to carry her out but only made it to the bedroom door. They found him shielding her body with his, but they were both dead."

His finger moved towards two women. "Karen and Paige. They were both artists. Karen was a photographer and Paige was a painter. When the fire hit Karen's darkroom, their apartment when up pretty quickly. They died in their beds. Next to them was Frank." He pointed to a guy in an army uniform. "He'd got half his leg blown off in Vietnam, and his wife left him. He was passed out on his couch. Didn't feel a thing."

His fingers pressed into the glass over an old Chinese couple. "The Wangs. I still don't know how old they were, but they were sweet. Mrs Wang would buy me a jar of lychees every month and leave them on my doorstep. They didn't speak a word of English, but they were always smiling. I don't think they had any children in America. They were the only couple who escaped their apartment. They made it to the stairwell before smoke got them. The firefighters got them out but they both died in hospital a few days later."

The last two pictures were of a woman in her early twenties, and Oz.

"My girlfriend, Vanessa. I ruined her life. Got her knocked up because I was too lazy to get a rubber out of my bathroom, so she dropped out of college and moved in with me. She was four months pregnant when I got super stoned, put cooking oil on the stove because I had the brilliant idea to deep fry Twinkies, then passed out on the couch waiting for the oil to heat up. It caught fire and killed twelve people. I went directly to hell for murdering eleven other people, twelve if you count my own unborn child, because I was a lazy, good for nothing, sloth."

His voice was rough. He swiped at the tears on his cheeks with the back of his hand, and cleared his throat.

"So now you know my tragic origin story."

I put the frame down beside me on the blankets and wrapped the big vulnerable man beside me in my arms.

"I'm so sorry." He turned in my arms and buried his face in my neck.

"Shh. It's okay. You are a different man now. It was a horrible accident that had terrible consequences. You just have to live better this time around."

I felt his nod against my neck. "I will." A deep breath. "Let me run you a bath. You have a date in the kitchen soon." He kissed my throat and rolled out of bed.

I shamelessly watched his ass as he left. My poor Oz. Such terrible guilt in his eyes, staining his soul. I would do whatever it took to save him.

A VERY LONG, luxurious bath later, where Oz washed my hair in a conditioner that was apparently made by some woman out in Cali who sold it through her new age shop, I left Oz's apartment in a pair of cut-off shorts and a tee.

I ran into Eli coming home from night shift in the elevator on the way to Valery's apartment.

"How are you feeling, Arcadia?" He asked, giving me a once over.

"I'm good. Actually, I need to ask you something. I, uh, well, Lux and I and then Oz and I…"

"Had intercourse?"

"Right. Should I be worried about diseases or whatever? I should have thought about it before but you know, my brain seems to switch off." I wasn't worried about babies. The treatment for the Hodgkin's Lymphoma had destroyed my fertility.

Eli smiled. "Don't worry. We are technically in suspended animation, zombies as you say. We can't give you anything as we can't contract anything. We also can't impregnate you for the same reason. We do not have the gift of real life so we can't gift life. Trust me, we would know. There would be literally hundreds of little Orion's in New York alone. Not to mention the other guys. Don't stress. I believe that until our mortality is regifted to us by being redeemed, we are as sterile as the dead. Have fun. But not so much fun that you put stress on your heart," he added sternly.

The lift doors opened at Valery's floor.

I stood on my tiptoes and kissed his cheek. "Thanks Eli!" That was a load off my mind. I didn't want to get a 70 A.D version of syphilis with no known cure.

I knocked on Valery's door, and he opened it shirtless, flour dusting across his bare chest. He wore a pair of black pajama pants.

"Uh, hey there."

"Cady, *bonjour*. Come in, come in." He ushered me into that amazing kitchen. I let out a long contented sigh. So pretty.

Ingredients littered the benches in organized chaos. In the center, on a beautiful china plate patterned with swirling pink roses, sat the most beautiful plate of bite sized French pastries and desserts. I was drawn to them like a moth to a flame. There was a mille-feuille, a perfect rectangle of opera cake, a chocolate dome that shone under the overhead lights like glass. There was also a thing that looked like a pastry doughnut stuffed with cream, some kind of double cream puff drowned in ganache and a mousse with a madeleine biscuit perched on the rim of the glass.

"Did you make all this this morning?"

Valery laughed. "No. Some I made yesterday morning. I am compiling my summer menu, and I would like your opinion on desserts." I sat down eagerly on a stool on the opposite side of the breakfast bar.

Valery went to the oven and pulled out a tray of golden croissants, moving them to the cooling rack with practiced ease that all chefs had. It's like they lose all heat receptors in the tips of their fingers.

I was totally going to fail redeeming Valery. I was probably going to end up in hell with him for the sin of Gluttony. Hey, at least I'd have a friend.

He picked up a spoon from the bench and came over to lean on the bench opposite me.

"I want your honest opinion, *mon chere*." He used the edge of the fork to cut through a section of the Mille-feuille. "White chocolate and raspberry mille fueille, or

Napoleon slice. Over 700 layers of pastry, a white chocolate and raspberry cream and finished with fresh raspberries." He held the spoon to my mouth and I obediently opened. As soon as the sweet cream hit my tongue, I let out a moan. It was perfect. Tart, sweet, flaky. I wanted another bite.

"That is amazing."

"*Merci*, but we are not finished yet. Is the dessert too simple? The combination too overdone?"

"I think it's classic, understated but incredibly well made."

He made a humming noise, and wrote in a notebook.

Next, he got a piece of the opera cake. "L'opera cake. Orange and cardamom flavor. A simple twist on a visually impressive dish." I eagerly took the spoon in my mouth. It was amazing. So delicate but packed with flavors.

"I think I may have just died and gone to heaven."

"There was never any doubt where you will be headed, my sweet."

Dessert after dessert he fed me, his hungry eyes watching my mouth as I wrapped my lips around the spoon. He'd watch my face as the tastes exploded on my tongue, and then he'd ask my opinion and write it down.

I didn't know foreplay could come in the form of Chantilly cream, but by the time we got to the mousse, I was ready for him to paint it on my body and lick it off. Slowly.

He'd moved around the bench after the Paris-Brest. Yeah, I'd giggled too. But apparently it's the name for the pastry doughnut thing. It was amazing as well, obviously. The guy could cook and he looked damn fine doing it.

I'm pretty sure the fantasy where he did me right here on the kitchen floor was becoming my new number one.

"You have to stop looking at me like that, *Ma Cherie*. I am trying to be a gentleman."

I raised an eyebrow. "Why?"

I meant it as a question, but somehow it came out as a seductive invitation. This sex kitten was totally getting claws. Accidentally.

"Because, we barely know each other. I want to be sure that you actually desire me, and it's not just Lucifer's magic that makes you want to make love with me. Also, if I'm not mistaken, you spent the night with Oz, no?"

I nodded, and blushed. Awkward.

"I have known Oz a long time. I think making love again this soon would put too much strain on your..." his eyes dipped down to my lap then back to my eyes, "heart."

A laugh escaped my lips, and grew until I was doubled over, trying to suck in breaths. Valery began to laugh as well, and I discovered that Valery laughed a bit like a goose; loud deep honks of sound. This made me laugh harder until I thought I was going to die from asphyxiation if I didn't get a breath.

I looked at the floor and deep breathed through my nose. I hadn't laughed that hard in so long. I leaned forward and kissed Val gently on the lips. He leaned into the kiss, his hand curling around my hip. He tasted of dessert, decadent and sweet.

His tongue ran over my teeth, and I bit gently, before his tongue darted in and his mouth was devouring mine.

The French really did know how to kiss. By the time he pulled away, I was panting.

"You should go now, before I forget why I was being so noble, *oui?*" He stood and there was a tent in his pants.

I'm pretty sure that there have been so many tents in this apartment building since you arrived that we should change the name to Dicks Sporting Goods.

I laughed.

THAT IS A GOOD ONE, ACEREZEAL. I HAVE MISSED YOUR SENSE OF HUMOR. I HAD A MEETING ON WALL STREET AND WISHED TO SPEAK TO MY CONSORT.

I winced as the Devil's voice hurt my brain.

LUC, PLEASE. OR LUCIFER IF THAT SUITS. THE DEVIL MAKES ME SOUND LIKE I'VE GOT HORNS AND CLOVEN HOOVES.

There was a subtle warning in his tone. I swallowed hard.

I'll try. It just slips out.

Ace snorted. *Don't worry, he's just being sensitive. Speaking of slipping out, do you remember...*

I blocked her out. That story was definitely not going anywhere g-rated and I had enough mental scars for the moment. I didn't need to imagine her and Lucifer getting freaky.

Valery was in front of me, concern etched across his

handsome face. Every time I saw him, the picture of him from the history book overlaid itself in my mind. Handsome, but his expression in the painting had been so arrogantly cruel.

"Are you okay? Are you in pain? You have gone very pale." His hands ran down my arms, searching for invisible wounds.

"I'm fine. Lucifer is in town. He just came to visit Ace inside my brain. It's like when you turn on the stereo and it's already up to the highest volume. Just a bit of a shock, that's all."

Valery wrapped me in a hug, and I laid my head on his shoulder. He was a little shorter than the other guys, not too much, but enough that I wasn't hugging his sternum like I was with Sam and Oz. We fit together almost perfectly.

"Come, I'll box the rest of the entremets up and walk you to your room. You look like you could use the rest."

I was suddenly exhausted. I was too busy living to give my body the rest it needed. Once again I felt resentful of the hand I'd been dealt. If I'd been healthy... but there was no point in falling into the abyss of 'what-ifs'.

As Valery gave me his elbow, the box of desserts in his other hand, I appreciated the Gallic handsomeness of his face.

I was what I was, and right now, that made me the luckiest woman on earth.

CHAPTER FIFTEEN

By the time I woke from my nap, it was already late afternoon. My stomach was bloated from far too many French desserts, I may have eaten them all at once, and my body was exhausted.

I laid in bed a second longer, before it dawned on me that it was a knock on the door that had woken me. I shifted out of bed, glad I was still in my shorts, and went to the door. I opened it to find Orion on the other side, looking awkward as hell.

I hadn't seen him much since the incident at the club, maybe once or twice with the guys, and in my apartment when Luc came to visit. Other than that, he'd been like smoke. He was definitely avoiding me.

I opened the door wider and invited him in. He pecked me on the cheek on the way past.

"Do you want a beer?" I asked, heading for the kitchen. Whoever did my grocery shopping left me some after Lucifer's last visit.

"Please."

He looked so nervous, and it morphed his whole face. Gone was the confident man who oozed sex through hooded eyes. He looked younger, and I revised my estimated age for him down a few years. He couldn't be that much older than my own twenty-one.

I handed him the beer and sat down on the arm chair across from him.

"Are you okay?" He was acting weird. I wouldn't say I was an expert on any of their behavior yet, but this was definitely weird for Ri.

"Yeah I'm good. I just wanted to come and apologize for what happened. You know, at the club."

I scrunched up my face. I'd kind of put the whole experience in a small box and stuffed it deep into the recesses of my brain, never to be thought about again.

"Okay? I don't know why you're apologizing, though. You didn't make those guys into perverted scum."

Ri stood, and began pacing around the room. "No, but I should have been taking better care of you, watching you better. That's my club, I should have known if someone was trying to roofie women on the dance floor. I completely failed you. Everyone thinks so. I know so."

Oh.

I'm not sure if this is sweet or pathetic. But I really need to help you develop some ass kicking moves so you don't have to spend the rest of your days surrounded by so much chest-beating testosterone. A girl needs to be able to handle herself. It's the first thing I'll do when I get my body back.

I laughed. *The first thing?*

Okay maybe the tenth thing, but still high on the list.

I could understand that. It was worse for Ace now, to be trapped inside my head. Now she remembered what it was like to be free, and the confines of my mind were chafing. *Soon, Ace. Then you can do whatever you please. Run naked through the bowels of hell eating a burrito, if that's what you want.*

That wasn't on the list, but it is now. Hell, I'm making that number four on my list of things to do when I regain my body. By the way, your boy over there is starting to look uncomfortable.

Whoops. I realized that I hadn't answered Ri. I stood and stepped in front of him, halting his pacing.

"Look at me, Orion." He stared down at me with his large golden eyes that usually promised pleasure but held nothing but uncertainty and perhaps a touch of fear now. "It was in no way your fault. You are my friend, hopefully one day something more. You are not my bodyguard. I'm a grown woman. I've been fending for myself for years. I don't need you guys to protect me every second of the day."

"But-"

"There were hundreds of people in Dante's that night, you can't have known that those dirt bags were planning on anything. I was having fun up until that point. I don't need another over protective lover. I'm dying, Ri. At some point I want to let go and have fun. Besides, Lux gave them an ass whooping they won't forget anytime soon."

A small smile curled on Ri's face. "No. They will think twice before trying to do anything against a woman's will ever again."

I narrowed my eyes. "What did you do after we left?"

His face was serious again. "Eli said it was best if I didn't tell you."

"Ri…"

He shrugged, and sat down on my armchair, pulling me onto his lap and snuggling me against him like a teddy bear. He breathed deeply.

"I've wanted to hold you for days. That shit with Luc would have shaved a decade off my life if I wasn't already, you know, dead."

I wrapped my arms around his chest, letting him indulge in the physical contact he needed. I felt better too, so maybe we both needed it. But when he was silent too long, I poked him in the ribs.

"Ouch. Okay. After I was sure that Lux had you safe, I followed those guys outside. You gotta understand, Cady that lust can result in something magical and beautiful. And I've always used my powers in that way. Well, most of the time. There was a time at the beginning that we were still trying to understand everything that resulted in a couple of accidents, but that doesn't matter right now. What I'm trying to say is that lust can be a positive thing.

"But it can also be a brutal, terrible thing. Something that destroys and punishes. I was so angry at those animals for trying to rape you, that I thought they should have a taste of their own medicine."

"Ri…"

"So I followed them out to the car park, and I waited until they got in their car, and I told them that they were never, ever to lay a hand on you or any other woman ever again. And then I hit them with a massive wave of lust. The only way they could assuage the urge was with each other. But neither was willing. It got...messy. Then the paparazzi happened to wander past. Did you know that they were the sons of popular congressmen?"

I was completely still in Ri's arms. I didn't know how to feel.

If I was there, I'd give Ri a big high five. Those scumbags got what they deserved. Just wait until they get to hell. I have a long memory. Oh, wait until I tell Luc. He's going to love that. He already had such plans for them. No one hurts his Redeemer. Ace sounded pleased and even a little amused. But she had spent centuries in hell, she was immune to this kind of barbarity.

Was it any different to Lux pounding them with his fists? I was willing to forgive Lux for that. But there was something horrifying about revenge being so intimate. Maybe my mind shied away from it because I was female, and that loss of control was always an all too real threat.

It was exactly what those guys planned to do to you, and have probably done to dozens of other women. God wasn't above an eye for an eye in the old days, so I doubt he would have a problem with Orion's punishment either.

Ace was right. It was poetic justice, even if it was wrong.

Ri was still staring at my face, and I realized he was holding his breath. "I can't condone using your power like that, but thank you for the spirit behind it. I pretty sure the dozens of other girls that were in my position would have gotten some kind of satisfaction from seeing those pictures in the paper."

"You're welcome," he said and kissed my head.

"But, you can never do that ever, ever again. No one should be subject to that."

He nodded. "Okay. I've also thought about what you said that night. About redeeming me even if I continue to sleep with other women."

I had said that, even though it grated against my heart. But I made it very clear that I wouldn't share. So he could be in a lot of beds, or just mine. Either way, I would help him.

"I don't want to sleep with other women. For the first time in forever, I only want to make love to one woman. And it's you."

I felt a grin stretched across my face. Thank god. I didn't like to share. Maybe that made me greedy, but the thought of Ri going out every night and sleeping with someone else would have driven me crazy.

I leaned forward and kissed him, falling into the softness of his full, pink lips. It briefly occurred to me that I should feel ashamed that I had kissed three different men in the space of a morning, four if you counted Eli in the lift, but surprisingly I felt nothing even close to shame. I felt alive. Cherished. Sore.

I let the kiss consume me, the whole world shrinking down to Ri's lips on mine.

Eventually, I pulled away and caught my breath.

"I'm so happy you are mine," I kissed his cheek,

dipping my tongue in his dimple. "And I'm sorry to be a tease, but I have to go see a man about a ninja."

Ri blinked. "Excuse me?"

"Actually I could use your help. But first," I walked toward the little sphere that was Mini-Oz, my home management AI. "Mini-Oz, can you tell me where user: Sam is?"

"User: Sam is on the 2nd floor with users: Oz, Valery and Tolliver." The automated voice replied.

"Thanks Mini-Oz. Can you unlock user: Sam's door for me?"

"Door unlocked."

I picked up the parcel that had been on my doorstep this morning. "Grab that box. It's on." I waggled my eyebrows and Ri laughed. It was time for me to save some Sins.

CHAPTER SIXTEEN

"Sam is going to be so mad when he realizes you stole his precious cologne. I'm pretty sure it's made with real tiger sweat or something. He gets it shipped here from Paris. Costs like $500 a bottle," Ri sounded positively gleeful about it.

I placed Sam's razors, face creams, the twelve different hair products, and other assorted beauty products in the box in Ri's arms.

"Who needs cologne that expensive? Sam needs to stop worry that he is the best looking person in the room. I googled the opposite of envy, and apparently it is kindness. That's why he has to stop being Sam the Model and start being Sam the Benevolent."

"He can't be benevolent and have smooth skin?" He asked holding up a jar of night cream.

I sighed, taking the jar and putting it back on Sam's vanity.

"I'm making this up as I go along. I'm petrified that

I'm going to screw it all up and get you guys condemned to the depths of hell forever."

Ri shifted the box to his hip and gave me a one armed hug.

"You're doing great. How about we leave him one of everything and steal all his shoes instead? Though we might need a bigger box. Or a shipping container."

I placed one of everything back on the counter. I held up the cologne. "Fine, but I'm keeping this. This is just lunacy."

"Agreed."

We dropped the box filled with beauty stuff, even after putting one of everything back, back at my apartment and headed down to Tolliver's floor.

I had Mini-Oz open the door, the package still tucked under my arm. The guys were sitting around playing poker. Everyone except Eli and Lux. I knew Eli was on his ED night shift rotation, but I hadn't seen Lux all day.

"Where's Lux?"

"His fight is coming up in a couple of days, so he spends most of the time at the gym training," Oz said, offering me a seat on his lap. I wasn't going to say no to that. I looked at Oz's hand. A pair of Kings, not bad.

I looked at the chips in front of everyone and laughed. "How long until Tolliver has everyone's money? Because I need to borrow him and Sam for the night."

Ri waggled his eyebrows, "The whole night? I'm not gonna lie, I'm a little jealous."

I poked my tongue out at him. "That's not what I meant, and you know it."

Oz's hand ran up and down my thigh soothingly. Well, kind of soothingly. His fingers kept brushing the inside of my thigh and the gesture was definitely climbing from soothing into something a lot hotter.

Sam and Valery folded, Oz showed his hand, and Tolliver revealed three of a kind. Oz let out a frustrated grunt.

"Don't worry, I'm out. Tolliver always wins. Greedy bastard," Oz grumbled and I kissed his cheek. He turned my face and kissed me softly on the lips, a contented sigh escaping me before I could suck it back.

"I think I am being struck with Sam's Envy. I want to be the one making her sigh like that right now," Valery groaned.

I blushed at the chorus of agreement. Despite Valery's words, there was no jealousy in their faces, just longing. This situation was beyond weird, almost unnatural, but I'd be damned (probably literally) if it didn't work just fine. They were happy to share and I was more than happy to be shared.

I stood, stretching slowly, feeling their eyes on me like predators observing their prey. But I didn't feel cornered, I felt powerful.

I passed the package that I'd been carrying around with me all night to Sam. "Can you go put this on? I ordered it online last night and got it express shipped. Yay for Amazon."

Sam looked in the bag, his pretty mouth turned

down in a frown. He pulled out the all black costume from the bag.

"Arcadia, why am I dressing up like a ninja?"

"You'll see, just get changed. Oz, did you find what I asked for?"

Oz shifted me on his lap, so I was pressed tighter against him.

"I did. It took some time to figure out the real ones from the phonies but I crossed checked it and this one fit you specifications perfectly and is legit. I found them on Craigslist, can you believe it?"

I watched Sam get undressed right there in the living room. I couldn't drag my eyes away as he slowly revealed smooth, hard muscles, his skin a creamy white. He ran his jeans down strong, muscular thighs and I forgot I had to breathe as he stood there in the nude.

"You don't wear underpants," I whispered, unable to drag my eyes away even though my brain said that I should.

Not this part of your brain. Stare all day long. I'm starting to appreciate what you see in the pretty ones. He certainly is quite anatomically perfect, Ace purred.

Tolliver cleared his throat. "Would you two like the rest of us to leave?"

I snapped my head towards him. "What? Uh, no. It's okay. I'm just going to close my eyes until he's done though." I scrunched my eyes shut to the sound of masculine laughter. Assholes. They knew how attractive they were.

There was rustling as Sam slid on the outfit. "Okay,

I'm covered from head to toe like a harem girl now, so you can look."

How anyone could still look attractive covered from head to toe in black with nothing but his eyes showing was beyond me, but Sam could achieve it. It didn't help that he had beautiful eyes that sparkled with mischief. I sighed. Still enviable. I would have to try harder.

"Let's go. Does anyone else want to come? Valery? Oz? Tolliver doesn't have much choice and Ri said he'd drive the getaway car, but everyone is welcome."

"I wish I could, but I must get to bed. I have to go to the fish market at 4am to get fresh Icelandic trout before those hacks from Gastronomy steal them all out of spite. But I wish to hear all about you adventures tomorrow, *oui?*" Valery said as he came to stand beside me.

Apparently the restaurant business was just as cutthroat as the modelling business. "I will." I kissed his cheek. Oz stood.

"I'm in. I just want to take a picture of Tolliver's face to show Lux and Eli. This is going to be good."

Tolliver scowled. "Just wait until it's your turn. I hope she makes you do boot camp or cross-fit or something."

Oz paled, but that was actually a pretty good idea. I'd look into it. I would kind of like watching him get all sweaty. I made a note to ask Lux if his gym did that kind of thing.

As a group we descended to the garage. One girl, one guy, one lumberjack, one model and one ninja. We made an interesting group.

We stood in front of Tolliver's SUV's. The Range Rover, the Escalade, the Explorer and the Jeep.

"Pick one," I told Tolliver, but I went over and held his hand. Although this seemed easy to me, what I had planned was going to be difficult for Tolliver. He had a compulsion that wasn't going to be easy to break.

He shook his head. "What am I choosing it for?"

I pulled out my phone and scrolled to the email Oz had sent me. I clicked on the photo of a woman with three adorable children sitting on the porch steps of a small house in the suburbs.

"This is Letitia Martin. She is a single mother of three. Her husband died two and a half years ago in a car accident. Six months ago, her youngest daughter, who is only three and a half, was diagnosed with a heart defect. Because it was classed as a pre-existing condition, Letitia's insurance refused to pay for the treatment. She had to sell everything to pay for this surgery. She lost her job because she had to care for her daughter. She lost the house where so many memories of her husband still resided. She is barely making ends meet. She catches a bus two hours each way to drop her kids off at their old school because she didn't want to uproot them after so many other changes. So today, we are going to change her life. We are going to give one of your cars to her and her family. What do you say?"

Tolliver stared at me for a long time. His jaw worked as he ground his teeth. Then he turned and walked back to the lift, not looking at me as the doors closed.

My shoulders slumped. He wasn't going to do it. I wanted to cry. I'd needed this to work. Maybe I'd gone about it the wrong way. Maybe I should have consulted him more, instead of dropping it on him.

I looked at the guys, who were all staring at me. "I'm sorry. Maybe I'm not the Redeemer. I thought this would work." I swallowed the lump in my throat, and blinked back tears. Sam was the first to give me a hug.

"Hey, it's okay. It was a good idea. And Tolliver will come around. He probably just needs time to adjust." He kissed my cheek, brushing stray strands of my hair behind my ears. "Besides, I totally rock this ninja suit."

I gave him a half-hearted smile. "I'm beginning to think you could rock a potato sack."

"I did a photo shoot once dressed in an indigo dyed hessian sack, so I can tell you from firsthand experience that I do indeed look great in a potato sack. Itchy as hell though."

We waited a little longer in silence, but Tolliver didn't return.

"Well, we may as well go back up."

I headed towards the lift when the doors suddenly slid back open.

Tolliver stood there holding a black workout bag. "Let's take the Escalade."

I ran into his arms and held him tight. "I was a little worried you weren't coming back."

He wrapped his free arm around my back and kissed the top of my head. "Cady, don't you realize that each of us would do just about anything to make you happy? I can give up a car to make you smile."

I screwed up my nose. "All you cars. And the boat. And the yacht, bikes and the Jet Ski."

His eyebrows rose. "All of them?"

"Well most of them. Except maybe two. We still need to get around too. But the rest… we'll be giving them to good homes. I promise."

Tolliver sighed. "You better give me this lady's details so I can sign the Escalade over." I handed him my phone with all of the details that Oz had retrieved about her from the web. It was a scary amount of detail really. Right down to her social security number, and her driver's license details.

Ri laughed. "I'll be damned. Well, damned again. I would never have thought that Tolliver would willingly give away something for nothing." He turned from the man in question back to me. "But what I don't get is why Sam is dressed in a ninja outfit?"

This was the second part of my plan. If the opposite of Greed was Charity, then the opposite of Envy is Kindness. And kindness doesn't need to be big and splashy with lots of recognition. Kindness can be just leaving something that would change a person's life on the doorstep. Kindness is helping someone with no reward.

"Sam is going to deliver the goods. But I didn't want him to be recognizable, which is hard considering his face is on the side of every bus from here to Alabama. I didn't think a hat and some glasses were going to be enough."

"Don't you think this lady is going to freak seeing a six and a half foot Ninja at her door?" Oz asked. Good point.

"Let's stop at the gas station on the way. We should fill up the escalade anyway."

Tolliver finally finished the paperwork. "Let's roll. It's almost nine p.m. She'll be asleep if we don't get a move on."

I piled into the Escalade with Sam and Tolliver, and Oz and Ri went in the Explorer so we had a lift back.

I paused as Tolliver placed the gym bag on the back seat. "What's in the gym bag?"

He held the door open for me so I could slide into the back. "Twenty thousand dollars and the number to a burner phone in case the baby ever needs any more surgery."

That moment right then, standing in the garage of the apartment building, I realized what the guys felt for me might be more than just longing or lust. And what I felt for them might be more than just an overactive libido and oodles of attraction. It might be another L word that scared the shit out of me. They'd forgotten - I'd forgotten - that I was only a temporary thing. My life was temporary. It's like some part of my psyche decided that I was here now, I was complete with all these guys around me, making sure I was cared for better than any woman could possibly dream of, so I had the right to love them and be loved in return. My psyche was wrong. They couldn't fix everything. I was still sick. I was still dying. And when I had finally redeemed them all, I would be dead.

"Hey, what put that look on you face?" Tolliver tilted my face up.

I forced a smile. "Nothing. I'm just really proud of

you right now. But you're right, we better get going." I slid in the back of the car, but could feel Tolliver's eyes watching me, before he shrugged and slid into the driver's seat. He shared a look with Sam, whose eyes sought mine in the rear view mirror. I gave him a smile, and he smiled back. Well, his eyes smiled back. His mouth was still covered by his ninja hood.

We stopped at the gas station, where Tolliver filled up the SUV with gas and I bought a bunch of flowers. A ninja was scary at 9pm at night, but a ninja with flowers couldn't possibly be a murderer, right?

We parked a block away, behind the Explorer, and Tolliver slid out of the driver's seat, handing Sam the keys. He gave the Escalade one last longing look, and slid into the back of the Explorer.

I handed Sam the flowers, and Oz laughed. "That didn't help, Cady. Now he just looks like a serial killer with a gimmick. You're going to have to go with him." He pulled a cap and sunglasses from the glove compartment and stuck them on my head. "There you go. A disguise in the tradition of every bad spy movie ever."

We pulled up in the driveway of a house that looked a little run down, but the flowerbeds were weed free and the yard was tidy. A single light was on in the living room, the rest of the house was in darkness.

I grabbed the duffle from the back seat and took it to the door with me, placing it on the welcome mat. Sam came and stood next to me.

"You should knock," I told him, and he reached over and gave three hard raps at the door.

"You knock like the police," I told him. "Or the repo

man." He rolled his eyes at me, and the door swung open.

Letitia Martin stood there, holding a baseball bat at her side. I didn't blame her.

"Can I help you?" She sounded suspicious, and rightly so. Her eyes never strayed from Sam's Ninja form.

"Uh, hi Mrs Martin. We are actually here to help you. We have heard about your troubles, and about the problems you've been having with the insurance company, and I think we can help you. Well, I know we can."

"Why is he dressed like a ninja?" she asked again, sounding even more suspicious if that were possible. If I knew I had to be at the door, I would have rehearsed a speech or something.

"I don't wish to be recognized," Sam said. "What I do want is to give you this car, and this money on behalf of a wealthy benefactor, in the hopes that we can make your life, and the life of your children, easier. The car is paid for, and legally transferred to your name. The papers are in the glove compartment. The money is all completely legally obtained. The Benefactor just wants to give back to society anonymously, so please don't try and track him down. Anonymity is important to him and this process. That's all we ask. The rest is yours, free and clear."

"There's no catch?"

I shook my head. "No catch. I know you are the kind of person who has a charitable heart, and it's only right that we can do the same for you, now that it's your time of need. I know that if you are ever in that position again, you will pay it forward."

"How could you possible know that about me?"

"I know that until your husband died, your family sponsored three children in third world countries, in honor of each of your own. I know even now you donate what little you can to the Red Cross in times of disaster of crisis. I know that you still give blood even though you are time poor. I know you give change to the homeless man near your bus stop every day, even though you are struggling to make ends meet. The internet is a scary place, Mrs Martin. You can find out all sorts of things about people. You are a good person, and you deserve this."

Letitia Martin burst into tears. Huge, wracking sobs that made my own well eyes well up. She hugged me so tight that I was worried I was going to crack a rib.

Then she fell into Sam's arms, and he held the woman as she cried tears of relief. Something shone in his eye, something that looked like pride, but not in the bad way. Letitia Martin finally pulled away with an uncomfortable clearing of her throat.

"I'm sorry. It's just… it's like God answered my prayers."

Huh. Well, it was actually Lucifer in a roundabout way, but I decided not to tell her that. There were fresh tears when she opened Tolliver's duffle bag and saw all the fat wads of cash stacked in there.

"I can't take this. It's too much."

She tried to hand the bag back to me but I moved

my hands behind my back. Not very mature, but extremely effective.

"You can take it and you will. You'll take it for your kids, and their futures. You can squirrel it away for emergencies, or you can pay off your medical bills, or you can just use it to keep you and the kids fed for a year. I don't care what you do with it, because I know whatever you decide will be the right thing."

"Don't blow it on strippers and cocaine though. And I'd avoid Vegas," Sam added, and I elbowed him in the ribs.

"We want you to have it. In fact, the Benefactor has left a phone number in the bag. He wants you to call if your babies ever need any more medical services. We are happy to pay, no questions asked." I turned to Sam. "We should go."

Letitia gave each of us one more hug. "Thank you. It doesn't seem like enough. I'm afraid that I've fallen asleep on the couch and this is all a dream."

There were a few more tears and a round of good-byes before we got to the end of the Martin's driveway.

We walked back to the guys in the Explorer a half a block away and the silence in the car was tense. "Was she happy?" Tolliver asked as I slid into the seat beside him, Sam bracketing me in.

"She was ecstatic. She said to thank you for your generosity. You did a good thing today, Tolliver. I'm proud of you."

"She made me want to cry," Sam said. "And I'm not really sure, but I don't think Ninjas cry."

I reached out and grabbed Sam's hand too, as Ri

pulled out onto the street. "Do you think she will tell the world, even though we kind of asked her not to?"

"Of course she will tell. I'd be surprised if she isn't already on Facebook updating her status," Tolliver sighed. "It's okay. The car was a company car, and it is almost impossible to trace the company back to us."

It was eleven by the time we all piled back into the apartment, and I was exhausted. I kissed everyone on the cheek and stumbled back to my apartment. Lux was standing outside my door, leaning against the door jamb, looking impossibly sexy.

"I've missed you." His quiet voice, with its low gravelly growl, sent shivers down my spine. "I'm tired, but I want to hold you. Can I stay with you tonight?"

I leaned in and kissed his lips sweetly. "You never have to ask." I took his calloused hand, which was sporting a fresh scrape across his knuckles, and wrapped it in mine.

There were definitely feelings that began with the letter L developing, and the thought scared the hell out of me.

CHAPTER SEVENTEEN

F riday rolled around too fast.

I'd spent most of the week with Oz, Tolliver and Sam, working out ways to spend Tolliver's money. Tolliver had been correct when he said Letitia Martin wouldn't be able to help telling social media about her late night visitors, and by the next morning we were trending, and two days after that we were a viral sensation and had been picked up by news stations across the country. They had dubbed Sam 'The Ninja Robin Hood' though I thought that was incredibly cheesy. We had researched different charities, dropping tens of thousands all over the place, spreading the wealth country wide by anonymous donation, signing it only "Ninja Robin Hood." Cheesy or not, we had to own it.

We hadn't done another home visit, but Oz had been researching worthy recipients whenever he wasn't making play-throughs for Twitch, whatever that was.

Tolliver was actually taking it rather well, and had

fallen into the role of philanthropic benefactor without too much trouble. Suspiciously easily. The businesses were still turning over a steady profit, and we were having a hard time spending the money faster than he made it. We were going to have to think of a longer term option sooner rather than later.

In fact, I'd rather be doing anything than what I had to do right now.

Eli had booked us a conference with two of my specialists.

I knew it was bad. It had to be. Because Eli wasn't just busy with work, like I'd thought, he'd been actively avoiding me. Subtly turning in the opposite direction if he saw me coming down the hall, leaving after a short, polite moment if I entered an apartment he was already in. I knew it wasn't because he didn't like me; hell when he did look at me there was such longing on his face that it was painful to see.

This only left one scenario. He'd received the results to the tests he'd ran, and they were bad. He must have said something to the guys at some point during the week, because while they were all extremely affectionate until I had the beginnings of a permanent beard rash, they never pushed to go further than second base, not since my night with Oz.

Speaking of Oz, he was pacing a circuit of the waiting room again. I was beginning to miss the old Oz, who laid down on any surface he could find. Pacing Oz made me nervous. Eli was already in the conference room discussing my case with the specialists, though even he had seemed reluctant to leave me. The rest of the guys had wanted to come too, but I put my foot down. My soul knew that this wasn't going to go well, and I would spare them the sucker punch of bad news if I could. I was even making Oz stay in the waiting room.

The phone rang on the receptionist's desk, and she motioned to me.

"You may go in now."

I kissed Oz's head and opened the heavy glass door to the conference room. I took the seat next to Eli, across from Dr Yao and Dr Herstein.

Dr Yao smiled. "It's good to see you again, Arcadia. How are you feeling?"

I smiled. "I feel good. Alive."

The muscle in Eli's jaw ticked.

Even Dr Yao shuffled some papers in front of her uncomfortably. "We've reviewed your tests with Dr August, and it appears that the Hodgkin's has returned. Unfortunately, this definitely removes you from the transplant list, and makes surgery unviable. However, if we get the lymphoma back into remission, there is an experimental procedure we can undertake that might prolong the viability of your current heart."

My current heart. She said it as though it was a phone service provider or something. Like it was something that wasn't an essential part of me, even if it was failing. My hands began to shake as my heart pumped harder and I moved them to my lap.

Eli slid his hand into mine under the table and squeezed tightly, though his face maintained an air of cool professionalism.

Dr Yao was still speaking, and I tuned back into her

words. "I suggest you start the chemotherapy again immediately. I'm sure I don't have to tell you that days could mean the difference in this kind of situation."

I shook my head. "No. I will start next week. I have somewhere I have to be this weekend, and it isn't hugging my toilet bowl. I will start them on Monday. I don't think a couple of extra days are really going to make a difference.

And it wouldn't. What everyone in the room knew but no one was saying, was that the chances of the lymphoma going back into remission were slim. For it to go back into remission for long enough that I could build my strength back up for open heart surgery before I died was an impossibility.

They were handing me a death notice.

The meeting went on, but I didn't hear much more. Just the same usual jargon of doses and the best anti-nausea drugs, so on and so forth. I trusted Eli to tell me the important things.

He looked devastated. Determined, but he was a scientist deep down. He knew that statistics game.

What felt like seconds and an eternity later, I was shaking hands with the specialists, and walking in a daze back to the waiting room. I hadn't registered a word Dr Herstein had said.

Eli had one hand under my elbow, as if he was worried I would drop dead right there on the conference room floor. He handed me off to Oz, whispering something in his ear, and Oz's face went white. But his jaw tensed, and he pulled me into his arms.

"Let's go get some ice cream. We'll binge watch

Game of Thrones, and tomorrow we will deal with it," he said against my hair, his words strangled.

He drove me straight home, despite the promise of ice cream, though maybe he stopped and I just missed it. When we pulled into the garage, Lux was there. He came around to my door and opened it, gently unbelting me and pulling me into his arm, cradling me against his chest like a child. Like he had so many other times already. Big, strong Lux; my savior.

Then I cried. Huge rolling sobs so like the ones that Letitia Martin had done only days earlier, but with a completely different feeling behind it.

He carried me to the elevator, whispering to me promises that neither he nor the devil could keep. We arrived in Oz's living room, and all five of the other guys were there. Even Eli had beaten us home. He must have driven as if the very hounds of hell were chasing him. Which they just might be now. If I died before they were redeemed, they would all go back to hell, except maybe Sam and Tolliver. I would have to work twice as hard to ensure that at least they were redeemed.

"I'm sorry," I sniffled, and Lux grunted. I assumed it meant, "Don't be stupid you have nothing to be sorry for," in Lux speak.

He laid me down on the couch, like Snow White and her seven sins, and the guys surrounded me immediately. So unlike the first time, where they all stood on the periphery, unsure of me and my intentions. Now I had developed a relationship with all of them, selfishly, and I was going to hurt every single one of them.

Watching someone die was not pleasant. It was raw and brutal.

"What if I run out of time, what if I don't redeem you all?" I sobbed.

Tolliver stroked the hair from my sticky face. "Hey, don't worry about that. You need to concentrate on you. We will figure out the rest."

"Why aren't you starting your chemo until Monday?" Lux asked. "Wouldn't it be better to start immediately?"

I guess Eli had told them all the basics already. I couldn't begrudge him that. It wasn't just my life on the line. If I died, we were all dead.

"I want to go to your fight."

Lux's jaw tensed, but he just nodded. "Okay."

Oz clapped his hands together loudly. "Okay lady and gentlemen. It isn't a pity party unless there's cake and ice cream. Fortunately for you all, I have ice cream cake in my icebox. Val, could you get it out to thaw a little, maybe grab some plates? Ri, can you please grab the fluffy afghan from the end of the bed for Cady. I am putting on Game of Thrones. Season one, episode one, so no spoilers, okay?" He sat down beside me and grabbed the remote of one of his consoles, hitting play.

Eli sat beside me and Tolliver beside him until four of us were jammed on Oz's couch. Oz grabbed a throw pillow from the floor and placed it on his lap, swinging me around so I was lying across the three of them.

Lux sat in front of the couch, so he could rest his head back against my hip. Ri sat beside him, as did Sam. They were all close enough that if they wanted to, they could reach back a few inches and touch me. I could sense their need for reassurance.

Valery returned with bowls and ice cream. "You need a bigger couch, Oz." He grabbed a bean bag and pulled it closer. Close enough that when I reached out my fingers, they brushed his cheek.

I felt instantly better surrounded by them. I hadn't lied to Dr Yeo. I was feeling healthier since I met them, despite actually getting sicker apparently. Something about them energized me, made me feel as if life was trying to burst from my chest. They healed me, spiritually. I would have to thank them for that. Not now though. That would sound too much like giving up.

Somewhere in the first few episodes, after Sean Bean got his head chopped off, while Oz stroked my hair and Tolliver rubbed my feet, I fell asleep.

I awoke to the sound of Tolliver and Eli arguing.

"There has to be something, Eli. Anything. I don't care what it costs, or how illegal it is, find a way to save her. Is your medical license really worth more than her life?"

Eli growled. Actually, physically growled. I felt the rumble of it against my body. "Don't be an asshole. It's not that and you know it. I would give up my license in a minute if it would save her. A heartbeat. But her specialists are the best in their fields. If she died because we rushed her into some back alley surgery that her body wasn't prepared for, could you live with her death? Her blood would literally be on my hands."

"She's going to die anyway. You said as much yourself. She knows it too, if that desperately sad look in her eyes is anything to go by. That look fucking kills me. Tell me what we have to do to fix this?"

"Pray."

I closed my eyes and forced myself to go back to sleep.

CHAPTER EIGHTEEN

I woke the next morning with a renewed sense of purpose. It was time to double my efforts.

I was in Oz's bed, pressed between him and Valery. I was pressed hard into Valery's back, my cheek smooshed up against his warm muscles. Oz was spooned around me, his hand on my boob.

God, I could get used to this.

I waited for Ace's inevitable smart ass comment about being the meat in a man sandwich, but nothing came.

Ace?

No answer. I began to panic.

Ace? Are you there?

I'm here, Arcadia.

I let out a relieved sigh. She sounded… wrong. Not snarky, or petulant, or perverted, which were her usual defaults. She sounded subdued. It was wrong on a fundamental level.

Then it hit me. If I died, she would die with me. No getting her body back, no being with Luc ever again. Would her soul just cease to exist? If I died, would Ace no longer be present in the fabric of the world. The panic set in all over again.

I'm going to try and hold on, Ace. For you. I will redeem the guys, because I have feelings for them that are confusing, and I think it might be what love feels like. But I know I love you. You are with me always. A part of my soul. I will carry a little piece of you always.

A small sigh echoed around my head. It sounded defeated despite her next words. *And I you. I am not worried, Arcadia. I have faith in very few things in this world. But I have faith that you will do everything possible to save those you love, even to the detriment to yourself.* There was a long pause. *Now I think you should wake these guys up and have a crazy threesome, because life is short. Actually, get the others in here and make it an orgy. A girl hasn't lived until she's had at least one orgy. Take it from me.*

My face flamed red at the thought. Other parts of me flamed as well. I willed my vagina to calm itself. I had a busy day that didn't start with me having sex with two guys.

Maybe.

I kissed Valery's spine, sighing at the way the muscles flexed under my lips as he shifted around to look at me with hooded, sleepy eyes.

"Good morning, Beautiful."

He pressed against my front, and he leaned forward to kiss me softly. It was a testament to my raging lust that

I didn't even worry about having morning breath. I kissed him back.

I could feel Oz's morning wood pressed against my ass, his hand squeezing my breast as he slowly woke.

Valery kissed the corner of my mouth. "The Doc has ordered that you do nothing more strenuous than lift a book until you start your chemo. However, I know a very relaxing way to wake up in the morning." He kissed down my jaw, down to my collarbone, then slid is tongue along the hollow of my throat.

"Just what is going on here?" Oz purred in my ear.

"I hear they call this the French Alarm Clock." I laughed, even as Valery sucked a nipple into his mouth.

Oz stroked down under my breasts, to my navel.

"Get to it dude. I'll handle the top half," Oz said, rolling me onto my back, pulling my tank top over my head. "Remember, go easy though. No undue strain on her heart." Then he kissed me. A slow, languid, delicious kiss that promised pleasure so good my toes would curl.

Valery had reached my hipbones, nipping one with his teeth and then tracing his tongue down the line of my leg. He shifted between my thighs, pushing them gently apart. He peeled my sensible cotton underwear down my legs and threw them over his shoulder. They landed on Oz's lightsaber lamp. Score one for the Sith.

Then he placed his head between my thighs and his breath tickled its way across my core.

Cosmo lied to me. It told me men didn't like giving head. My guys had practically made it the national sport, and damn they were good at it.

He ran his hands down my thighs, placing one leg

over his shoulder and putting a large hand under my butt to angle me to his mouth.

Oz broke our kiss and looked down, and so did I. Valery's intense eyes never broke contact with mine as he lowered his mouth to my pussy and swirled his tongue around my clit with expert ease. I sucked in air as my pussy clenched.

Oz chuckled. "Bon appetit, man."

I felt Valery smile, then he sucked my clit into his mouth. "Oh god."

"Not today. That's the sin of Gluttony for you, he really knows how to eat," Oz laughed at his own joke, and then his eyes fell to my breasts. "You have the greatest boobs I've ever held." He slid his hands up to cup my breasts, his thumb coming out to rub over my nipple until it peaked at his attention.

Then he lowered his mouth and bit it, hard. I bucked against him, and he spread one large hand against my hip to hold me still as he lapped at the hurt.

Valery flicked his tongue against my clit again before sliding his mouth down my slit and thrusting his long clever tongue into my aching hole.

He swirled and stroked while Oz did the same on my nipples, and I was a mewling, panting mess of need. Valery moved back to my clit and slid a finger into my pussy, then another, filling me slowly, stroking as if he already knew each and every one of my hot buttons.

"Oh, oh."

I moaned over and over again. Valery slid out his finger, moving it down the crease to my ass, using my own juices to moisten the ring. I tensed, but Valery looked up, meeting my eyes.

"You will like this, *Ma Cherie*. I promise." Then he went back to worshipping my pussy with his tongue, until I was nothing but a throbbing ball of pleasure.

"I'm going to come," I moaned. They double their efforts, Oz pinching and suckling my nipples as I ground my slit into Valery's face, wanting, needing release.

Then Oz sucked my nipple hard into his mouth, pinching the other one, and Valery pressed hard into my clit with his tongue as he forced his finger into my ass. I thought my body was going to fly apart.

Valery moved his finger slightly, the odd new pleasure tipping me over the edge.

I screamed as the waves of pleasure hit me, slamming my thighs on either side of Valery's head, my hand wrapped tightly in Oz's hair.

I didn't loosen my hold on either of them until the final pulses of pleasure left me, and I flopped back against the bed.

"Fuck," I panted. Oz was looking down at me, a massive grin on his face. God, he was cute. "High five?" I half-heartedly held up my hand for a slap.

Oz laughed and kissed me. "You are the most beautiful, adorable woman I have ever met, Arcadia Jones." But he still gave me a high five.

Valery climbed back up my body and I snuggled against him, kissing his chest as his arms came around me.

"Good morning, sweet Arcadia." He whispered

against my hair. I don't think 'good' was a strong enough word for it.

A LONG, delicious shower later, I was sitting in Valery's apartment at his dining table eating a breakfast that he'd made me during my soak in the shower. Sausages, eggs and biscuits. High calorie foods for when the chemo started. Val said he had a weekend to fatten me up a bit. I suggested he build a house made out of candy. Instead he gave me the world's worst smoothie. It was green and tasted like ass crack, but apparently contained high levels of essential vitamins and nutrients I would need in the coming week.

"You should try to enjoy the taste. There will be plenty more healing smoothies to come," he said as I screwed up my nose. When Valery put a second plate of food in front of me, the other guys walked into Oz's apartment. Everyone looked exhausted and drawn. They each kissed me before heading to get a plate of food and sitting down with me.

"So what's the plan for today?" Sam asked. "Hashtag Ninja Robin Hood is trending on twitter you know."

"I want to drive out to Connecticut. There's a couple there who could use our help, I think."

"In Connecticut? Okay. Should I wear the ninja suit?" Sam grinned. I was beginning to think he was enjoying playing Santa. The other day he walked to the grocery store dressed in the gear and gave fifty bucks to every panhandler he could find. He'd gone to the projects, and asked the kids down there if they could think of anyone who needed his help. We'd been prepared for the inevitable me, me, me's but they had been pretty thoughtful in their responses.

Several kids had mentioned a mother whose son had been killed gang violence, who was barely scraping by for the rest of her kids. One boy mentioned a girl his age, which couldn't be more than fifteen, who painted graffiti murals in the hallway of the project buildings. Beautiful, inspiring pieces. She got rejected for a scholarship to an art school because the state had pressed charges, insisting that her graffiti was public damage.

Twin boys, who were nineteen, who'd gotten custody of their siblings when their mother had OD'd in some filthy back alley, who put aside their own futures to ensure their siblings could stay together.

That one had made me cry later, after I'd made my way up to their tiny apartment, looked into the faces of the exhausted teens, and everyone with eyes that were too old for their youthful faces.

Tolliver, who listened into our conversations through my hands free earpiece, told me to tell them he was setting up a trust for the family. Enough for the kids, of which there were four aged between 3 and 15, as well as the twins, could go to any college they wanted. Enough for the guys to hire a housekeeper for during the week, to pay for food and power for the next ten years so the boys didn't have to work so hard and could go to college part-time if they wanted to, so they could become whatever they wanted to be. Once they got past their general distrust, like we were trying to buy their siblings, I could see the age drain away from their faces. Relief made their faces younger, their eyes more hopeful. Their fifteen year old sister cried uncontrollably.

Tolliver told his lawyers to take care of it all, including the girl who wanted an art scholarship. We talked to the girl, who'd been painting another mural in the dingy lobby of a broken down building, and asked her what college she'd wanted to go to. We spent twenty minutes more talking about her life, her family were Bosnian and had come as refugees during the war. She talked about how she was always viewed with suspicion, even in the projects.

By the time we'd finished talking to her, Tolliver had paid for three years of art school at the school of her choice, as well as a trust allowance for the first year.

We just deposited twenty grand into the bank account of the woman whose son died senselessly by gang violence. She wasn't a kid who we could start on the right path. She was an adult with the ability to make her own decisions. She would use it how she would.

It had been a busy day, and I'd been exhausted when we'd gotten home. But word had spread about the ninja who helped the downtrodden, and now he was practically an urban legend.

I finally saw changes in Sam and Tolliver, ones that told me I had set them on the right path. Sam interacting with those kids, so far from his former life as elite male model, boosting them up, telling them they could be anything. He'd changed. It wasn't a big change. I wouldn't be able to pull out before and after photos, but something had shifted in his heart. Tolliver was harder to read, but I could tell. It was the small things. He started suggesting causes to give his money too. He talked about setting up charities and trust funds and chairing them himself. We already had a list that Oz had compiled of worthy recipients, and they came from wide and varying backgrounds. The young, the old, families and singles. But each one had an obstacle that couldn't be overcome without the necessary evil of money.

Oz had tracked them all down through less than legal means, hacking insurance databases, college mainframes, and social media. We couldn't help everyone, so it became a bit of a lottery of the neediest.

Tolliver had been adamant about setting up some kind of Robin Hood fund for people whose insurance rejected them for life saving medical treatment. Eli would spread the word through the other doctors he knew. He'd also donated quite a sizable chunk of money to both the heart foundation and for cancer research.

Apparently, there was no end to Tolliver's money. But at least it was funding something worthy now. He'd spent days in meetings with his lawyers, redirecting the vast majority of the profits from his business ventures into different accounts to be spent on his charitable endeavors with Sam. I didn't think they'd been redeemed yet, I wasn't naive enough to think you could wipe a lifetime of bad deeds in a week, but they were on the right path. They would go on without me.

Now, sitting around the breakfast table with them, I was suddenly incredibly grateful that I could experience this small moment with these guys.

I looked between the two of them, and then the rest

of the guys around the table. If there was ever a time to give yourself to emotion with abandon, it was now. I loved them. Whether part of that love had been preordained or not was irrelevant. I felt what I felt.

"I love you guys. You know that right?"

Lux kissed my temple. "We know. And we will have a lifetime to show you how much we love you too. Got it?"

I gave him a small smile. "Got it. Okay, enough morbidness, we've got some cows to tip," I gave the room my best smile.

"Seriously?" Tolliver raised his eyebrows.

"No, not really! Who actually does that?"

Oz raised his hand. "But only once. And it was a dare. I honestly was petrified the whole time."

I gave him my most 'I'm not angry, I'm just disappointed' face, but it was hard to hide my smirk.

Valery packed us a picnic, and left for work with a very hot kiss that made Ri wolf whistle. Not to be outdone, Ri kissed me until I forgot how to breathe.

Eli held my face and kissed me lightly on the nose. "Take it easy, nothing too strenuous." He gave me a stern look, and then gave the same look to Sam and Tolliver.

"Dicks to yourselves," Lux growled as he kissed me gently on the lips and left.

That just left Tolliver, Sam and Oz. I walked over to Oz and leaned against his chest. He wrapped his arms around my back and pressed me tight into his chest. This was my favorite place in the whole wide world.

"Are you coming to Hartford?" I asked him.

"I'm scared of cows."

"You just said you tipped one," I said, poking him in the ribs.

"Yeah, but I didn't quite make it and it was pissed. I nearly got stomped into the ground. I'll just stay here in civilization, maybe do some more research. You guys have fune." He kissed the top of my head and left.

Both the guys got changed into their disguises. Tolliver wore thick rimmed glasses and a fedora. He looked like a spy trying to act casual in a cheesy sixties film. Although, to pay him his due, no one ever recognized him, but he did look a little like Clark Kent with bad taste in hats. Not exactly subtle.

We took the Range Rover, though I'd had to talk Tolliver out of taking the Jag for one last spin. There just wasn't enough room in it for the three of us. It was essentially a penis with wheels.

Tolliver drove, still the control freak, and Sam sat in the back with me. He made sure I was strapped in, before strapping himself in.

"You know I have been belting myself into cars for nearly a decade and a half now. You don't have to check my work," I teased.

"I know. Just makes me feel better to know your safe."

"Mini-Oz, play Classic Old School playlist," Tolliver said.

"Mini-Oz reaches to the car?" It made sense. If my health tracker worked off my cell phone, I guess Mini-Oz really could go anywhere. I still wore the bright pink wristband everywhere, and I had no doubt that Oz was really at home fine tuning it so that he would know if I so much as sneezed. I was going to have to start taking it off when I got...frisky. Otherwise, we'd have a repeat of the first night with Tolliver and Sam. As much as I adored the guys, I didn't need an audience every time I got naked and did the horizontal Merengue.

Mama Cass started crooning quietly about dreaming a little dream, and I relaxed into the plush leather, my head resting against Sam's chest as he tucked me into his side.

"Sam?"

"Mm?"

"Can I ask you a personal question?"

He kissed my hair. "You can ask me anything."

"How did you get sentenced to hell?"

Wow, Cady. You can't just ask someone how they got damned. Ace had been quiet the last day or two, and hearing her snark made something unclench inside me.

How else will I ever find out? Besides, after Oz's accidental pyro story, pretty sure nothing could surprise me now.

Ace scoffed. *Still so naive.*

"I murdered my family to become Chieftain of my clan."

Well, that was one point to Ace. "What?"

"I was the third son of a war chief of a Viking clan. I was never going to inherit the mantle. I wanted it. I had all the men of my family killed in one night, most of them had their throats slit in their beds. I fought my father fair and square. His last words to me were of pride."

I pulled away. "Dude, that is seriously fucked."

Sam gave me a sad smile. Pulling away would have stung, but I couldn't make myself cuddle back into his arms right now.

"You have to remember, Arcadia, this was a different time. A different culture. A culture of barbarity cloaked in the facade of civility. This was how generations of Chieftains had gotten their positions for centuries before me. It is how Chieftains were expected to die. Indeed, my own cousin killed me not too long after I took the mantle. He killed my children, my wife. He murdered my brothers' wives and children, the ones that I had spared when I took the lives of their fathers. That was nearly unheard of; you don't spare a future adversary."

"Wow." I was stunned. I looked at Sam, with his clear blue eyes the color of icebergs in the sun, and saw him in a whole new light. Gone was the model. In his place was a Viking. Someone who had once been coated in the blood of his enemies, as well as his family.

"When was this?"

"Around the same time as Lux."

"What about you?" I asked Tolliver. Surely, his couldn't be as barbaric.

He hesitated for a long moment. If anyone would hold back, it was Tolliver.

But eventually he cleared his threat and began.

"I was born in Brazil to a rich plantation owner, powerful and a leading proponent of the slavery movement. They would lure the Japanese people to Brazil with promises of a better life, and then trick them into slavery. They had no other options. My mother was one of the Japanese slaves that my father had raped. His own wife was barren, so he took me from my mother at birth and groomed me as heir. After he died, he left the plantation to me, and I could have emancipated them all. Or even paid them for their labor. I was filthy rich. Yet I still subjugated my own people for profit. My own mother, though she was never allowed to raise me, worked my fields until she could no longer stand straight. I worked some of them to death in my fields. They eventually overthrew me, cut off my head with a katana. My mother watched emotionlessly."

His jaw was tense. As was Sam's. They were waiting for my rejection. Every part of my morality rebelled against their stories. The sheer horror of it.

They were sentenced to hell. Did you think it was because they kicked a puppy?

Ace had a point, but Oz's story had kind of lulled me into believing that perhaps they were all semi-innocent bystanders to their sins. Even Valery's story was a sin of omission. Of selfishness. He didn't starve his fiefdom out of cruelty, but rather self-absorption. I had even forgiven Lux for his sins, and he'd murdered thousands on the order of his General.

But Sam had willingly, of his own volition, murdered his kin. Tolliver had knowingly enslaved his own people and worked them to death. There was no escape from the culpability there.

But they had changed. Hell had changed them. I was changing them. They were not the same people they were in their former lives.

I repeated this to myself, as I wrapped my fingers in Sam's, and leaned forward to squeeze Tolliver's bicep.

"It's a lot to process. Who you were is not as important to me as who you are now."

Sam nodded, but turned to look out the window, and Tolliver's jaw tensed periodically, but he too was silent. Although, eventually Sam cuddled me back into his side, he didn't speak, too lost in memories.

CHAPTER NINETEEN

W e reached farming country after a couple of hours. "Turn up here. At the Turner's Dairy sign."

Tolliver turned down a dirt road.

"Who lives out here?"

"Ewan and Ethel Turner. Fourth generation farmers. They had three healthy, strong sons who would take over the farm when they retired. But then 9/11 happened, and all three sons enlisted. Two died in Iraq. One was critically wounded and lost a leg and an arm. Now Ewan and Ethel are in their late seventies, and the farm is about to go under, like so many other farms around the area. Years of profit have been eaten away by medical bills. The house has been re-mortgaged. The dairy employs most of the young people in this town. If it went under, it would be catastrophic to the town and its economy. Lieutenant Austin Turner can't afford correct fitting prosthetics, so his life is a shadow of its former self. We can do a lot of good here, if we can convince them to accept our help. They are proud people."

Tolliver threw his phone over his shoulder to Sam. "Call Eli and get the name of the best prosthetics specialist in the country. Then call that guy and get the son an appointment. Then call the lawyer and see if we can't buy their debt from the bank."

"Say what now?" Sam asked. Tolliver sighed. "Just do the Eli part, I'll handle the business while I'm waiting for you two."

We drove through a gate with a Turner's Dairy sign on the front, and pulled up in front of a ranch style house.

Sam and I slid from the back of the car, just as the Turners walked out onto the porch.

"Can we help you?" Ewan Turner asked, eyeing Sam's ninja mask with something between suspicion and humor.

"I hope we can help you."

"I've heard about these guys. They go around handing out money, hoping to get famous probably." The younger Turner sounded bitter. A bitterness that can only come from the knowledge that life does not care about you and your feelings. I knew that kind of bitterness. I'd fought it back when I was a teen, and again when my parents died. If it hadn't been for Ace giving me a proverbial ass kicking, I probably would have wallowed in it forever.

You're welcome, by the way.

I rolled my eyes. Don't expect self-deprecation from a fallen angel.

Sam slid off the hood of his outfit, revealing his face. All the moment was missing was dramatic keyboard music.

Ethel patted her sons arm. "I don't think he's doing it for the fame, Austin dear. Even I know who this man is. Though he is slightly harder to recognize fully clothed."

Oh, Ethel is a salty one. I like her already. I had to agree with Ace.

Ewan shook his head at his wife bemusedly. "What can we do for you folks today?"

"We are, uh, looking to invest in the Connecticut dairy industry, and we were hoping that you might be open to a little cash injection for a small stake in the company."

"How small of a stake?"

"Uh, like one cow worth? But I get to name it." I was totally going to name the cow 'The Ozinator'. Ace groaned.

"They want to give us charity, Pa," Austin said, still eyeing us suspiciously. He subconsciously rubbed his thigh where his prosthesis was strapped to his leg.

"Oh, now there are people much more hard done by than us. You should use your money to help some of them."

Tolliver slid out of the car and walked over.

"Oh my, it's the Armani model too. I need to call Cathy and Sue. They will never believe I had two boys from those billboards in Hartford on my farm." I was surprised that Hartford had Armani billboards.

Sam gave her his most winning smile. He should probably turn it down a notch or he was going to give Ethel a heart attack. "We'd prefer you didn't, Ma'am. Our identities are meant to be a secret. We don't want the press. We just want to help people and be on our way."

"Good afternoon, Gentlemen. Ma'am." Tolliver gave a half bow. Sometimes his old world manners reared their head. "I've been discussing with my lawyers, and we believe it would be best if perhaps we entered into a co-operative arrangement. You would be in charge, and the company would remain in your name. You would continue to have full ownership of your farm. We would just like first rights to part of your product and the option to add more companies to the co-operative."

I frowned. I wasn't sure what he was doing, but I just had to trust that he wasn't screwing these hard working people over.

"What percentage of the profit would they receive?" Austin asked,

"While they are the only farm in the cooperative, they will get 100% of the profit, minus lawyer's fees. When more businesses are added to the cooperative, profit distribution can be agreed upon as they see fit, but I would suggest by production levels and sales percentages."

Austin nodded. "Seems fair. Let's go inside and talk it over."

Tolliver nodded, and we all followed Austin into the house, to the formal living room, where overstuffed lounges and threadbare rugs fought with photo frames and knick knacks.

I walked past a photo of three boys, barely out of their teens, in their uniforms, smiling widely for the camera. Such a waste.

I sat down on a large sofa between Tolliver and Sam.

"Would you like some coffee? I just made cake?" Ethal asked, her warm, smiling face making me feel instantly at ease.

I smiled politely. "No, thank you. We have a picnic in the car for the way home. Wouldn't want to spoil my appetite for this beautiful countryside you have around here."

Tolliver steepled his fingers. "I have one condition."

Austin frowned. "Let's hear it."

"You go and see the prosthetic specialist that owes me a favor. Your parents deserve to enjoy their retirement, and this place will need proper hands-on management. You can't do that in the poor quality prosthetics that the VA has given you. I'll pay, and consider it an investment in the co-op."

Austin raised an eyebrow. Tolliver's roundabout talking wasn't fooling him. He looked set to decline.

"Take the offer. Only a fool turns down free medical care, especially when so many people are relying on him. If you won't accept the offer for yourself, do it for your folks and this town. Your suffering doesn't make their deaths any more meaningful," I told him.

"What would you know of it?" Austin snapped, hurt making him angry.

"I know more than you think."

Ethel looked between Sam and Tolliver's faces, understanding lightening her expression. "Oh dear. That's… I'm so sorry dear."

I smiled at the lovely old woman. "It is what it is. Can't change the way things are. You just have to believe that things will get better."

Both Ewan and his son looked confused and Ethel rolled her eyes. "Men are so dense sometimes. You would think they'd get more wise with age, but I can promise you that isn't the case. She's dying, you numpties."

Confusion gave way to embarrassment on their faces, settling on pity, as it always did. My guys just looked sad. I squeezed their hands three times. It would all be okay.

"Actually Ethel, I think I might take that coffee after all."

We spent the afternoon talking and laughing with the Turners. I met my one cow, the Ozinator, and the name didn't suit her at all. She had big, dark, shiny eyes, and she chewed so slowly that I thought the hay would fall from her mouth. She wasn't likely to stomp anyone into the ground, though I still took a photo and sent it to Oz.

By the time we finished the tour of the plant, I was dead on my feet.

Ethel hugged me tight as we left. "You stay strong, okay? God doesn't give us more than he thinks we can handle."

I wasn't so sure about that, so I hugged the old woman back just as tightly. She smelled like violets.

Austin smiled and shook my hand. He looked years younger, and so much more handsome when he smiled, that I was a little dumbstruck. Tolliver gave him a cool look and hustled me into the car. Apparently his ability to share only extended to his fellow Sins.

I waved out the window as we drove off in a cloud of dust.

"Do you think they realize you essentially just gave them the money? That there'll never be another member of the co-operative?" I asked Tolliver sleepily.

"Never say never, Arcadia. But yes, Austin at least knew what we were doing, but it was a solution that wouldn't prick his pride too much and kept everyone happy. I think he would do just about anything to make his family happy again."

I knew the feeling. A deep sense of satisfaction filled my soul. Tolliver would be fine. So would Sam. I'd done enough. I wouldn't be there every step of the way, and I would never see what happens at the end, but I'd set them on the right path at least.

"Don't forget our picnic," I told Tolliver. I'd never been on a picnic in the country before. The closest I'd come was hotdogs in Central Park.

We pulled over at a rest stop in the middle of nowhere, which had a barely used pathway from the car park down into a heavily treed area. Sam grabbed the cooler filled with lunch, well afternoon tea now, and Tolliver grabbed the picnic rug from the back. Then he tucked my arm in his and we walked down the track.

It was beautiful. So quiet and peaceful. There wasn't the sound of city traffic that was a constant buzz in the back of your head. There weren't any people yelling, or construction sounds, or the smell of dumpsters and pollution. It was fresh and pure.

We walked fifty feet before we heard a stream and the track dropped steeply, so that we had to climb down an embankment to continue. Tolliver went down first, his feet nimble like a mountain goat. He reached up and wrapped his large hands around my waist, lifting me down. Sam scrambled down after us, a little less gracefully. The track turned sharply left, and there through a thick stand of trees was the stream and the world's most perfect picnic spot.

A huge tree spread out its branches over the banks of a small stream that was not even six feet across. Tolliver laid down the blanket under the canopy of the tree, out of the harsh late afternoon sun. I took off my shoes, and sat on the edge of the embankment, my toes only just touching the surface of the stream. Sam unpacked the cooler as Tolliver came to sit beside me, his pants rolled up his calves.

"It's beautiful out here," I said inanely, but it was true. There was a peaceful calmness out here that I could never achieve in NYC, even in the luxury of our home. It was easy to lay out here and pretend that we were the only three people in the world, and that life was some idyllic painting.

"Come and eat before the ants beat you to it," Sam called, and I walked hand in hand with Tolliver back to the rug.

If spending the day in the company of the Turners had taught me anything, it was that life was too short to stew on past mistakes and what-ifs. I'd come to terms with the guys pasts eventually, and until that point I was only going to judge them on how they were now, not how they were in another life, and in Sam's case thousands of years ago, before being sent to hell.

"What was hell like?"

Sam groaned. "Geez Cady-Lady, you aren't holding back today, are you?"

I shrugged. "My time frame to ease the answers out of you just got reduced. I don't have time to go gently-gently anymore."

Tolliver was tense, but he answered. "Worse than you could ever imagine. But the longer we are away, the more the particulars fade from our memories. Now you just get this crawling feeling under your skin when you think about it. Like thousands of ants are trying to burrow into your bones. Your body is instantly on high alert from muscle memory of the trauma. But I know, with utter conviction that I never, ever want to go back." He had become more agitated as he explained.

I ran my hand over his hair, trying to sooth the ravages of memory.

"I'm sorry." I grabbed a strawberry from the container in the center of the rug and held it to his lips. "No more hard questions today, I promise."

Tolliver took the berry between his teeth and bit down, making strawberry juice run down my fingers. He grabbed the stem of the strawberry from my fingers and threw it over his shoulder, then he took my fingers, still dripping with strawberry juice, and sucked them into his mouth. His eyes held fiery heat, and as my fingers popped out of his mouth with a loud smack, I crawled across the rug towards him and into his lap, wrapping my legs around his back. He kissed my temple, my cheek, the corner of my mouth before plunging his tongue between my lips. My fingers curled into his hair as he branded my mouth with his own.

A heavy sigh behind us made me look over my shoulder at Sam, who was packing the food back into the cooler.

"We'll want this after we're done," he grinned, leaving the strawberries and chocolate dipping sauce out. Tolliver grabbed my jaw, turning me back towards his lips, kissing me again, his hands sliding up under my shirt to wrap around my ribs, his thumbs venturing up to rub over my nipples through my bra.

I gasped as hands grabbed the edges of my tank top and pulled it over my head, then Sam's mouth was on my neck, trailing kisses down my spine. Tolliver dipped me backwards, so his mouth could trail kisses between my breasts before moving to one lace covered nipple and sucking it hard into his mouth, the pressure sending pain and blinding pleasure right to my core.

Sam came up behind me, turning my head to the side so he could kiss me too. He kissed differently to Tolliver, softly where Tolliver plundered. Long strokes where Tolliver nibbled. The dichotomy was mind-blowingly arousing. By some unspoken agreement they laid my on the rug between them.

"Do you feel okay?" Sam asked as his hands went to the button of my cut-off daisy dukes even as Tolliver unsnapped the front clasp of my bra.

"Amazing."

His grin was infectious and I couldn't help but smile back. "Good. Now lay back and let us love you." He leaned forward and kissed me lightly on the lips. "I've wanted to do this for so long now." He dipped a strawberry in the chocolate sauce and ran it over my lips, tutting as my tongue darted out to taste it. Tolliver leaned forward and kissed the chocolate from my lips, pulling my lower lip into his mouth and sucking gently.

The strawberry meandered down over my collarbone, the swell of my breast, circling my nipple, leaving behind a sweet trail of sticky chocolate. Sam and Tolliver watched the strawberry with single minded focus, devouring my body with their gaze. Sam re-dipped the strawberry and moved to the other nipple, before swirling down my stomach and dipping into my navel before running into the roadblock of my shorts.

"Allow me," Tolliver positioned himself between my feet, tugging my shorts and panties down until I was exposed to them and the world. The breeze kissed against my body, cooling where the chocolate made a path.

Sam re-dipped the strawberry and handed it to Tolliver, who ran it up the inside of my left leg, venturing off behind my knee before swirling up my inner thigh. He swept around, over my hip and meeting up with the trail of chocolate on my abdomen.

Sam took it back, dipped the strawberry one last time and then ran it down my other thigh then up, over my folds of my pussy to my clit. I moaned at the sheer eroticness of the moment, and the sound echoed around the clearing. Sam watched my eyes as he removed the strawberry, licked the remaining chocolate from it and then ate it.

I wasn't ever going to look at strawberries the same way.

Tolliver grabbed my attention as he lifted my leg and ran his tongue over the trail of chocolate that ran up my calf muscle.

Sam did the same, the flat warmth of his tongue traveling down my collar bone to my nipple, and sucking it gently into his mouth, his tongue flicking my aching bud. I pushed against him. My breath was coming in pants now, and I needed them to hurry. I wrapped my fingers in Sam's hair and moved his head to my other breast, even as Tolliver's mouth ran up to the inside of my knee, his tongue almost rough against the sensitive skin. My leg went over his shoulder as he crawled further up my body his tongue following the intimate pattern he had traced.

Their heads met at my lower belly, and I was going to come apart right there and then, the sight of them both looking up at me, Sam with a sultry grin and Tolliver with burning intensity, light and dark, but both intent on giving me pleasure. It was heady.

Sam smiled. "After you."

So damn polite.

Tolliver stroked his tongue between my folds in one hard, long stroke and I came undone, my moans captured by Sam's mouth. Tolliver lapped at my orgasm and kept going, his tongue flicking over my clit in the perfect rhythm, driving me higher. Sam followed his pace with his kiss, his tongue stroking mine in a sexy imitation of Tolliver's on my other lips.

Suddenly, the warmth of Tolliver's mouth was gone, and Sam drew back.

Somehow Tolliver had gotten rid of all his clothes in seconds, and knelt between my knees, naked and so glorious he took my breath away.

"Are you ready?" Sam whispered in my ear.

"Yes," it was more a moan than a word, but it was signal enough. Tolliver leaned forward, lining his body up with mine, and kissing me as he pushed his cock into me.

I sucked in a breath as he filled me, momentarily forgetting I needed to breathe, until Tolliver began to move. Then my breath came out on loud moans and in on sucked gasps.

Sam stripped out of his clothes, and sat back down beside us, on hand stroking his stiff cock while he watched my face.

"It's been so long," Tolliver whispered. "This is going to have to be hard and fast, baby, because I just won't last." He slipped my legs over his shoulders, hitting every happy place inside me and I let out a feral noise as he began to drive himself into my body on an increasingly discordant rhythm. He was moaning something, but I couldn't understand. Maybe it was in Brazilian or maybe it was in English, but I was beyond comprehension as my body became a mass of nerves and sensations, the pleasure swelling in my body as Sam came over me, sucking the mewling sounds from my mouth, and I anchored myself in his hair.

"Oh, oh, oh," I said, my pleasure cresting as my orgasm swept over me and my screams were muffled against Sam's lips. I bit hard, and he yelped even as he moaned.

Tolliver came on a grunt, his movements' wild. Finally, he pulled out and collapsed, his head on my belly. My heart was beating sluggishly, but I was okay.

Tolliver raised his head and looked around the surrounding forest.

"What?" I asked.

"Just looking for Lux. I keep expecting him to appear out of the trees and pound me into dust as he lectures me."

I laughed, running my hands through his hair. I lifted my other wrist. "I slipped the health monitor off when you guys started with the strawberries."

We all laughed, and then lay on the picnic rug in silence, Sam's head on my chest listening to my heart beat out of time, and Tolliver's head on my abdomen after he'd cleaned me up with his shirt.

When my heart rate had calmed back down, Sam raised his head. "You know we aren't done right, Cady-Lady?"

I laughed. "You guys are trying to give me a heart attack."

All heat left his face. "Are you okay? Is this too much?" He looked at my eyes, my face, my chest, as if I had a 'battery low' sign somewhere.

"I was kidding. I'm fine," I brushed his hair out of his face.

"Scary." He kissed me in a punishingly hard kiss. He

flipped me over and pulled me to my hands and knees in an effortless move that had to be the result of giant hands and years of experienced. I held in a little yelp of surprise.

He pushed the hard head of his cock along my still wet slit. He ran one hand along my back, angling me down a little, his other hand holding my hip steady. Then he slid into me in one long movement. Tolliver, who is still lying sedately on the rug beside us, ran a hand along my stomach until he reached my clit. He flicked a finger against it, and I let out a long moan as I slam back against Sam's body.

Sam, his strong pale body moving in perfect harmony with mine, sped up until my forehead was pressed against the rug and I was holding on for dear life.

Tolliver circled my clit in time with Sam's thrusts and an orgasm snuck up on me so fast I had no time to prepare. It blinded me as my body continued to milk Sam's.

"That's it. Come for me, Arcadia. Fuck you are so beautiful," he moaned as he slammed into me, his fingers digging into my hips. Another orgasm was building and I wanted to scream at the top of my lungs. Sam reached forward, tangling a strand of my hair in his fingers and tugged as he came. The edge of pain when my body was a mass of pleasure did something to me, pushing me over with him.

I collapsed onto my stomach and Sam lay down next to me. He ran his fingers gently up and down my back. Tolliver pressed his body along mine, his hand stroking my hair. "You are the most precious thing I have ever held in my hands, Arcadia Jones."

"We are going to cherish you until we draw our last breaths," Sam added, leaning in to kiss my cheek. "Now how about lunch?"

I fell asleep in the car on the way home, and only woke when Sam carried me into the lift. "I'm awake. I can walk you know."

"I like you in my arms. You weigh practically nothing. I'll have to talk to Valery about providing higher calorie meals."

My eyes drifted closed again of their own accord. I let my body do its thing. It would need all the rest it could get in the next couple of months.

CHAPTER TWENTY

Fight Night. I was so excited; I was basically bouncing around Lux as he gave Oz, Tolliver, and Sam last minute instructions/threats. It was the first time I'd been out in a crowd since the incident at the nightclub.

"She doesn't leave your sight. One of you is with her at all times. Do not let her near the cage. If she looks pale, take her home. I don't care how often she says she feels fine."

I grinned, jumping into Lux's arms. "Don't be such an old hen. I'll be fine. We'll be fine. Now kiss me."

He did, grabbing handfuls of my ass while he kissed me like it would be our last.

Unfortunately, Ri and Valery would miss the fight. They were buddying up today. Ri would catch a nap in Val's office and Val would sit around with Ri until Dante's closed at four. Depending on how the fight went, we'd join them at Dante's afterwards. I was excited. I was going to enjoy my last night of freedom before my thoughts we consumed by cell counts and chemo appointments.

Eli walked through the side entrance to the arena, stopping to talk to the security guard.

"Sorry. My surgery went longer than expected." He leaned in and kissed me, despite me still being in Lux's arms. The security guy's eyebrows rose, but then he politely looked somewhere else.

"Ready?" He asked Lux.

"Yeah. I feel better leaving her now you're here and I don't have to leave her with the three horny amigos."

Tolliver flipped him off with both hands.

I laughed and kissed him again. "Break a leg. Hang on, don't do that! How do you wish a fighter good luck?"

Lux chuckled. "You kiss him and say good luck."

I gave him another hard kiss, my tongue dancing with his. "Good luck."

He slid me down his body slowly, and I felt every bunched muscle on the way down. Delicious. I wondered if I could talk him into victory sex later.

He strode through swinging doors that indicated the locker rooms, and he gave me one last finger wave goodbye.

Eli took my hand in his. Happiness spread through me. I'd missed Eli. He led me to a VIP area with the best view of the octagon, the other three guys at my back like my own personal bodyguards. Well, until someone pinched my ass. I threw them a stern look and Oz waggled his eyebrows.

The chairs were plush and reclined. Ah, how the rich lived. Tolliver went and spoke to the promoter, a guy who basically oozed new money, and pretty much lived up to every sleazy stereotype of a promoter I had. Sam handed me a glass of champagne.

"To us. To the long life we will all have together," he said as a toast. I bit the inside of my cheek. They were being positive, but the power of positivity wouldn't be enough this time.

"To us," I murmured as I sat between Oz and Eli on the couch overlooking the octagon.

There were thousands of people in the arena, screaming for blood. The pair of fighters in the ring pummeled each other, one getting the other to the ground and wrenching his arm back in a hold that looked as if it was about to pop the shoulder out of the socket. I grimaced. Maybe this wasn't such a good idea after all. The guy tapped the mat, and the ref jumped in, holding them apart as the siren sounded

The referee held the winner's arm in the air, and the crowd cheered. I downed my champagne in one gulp. I was going to need a few more of those before Lux came on.

Tolliver came over and pulled up a chair to sit beside us.

"How much does Lux earn a fight?" Surely getting pummeled like that was hardly worth a couple of thousand dollars.

"About 900k per fight."

My mouth literally snapped open. "No way?"

"He's a drawcard fighter. People come to watch him.

He gets a cut of the pay-per-view as well. He's actually quite a bargain. Some of the other big names get well into the millions, but Lux doesn't like the publicity that comes with those kinds of fights. He hates all the interviews and the show-ponying."

I could imagine my softly spoken warrior would hate being the focus of attention. Sam grabbed another tray of champagne from the roaming waitress.

"Lux doesn't fight for another hour. May as well enjoy the luxury."

He must have meant the free champagne, because it wasn't as if we lived in a cardboard box under a bridge. I sipped at my bubbles and sat silently as the guys talked. We'd been going from one drama to the next; I rarely got time just to appreciate them being themselves. Eli was smiling as he told us of a case that came into the ER of a guy who had accidentally shot a nail gun at a steel beam and the nail had ricocheted into his temple. The guy drove himself to hospital, and walked up to the triage smiling.

By the time Lux's fight was announced, I'd become a little more desensitized to the violence in the octagon. The sounds of fists hitting hard flesh, and the bright red streaks of blood that didn't seem to bother the fighters and only stirred up the crowd, none of that made my stomach turn anymore.

But it was probably going to be different with Lux.

"I wonder how he'll fight with Cady here," Eli asked Sam, and I tilted my head towards them.

"What do you mean?"

"Well, he was Wrath. Before you, he was a different

kind of guy. I mean, he still had a good nature, but he was angrier, more brutal, and even more bloodthirsty in the ring. But since you've been on the scene, he's basically a six and a half foot pussy cat," Sam explained as music blared and Lux walked up to cage.

He was something to behold. He wore black shorts that skimmed his mid thighs, and some kind of compression tights underneath those. Every inch of his scarred skin, each hard cut muscle shone beneath the lights of the arena. His hands were wrapped in bright red wrappings, and a red mouthguard cradled his smile.

He entered the cage as they announced his name and stats, and then he looked up at the VIP area, finding me despite the crowds and the lights.

He placed his gloved hand over his heart, his eyes never leaving my face. I pressed two fingers to my lips and blew him a kiss. He winked and faced the ring where his opponent was entering. The guy he was fighting was slightly shorter but only by an inch or two, as fair as Lux was dark. He wore golden shorts, and white gloves. His reddish blonde hair shone. But he had a face that looked like it had taken one too many hits over the years. He looked like the fightin' Irish and I dubbed him that in my mind. Lux's opponent bounced around on his toes like a jackrabbit, where Lux moved with an easy grace of a man used to fighting under armor. He held himself as if gravity had no hold on him.

The siren buzzed and they started, bouncing around each other and sizing one another up. Then Irish moved in with frighteningly fast speed, getting a good punch into Lux's cheek. I winced, but Lux hardly moved. While Irish was getting his footing back after the punch, Lux's leg whipped out and cracked across the guys thigh, and Irish turned a little too late to avoid the blow completely. His leg buckled, and with a speed that was almost too fast for my eyes to follow, he was on the ground and Lux had his arm in a hold so tight I was worried not about dislocation, but that his arm would literally tear right off. Irish wiggled and squirmed, trying to get his arms up under Lux's to break the hold, but it was no use. But I had to hand it to the guy.

The referee tapped him, and they moved back to opposite sides of the cage.

"Huh. Normally he plays with them more," Tolliver said to no one in particular. If this was playing fair, I would have hated to see Lux at his brutal best.

Irish got a couple of good kicks in, making Lux dance away but not enough to take him to the ground. Lux punched the guy in the face once, before he could get his hands up, then punched him one-two in the ribs, backing him into the side of the octagon before laying the punches in hard until the referee broke them up again.

They came back out into the centre, and Irish attacked again, aiming kicks at Lux's ribs, trying to get him on the ground, but Lux punched and got him hard on the cheek.

His head snapped back with sickening speed, and the guy went down to the mats, out before he even hit the blue vinyl.

I closed my eyes, and Eli held my hands. "Is the other guy alright?" I asked.

Eli was silent for a bit. "The medics are in there. His eyes are open. Yeah, he's up. He should be fine. The medics will check him out and send him for treatment if he needs it. You can open your eyes now; your boy is looking for you."

I opened my eyes and found Lux's intent gaze honed in one me. I gave him a shaky smile and clapped. He bowed his head as the referee held up his arm and declared him the winner, the crowd chanting his name like he was a gladiator of old.

"We can go and see him in the change rooms if you like?" Tolliver said, and I nodded.

"Okay, but I want to go to the ladies room first."

Oz put down his beer. "I'll take you."

I screwed up my nose. "I can pee by myself."

Oz laughed. "I know that. But if anything happens to you and we weren't at least close by, I'd be eating out of a straw for a year. I'll just stand outside the door." He guided me through the crowd, one hand on my lower back."

The ladies room was empty, yay for the VIP section, and I did my business in record time. I stood in front of the mirror, and assessed my appearance. The bags under my eyes were a little darker, my skin a little duller. It might have been the fluorescent lighting, but I didn't think so. I wasn't at walking corpse stage yet, but it wouldn't be long. I fingered my short hair. That would be gone again soon.

A man appeared in the mirror behind me. I looked again. Not a man. An angel.

Ace hissed. *Azriel.*

I gaped. As in, the Azriel who parted her immortal soul from her body? I spun around and backed up against the sinks. I needed Oz.

I opened my mouth to shout, but the angel grabbed my face and then I was rushing through time and space to somewhere else.

Central Park. I recognized the statues.

I leaned over to the left and puked onto the grass.

"Apologies. I needed to talk to you."

"And kidnapping me was your answer?" I said between dry heaves. It felt like the worst hangover I'd ever had.

What do you want Azriel? Ace growled. But beneath the boiling anger, I can sense her hurt. The festering wound of her betrayal.

"I will speak out loud. I do not want to cause more distress to your host." His voice was perfectly modulated. It was a nothing voice. Neither too low, nor too high. It was completely without character.

"I'm with Ace on this; what do you want?" I frantically willed my stomach to stop somersaulting.

"Merely to talk. To fill you in on some carefully omitted facts. For better or worse, Lucifer has set you up as the queen in his game of chess with the Father, and I believe the queen should be able to see all the pieces on the board."

"I'm really getting tired of the chess analogies. You

are talking about living human beings here. And their immortal souls."

"Hardly living beings, are they? Your sinners?"

Jesus, Azriel, you didn't get any less verbose in the last two thousand years.

"So eager for me to spill your secret, Acerezeal? So be it."

I could feel Ace's sudden apprehension.

I frowned. "What secret?"

Arcadia… Ace sounded cagey.

What secret? I asked her.

"It's Acerezeal's soul in your body that is making you sick. Her immortal soul inside you is literally killing you, like a parasite feeding off its host. A body was not made to house two souls. What Lucifer has done is an abomination, and nature, in all His glory, is trying to right the wrong by killing off the anomaly."

I blinked, my mind suddenly filling with white noise as I struggled to grasp what he was saying. "But I have lymphoma?"

"Your body is attacking itself, because it can't find the foreign body that is feeding off you. The rapidly enlarging hole in your heart is because it is working twice as hard to sustain you both, even though you possess only one body."

Ace? Did you know?

There was a long silence. *I suspected after the doctors said that your cancer had come back. I didn't think it could be a coincidence.*

"I am here to save you, Arcadia. I can remove the parasite from your body, and you will begin to heal almost immediately. However, if you do not, I am afraid you will not last the year."

I slumped to the ground. My mind was just empty. Ace had saved me so many times over the years. I couldn't just abandon her. Let her soul be ripped from a body again. Her scream as she remembered that moment still haunted my dreams sometimes.

But keeping her was an inevitable death sentence. I would die, and any chance of the guys being redeemed would probably die with me. At the very least, I would break their hearts.

But at least they would move on. Ace would be gone forever, from the very fabric of existence.

I couldn't let that happen. Ace deserved to be saved as much as the guys did. I couldn't let Azriel have her.

"No. I believe that I can redeem the guys in enough time that Luc will win the bet and Ace will get her body back. You don't sell out the ones you love when times get tough. Ace has been with me through the toughest times, and I won't abandon her out now."

Arcadia…

Why did Ace keep saying my name like that?

The Angel grinned, and it was disorientating. He was so beautiful, but his face was almost cruel in its perfection. His huge white wings sat high on his shoulders, the snowy feathers a whisper from the ground.

"Humans. Sometimes I can understand why Acerezeal fell, though it was mostly Lucifer's doing. But you are so pure in your love. It's breathtaking in its innocence." He was still smiling. "It is commendable that you would sacrifice your life for the Fallen Acerezeal.

But are you willing to sacrifice the life of your unborn child?"

My world shrunk. Blood rushed in my ears. I ceased to breathe even as my heart thundered in my chest. "What?"

"The child that grows now in your womb. You cannot sustain both. Is Acerezeal's life worth that of your child?"

PART III

I couldn't breathe. Black spots danced in my vision as my heart beat in a discordant rhythm. I was going to pass out. Or vomit. Or both.

Call for Lucifer, Ace yelled in my head. She seemed really far away. I ignored her. *Lucifer!* Her yelling wasn't helping the encroaching darkness.

"Well?" Azriel asked, stepping closer. I scrambled away out of instinct. I didn't want the angel to touch me.

I was pregnant. Ace was killing me. Those two thoughts just went around and around in my head.

"I can help, Arcadia. Ace would understand. All I need to do is touch you." He reached out a hand. His long, beautifully sculpted fingers snapped me out of my shock. I didn't know what I was going to do, or even what I was thinking, but I knew one thing for certain; I didn't want anything to happen right now.

"LUCIFER!" I yelled with every ounce of will I could muster. The danger of calling for the Devil wasn't lost on me, but the only people I could trust were across town and couldn't just teleport themselves around like angels and devils.

Luc appeared in the time between one frantic beat of my heart and the next.

"Azriel. It's been a long time." He positioned himself between the angel and I, and I instantly felt better. That was all kinds of messed up, but right now I was all kinds of messed up. There was nothing okay about this situation.

Today, Lucifer had wings. The shone like polished onyx in the sun, soft and smooth, and a discombobulated part of my mind wondered what they felt like. Could I touch them? Where had he put them all those other times he'd come to visit? He spread them wide, hiding me from Azriel's view.

"Lucifer Morningstar. Did you think you could hide her from him, that He would not know?"

"She needed a chance to live."

"Arcadia or your precious Acerezeal?" Azriel almost sneered.

"Both."

Luc knew. He knew that placing Ace in my body would slowly kill me. If I was expecting guilt, I would be disappointed; expecting guilt from Lucifer was useless.

"You stole her from me once, Azriel, I will not let you do so again." Luc lost the pleasant edge to his voice, and almost growled.

"She will die with your Redeemer, anyway. The seed of life sits in Arcadia's womb. It will accelerate the only gift you really have to give, Lucifer Morningstar. Death."

Lucifer laughed. "Oh Azriel. The Angel of Death, lecturing me? You always did have a great sense of humor, even if you are oblivious. You have not spent enough time amongst these children of the Father. You do not understand their medicine or their hearts. I believe that Arcadia will redeem the Sins. She will restore Ace to her body and she will hold that child in her arms. The fact she carries that life at all means she has already redeemed one of them. Maybe she will even name the baby Luc."

Un-fucking-likely. Azriel tsked at my mental bad language, and I did something that the old Arcadia would never have contemplated doing. I flipped him off. The angel Azriel. A messenger of God, even if he was rude and creepy as hell.

"It is always a pleasure seeing you, Azriel. Every time we meet, I see just how close you are to falling yourself. Soon, you will be in my domain, old friend." The promise of pain tripped silently off his tongue.

"Unlikely, Lucifer. Arcadia, call me when you are ready to save your child."

Luc turned quickly, wrapping me in his arms and his wings, and the whirling motion sickness returned.

He materialized us back in my apartment, in the bathroom, and I promptly leaned over the toilet bowl and dry heaved as my body succumbed to the worse form of vertigo imaginable. I wiped my face on my sleeve. Luc stared down at me patiently.

"You knew all along."

Lucifer nodded. "Yes. But you are strong, body and

soul. I knew you could survive sharing your mortal body with Acerezeal."

"And the baby? Did you know about that too?"

This time he grimaced. "No. That was a surprise from the other side of this chess match. For what it is worth, I am sorry."

And you? Are you sorry too? I trusted you above anyone else. I trusted you more than I trusted myself. And you betrayed me, I couldn't keep the accusation, or the hurt, from my voice.

I'm sorry. Ace's voice cracked a little. *I truly wasn't sure until Friday either.*

But you've suspected since you got your memories back and you said nothing. Nothing, I hissed.

I wanted to slam out of the room, away from them both, but you can't escape yourself. I heaved a few more times and Luc made a bottle of sparkling water appear in his hand.

"Drink this. It will help."

I took it from him, scowling, but desperate to settle the churning in my stomach.

I pushed to my knees, and then to my feet. I had to call the guys. They would be frantic.

"Mini-Oz, message User:Oz and tell him that I am okay and at home. But I need them here as soon as possible."

I needed a time out away from them all. Ace, Luc and maybe even the guys. I needed to be alone, but I was never actually alone. Until now, that fact had comforted me. Now it felt like shackles.

"I'm going to bed. Don't talk to Ace. I don't want to hear anything from either of you right now."

Ace said nothing and Luc nodded. "If it is okay with you, I shall wait for the return of the Seven in your living space."

"Whatever." I shut the door in his face and crawled into bed, pulling the pillow over my head and hoping it would all just go away.

Twenty minutes later I heard the door slam open and voices yelling in the living room. I tensed, expecting Azriel's return, but then I recognized Tolliver's angry baritone. The bedroom door slammed open too, and the blankets were yanked away. Lux stared down at me with wild eyes that roamed continuously over my body, which was curled in a ball protectively around my belly.

"Are you hurt? Eli!" His voice was strained, and I could see fear in the whites of his eyes.

"Lux, I'm fine." Well, that was probably a matter of perspective but I wasn't going to say that to the man who was still shirtless and in his shorts from his fight. They must have gotten him straight from the change rooms.

Eli appeared in the door anyway, and was at my side in a second. "Where is the pain?"

I laughed, but it wasn't a happy sound. If I didn't think it would result in him calling the paramedics immediately, I would point to my heart.

"I'm not in any pain, Eli." I wouldn't say I was fine though. That would be a lie.

"Luc says you were abducted by an angel?" Eli pressed.

I sighed and slid out of bed. Best to get this story over and done with so we could plan. The thought not to tell the guys about Ace's role in my sickness, and even the baby, crossed my mind, but I dismissed it completely. I'd promised Eli no more secrets, and I meant it.

I saw Oz's guilt-ridden face first and I walked straight into his arms.

"I'm so sorry. I'm so sorry." He repeated it over and over into my hair.

"You couldn't have possibly known that I'd be abducted by the Angel of Death from the women's restrooms. Don't apologize."

"I should have gone in with you."

"No, you shouldn't have. I'm fine."

Valery and Ri burst through the door, their relief palpable when they saw me in Oz's arms. Ri cast a look at Lucifer, then strode over, gently taking me from Oz's arms and pulling me into his own.

"If this keeps up, I'm the one who is going to have a heart attack." He pressed kisses to my forehead and cheeks and lips.

Valery came over and ran a hand down my hair. "What happened?"

I sighed and snuggled deeper into Ri's arms.

"You all better sit down."

Lucifer cleared his throat awkwardly. "Should I take my leave?"

I wanted to shout yes from the rooftops, but instead I shook my head. "Stay. There'll be questions that I just can't answer."

He eyed Lux warily. Yeah, Lux was not going to be impressed.

Ri sat with me in his lap, the solid warmth of his body dispersing the chill from my bones. The others didn't sit beside us, instead standing in a small semi-circle facing me, six equally concerned faces staring down at me.

"So, there's good news and bad news. The good news is that I know how to cure my sickness. I could be better within a year."

Broad smiles broke out on their faces and Sam sat down beside me, his hand on my cheek. "That's great news."

I frowned sadly. "It gets better, and then so much worse. Also, one of you has been Redeemed. I'm not sure which one."

Eli was frowning. "Go back to the miracle cure. What did Azriel tell you?"

Ah, my sexy scientist. Always needing to know the why.

"Ace is the one making me sick. Possessing two souls in my body is unnatural, and nature is trying to resolve the issue by having my body attack itself. My cardiomyopathy is from the overworking of my heart to sustain two life forces. Azriel offered to remove her for me, and that once gone my body would begin to win the fight. As it is, he said I have less than a year."

"You said yes, right?" Tolliver asked.

Lucifer growled. "Watch it."

"No Tolliver, I didn't say yes. Ace, despite our differences, is someone I love. I don't give up on the people I love."

Lux grunted. "So we all work hard to be redeemed

in months, and then Ace goes back to her own body in hell and you get better."

"That was the plan. There was a problem though. No one has asked how I knew one of you was redeemed."

I watched the color drain from Eli's face. He went ashen. "No."

I nodded sadly. "Yes. I'm pregnant."

CHAPTER TWENTY-TWO

I f the situation hadn't been so tragic, their response would have been almost comical. Orion, who had been hugging my torso tight against his body, dropped his arms like they were on fire, moving down to grip my thighs tightly. Sam and Tolliver had similar looks of shock. Valery began to swear in French, cursing everyone and everything, well, at least I thought that's what he was saying.

Eli was still pale and Lux was completely blank. His face was devoid of any expression like he was a Greco-Roman marble statue.

But it was Oz who took it the worse. His face went deathly white and he swayed on his feet like he was going to pass out.

"Sit, Oz."

He sat without question. Without a word, Eli turned and left the silent room.

"Where's he going?"

"To get his medical bag, I would think," Luc

answered. He was the only one who didn't look like he'd been hit by a bus.

Unfortunately, speaking drew Lux's steel grey eyes to him. It was Lux who looked like the angel of death as he prowled toward Lucifer.

"You."

Lucifer tensed for a fight. This could not end well. I moved off of Orion's lap, stepping toward them. Lux ignored me.

"You knew this would kill her and said nothing," Lux growled.

"She was so strong of will. She would have made it."

Would have. Past tense. Another blow.

"Take your consort out of her now."

"That will not happen. She will redeem you, and Ace will have her body restored. How about you help her help you, instead of falling back into old patterns, Lux of Taygetus."

There was another deep growl from Lux and I moved closer, ready to put myself in the way. Orion was there in an instant, holding my arm.

"Don't endanger yourself. Or the baby," he murmured to me. "Lux in this mood can be... unpredictable. He is more animal than man."

I didn't care how unpredictable Lux got, I knew he would never hurt me. Lucifer on the other hand would probably snap me without a single thought.

I had to stop this. I stepped around Ri and reached out for Lux's hand.

Those cold gray eyes snapped to mine, and immediately warmed with such love that my breath clogged in my throat. I gave him a watery smile.

"The baby could be yours. I need you." Conflict contorted his face, until he put his back to Lucifer and placed a hand on my stomach, his fingers curling over the light curve that probably had more to do with Valery's food than a baby.

"I'm yours. Both of you."

Eli returned, wordlessly indicating I should return to the couch. Lux picked me up in his arms and went back to the couch, sitting me on his lap.

Eli didn't waste any time checking my vitals, including my blood pressure. He handed me a cup and a white packet with a pregnancy test inside.

"Just to make sure."

"It might be too soon to come up on tests," I argued.

"I know. But it might help us narrow down who the father might be," he said softly. Or who was redeemed.

"She shouldn't keep it. She will die. Is no one else catching the sub context here?" Tolliver argued.

Oz shot to his feet. "Don't you ever listen? There's no way she's going to get rid of the baby. She won't even get rid of Ace, who is killing her slowly. There is no way she'd get rid of the baby. Besides, it could be yours. Are you so eager to get rid of your own flesh and blood?" He came over and knelt in front of me. "I don't care who's baby it is, Tolliver's or Sam's. I will look after you and him until the end of my days."

I leaned forward and kissed him gently, his rough beard chafing my chin.

"It could be Lux's. Or yours."

Oz smiled sadly. "I don't think so. You haven't tried to redeem either of us yet."

"But you have changed. Both of you." I set my chin stubbornly. I hated making him sad. I wanted him to be redeemed. My sweet, caring Oz.

"Not enough. But it doesn't matter. We all will be, because we are going to work twice as hard to redeem ourselves while you rest. Aren't we Lux?"

Lux gave a stiff nod, his hand still resting on my stomach. His eyes found mine and burned with an intensity that made my heart jump into my throat.

"I, Lux of Taygetus, swear upon Diana, Goddess of the Hunt, to protect you and yours until my dying breath." His tone was solemn and hard, determined in a way I had never heard before. It was the voice of a warrior. A vow.

"Thank you," I whisper against his cheek, my hand reaching out to run down Oz's face. "Thank you both."

Lucifer cleared his throat. "Avowing another god in my presence is a bit of a faux pas, don't you think?" Lux just narrowed his eyes in Luc's direction.

Luc had a small smirk on his face. That face made me suspicious.

"Do you know who's baby it is?"

Lucifer laughed. "Always such the clever one. I have my suspicions, but that is all they are." He cocked his head, as if he was listening to music in another room. "I must go. Give my love to Ace."

"Fuck you," I said pleasantly, and he laughed again.

"You'll be fine, Arcadia. You spit in the eye of the Devil and stare down the Angel of Death. If there is anyone who can survive this with everything intact, it will be you."

With a crack of air, he was gone.

I shifted from Lux's lap and moved toward the bath-room, cup and stick in hand.

Time never goes slower than when your are waiting for water to boil or a pregnancy test to work.

When the pregnancy test came back negative, I was a little relieved. But it was short lived.

You are definitely pregnant, Arcadia. It is just too soon for human tests to detect. Ace's voice was quiet, respectful.

Do you know who's baby it is? Who has been redeemed?

Ace sighed. *No. It could be any one of the four you've slept with.*

Normally, she would have called me a hussy or something. I was already regretting the distance between us. It was like losing my best friend. Sure, it was a best friend I refused to talk to for a couple of years, but still.

I walked back into the room, every pair of eyes following my movements.

"It's negative. But Ace says that Azriel was right. I am pregnant despite the test."

Eli sucked in air through his teeth. "Never trust the motives of the Devil, Arcadia. Or Angels in general. They always play the bigger game. We will continue as if they are correct, but I won't believe it until the tests say it is so."

"If the baby was Lux's, would the test have been positive?" Lux went still at my words.

"Not necessarily, but it would have ruled out Sam and Tolliver. Now, it could be any of the four."

Valery walked over and took my hand, pressing a mug of chamomile tea into my hand. "No one has asked what Arcadia wants. You've all made assumptions on her behalf, and told her what you think she will do." He wrapped an arm around my shoulder and pressed me gently to his side. "I do not have any grand Roman vows to make, and I may not be invested in this situation to quite the same degree as Lux, Tolliver, Oz and Sam, but know that I am with you every step of the way. I will support you no matter your decision," he murmured against my hair.

"I want to keep the baby. And I want to help Ace if I can."

Ri laughed, and it sounded wrong. "Well, that's the least surprising thing I've heard today."

Valery sat me at my bench, and pulled open my fridge, getting out the bread and some strawberry jelly. Then he got down the peanut butter and started making me a sandwich as I gaped. Valery never made anything as mundane as a PB and J.

He cut it into two triangles and set it down in front of me.

"You need the calories. You are eating for two now, and you are desperately thin. We need to feed you as much as possible before the baby gets bigger." And before I got sicker. The words hung in the air.

Even though the food tasted like sawdust, I ate it. Val was right. I would need the calories.

Eli had out a notepad and was scrawling things down.

"We need a plan. If you are keeping the baby, obviously chemotherapy and other cancer treatments are out until late the second trimester. But we need to keep you as healthy as possible. I suggest bed rest and only light activity for the next nine months. I know a great obstetrician to add to your team of specialists. "

"I'm not spending nine months in bed, Eli. We'll just get on with it until I can't, and then we'll work it out again."

"Doing more will only deplete your reserves quicker. We need you to retain as much of your energy as possible. Optimally we need the baby to make it to thirty weeks to be viable and healthy. We can do this." He dropped his head to his chest. "We can do this. I know we can. I just need to think of something."

Actually. I have an idea. Ace's voice surprised me. *But you can't tell the Seven. And you definitely cannot tell Lucifer. Ever. It would not be worth the grief to both of us. He is sexy as hell but he has a killer temper.*

Not tell any of them? *But-*

I know. You promised Eli no more secrets. Okay, you can tell Eli, but that's it.

She explained the plan, and I remembered why I loved my fallen angel so much.

CHAPTER TWENTY-THREE

E li tucked me into bed like I was a piece of porcelain. Then he hopped in beside me. I didn't protest. I wanted him with me. I needed to feel one of them there, touching me, comforting me. The rest of the guys had gone to bed after much protesting.

"You need to get Ace explain this to me again. It doesn't make sense in any scientific terms."

I could feel Ace's exasperation. *Damn men of science. If it isn't in a peer reviewed medical journal, it can't be true. Well, I have news for him. Seeing isn't always believing. Heaven doesn't give a shit about his science. They deal in miracles. And by extension, I deal in miracles. Try and explain it to him again. Go slower. Maybe use smaller words.*

"Ace said that she is going to use her own life force to sustain the baby until thirty weeks, taking the added pressure off my body somehow. She believes that she has enough reserves to last that long without exhausting it and therefore ceasing to exist. She said it isn't based in science. It's something more divine."

Don't forget the last part.

"And don't tell the other guys or Lucifer. If he knew, he would lose his shit. Direct quote by the way."

"And why would she do that?"

"Because she is mine. The baby is part of her, so he will be mine too. I protect what is mine," Ace's voice came out of my mouth in a booming thunder, her ethereal tone raising the hairs on my arms.

Eli's eyes went wide. "What the hell was that?"

I began to shake. That had never happened before, Ace taking control. "It was Ace."

I'm sorry, Arcadia. I did not mean that. It's a sign that your life force is weakening. It's good that we have chosen this course of action. I will protect your child, lowering my life force to similar levels as yours. If we didn't, by the end, there would be hardly any Arcadia left.

She sounded genuinely remorseful. So full of love. Fallen or not, she was my protector. *I love you, you know that right? I'm sorry for what I said earlier.*

She chuckled. *Your capacity for forgiveness knows no bounds. I love you too, Arcadia. And I will help you protect what is dear to you.*

A hole in my chest opened, a sensation that made me gasp. A fullness that I had always had, but never noticed, left and settled around my womb.

Ace? I whispered.

I'm still here. She sounded further away than normal, like she was yelling down a long tunnel. *He's so beautiful. His little life force barely a flicker, yet so pure. He will be like you,*

Cady. A beautiful soul. She began to hum something in a language I couldn't understand.

What are you singing?

A hymn of the angels. She laughed. *He likes it.*

He was barely more than bubbles right now, but I took Ace's word for it. My eyes welled with tears.

"Arcadia? Are you alright?" Eli's concerned voice snapped me back to the external world.

I nodded. "I am now. Ace is singing to the baby. It's beautiful."

Eli pulled me back into his body, curling his tall frame around mine protectively. "Sleep, Arcadia. Rest."

I closed my eyes and listened as Ace sung to my baby. Maybe it would be alright.

THE NEXT WEEK, the week I was supposed to start chemo, did not go exactly as planned. The first surprise that I didn't see coming was Valery quit as head chef at Epicurean, handing over the reins to his sous chef. Now he spent most of his time in my kitchen, making green smoothies and calorie dense junk food to help me put on weight. When he wasn't cooking in my kitchen, or sometimes his if he needed a decent oven, he was watching Ellen with me on the couch.

Actually, one of the guys was with me at all times. Subtly ensuring I rested, and keeping me entertained. Completely platonically.

I was going insane. My hormones were beginning to go a little fritzy. Eli's pregnancy test had confirmed what we all already knew. I was pregnant. Two blue lines. We wouldn't know the exact date of conception, and we couldn't run a DNA test until after he was born. So until then, the baby was Schrodinger's baby. Everyone's and no-ones, but mine. Well, Ace's too. She loved that baby as much as she loved me now. The thought made me smile.

But I was still going stir crazy.

Today, Ri was sitting with me, watching Superhero movies, and I was tucked under his arm.

"You know, we could go to my room and I could show you my Spider-Man underoos." I waggled my eyebrows at him.

Ri gulped. "Nope. The Doc said no physical exertion. What the Doc says, goes."

I pouted, but then smiled. "You know I'm not holding you to your monogamy vow, right? Asking you to stay celibate for nine months, especially if I…"

He kissed my head, and then my lips, gently. "I meant what I said. Besides, I just jerk off, like, twelve times a day."

"Does that still count as lust?"

Ri scoffed. "If so, hell would be full to overflowing." His eyes flicked back to the screen as the superheroes accidentally demolished another city block.

"You sure? Because soon I'll look like I swallowed a watermelon."

He stared at my eyes, and I saw the sincerity shining out of them. "You will be the most beautiful expectant mother I have ever seen. Pregnancy is one of the most wondrous experiences gifted to mankind."

"I bet you say that to all the watermelons," I said as

I climbed onto his lap. I kissed his temple, the hard angle of his jaw and then gently nipped at his neck.

His hands ran up under my shirt, his fingers tracing the smooth skin of my ribs. "Only you."

I kissed his full lips, tracing the line of his straight, white teeth. He was already hard and ready for me, and I could feel the hard swell pressing between my thighs.

"Eli only said no physical exertion. It doesn't count if we take it really slow and very easy, right?"

Ri bit my lip. "Totally doesn't count." He pressed down on my hips, grinding himself against me and I let out a moan. I kissed him hard, and Ri kissed me back with so much sexual frustration that we were going to spontaneously combust if we didn't get to my bedroom right now.

I broke the kiss. "Bed. Now." It came out almost as a pant. I slid off Ri's lap and basically sprinted for the bedroom, throwing my clothes off on the way until I stood naked in the middle of my bedroom floor.

Ri was just in his boxer briefs, his tattoos curling down his body, over his abs and down his hip. I loved his tattoos. Every time I traced them with my fingertips, I found something new.

Ri pulled me to his body, wrapping his arms around my waist and just holding me close.

"Slow down, Beautiful Girl. I'm going to make love to you properly."

I didn't want slow. I wanted to satiate all my needs right now. But I let Ri lay me down on the bed, and when he kissed me softly, I melted into his embrace.

He laid beside me, turning me on side so his body

was curled around mine. His fingers skimmed my shoulders, my collarbone, and down to my breasts. I moaned as his slightly calloused fingers brushed my nipples, and then pressed back into him as he rolled them between his thumb and forefinger.

"You are a Queen, Beautiful Arcadia, and I intend on worshipping your body every day for as long as I live."

His fingers roamed lower, his finger dipping into my navel before tracing the round curve of my stomach.

"Glorious." His fingers brushed down, over my hip and up my inner thigh.

I was aching. "Ri…"

"Shh, I'm going to make it all better."

Good on his word, he slipped his fingers between my folds and stroked my clit. I bucked against his hand, moaning, as he rubbed gentle circles on my clit. The sensation was off the charts. I needed more. Now.

I must have whimpered something to that effect, because the head of his cock was soon pressing against me, asking for entrance. He didn't need to ask.

I pressed back hard, and Ri's cock slid into me like it was made to be there. I moaned as the sensation rippled through my whole body.

Ri slid back out all the way, before entering me again in one long, slow thrust.

"Oh," I whispered. "Fuck."

Ri repeated the slow, deep rhythm, showing better restraint than the sin of Lust should possess. He arched back and pressed kisses down my nape and across my shoulders as he picked up the pace. He wrapped a large hand around my thigh, spreading me wider so he could get deeper again, and I thought I was going to hyperventilate as he hit pleasure zones I wasn't even aware I possessed. He rocked in and out of me, and I was getting so close.

"I want you to touch yourself for me, Beautiful Girl. I want feel your pretty pussy clench around me as you climax," he whispered in my ear, and I was helpless to resist. My hand slipped between my thighs, and I flicked my clit, coaxing out the orgasm that was right there within my reach. Ri plunged into me harder as my body shuddered and I came on a yell. Ri was close behind, his hand slipping back to my hip as he thrust into me wildly, coming on a satisfied moan that was muffled against my shoulder blade.

He rolled onto his back, a slight breathlessness to his voice. "Sorry we didn't go for longer. It's been awhile."

I turned toward him and kissed his shoulder. "It was perfect."

He kissed my lips gently, and gave me that sexy grin, complete with bedroom eyes, that made me want to throw my panties at him from the first moment we met.

"Let me just get something to clean you up."

Five minutes later, in which Ri cleaned and I tried to reconnect my synapses, we were back in bed and I was curled in Ri's arms. He stroked my belly with such tenderness it made me a little weepy.

"Did you have kids in your former life?"

"Uh huh. Fifty-two."

I jerked upright. "Get the fuck out? Seriously?"

Orion laughed, a little sheepishly. "Well, fifty-two

confirmed children. There was a few more I suspected weren't legitimate heirs, if you catch my drift."

"You can't have been more than twenty-seven when you died."

"Twenty-three. But this was before easily available contraception on the islands. They kind of considered me a fertility god. If people were having trouble conceiving, I would come, make love to their wife, and then poof, nine months later they would have an heir. I was part of no tribe and every tribe in that way. I just travelled from island to island, and they would have a huge feast and I would bang my way around the village. It was a good life, well until I died in a freak storm at sea, that is."

"How old were you when that started?"

He pulled me back down into his arms. "I was fifteen when my first child was conceived. But it was a different time. I was considered a man."

"That's six children a year!" The idea both fascinated and horrified me.

"Yep. Many Pacific Islanders can trace their ancestry back to me. From Hawaii to New Zealand."

"Hardly seems worth sending a person to hell for though, right? Besides, they wouldn't have been your gods."

It was something I'd been thinking on. Lux's wouldn't have followed Christianity nor would have Sam. Some of those religions celebrated sex and life.

"That's true. But they are all derivatives of the same thing. Some worship one over the other, some worship many, but in the end, they are all stories created by man to explain something divine. Even hell is just a convenient name from the place where you go when you do things that aren't morally acceptable in most religions. And no Parthenon likes you to set yourself up as a false idol. I'm almost positive that is why I ended up in Hell."

Confusing. But it made a strange sort of sense. If I had met Lucifer in a 1000 BC tavern in Sweden, wouldn't I have thought him a trickster god? If I had seen Azriel on a battlefield, would I not think he was a God of Death?

"Okay."

"Centuries of theological debate and countless wars, and she accepts the whole thing with an okay?" Ri waved his hands at an invisible audience. "Want me to start the movie back up in here?"

I shrugged and snuggled back in as Ri turned on the tv and pressed play on Netflix again. I didn't need Clark Kent, I already had my superheroes.

CHAPTER TWENTY-FOUR

O z laid with his head on my thighs, and the others were scattered on the beanbags and couches around Oz's apartment.

"What about Englebert? My dads name was Englebert."

Tolliver choked on his beer. "We cannot call a baby Englebert. Actually, no one should be named Englebert. Ever."

Oz huffed as he rubbed his cheek on my bump. It actually looked like a pregnant belly now, rather than like I had a really big burrito for lunch. But the bigger my belly grew, the fainter Ace sounded. I was worried, though I didn't let on to anyone but Eli. The only time she moved away from the baby was when Luc came to visit, which was pretty infrequently since they'd arrested a terrorist cell in Tanzania, which meant there was a lot of last minute deals with the Devil.

"Well, what do you suggest? Tolliver Junior?" Oz

screwed up his nose. "I don't think so. Poor kid might already have to put up with your face."

"I was thinking Axel."

It was Sam's turn to screw up his nose. "Why don't you just call him Bruiser if you want him to join a motorcycle gang that bad?"

They bickered about the name, what color to paint the nursery, whether the baby should have a walker, what school he should attend.

Only Lux believed it was a girl. He'd pat my stomach from time to time, and murmur, "Hope."

It was the perfect name if it was a girl. Ace wouldn't tell me, saying she didn't know, but I suspected she did.

I was three months along, and getting weaker by the day. Eli cut down his availability at the hospital to care for me, and spent several hours a day talking to doctors all over the world about research into cancer treatment of pregnant women. Every night, he would attach a drip filled with god knows what to keep me healthy, and then he'd sleep beside me. Or if one of the other guys filled that spot, he'd sleep on the couch in the living room in case the machine beeped during the night.

Most of them had cut down their working hours, or given it up all together, to stay with me, or try to do things that would hopefully negate their sins. Oz was even doing cross-fit five times a week. He looked like sex on a stick, his wide shoulders now bulging with muscle.

On the advice of Tolliver's lawyers, Sam and Tolli had set up a charitable foundation, but they still went out once a day to give money directly to people, or to homeless shelters, or soup kitchens. They'd eventually been outed as the Robin Hood Ninjas, so they used their public profiles to encourage more of the rich to give to charity. I was sure they would be fine. They even seemed happy in their roles. Sam didn't even miss modeling, though it probably helped that he kept getting spreads in newspapers and magazines. The publicity went back and helped the poor, so surely that would be okay, right?

Ri sat with me most days, or took me up to the rooftop pool to swim, and worked nearly every night. He looked like crap though.

Despite my offer, he was sticking to his celibacy unless it was me. And he refused to make love to me unless Eli said he could. And Eli was against me doing anything but my best impression of sleeping beauty.

"What do you think, Cady?" Sam asked, bringing me back to the present.

"Mmhm? I was daydreaming. Sorry. What was the question?"

"We're back to names. Have you picked one yet?"

I shook my head, although I had some distinct favorites. But I knew if I suggested anything, they would agree with me just to make me happy, and I liked this little slice of normalcy.

"I want to wait and see what the baby looks like."

"It will look like a tiny, wrinkly alien. You can't call the poor kid Wrinkles," Ri quipped, getting in on the action tonight. Normally, he, Eli and Valery stayed out of it. They all knew they couldn't be the father, because I'm pretty sure the baby wasn't an immaculate conception, but I purposely drew them in. This was our baby.

The eight of us. I wanted everyone to feel connected, included.

Valery put down several trays of piping hot nachos on Oz's coffee table, one tray just for me. I didn't know what it was about nachos, but I craved them all the time. It was the only thing I could stomach after the morning sickness, that for some strange reason, always struck in the late afternoon. What kind of false advertising was that?

I dug into my nachos furiously. No one tried to take them from my tray now, not after I almost stabbed Oz in the hand with a fork.

Sometimes my body felt like it was possessed.

Speaking of possessed, something pushed against my stomach. I held my breath. I'd been feeling the flutters of movement for a few weeks now, but this one felt different. Stronger.

Ace, was that you?

I could hear Ace's happiness. *No. Wait for it.*

A kick.

"Ace or morning sickness?" Valery asked.

"Morning sickness. She hasn't thrown up yet today," Ri weighed in.

"No. It's Ace," Lux said. He didn't elaborate. He just knew.

I grinned at them. "Come here, come here, come here," I said giddily. I grabbed Lux's hand and placed it on my belly, and Oz did too. I moved their hands to where the baby kicked. Seconds went by, and there it was again. A huge grin spread across Lux's face. It was so rare, especially these days, that I was temporarily blinded by his happiness.

"She kicked."

"He kicked," Oz corrected, laughing happily. He moved back so the other two could try.

We waited and waited, and I could see Tolliver's face fall with disappointment.

"Maybe it likes those two better?" Sam teased, but I could sense real disappointment.

As if the baby could too, it kicked again. Such a kind little heart already.

Sam laughed. "It has been so long since I have felt such a beautiful thing."

Tolliver just rubbed circles on my belly, his eyes a little wet.

They stepped back and Eli came over, stethoscope in hand. He blew warm air over the end and placed it on my stomach where the baby was kicking.

"Nice strong heartbeat," he smiled, offering the stethoscope to Valery, who listened with a wide smile, and the Ri, who I could see counting the beats under his breath.

"Should it be that fast?" His brow knitted in concern.

Eli nodded. "It's perfect. The ultrasound tomorrow should confirm that."

I wish I could use the ultrasound to narrow down who the father was, who was redeemed. They'd all become so invested, and I worried that they were going to be upset if it wasn't them.

Sam must have seen the worry on my face.

"Don't stress. We won't care if we aren't the father. The baby is yours and we are yours and we will love it. Even if it is called Englebert. Or Wrinkles."

Then I cried. Because apparently being pregnant made you a mess of hormones that means you cry every time a toilet paper ad with a kid or a puppy comes on.

Used to my tears by now, Lux just rubbed my back and handed me a tissue. The guys all carried purse packs of tissues around.

"I think it is time for Arcadia to go to bed. Start the tournament," Eli ordered

The tournament of Scissors, Paper, Rock happened every night to determine who got to sleep next to me. I suggested drawing up a roster, but it disadvantaged the guys who were on call and weren't always here at night. This way it was down to skill and a little bit of luck. It was always fun to watch, anyway.

Oz and Ri were up first.

"Scissor, Paper, R-"

"Hello, Arcadia."

We all whipped around to see Azriel standing by my front door.

"I apologize for letting myself in." His tone was completely unapologetic.

Lux was up and between us in seconds, a knife appearing from somewhere on his body. Where had he been hiding that all this time?

"What do you want, Azriel?" I asked, as the guys huddled around me protectively. It was probably pretty useless actually. He was the Angel of Death. He didn't really need to be anywhere near me to kill me, right?

"It is an interesting solution that Acerezeal has concocted. I did not believe she had such selflessness left in her, since her fall to hell. I wonder what Lucifer Morningstar would say about it, hmm? I do not believe he would be quite so supportive of this newfound sacrificial side."

What do you want? You are not welcome here, Ace growled

Azriel laughed. "I am an angel. I am welcome everywhere. I have come to offer Arcadia a choice once more. Despite your little solution, the cancer is eating its way through her body, and soon it might be too late for her to ever recover, irrespective of your salvation, or theirs." He indicated the men standing in the room. My men.

"The answer is still no. Ace stays and you go."

He was in front of me in a flash, disappearing and reappearing inches from my face.

"Father has ordered me not to take Acerezeal from you by force, even though it would be a simple thing and it would cure you. But you will not talk to me with such disrespect. I am an angel. People beg me to save them every day, and I comply. What are you saving?"

With that, he vanished completely from the room.

Fucking uptight asshole. If I still had my body I would show him "respect" at the end of my sword.

My knees buckled and Eli caught me, scooping me up and walking me out of Oz's apartment but he didn't hit my floor number in the lift, instead going down to Lux's floor.

"Why are we going to Lux's apartment?"

"His has the most weapons, and he's the best equipped to protect you if Azriel comes back."

I looked over Eli's shoulder and saw that Lux was there. He nodded once.

"Lux can't stab an angel, Eli. I'm pretty sure they can't die, plus I'm trying to redeem him, remember? Getting stabby on an angel has the opposite effect."

"You're life is more important than my redemption," Lux growled.

"You guys are being purposefully dense. His redemption is my life. I need Lux to be the opposite of wrathful so we can all survive." I wiggled in Eli's arms and he just held me tighter. Eli wasn't as big or as buff as Lux or Oz, but he held my weight effortlessly against his strong body.

"Be still." He used a tone that I hadn't heard from him before. Not caring doctor, or educated man of science, or even his normal, relaxed demeanor.

It was authoritative, dominant and sexy as hell. I found myself complying without conscious thought.

"You will stay with Lux, and Lux will protect you if you need it, and you will be saved, right along with us even if I have to try every single procedure known to modern medicine to achieve it."

There was no doubt in his voice, no hesitation. He would save me. He was determined.

Pride, thy name is Elias.

I didn't know what to do about his redemption. Pride was integral to his very existence. He'd gone into the too hard basket, but I didn't have the time left to procrastinate. It wasn't as easy as Tolliver and Sam. I couldn't just ask him to quit his job. Literally hundreds of people would die without access to his neurosurgical abilities.

It wasn't like Valery, who was kind of redeeming himself, though I didn't think he knew it. More and more often, he was cooking basic meals for me, things that my stomach could handle. But he wasn't cooking extravagant things, he wasn't partying or sleeping around or doing the other things that the guys said he used to do to excess before I came onto the scene. I found those stories hard to believe. I'd never met that version of Valery. My Valery was hardly eating, because he was too busy ensuring I ate.

No, Eli was the quandary.

We got to Lux's floor, and the front door buzzed. I looked at my health tracker, that handily came with a watch feature. Who would be here at eleven at night? All the big bads could just poof themselves into the room, so I wasn't worried about it being Azriel again. Did Oz order more pizza?

Eli pushed the intercom by Lux's door. "Can I help you?"

"You bloody well can help me," a slight Irish accent came through the speaker, the quality crackling and distorted. The voice sounded familiar, and my heart lifted.

"Who's this?"

"This is Clary Mulligan and I want to know what the hell you've done with my best friend."

Ace gave a little squeal of delight. *Yay, Clary's home. Oh, this is going to be fun to watch. Get your popcorn and put on your big girl panties, because shit is going to go down.*

CHAPTER TWENTY-FIVE

Clary was quintessentially Irish. She had the small round face, the mouse brown hair that glinted auburn in the sun, a small snub nose that turned red when she drank too much, and big apple cheeks that made the corners of her eyes crinkle when she laughed. She was also so pale that you'd lose her during a snowstorm. Why she'd chosen to go to Africa, I had no idea.

No that was a lie. She went because she was needed, and if there was anything the youngest child in a family of ten children wanted in life, it was to be needed.

I hugged her close, admiring her almost tan.

"It's so good to see you, Clary. I've missed you so much." She hugged me back, and then jumped away like a scalded cat.

"Arcadia Jones, you are pregnant under that sweatshirt!"

I nodded slowly. This is where things were going to get sketchy.

"Which one of you good-for-nothings knocked up my sweet, innocent Arcadia? I'm going to chop off your balls and wear them as earrings!" She stood toe to toe with Lux, even though he towered over her average five and a half feet height.

"It's not that straight forward, Clary. How about we go into my apartment and talk?"

The doors to the lift opened and the other five guys strode out, in various states of late night dishevelment.

"What the hell is this place? Did you start a cult for hot hipsters while I was gone?"

Ace chortled in my head. Ace liked very few humans. Me, and now the baby, and the old guy who made subs at the deli on the corner near my old apartment, who flirts outrageously with every woman, or man for that matter, who came in for a sandwich. But she loved Clary. They were kindred spirits, even if Clary didn't know that Ace existed.

"Umm, no. These are my, well boyfriends I guess you could say? Soulmates is probably a better term." I rattled them off. "Orion, Oz, Valery, Tolliver and Sam. You've already threatened to castrate Lux and Eli behind you. Guys, this is the best human on the planet, Clary Mulligan, formerly of the Boston Mulligans, holder of the record for most Irish whiskeys consumed at the NYCU student bar. Clary, these are my guys."

"Your guys? As in plural?" I nodded. "We need to make some tea and you need to tell me everything. Starting with this," she pointed to the roundness of my abdomen. "Which one is the father?"

"Umm, we've narrowed it down to Oz, Sam, Tolliver," I pointed as I said their names, "or Lux."

Clary slow blinked. And then once more. "I'm going to need a big set of surgical scissor and a tourniquet."

I winced and Eli chuckled, the only one to get her mass castration joke. I grabbed her by the arm. I'd heard stories. I wasn't going to put it past her.

"Lets go have that tea, hey?"

HOURS LATER, I'd laid it all out for her at my breakfast bar. She leaned on her elbows, sipping Valery's fancy Bordeaux wine, and hadn't said a word in comment, even when I got to the part about Ace and Lucifer. She gave me the face I imagine you would give to a man who was bleeding to death. Not overly concerned, just warm nonchalance.

"You know, in Somalia, I saw some terrible things. Girls coming in pregnant at thirteen because they'd been raped, whole villages decimated, babies starving at their mothers breasts. Some of it will haunt me for the rest of my life. But you are telling me now, that there is a God and he was sitting around playing chess with the Devil while people were literally hacked to death with machetes? Bargaining for the souls of murderers? That these 'divine' beings really exist, and therefore must just turn a blind eye to all the suffering in the world? And the only person who is trying to alleviate the eternal damnation is the Devil? That's some seriously fucked up shit, Arcadia."

"It does sound pretty preposterous, I know. But it's real. It takes a little getting used to, is all."

"You think?" She downed the rest of her wine. "Let's get back to 'your guys'. They are zombies masquerading as the Seven Deadly Sins and it's your job to save them, and in doing so you get what exactly? To not die? Sounds like a lot of hard work and a pretty shitty prize to me."

You should tell her about the mind blowing orgasms, Ace suggested. Err, maybe not just yet. "Plus the reconsideration of the eternal damnation of souls for merely sleeping with your neighbors wife."

"Mmphf. Maybe. Now tell me what you left out."

Damn Clary. She knew me too well. "I'm really sick. The leukemia is back, my myocardiopathy is at a critical level, and I might not make it to the full term."

Clary's eyes got wide. Huge, shining hazel orbs. "What?"

I continued. "And I need you to promise me something if that happens. If everything goes pear shaped, and let's face it when you are playing in a game of angels and devils, that has a high likelihood of happening, I want you to take the baby and raise it. There is no one I trust more than you and yours. I need to know that the baby will have a good future, in a big family with lots of love, no matter what happens. I know that's a lot to ask, I'm essentially asking you to give up your life. But you are the only person I know who would love the baby like it was her own, no matter what."

Clary was still blinking, stunned. "You know I will. You don't have to ask. How could you not tell me you were sick again? I would have come back in an instant. I could have been here for you for the last three months."

I rubbed her arm. "I've been in good hands, and I wanted to keep you out of this if I could. I got Tolliver's lawyers to make you the baby's next of kin in case of emergencies, as well as my own. I hope that's okay. The guys, well, they have all the best intentions, and I know that they will love the baby, all of them. If anything happens, I need you to give them the chance to parent the baby, too. I'm asking for too much, I know, it's just that you are the only one removed from this situation."

Clary nodded. "Of course." I leaned across and hugged her, my stomach brushing on the edge of the bench, and the baby kicked in response. I laughed and held her hand to my stomach. "Isn't she wonderful?"

"She? It's a girl?"

I shrugged. "I don't know, but I have a feeling."

Clary nodded. "And just to clarify, you've slept with all of them?"

I laughed and shook my head. "No, only five of them. But I would have, if I hadn't gotten sick and then the whole baby thing. Eli went into super doctor mode and banned anyone from having sex and causing my body 'undue stress'."

"So they are all just hanging around, being faithful to you, hand feeding you peeled grapes? Bitch, I don't know what Kool-Aid you fed them, but give me some. I want me a harem filled with sexy dead guys." She waggled her eyebrows suggestively.

I laughed and laughed until tears streamed down my face. God, I'd missed her.

. . .

I MOVED Clary into my apartment. I hardly used it anymore anyway, I was always in Eli's apartment. I kind of presented Clary moving in to the guys as a *fait accompli*, but I needed her, and the guys knew it, so no one protested. Besides, she took some of the nursing burden from Eli, so he could actually sleep at night.

I ran a hand over my stomach.

How is she today?

Ace's reply was immediate, though her voice was weakening. *The baby is getting stronger every day. He learned how to suck his thumb today. He will be strong and healthy at thirty weeks. Mark my words.* The warmth and love in Ace's voice made me tear up. Actually, everything made me tear up, but this was pretty special.

Thanks Ace.

Ugh, hormones. You don't have to thank me every day. I put you in this position. It's me who should be thanking you, really.

I opened my laptop and went to Google. This is what it had come to, googling for solutions. Unfortunately when I googled 'how do you redeem seven guys who are the embodiment of the seven deadly sins before you die of a heart attack or cancer?' There were zero results.

Hold on. Ace's tone was calm. Too calm. *Oh. Don't panic, but you need to call Eli right now.*

"Call Eli!" I shouted to Clary and Valery, my voice edged with hysteria. Clary bolted around the counter towards me and Valery, who'd been making me juice in the kitchen, bolted out the door, his phone already to his ear.

"What's wrong?" Clary's tone was calm and in control.

But I wasn't. "Ace said there's something wrong with the baby."

I said no such thing. What I did say was not to panic. Breathe.

"I'll fucking breathe when you tell me what's wrong," I said, out loud. Clary's eyes went wide. "Not you," I said to her. "Ace."

Clary had her fingers on my wrist. "Well, Ace is right. Your heart rate is erratic. You need to calm down and breathe."

Eli burst through the door, and Valery came in behind him holding his medical bag.

You need to tell him it's twins.

I blinked. My breathing stopped. *What?*

Eli was there, his stethoscope out listening to my heart. "What is wrong?"

"Ace says it's twins."

He jerked back as if I punched him. "What?"

You've been monitoring the baby for months, how could you not know I was having twins?

I don't know! She's small, smaller than her sister. Her sister's life force is so strong, it encompasses them both. Their heartbeats are in sync. If I hadn't felt her interest in her sister's thumb sucking, I would never have known she was there.

"Grab the fetal monitor," Eli ordered, and when Ri went sprinting out of the room, that's when I realized they were all there. Staring. Gaping really.

But Eli look devastated.

"What does this mean?"

"Complications. Your heart is already taxed when pregnant. This increase significantly with twins. Given the condition of your heart, I'm worried it will fail before you reach thirty weeks."

Ri returned with the fetal monitor, and Clary helped Eli put it around my stomach.

The room went silent as we listened to the rapid flutter of the babies heart beat. But we could only hear one.

"Is Ace sure?"

Yes. Listen closely. Their heartbeats are synced, but the little ones is just a fraction of a second behind.

I listened. There it was. A strong thump followed by a tiny flutter.

Hang on, did you say 'she'? Am I having twin daughters?

Yes, I wanted the sex of the baby to be a surprise.

Oh, I was surprised alright.

"Congratulations, guys. We are having two baby girls." My stomach rolled. "I think I'm going to throw up."

CHAPTER TWENTY-SIX

The next week was a wave of appointments. High risk obstetricians, heart specialists, my oncologist, scans, ultrasounds, blood tests. A lot of serious faces and serious decisions.

No one would let me walk anywhere. They practically carried me to the car and back. Oz hovered over me every second of the day until I wanted to punch him in the throat if he asked me how I was one more time. It was probably the hormones. Probably.

Ace told me that the littlest baby was getting stronger as she channeled her life force into her, but as a result Ace was getting weaker. I didn't know how I was so sure, but there was an emptiness that I felt in my soul. An emptiness that I knew had once been filled by Ace.

"We have to tell Lucifer what Ace is doing."

"Tell Lucifer what," Lux said, his head whipping towards me. Oops, I'd forgotten only Eli knew about Ace's involvement. Dammit baby brain.

"Uh, Ace is channeling her life force into the babies to take a little of the strain from me."

Lux nodded like that was the most logical thing in the world. "But she's getting really faint. I think she's overtaxing herself with the extra baby. We need to tell Luc before he finds out himself."

"That's a bad idea."

I'm with tall, dark and deadly over there. Bad, bad idea.

"Ace can't sustain both babies. He's going to notice and be angry. We should tell him now, before it's too late."

I can and I will. You will not tell Luc. It is better to ask forgiveness from the Devil than permission.

"Ace is a fallen angel. Let her do her thing. She deserves the chance."

The rest of the ride was silent as I wondered how the hell I'd gotten to this place. Life, or fate, had a lot to answer for. I was exhausted, and didn't protest as Lux hefted me out of the car and into his arms. We rode the lift up to Eli's apartment. Eli would make me go straight to bed. His bed.

I briefly thought of that sexy flash I'd seen from Eli the night Clary had arrived. The dominant, commanding Eli. I wondered if that was the voice he'd use in the bedroom?

Would he tie me to the headboard with one of his ties? I imagined him leaning over me, commanding me not to cum until he gave me his permission. He would explore my prone body at his leisure, kissing some places, biting other places, explaining what he wanted from me in that steady voice, so filled with authority. He would call me Miss Jones, and not Arcadia, as he bit the inside of my thigh, hard enough to leave a mark. He'd soothe the hurt with a swirl of his tongue, that would move up to explore the folds. And when I'd get close to coming, he'd stop, tsk, and move back to exploring my body. He'd do this over and over, until I was begging him to give me release, and only then would slide his delicious cock inside me, taking my nipples in his mouth and biting the sensitive buds as he rode my wet and ready body, until I screamed in pleasure.

"I don't know what the fuck you are thinking about right now, but you need to stop," Lux's voice was hoarse and strained, and I realized I was breathing heavily.

"I can feel your wetness on my arm, and it makes me want to make love to you here in the elevator. But we cannot." I didn't know if that last part was for my benefit or his. It had been so long since I'd had sex, I might actually be going insane.

Who knew there was a dirty little submissive inside that prim and proper exterior? Ace laughed quietly.

"It's the hormones," I whined to both of them.

Sure it is. Liar, liar pants on fire.

Lux just grunted as the lift shuddered to a stop. He knocked on Eli's doors, and when the man himself opened it in only his boxer shorts, I blushed the brightest shade of pink ever. Lux pushed me into Eli's arms.

"I'm going for a swim. Then a cold shower. Call me if you need me," he said gruffly, and almost ran to the stairs.

Eli placed me on my feet, sliding me gently down his

delectable body. He was all lean muscle, smooth and sculpted. I gulped.

"What's his problem?" Eli asked, as he held my elbow, guiding me toward the bedroom like a dementia patient.

"Blue balls."

Eli let out a choked laugh. "It seems to be an epidemic. Ri came to see me with a sore wrist today. RSI."

I blinked. "That's a joke, right?"

Eli just laughed as he pulled back the covers, hooking me up to my obs machine and then tucking me in.

"Still on nights?" I asked him as he climbed in beside me.

"Mmhmm." He said as his eyes closed.

"Have you ever thought of tying me up?"

HIs eyes snapped open. "What?"

"Never mind."

He reached over and flicked my taut nipple. "I asked what you said." The sensation rocketed through my body.

"I said have you ever thought of tying me up?"

He leaned over and sucked my nipple through my shirt and I arched off the bed towards him.

"Every night since you arrived here four months ago. But now is not the time. We will have the rest of our lives for me to do all the things I dream of doing to you. Now rest, Arcadia."

I did as I was told. Just this one time.

· · ·

SAM AND TOLLIVER agreed to live together, so I could have Tolliver's apartment and Clary could have mine. I wanted to nest, and I couldn't do that in Eli's smaller apartment. Oz and I spent hours online shopping, and the delivery guy knew me by name now. Tolliver's apartment had once been decorated with modern lowline furniture made from chrome and glass but was now a mass of amazon and IKEA boxes, and a mountain of onesies. It was like Babies'R'Us threw up all over the place.

We'd turned Tolliver's second bedroom into a nursery and Orion had painted it like an island paradise, complete with coconut trees, brightly colored tropical birds, the deep blue ocean and golden sand. Ri turned out to be quite the artist. When I'd said so, he'd just given me a lascivious wink.

"I'm good with my hands. When this is all over, I'm going to paint you with my tongue from head to toe, tasting every delicious inch of you." It was a standard Ri kind of comment that he used to flirt all the time; a blend of teasing promise and smoldering sexuality. I was used to them now, and although I found him incredibly sexy, I'd learned to ignore the pickup lines and look for the subcontext of what he was saying.

But not today.

Something possessed my body, and I had him backed up against the still wet paint, my hands under his shirt and my body pressed tight against his. As tight as it would go with my bump.

It was like I'd turned into some sex crazed monster,

but then he was kissing me back, and all thoughts left my brain.

I tore his shirt off, kissing my way down his hard smooth chest, and he did the same, kissing my neck and biting the vein there hard. I moaned and pressed closer to him. His hands ran down to my ass and squeezed, and I could feel the hard length of him beneath his jeans.

He jumped away as if he'd been burned. "We can't. The cardiologist said no undue physical exertion, and that includes sex. Fuck, does that include sex. Your health, and the babies, are more important. You feel so good though," he groaned, running his fingers over my cheek and down my jaw, the back of his hand brushing over the hard bud of my nipple. I moaned and Ri took another two steps back.

"Soon, Beautiful Girl. Soon." He reached forward and rubbed my belly, as if reminding himself why. "Let's just get this little family into the world first."

It was then that I realized I didn't need to worry about Orion. He would be fine.

He led me to the bedroom, his hand around my back. "How about I give you a foot rub, and you have a rest."

Actually, a nap sounded good right now. I sat on the bed, and Ri leaned down, pulling off my fluffy slipper socks, and laid me back on the bed.

"Ri, do you ever regret how you lived? Before you died the first time, I mean."

Ri took one of my feet into his hands, and pressed his thumb into the arch. I moaned with happiness. My eyes felt like lead weights, as if they were just waiting for the comfort of a pillow to relax.

"I made a lot of people happy, if I do say so myself. But yeah, I regret it sometimes. Hell wasn't a party. And I never got to have a family of my own. I would have liked that."

I opened one eye and gave him a sleepy smile. "You will. I promise."

CHAPTER TWENTY-SEVEN

I sat on Oz's lap, his laptop open on the table in front of us.

"We need a plan. And a spreadsheet. I can't leave the house, so you guys need to redeem yourselves and help each other. Let's start with Val. What's the opposite of Gluttony?"

Oz typed it into the search engine. "Uh, temperance."

I groaned. This one was hard. Given the fact I nearly mauled Ri earlier, apparently temperance, or self-restraint, wasn't something I had in abundance.

"Let's leave him until last. What about Pride?"

"Humility."

Clary, who was sitting across from us, scoffed. "Send him to Africa. There is no place for ego there."

Oz screwed up his face. "Eli cant go to Africa. Cady needs him. She comes first, always."

I leaned back and kissed his cheek.

Somewhere between kissing Oz's rough cheek and turning back to the computer screen, I had an epiphany. The answer was so simple, I couldn't believe I hadn't thought of it before. Eli didn't need to go to Africa to see tragedy and learn humility. There was plenty of tragedy right here in NYC. There were people he could help, with the aid of Tolliver and Sam's new charitable foundation. We could provide life changing care to the uninsurable. But would it be enough?

I explained my idea to Oz and Clary, and Oz's fingers flew across the keyboard to find already established facilities that Eli could work out of, or maybe we could even build our own if we needed too?

As Oz did what he did best, well maybe not what he did best because he was pretty clever with certain parts of his anatomy, I turned to my best friend. "What about you Clary? Are you going back to Africa after all this is over?"

Clary stared at a spot in the distance, the place where memories play on a nightmarish loop, then she shook her head. "No, I'm not going back to Africa. I'm needed here, with you. Like the lumberjack said, you are the most important thing right now. Maybe I'll join Doc McBuffins in the projects. He'll need a nurse."

A selfish part of me was glad Clary wasn't going back. I did need her. And if not me, the babies would need her. She would never say anything, but sometimes I would catch her looking at me with the saddest eyes. She didn't expect me to make it through. The odds were too stacked against me. I literally felt weaker every day. My body wasting away except my big, round belly filled with life. When I was being honest with myself, I didn't expect it either. But I would fight, and so would everyone else.

"That's a great idea. He will need the help, and it's easier than finding work in NYC. The foundation will pay you a wage, of course."

She'd be fine after I was gone. She'd have a steady job. And if I didn't redeem Eli... I shut down the thought. I would redeem them all. But if the worst happened, I knew the guys would take care of her. Make sure she wanted for nothing, because she had loved me too.

There was a knock at the door, and Clary got up to open it. Valery walked in with a huge casserole dish.

"I just need to put this in your oven, *Ma Cherie*."

"I think she has enough in her oven, don't you?" Clary teased.

Valery muttered something unflattering in French, but his mouth tilted up at the corners. He put the dish into the oven and then walked over, kissing me gently on the lips, one hand rubbing my belly like Buddha.

"Beautiful. Now I must get back to the buns in my oven."

Clary choked out a laugh. I smiled and smacked him on the butt on the way out.

We were having a family dinner, which was just a fancy way of letting them all see me eat. The idea of food turned my stomach, but I didn't care. I was eating for three. Much to everyone's disagreement, I'd even invited Lucifer.

Ace sounded weak. My gut said she needed Luc.

And the babies would be fine for a night. She was like a mother hen with her eggs though, so she was pouting about it.

I'm not pouting, she said in a disgruntled voice. She sounded stronger already, and I tried not to grin.

"When's the Devil arriving?"

I hushed her. "Don't call him that. He's Luc. I don't think you get my leeway."

He'll chew her up and spit out her bones, Ace added

Metaphorically, right?

Ace just laughed.

"Luc should be here after the other guys arrive. At 6 minutes past 6, or at least that's what his RSVP said."

I stood and waddled toward the table, ensuring once more that everything was perfect. I wanted this one happy memory. I was wearing a beautiful wrap dress that Sam had bought for me, the latest in maternity fashion. In all honesty, it looked like a tent.

I straightened the silverware once more, adjusted the bouquet of tulips that Tolliver had had delivered this morning, and fussed with the napkins. It was only five.

"It's as perfect now as it was ten minutes ago. For Christ sake, just sit down. Oh crap, can I say for Christ's sake? I'm going to have to get Mammy to light a candle for me. I'm going to hell," Clary said as she crossed herself.

"Don't worry, it's not as bad as everyone says," a voice said from behind me, making Clary jump and whirl around. Lucifer stood at the doorway, leaning against the door jamb, a, well devilish, grin on his face.

Always with the dramatic entrances, my love. Ace said, and she sounded happier and stronger already. She may not have wanted… I snapped down on my thoughts immediately.

Luc tilted his head at me. "It's hard to guard your thoughts all night, Arcadia. You should just get it off your chest now."

"There's nothing on my chest." I gave Oz a stern look, cutting off the inevitable Oz boob joke. "Come in Luc, sit down. This is Clary."

"Yes, of the Mulligans of Boston. I've met more than one of your kin, despite their strict Catholicism. Usually only the men, though. The women are practically in line for sainthood." He laughed at his own joke, and looked Clary up and down. "Your heart is way too good. You won't be heading to my domain unless you intend on taking over the family business? Cracking skulls doesn't seem like your style."

Clary's face went carefully blank. "I'm sure I don't know what your talking about."

Luc laughed. "You don't have Ace boosting your mental shields like Arcadia does. But don't worry. I don't care. You aren't your family, and you always get judged on your own actions. Blood does not matter in the end."

I just stared. If Luc was insinuating what I thought he was, he was trying to say the Mulligans were part of the Irish mob. I looked from one to the other, and the silence was stifling.

"Luc would you like a beer?" A beer appeared in his hand from nowhere. "Okay then."

Quit showing off for the mortals. You're early, by the way. Since when do you turn up early to anything?

Since my consort was reborn into a mortal body and I don't get to spend nearly enough time teasing her delicious body, Luc crooned and I grimaced. Ew.

Come on guys. There's kids present.

Kids?

Ace groaned. *Seriously. It's like the babies are draining you of your IQ. Yes, Arcadia is having twins.*

Oz felt me tense, and his own body tensed in response.

"I wonder where the rest of the guys are? Mini Oz, call All Users and tell them that it is time to get to Arcadia's apartment for dinner. We will need help with the serving."

Clever boy.

"You look well for a woman carrying twins, Arcadia." Luc's tone was pleasant.

"Thanks, Lucifer. Valery has me on these kale shakes that some Italian doctor swears will cure everything."

Luc laughed. "If there is a more angelic food then kale, I'm yet to find it. All goodness and purity, not taste."

I gave him a smile. He was kinda of charming when he wasn't being scary.

That's your mistake, Arcadia. He is always scary, even more so when he is smiling, Ace said, her tone affectionate, with a little fear.

"I'm not going to lie, I think Azriel is scarier. All that perfection isn't natural. He looks like a store mannequin come to life." I shuddered with exaggeration. "It's just not natural."

"I wouldn't say his name too often, Arcadia. He is

likely just to appear in the mirror like Candyman. There's a Yankees game on, mind if I watch? We don't get ESPN down below. Bad reception."

"Probably the brimstone. Go for it. Mini-Oz, turn on TV and switch to ESPN."

The TV turned on. "Sometimes I think you humans do possess magic," Luc said as he walked over to the couch. I let out the breath I'd been holding.

The door opened and Lux strode in, looking fine in a tight white shirt and black jeans that molded to his thighs like latex. He came over and kissed me.

"Everything okay?" He whispered in my ear.

"Yes, for now."

Clary looked pale, and I grabbed her arm, dragging her into the kitchen. It wouldn't help much in the way of privacy, but it was something.

"Are you okay?" I asked, rubbing her arm reassuringly.

"He looks so… normal? Hot, for sure, as sexy as he is scary. But I was expecting something more…"

"Pitchfork-ish?"

"Uh huh. And less average. He's drinking beer and watching baseball. He makes pop culture references. That's just weird."

"Yeah. I found it was best if you just threw out everything you thought you knew about the world and started again."

Clary stared at her fingernails for a minute.

"Clary. What Luc said about your family, you know none of that matters to me, right? Hell, I find it hard to even imagine. I mean, they are loud and boisterous, but mob? I wouldn't have known in a million years."

Clary shrugged. "They are old school like that. Keep the women pregnant in the kitchen, and out of the family business. They aren't like you see in the movies, though. It's not that brutal, well the Mulligans aren't anyway, and the Irish mob is losing ground, going more legitimate. But I went to a lot of funerals when I was younger."

I gave her a hug, and a baby kicked. Empathetic little things.

Valery and Ri walked in, saw Lux and Luc sitting at opposite ends of the couch and Oz in the rocking chair we'd gotten, and headed towards the kitchen with arms full of food. Then came Sam and Tolliver, with the drinks and appetizers. Eli wouldn't be home until six, he had a surgery.

The party had started. Ri placed the food on the breakfast bar and leaned over, kissing me gently, nipping my lip.

"You look sexy as hell."

"If orcas are your thing, maybe." I kissed his cheek and he headed off to the living area. Tolliver kissed me, and then my stomach, and Sam did the same.

"Hey babies," he whispered at my belly, and I smiled happily. What a weird family we would be.

The smell of food permeated the apartment. Even my mouth watered, and I'd lost my appetite weeks ago.

I dipped my finger into the gravy boat and stuck my finger in my mouth. I let out a little moan. "You are an artiste, Valery. This is amazing."

"I will make it for you by the gallon if that is what you desire, *Ma Cherie*. Now, please, go rest. Tell one of those good for nothings to give you a seat." I had no doubt that someone would be quick to offer me a seat, but it was usually on their lap. They needed to touch me, and I didn't mind. I felt the same pull to touch them as well. But tonight, I needed to stand on my own two feet. Or sit on my own two butt cheeks, in this case.

I walked out to the lounge room and sat in the large empty space between Lux and Lucifer.

Luc turned to me. "What is the gender of your babes? I had children once."

"Really?"

Yep. It's why he fell. He questioned god, lay with the daughters of men. Reproduced a bunch. And then came ruler of hell. He's been a busy boy. Ace sounded amused again, almost like she was proud.

"Uh, they are girls. We are having girls."

"Ah, wonderful. Females are a gift. The vessels of life. A fact beings like Azriel fail to understand. Angels cannot reproduce with other angels. To experience the joy of creating life, you must fall. The problem with this religion, the one that casts me as the devil, is that they've demonized women for far too long, as betrayers and temptations. They are the givers, not the takers." He smiled at me. "You know what's a nice name? Lucia."

I stared as he went back to watching the baseball. Huh. I was beginning to see why he fell.

"I'm not naming my kids after you, you know that right?"

"Well, if it wasn't for me, they wouldn't exist. These

guys wouldn't exist. They would still be dead souls, being tortured in the pits of hell. Did you know one of the gifts I acquired when I became Satan was the ability to see the various strands of a person's fate? All the better to deal with, if you catch my drift. For instance, I can see that if it weren't for my interference in your life, you would still live in your little hick town of Nowhere, and you never would have come to the bright lights of NYC. In fact, you would have married your high school sweetheart, become a bank teller, had 4 boys, all who would get caught up in the drug epidemic that would sweep the town when they were in their teens, two would go to jail, you would hit the bottle and die from cirrhosis of the liver at 55. Your husband would marry his secretary, with which he'd been having an affair for three years, as soon as your body was in the ground. They wouldn't let your sons out to attend your funeral."

My mouth fell open. "I can't believe you can see the future. I can't believe I became a bank teller. I hated math in high school."

"It was one of many possibilities. You may still die, but at least you will know happiness. You have free will. What happens in this life is up to you. I can only tell the outcomes of the lives that did not happen."

That was a scary ability, to know what could have been.

"In any did I live to be an old lady?"

Lucifer shook his head. "No. Though the possibilities are infinite, balance is balance. But when I put Ace into your body, I threw out the balance. Now your life is your own, your fate is whatever you want to make it."

"Is it though?"

Luc laughed. "No. Not entirely. But more so than if you had never entered this life." He put two hands over my stomach, and everyone in the room tensed. Lux's body was poised to leap over me and tackle Lucifer. I held out a hand to him.

"Wait. Luc will not hurt my babies, will you?"

"And risk Ace's wrath? Never. She's quite the little hellion when she's angry." He tilted his head to the side. "Ah, strong and healthy. Even you, Arcadia seem to be better than expected, even with the kale." He looked into my eyes, but he wasn't looking at *me*. He was staring directly into my soul. "Acerezeal, what have you been doing?"

I have no idea what you are talking about. Ace sounded perfectly perplexed.

I AM SATAN, THE GREAT DECEIVER. LIES DO NOT WORK ON ME ACEREZEAL. WHAT HAVE YOU DONE?

I am protecting the one who gave me the chance to live again. She stared down the Angel of Death and protected me. Have you lost your sense of honor, Lucifer? Have you fallen so far?

I WILL ASK AGAIN, MY BELOVED AND ONLY ONCE MORE. WHAT HAVE YOU DONE?

The temperature in the room dropped suddenly, and Lux was on his feet in front of Luc, a sword that appeared from nowhere pointed at the Devil's chest. Luc still had his hands on my stomach and I was frozen in fear.

"Holy fuck, is that a sword? Did it just get cold in

here? What is going on?" Clary asked, her voice high pitched.

I felt Ace rise up, and like last time, she possessed my body and pushed me back until I was just a passenger.

"I am feeding my life force to the infants. I will continue to do so despite you disagreement. Feel them Lucifer, see their futures. Because I know you will sense what I do, that their lives are important."

Luc was silent, unperturbed by the sword at his throat or the tension in the room. "You will die!" He burst out into the silence, and Ace's voice, my voice was gentle. "I will not die, my beloved. Not after everything you have accomplished to save me. I have thought this through. Cady means the world to me, she is your Redeemer. These babes are as much mine as they are hers. They must live, and they will. And then I will come back to you. We will be together again, one way or another."

The look on Luc's face broke my heart in two. Such a mask of tortured pain that my eyes welled. But then the moment was gone, and back was the rage. "You will do what you will, Acerezeal. You always have, and losing your immortal soul obviously hasn't taught you anything." He stood, the point of Lux's sword drawing blood from the hollow of his neck. He looked at us all, and I'd never felt so small, so fragile. "But know this. If Acerezeal fades into oblivion, you will all promptly follow her."

Flames burst up from his feet, smoke swirled around his body and with a crash of thunder, he was gone. All that remained was a scorched glyph on my favorite rug.

Ace shrunk back into my body, swirling around the babies. I could sense her exhaustion, her torment. That show of defiance had cost her. I left her to her pain. She didn't want to talk, and I wouldn't know what to say anyway.

Clary was muttering the Lord's Prayer, and the guys looked tense and confused.

"Well, it's not a good dinner party until someone storms out, right?" I said into the silence, and Valery gave a startled smile.

"Can you please tell Ace that the whole possession thing is really not cool?" Oz said weakly.

I shook my head sadly. "I don't think she will be doing it again anytime soon."

Tolliver rolled up the singed rug and put it outside the door. Out of sight and all that. Sam began putting the food out on the table. "We should eat. We can figure this all out over a nice meal. No need for all this hard work to go to waste."

The guys all glanced between Val and Sam. "I think they've been body swapped," Orion muttered, and Oz laughed. "Maybe Valery has possessed Sam?"

Valery just rolled his eyes. "Ha ha, guys. But Sam is right. It's time to eat."

Clary slammed a hand down on the table. "Eat? How can you guys even think of eating? You were just threatened by the Devil. Cursed by Satan himself. How can you even think of eating?"

Sam shrugged. "Happens every time Luc visits. It's just the way he likes to end his conversations. Though the flames were new. I'm pretty sure that Cady and

Ace's little gambit has really pissed him off." Standing across from him, I could tell Sam was more concerned than his light tone conveyed.

The front door opened and everyone tensed again, only relaxing when Eli walked through. His eyes took us all in. "I'm going to assume from the look on everyone's face and the fact there's a burned rug outside the door, that I missed something big?"

I ran over and hugged him tight. His arms came around my shoulders and held me close to his chest.

"Ace told Luc about her plan to ensure the babies are delivered healthy. He didn't take it well. There were swords and flames."

"So just another day at the ranch?" He squeezed me tightly.

I laughed at the truth of the statement. "Pretty much."

CHAPTER TWENTY-EIGHT

I was restless. There was only so much online shopping and nesting a girl could do. I missed being able to leave the house without an entourage. Or having thirty-four pee breaks between my front door and the garage. I missed alone time. I missed not needing three naps a day.

Oz had assembled all the baby furniture, and Sam and Tolliver had bought every stuffed animal they could lay their hands on until the nursery resembled a plush zoo.

I stared sightlessly at the television, my head on Lux's lap. He stroked my hair with one hand, the other resting on my protruding belly and one of the babies kicked at his hand. Oz was coding on his computer, sitting on the floor in front of us.

"I want to go on a date."

"We can go out to Epicurean if you like. I'm sure Val is itching to check up on the new head chef," Oz offered, his eyes not leaving the screen.

"No, I mean I want to go on a *date* date, with each of you." I tried to sit up, and failed. Lux put a hand under my back and helped me up. I used to have core muscles, kinda, now they were 80% infant. I was beached without assistance. "We all kind of fell into this weird romance thing. I never got to go on a real date with any of you. I want to have one perfect night alone with each of you before…" I died. But I couldn't say that. Everyone was firmly in denial for people who were essentially the rean-imated dead. "Before the babies are born."

Oz closed his laptop and turned toward me. "Eli says you are meant to be taking it easy, especially because they want to start you on chemo next week."

"So we won't climb any mountains or run a marathon. I'm sick of being cooped up in this house." And then I burst into tears. Again.

Lux pulled me into his lap and held me close. Even though I cried all the time, Lux responded like my heart was breaking every single time, though it was mostly hormones. I cried harder.

"Hey now, we will go on hundreds of dates as we all grow old together. But if you want a special date with each of us now, then that's what you'll get," Oz said, wiping my eyes with a tissue. "I'll start. We'll go to the baseball, or the gallery or whatever you want to do as long as you stop crying, okay?"

You should totally milk this, make them take you somewhere fancy. Or S&M night at Dante's. Ri owes you one.

I look like the old lady who swallowed a cow. I'm not going to an S&M club, I scolded Ace half heartedly. I was just glad to hear her voice. She'd been so faint lately, I was almost alone in my own head.

Are you kidding? You are like a fetish dreamboat right now. Look at those cankles. The foot fetish guys will crawl through hell to get you to tie them up and dip those chubby little tootsies in their mouths.

I screwed up my nose. Not to kink shame anyone but ew.

I think I'll pass.

"Let's do something you want to do. Take me on a date to your favorite place in all of NYC."

Lux stroked a hand along my back. "I'm already here."

Ace sniffed, *I think your hormones might be contagious. Damn, that guy looks like sin personified but he has some seriously sweet lines.*

I snuggled in closer to Lux, kissing his chin before tucking my head beneath it. I was exactly where I wanted to be too, but a girl needed to leave the house once in a while.

"I'm with Lux on this one. Before you came along, I rarely left the house. Hell, I rarely put on pants." I was failing to see a problem with that last part. "So I don't really have a favorite place in New York. But we can go somewhere I've always wanted to go?"

I nodded, my spirits already lifting. This would be fun.

I STOOD hand in hand with Oz in front of a store in

the Rockefeller building. "This is where you've always wanted to go?"

"Yep."

"You want to go on a date to the Lego Store?"

He began to look a little uncertain, so I smiled. "It sounds perfect. Let's go."

For an hour, Oz whirled around me like a satellite, always within arms reach but he wanted to see everything at once. The stupidly big grin on his face made my heart lift. I had to admit that some of the large LEGO sculptures were amazing.

The store was filled with tourists, but I didn't mind. It was just nice to be out amongst humanity again. Oz decided he wanted to build the babies a two foot tall LEGO sculpture of a unicorn for the nursery, and set about finding all the bricks he'd need. I sat down on a chair, thankfully not made of LEGO, and rested. My belly was so big that I'd gotten a few curious looks, but so far no one had stopped to ask questions. That was probably thanks to Oz's looming presence. He wasn't nearly as terrifying as Lux, but he was still tall and built and had a big ginger beard.

"May I sit too?"

I looked up at a pleasant looking man in his late forties.

"Uh, sure." I scooted over a little, and the man sat down.

"You're just a wee little thing, aren't you? All baby belly." He smiled. It was a nice smile, one where you couldn't help but smile back.

Holy shit! Ace roused herself for long enough to say.

The man tsked. "Acerezeal, such bad language."

I scooted away a bit more, my hands protectively around my stomach.

Apologies, Michael.

"Michael, as in Archangel Michael." I had to work hard to control my own expletives.

Michael laughed. "Yes."

How can we help you? I'd never heard Ace so cordial to anyone. She basically spit it the face of Azriel.

"Oh, I was just in the neighborhood and wanted to see what all the fuss has been about. Azriel has been quite vocal about your situation. Although, I do not know what he thinks I will do about it. It is the Father's will after all."

Azriel is just a whiner, Ace replied and Michael laughed and it was the most beautiful sound I'd ever heard. I wanted to cry and laugh and fall at his feet.

"Well, perhaps, but we all have our strengths and purposes. You are even causing a stir in the depths. Word has gotten around that the fallen Acerezeal is not dead, but alive in the body of a mortal. I see you are protecting the infants even now. From me." He sounded amused.

"No disrespect, Sir, but we have learned to be cautious," I said. He just inclined his head.

Have you come to heal her? Ace asked, her voice barely a whisper.

"No, Acerezeal. That is not the Father's will either. I am merely here out of my own curiosity."

Angels don't get curious.

"And Fallen don't protect the innocent. But all things

change, do they not? Not even angels stay in stasis forever." He stood, briefly touching my belly. "Ah. I see now. Good luck, Arcadia. Acerezeal, give my love to Lucifer."

Ace scoffed. *I probably won't do that. He still hasn't forgiven you.*

Michael laughed again, and between one breath and the next, he was gone.

Oz appeared next to me, three bulging bags of LEGO in his hands.

"Hey, are you okay? You've gone a little pale? Maybe we should head home." He lifted me from the chair with ease. I shook my head. I went to tell him about Michael, but changed my mind. I didn't want our date to end. I wanted to cling to this little piece of normalcy for a little while longer.

I shook my head. "It's fine. I'm just hungry."

Oz wrapped an arm around my waist. "Well luckily, I know the greatest diner where they sell the kind of food that would horrify both Eli and Valery."

"Are their shakes green?"

Oz leaned in and kissed my temple. "Nope. They make the best Blue Heaven milkshakes in America, though. And the best chili fries and their hotdogs are orgasmic." He moaned.

"Sounds perfect."

Normal.

I STEPPED INTO THE ROWBOAT, Eli's hand steadying me. Maybe maneuvering would be a better word. It wobbled a little but we were still close to shore, so I wasn't worried about tipping. I sat down, taking the picnic basket from Eli as he stepped off the dock and onto the boat with nimble ease that made me jealous. The kid who was working the boathouse pushed us away from the dock with a heave, and we drifted to the middle of the lake in Central Park.

Lux had informed everyone of my desire to have a serious date while I'd been out with Oz the day before. Obviously Oz didn't get the serious memo. But serious isn't his style and I loved him just the way he was.

Eli had had today off, so it was decided he would have the next date. And here we were, Eli rowing a boat to the center of the lake, and I perched on the seat with a large hat. We were like a picture from a nineteenth century photo album. I loved it.

I'd even brought a book, so we could just drift around and relax in the sun. All that was missing was my parasol.

Val had packed us a picnic of baguettes and sparkling grape juice and chocolate fudge brownies, and the thought made me hungry for the first time in weeks.

Eli rowed us to a place where the branches of a large willow tree shaded the edges of the lake shore.

"This is bliss," I sighed leaning back on my hands. My back was beginning to ache, but I didn't care.

"Come here and sit with me," Eli said, and I shifted slowly from one bench to the other, sitting between his thighs. "You can rest against me."

I leaned back into his chest and sighed. I didn't know how he always knew when I was uncomfortable, but he did and he inevitably had a solution to make it better.

He leaned forward and kissed my hair. "Now, this is bliss."

We sat in silence for a while, appreciating the sounds of laughter from the shore and the butterflies that seemed to make their home in the middle of Central Park. Everything seemed brighter, better.

We drifted on the water, the slight wind drifting us back toward the middle.

"Is this what courting was like in your day?" I asked, taking a deep inhale of his fresh, clean scent. Eli didn't wear expensive cologne like Sam, Tolli and Ri. He didn't smell like sugar cookies like Val or that sexy musk of Lux. Eli smelled like new beginnings. Like soap, and crisp mountain air and maybe a touch of antiseptic.

"Somewhat. Mostly we would take chaperoned strolls through manicured gardens. Or carriage rides, that kind of thing."

"Did you have a wife?"

Eli shook his head. "No. I was married to my work. I was determined to be the Da Vinci of my age. It didn't quite work out like that, though."

I rubbed my stomach. "I guess not. You must have died fairly young."

"Thirty-six."

I wanted to ask why he was sent to hell. I was desperate to know. Who wouldn't? I knew the rest of the guys stories, but Eli kept things closer to his chest.

He gave a chuckle, but there wasn't a lot of humor in it. "Ask your question, Miss Jones."

"Why were you sentenced to hell?"

"Because I sold my soul to the Devil to save my home from the plague. Well, the whole County actually. Lucifer was fairly generous with his definition of home."

I watched a dragonfly land on the water, skimming the top as if gravity did not affect him. "You went to hell for saving people. That hardly seems fair."

His hands reached down to stroke my stomach. "When it comes to the affairs of Heaven and Hell, things are rarely ever fair."

I tilted my head back for a kiss, and Eli happily obliged. His lips were firm but there was tenderness there, such caring that it made my eyes water. He pulled back and stared into my soul. "I love you, Arcadia. You will live. I will save you."

My body felt tired. My mind felt tired. My heart was exhausted. But Eli said it with so much self assurance that I was almost certain I would. "I know you will."

We sat in silence again, lost in our own heads. My eyes lulled with the gentle rocking of the boat. My body was more relaxed than it had been in months, even given the uncomfortable bench seat. I was safe in Eli's hands.

"Want to hear the strangest case I ever had as a young physician?"

I nodded. I was desperate to hear anything and everything about this man.

"They brought me a boy they pulled out of the frozen lake, much like this one, in the middle of winter. It was bitterly cold that year. I'd amputated so many toes from frostbite that I could practically do it in my sleep.

The kid came in and was blue, the same shade of blue as Sam's eyes. I placed him on my table, and did my checks. I took one look at him and pronounced him dead. No heartbeat, no breathing noises. The men that had brought the boy to me then went in search of his parents and I went back to staring into my microscope. Two hours later, they still hadn't found the parents, but the boy sat up and told me he was hungry. I screamed like a maiden who'd seen a mouse. I checked the boy over and other than a bad case of frostbite, he was fine. I, however, learned not to assume anyone was dead until they were warm and dead. I had to convince his parents that he wasn't a demon, and that it was actually a miracle. It was a tough sell but he went home and grew into a fine young man."

I giggled at the image of Eli jumping and screaming. And the irony that Eli himself would actually come back as the reanimated dead from hell made me laugh harder.

We ate our small picnic, and we talked in a way we rarely go the opportunity to talk. We talked about his life before and after he went to hell, and his family. And I told him about my parents, and the hospitals stays and my adventures with Clary while she was in college. This is why I had wanted these dates. I wanted these perfect memories, this closeness, with all of them.

By the time we were rowing our way back to the dock to return the boat, I was warm, relaxed and exhausted.

It took both the boathouse kid and Eli to pull me out of the boat and onto the dock, and I couldn't even find the energy to be embarrassed. We walked back to the carpark, and I slid into Tolliver's Jag. He still hadn't gotten rid of it yet.

He went around the other side and buckled me in. Now it was actually getting a little tough to belt myself in, I'd stopped complaining about it. I rested my head back against the warm leather seats.

"Eli?"

Eli turned over the Jag and she purred to life. I could see why Tolliver was so reluctant to get rid of it.

"Yes, Arcadia?"

"I love you too, you know."

He put the car back into park and unbelted himself. He leaned over and cupped my cheek, giving me a whisper light kiss. "I know."

CHAPTER TWENTY-NINE

I hugged the toilet bowl as Tolliver sat on the edge of the tub and watched as I lost everything I'd eaten this week. Chemo sucked.

"Can I get you anything?" He asked for the thirtieth time.

"I just want to be alone." He didn't move. "Are you deaf? Go," I yelled, the words harsh to my own ears, but I didn't have it in me to apologize.

I didn't even raise my head as he walked out the door, closing it gently behind him. I'd probably hurt his feelings. Fuck. I didn't want to do that, but I didn't want anyone to watch my relapse into misery either.

I burst into tears and sobbed in between dry retches. I missed Ace. She was so quiet now. I was lucky to hear from her once a day. I laid on the floor and curled around my belly. And I cried some more.

The door opened, and I saw Clary's feet come into view. Or maybe Oz had taken to painting his toenails pink.

"Go away."

"No."

I looked up at her. "I mean it, Clary. Get the hell out."

"No. I sat with you through this once, and I will do it again. Now get your whiney big baby butt off the floor. I bought some of those crackers that you could stomach last time." She was using her nurse voice, and I sat up. I didn't doubt she would make me if I said no again.

"Lets wipe you down, and then you can eat. You live in a house full of men. I'm pretty sure not every single one of them aims right. Men are gross."

She got a washcloth from under the basin and filled the sink with warm soapy water. She wiped my face, my neck and then my hands.

"I don't know if I can do this again, Clary. It's not the same as last time. I'm weaker."

Clary scoffed. "You might be physically weaker, but you are mentally stronger. You are a badass bitch with everything to live for. You will fight, and I will be right there in your corner."

She handed me a cracker and I nibbled it slowly. I was just so scared.

"I'm really glad you are here, Clary. I don't know if I've told you that enough. I've been distracted."

Clary pulled me to my feet and hugged me tight. "There is nowhere else I'd be. Now let's get you to bed. At least you'll never be short of bed warmers."

I gave a half grin. "A lot of good that does me. Hopping into bed with one of them is like walking into a candy store on a diet."

"Mm, but at least they smell good. Speaking of smelling good, have you met Tolliver's lawyer? The guy looks like sex in an Armani suit. I went to sign my employment contracts for the clinic, and the whole time I had these crazy fifty shades fantasies."

I laughed. She was trying to distract me, and I was more than willing to be distracted. "He couldn't possibly be hotter in Armani than Tolliver. The guy was literally on the billboard."

She led me out of the bathroom and straight toward the bedroom. I could see all the guys hanging around my living room, looking worried. I gave them a half hearted smile and a finger wave. I didn't have the energy to reassure them.

"I don't know. He must work out or something, because his ass looked like two melons in a sack."

I laughed. I couldn't help it. "You know that isn't an attractive comparison, right?"

I slid between the cool sheets and sighed. My body was exhausted.

"Rest. I'll get Val to send you in something white and bland later, and I'm not talking about Doc McBuffins."

"Eli isn't bland," I defended weakly and she just laughed as she walked out my bedroom door.

Randomly, it was Valery that Clary got along with best, probably because he was always in the kitchen, and to her Irish roots, the kitchen was the heart of the home. So I'd often find Val and Clary in the kitchen, discussing the effect of green juices on my white blood counts or something or other.

I wasn't jealous. Okay, maybe a little at first but it soon wore off. I was their only topic of discussion, and Valery would take me in his arms and kiss me any time he got within three feet of my person. Plus, they bickered like siblings. Even now, I could hear them arguing in the kitchen.

"I'm telling you, there is an Italian doctor who swears by kale juice as a tonic for all ills, and counteracts the toxicity of the chemo," Valery said, his French accent getting thicker as he got riled up.

"Oh sure, because an Italian kook who did a TED talk is much more trustworthy than sound science," Clary scoffed. I hoped Clary won this battle, because I hated the kale juice.

I dozed off, and when I woke it was to Tolliver and Sam climbing into bed with me, one on either side. I snuggled in between their bodies, and let their warmth chase away the chill of the chemo.

I pressed my lips to Tolliver's chest.

"I'm sorry I yelled."

"You never have to say sorry to me, sweet Cady. Go back to sleep," he kissed my forehead.

Sam rubbed my back. "We'll be here with you, always."

I fell back into the blackness of sleep, exhaustion chasing away my dreams.

I WALKED between the velvet ropes of premium class at the movie theater, my hand wrapped in Valery's. We entered the restored playhouse, with its ornate ceiling and tiered seating. It was classic movie Tuesday and we were here to watch *Casablanca* for our date. I didn't want the chemo to slow me down. I wanted my dates, not only to spend time with the guys, but ensure they were on a path of a redemption that would go on without me.

"You know, when we were spat out of hell, it was the cinema that fascinated me the most. Television too, of course, but there was something magical about watching people moving in front of you, affixed onto film and then played to the world, and sound was somehow woven in as well. It was breathtaking, and it was the first time I'd felt pleasure in hundreds of years."

His eyes lit up as he spoke, and I could only imagine what it had been like those first couple of weeks after they had been placed here by Luc. Especially for Lux and Sam, who'd had to adjust to a couple of thousand years worth of technological advancement and social reformation.

We found our seats, and Valery raised the arm rest between us so I could snuggle in close.

We'd all decided that I would go on one date a week so I didn't exhaust myself, and if I timed it right, I would be feeling okay after the chemo too. Valery handed me his popcorn, and I took a handful.

The cinema was beautiful, its restoration done perfectly. Heavy midnight blue velvet curtains sat either side of screen, and even from here I could see the intricate gold embroidery along the bottom edge.

Valery slid an arm over my shoulder and I rested my head on his chest, listening to the steady thump thump of his heart that defied nature itself.

He popped a milk dud in my mouth, and I let it melt on my tongue. People were still finding their seats, but the cinema was mostly empty. It was mainly hipsters and couples. The odd lonely soul sitting by themselves in an acoustically correct position.

"What are you going to do after I have the babies and get better and everyone is redeemed? Will you go back to being head chef at Epicurean?" I asked into his chest. He rested his head on my hair.

"Maybe, part time. I'm very fond of my restaurant, but not as fond as I am of you and what will be our little family." He laughed. "Well, perhaps not so little, not with so many papa's. They will be well loved *bebe's*. I have already begun researching how to make the tastiest, nutritionally dense baby foods. My *bebe's* will eat gourmet."

I smiled up at Valery, his handsome, guileless face holding nothing but love for me. "You really don't mind that the babies aren't biologically yours, do you?"

"No, *ma cherie*. Because they are yours, and you are mine. I will love them like they are mine. They are a miracle, no matter who fathered them."

The lights went down and the opening notes from *Casablanca* came up. I'd always loved this movie. Humphrey Bogart being suave as hell, and Ingrid Bergman just had a timeless beauty that made me seriously question my sexuality. When *As Time Goes By* played, my eyes misted over and stayed that way until the final scene.

Valery turned to me as the credits rolled, and kissed me softly. I kissed him back with an urgency that appeared out of nowhere, inspired by the loss, the time wasted, the long goodbyes that happened in the movie. Valery groaned and slid a hand into my hair. And came away with a chunk.

He pulled back and stared at the blonde strands still wrapped in his fingers, his face horrified. I stared at them too. Then I cried. Again. Fucking hell. Valery got out his handkerchief- who still used those?- and placed my hair in the center, bundling it up and stuffing it into his pocket.

"I am sorry, *Ma Chere*. I should have thought..." He trailed off. I didn't know who was more traumatized right now. "Would you like to go home?"

I wanted to be tougher, and say I was fine. But I wasn't and all I wanted to do was go home, have Valery wrap his body around mine and sleep, hoping that I'd wake up tomorrow cured.

My lip quivered, and I pressed it between my teeth. "I'm really tired. We should go home."

"*Oui*, my love. I will take you wherever you need to go."

He stood and wrapped his arm around my shoulders, sheltering me against the world. "Will you sleep with me tonight?" I asked, and my voice was nearly lost in the happy chatter of the foyer.

"Always."

CHAPTER THIRTY

Unlike last time, my hair all fell out almost all at once, in large chunks that were left behind on the pillow every morning. I'd get up, heave myself to the bathroom, and by the time I got back, the offending pillowcase would be gone, and the bed would be made. I was pretty sure Clary had taught someone how to do that speed bed changing that nurses somehow managed. It was almost magic.

I struggled back into bed and onto fresh pillows. The only problem with magically changing linens was that it wiped away the scent of whoever had slept beside me. Luckily for me today, Oz was still there, arms folded behind his head, displaying a very impressive chest. Cross-fit had honed him into hard muscle, and I wanted to find the creators of the regime and kiss their feet. My eyes followed the slight dusting of hair that trailed down past his navel, and his grin got cocky as he caught me in my blatant perusal.

He waggled his eyebrows. "Don't let me stop you. I could move the blanket if you want."

I made a face at him and moved toward the bed, lowering myself down without much finesse and snuggling back into his warmth. Today, I was determined to be my old, happy self. Death be damned. Perhaps literally.

Today the babies were officially 28 weeks. While not ideal, we were in the safety zone. Though little Hope still needed another week or two of baking time. I was going for a 4D ultrasound, and I couldn't be more excited to see my babies.

But first.

I laid a kiss on Oz's shoulder, then his jaw, until he turned to kiss me back. His hand slid over my ass and up to my swollen breasts. He juggled them in his hands like they were the world's most mesmerizing stress balls.

"Oz."

"Hmm?" He still hadn't taken his eyes from my breasts.

"Are you going to stare at those all day, or are you going to do something with them?"

He pulled down my tank and kissed one nipple then the other. "Sorry, Cady Lady. We are at DEFCON 3. Nothing that could put undue strain on your heart or bring on early labor." His eyes went back to my breasts. "Soon, my pretties. Soon."

With that he heaved himself out of bed. Oz slept naked. Well, most of them slept naked, except Valery and Eli.

Oz stood, stretching his arms above his head, and

his back muscles tensed in all the best ways. My pulse rate sped up, as my eyes slipped down to that glorious ass. I wanted. He turned and smiled over his shoulder, the cocky showoff, and I made grabby hands and pouted.

"Not today, sexy mama. Now watch this butt wiggle as I walk away." He strode out of the bedroom door with an exaggerated sway of his hips. I got up and walked to the shower. At least I could still do this on my own.

I was so sure of myself. And then I dropped the soap. I kicked it around with my toe, trying to get it into a reachable position. No such thing existed for me now. The soap was gone.

Half an hour later, I walked into the kitchen, clean-ish. Eli was at the stove and Valery was reading the paper.

"Did Valery do a body swap? How did you get him out of the kitchen? Did Lux get out his sword again?" I leaned over the newspaper, and kissed Val good morning.

Lux huffed around his cup of coffee.

"You'll know when I get my sword out, Arcadia." Then he winked. It was official, they'd gone crazy.

I kissed Lux and he pulled me onto his lap and kissed me back, with the added bonus of tongue. "Good morning. You look beautiful today."

It was a lie. I had no hair. My stomach protruded from my too thin body like I'd swallowed a torpedo. But there was no artifice on Lux's face. He meant his words.

"Thank you. I feel good today. Ready to see the

babies." I stood, with a little help from Lux, and went over to the kitchen.

Eli was cooking bacon, sausages and eggs. The smell didn't make my stomach turn, and I gave the universe a silent high five. "This looks great," I said, standing on my toes for a kiss. "Can I kiss the cook?"

"Of course." He kissed me with delicious softness, then handed me a mug of peppermint tea.

And in that moment, I felt like I had a touch of Lucifer's precognition. This could possibly be our future. Sure, having seven partners sounded exhausting at best, and untenable at worse. But I could be happy like this.

Sam walked in, and I nearly dropped my tea. He'd shaved his head, down to a fine pale fuzz. All gone.

"Your hair!"

He ran a big hand across his scalp. "I wanted to donate it to you, but the hairdresser said it wasn't long enough. So I just shaved it off in solidarity." He came over and kissed me, and I ran my fingers over his scalp.

Tolliver wasn't far behind, usually where there was one, there was the other, and he shut the door behind him.

"I told him he could have just kept growing it, until it was long enough." He slapped the back of Sam's head and then kissed my cheek.

"And like I told you, she isn't going to be still sick by the time my hair gets to twelve inches long. We'll be sipping mojitos on a beach by then with the kids," he said stubbornly.

No one spoke. Nothing needed to be said.

"Well. That'd be the only thing that got twelve

inches long for Sammy," Oz said into the silence. I laughed.

"That's two dick innuendos and its not even-" I looked at the clock on the wall. "Holy hell, it's nine o'clock. I slept in! We have to go. We'll never get through peak hour traffic at this rate." I raced/waddled into the bedroom and threw on yoga pants and one of Oz's shirts with Chewbacca on the front. It said '*love bites only*'.

Ri stumbled into the room just as I hustled back into the kitchen/dining area. Eli handed me a lunch bag and a travel mug of coffee. I thrust the cup at Ri and shoved him back towards the door.

"No time to stop, we're running late."

"Good morning to you too, Beautiful Girl." I grabbed his hand and pulled him along. I didn't blame him for sleeping in, he'd worked until late. But today was the day I was going to see my babies in 4D and I was excited.

He opened the lift door and I walked past him. He smacked my butt on the way past, making a little hum of appreciation even though it was now twice as big as it was. He pulled the cage door closed and hit ground. Then he wrapped me in his arms and kissed me like he hadn't been laid in seven months. Which he hadn't, the poor bastard. His expert lips made me breathless, or maybe it was that he didn't come up for air until we reached the ground floor.

"Who needs coffee when I can wake up like that every day?" He gave my nose a small peck and then we were in the garage. The guy could kiss. Every single time it was like being consumed by red hot heat. I kept waiting for the day he fell flat, but it never came.

He led me toward the Escalade. "Not the Jag?" Yep this was my life now. Having to choose between my luxury coupe and my luxury SUV.

"Nah. Not enough safety features. I was watching a news report about it the other day. Escalade only from now on."

I raised an eyebrow. "Tell that to Tolliver."

The thing about the Escalade, or maybe it was just my circumstances, was that I fell asleep like a narcoleptic every time it began to move. Lights out.

When I woke up, the girl in the ticket booth in the hospital car park was trying to chat up Ri.

Seriously. It made me irrationally angry. I wanted to climb out of the car and punch her in the face. He was in the car with a heavily pregnant woman. Where did she get off trying to hit on my guy? Though Ri, bless his heart, was nothing more than polite, waiting for her to give him a ticket and leave.

"You know, if there's a long wait in the waiting room, you're welcome to come down and chat with me," the ticket booth bimbo said. Seriously, who the hell did she think she was, with her high vis vest tied up like she was Daisy-freakin'-Duke? I snapped my eyes open, and fumbled around for my seatbelt. I was going to smack some manners into this fake-boobed wannabe meter maid. If I could just find the seat belt release. As I fumbled around, I could hear Ace's hysterical laughter in my head. It was so nice that she was there that I momentarily stilled.

Oh, that's the funniest thing ever. I can just imagine you stomping up there like a baby hippo and doing what? She wouldn't even have to run away. She could power walk away and you wouldn't be able to catch her. More hysterical laughter. I wanted to be mad but I was just happy she was happy.

I do not look like a baby hippo, I pouted back. Ace had distracted me for long enough that Ri had managed to extract the parking ticket from Bimbo-Deluxe and pulled into the multilevel carpark.

"Whoa Cady, that look isn't directed at me right? 'Cause I'm innocent. I wasn't using any of my lust juju or anything."

We pulled into the empty parking space, and Ri leaned over to unbelt me. "No. I'm not even mad. It's just-"

"The hormones. I know, sweetheart." I leaned over and kissed him again. I could never get enough of him. We held hands all the way to my high risk obstetricians waiting room, and by a minor miracle, they were running on time and we went straight through.

The nurse had me undress, and I hopped up on the bench. Well, maybe hopped is a bit of an exaggeration. I used the step and Ri's arm and wiggled my way up. Gravity was now my foe.

The doctor bustled in, a middle aged man with attractive graying hair and artificially white teeth, but extremely kind eyes. Ri gave him the stink eye. My seven hadn't been impressed that the man rummaging around in my lady parts was attractive. If he hadn't been the best in the State, they probably would have protested more. To Doctor Hamilton's credit, he didn't even seem shocked that there was a different man with me at my ultrasound. The guys had a steady rotation taking me to my appointments, so it was unusual to see the same face twice, except maybe Oz or Eli.

"How are we doing today, Arcadia? I see in your notes that you've started chemo."

"Well, being bald wasn't a fashion choice, Doc." I pointed to my nearly smooth head. "But yeah, I'm heading into my third week."

He checked my vitals, and then listened to my belly. "Sounds good. Let's have a look at the little ones, shall we?"

He got the ultrasound wand and squirted jelly on my stomach.

I held my breath. The first beats of two little heartbeats was always a relief. They'd unsynced, so identifying the two was easy now little Hope was bigger.

"You're in luck, both babies are facing outwards, ready for their close-up." And then I saw the most beautiful thing I'd ever seen. A perfect nose, closed little eyes, curling tiny fingers. Ten of them.

"Baby one. She's got good growth. A miracle really, considering your overall health." A miracle named Ace.

Are you seeing this, Ace? This is all your hard work. I can't thank you enough.

Silence for a moment. *I see her. She is beautiful.* The level of awe in her voice made my heart swell.

"Okay, and here is Baby Two. She's a little smaller than her sister but she's still a good size. Everything looks good, developmentally, for both babies, but how about we just have a tour around the womb to get a good look."

Hope. My beautiful little Hope. I smiled at Ri. His eyes were brimming with tears, and he wiped them on the back of his arm.

"They are perfect, Cady. Just like their mama." We sat there for thirty minutes, counting toes, and watching tiny limbs kick, and when Hope yawned, I thought my heart would burst.

Thirty minutes went way too fast, and soon the doctor was handing me a disk.

"Okay, the babies look good. Your heart rate is a little fast, though. Do you have an appointment with the cardiologist soon?"

"Next week."

Doctor Hamilton scribbled notes on his file. "That should be fine. As the babies get bigger, the strain on your body will increase. Now is the time to be vigilant. Bed rest will be important from thirty weeks, so be prepared for total bed rest until the babies are born. Can you do that?"

I screwed up my face and nodded. Six weeks in bed was a small price to pay.

"Other than that, your pregnancy is going perfectly, even for a healthy mother. For you, it's practically divine intervention."

I laughed. "Doc, you have no idea. Thanks so much for the scan."

"My pleasure, Arcadia." With that, he left me to change. Ri was practically dancing with excitement as he helped me get my feet into my yoga pants. Sexy. I hadn't seen my toes in a month, and my belly poked out like I'd eaten Shamu.

"Did you see the baby suck her thumb. We need to name her. Hope has a name, and our big girl needs a name too."

I agreed. Maybe tonight we could decide on a name. Between the eight of us, nine including Clary, we could pick a name.

"LADIES AND GENTLEMEN, and Oz. Welcome to the Naming Knockout Tournament. The rules are simple. Everyone gets one suggestion including Ace and Clary, so make it count. We will have sudden death rounds with votes, and in the case of a draw, Cady's vote prevails, because she's the one doing all the hard work. Are we ready to rumble?"

Ri was way to into this. The guys were all sitting around with beers, and Clary had a glass of red wine. We'd watched the ultrasound DVD in preparation, twice.

No one had a hat on hand, so the suggestions went into one of Oz's replica Hulk gloves. I liked Sasha, so I wrote it down on the small slip of paper Ri had handed around.

How are you feeling, Ace? Are you going to play?

There was a snort, and then Ace was filling my chest. It was comforting to have her back.

Of course. If I don't get compete, she'll end up with a name like Sasha.

Hey!

"Is everyone nearly done? Beautiful Girl, do you want a sparkling water or crackers or something while we're waiting?" Ri asked, heading toward the kitchen. Sweetheart.

"Sure. I'll have a scotch on the rocks please. Hold the rocks."

"Soda and ice it is."

Estrella, Ace said.

I wrote it down and put the squares of paper in the Hulk hands.

That's really pretty. What does it mean?

Ace was beginning to fade away, her voice barely audible over the sounds of the room. *Estrella means Star. I thought Ace Junior might be a hard sell.*

I smiled. I mightn't have been too hard to convince. I felt a lot of gratitude.

"Alright, alright, alright! Everyone's in. Let's go." Ri handed me a drink and I snuggled between Sam and Eli. He picked up the hulk hand and pointed toward me. I plucked out two folded pieces of paper.

"First contestants are..." I wrinkled my nose. "Zelda."

Lux smacked Oz in the back of the head. "Seriously?"

Oz scowled. It was adorable. "What? It's a good name!"

I pulled another out of the glove. "Shae"

I winked at Clary. Such a traditional Irish name could have only come from one person.

"All in favor of Zelda?" Oz raised his hand. He was

the only one. He threw me a mock hurt look. I mouthed *I love you*, and he blew me a kiss.

Ri wrote down the winner on the tournament sheet.

"Well, that was easy. The next contestants are…"

"Isadora and Wilhelmina. It says in brackets that they will accept Billie."

Eli leaned over and kissed my cheek. "It was my mother's name."

This time the votes were split. I liked both, but in the end I'd voted for Billie. "Billie it is." He held out the hulk hand to Clary.

She pulled out Estrella and Sasha. Ah damn. I voted for Estrella, even though Sasha was my nomination.

Estrella won easily, and I was glad we were doing this anonymously.

It was back to my turn. "Lulu and Odette."

"I vote for Lulu. That ones mine. It means pearl in my native language. I'm going to go out in a limb and say the French one belongs to Valery," Ri suggested.

"These are meant to be anonymous, Orion," Valery scowled, but nodded.

This one was tough. I liked both but… "Odette."

Ri pouted when Odette won.

Ri pulled the last two out. "Okay, we have Lara and Bryn."

Sam kissed my temple. "It's short for Brynhilde. A fighter who wears chainmail. A name worthy of our tiny warrior."

Ri whacked him with the hulk hand. "No trying to sway the swing vote." Even though he'd literally just done the same thing.

"I like Bryn. As long as she's never Brynhilde," I shuddered.

Honestly, they shouldn't let you lot name a puppy let alone a child. Wilhelmina and Brynhilde. Seriously. You may as well buy them a crazy cat lady starter pack for their first birthdays.

The vote went the other way, Lara coming out on top, and Tolliver gloated a little that his suggestion trumped Sam's.

"So our options are Shae, Billie, Estrella, Odette…"

"I like Estrella," a voice said from the kitchen.

Luc, Ace whispered.

Luc swaggered out of the kitchen, a leather jacket open on a bare torso and his abs rippling in a way that can only be supernatural. He was devilishly sexy.

Does that count as calling you the Devil, because if it is, I totally meant it as a compliment

I'M OKAY WITH THE ADJECTIVE. MY LOVE, YOU ARE HARDLY EVEN A FLICKER. PLEASE GIVE UP THIS NOW. YOU HAVE ENSURED THE BABIES WILL SURVIVE. THEY COULD BE BORN TOMORROW AND THEY WOULD LIKELY SURVIVE WITH THE CURRENT MEDICAL ADVANCEMENTS THE HUMANS HAVE.

I'm almost ready, Lucifer. One more week and Hope will be safe.

Luc sighed as he walked toward me. There was such love, such heartache, that I almost cried for Lucifer.

He placed a hand on my stomach, looking past me to Ace. "Okay, Acerezeal. Okay. But remember, I need you too." It was a plea.

I need you, as well. And I need to do this. We will be together again.

"I like the name Estrella. You should name her that," Luc said again, this time to the room. A glass of scotch appeared in his hand.

"Well, it's better than Lucia. No beer today?"

I edged toward Sam, creating a space for him to sit. Luc sat down and Lux eyed the space between us, which was barely inches. A nerve in his cheek twitched, and his hand flexed, like he was imagining slicing Luc in half.

"Today is definitely a scotch day. Relax, Lux. I have made my peace with this situation. The irony of it all isn't lost on me. I grant the Redeemer freedom from the master plan, free will in its purest form, and now she's the greatest threat to the love of my life. The Father would be having a good laugh up there."

I reached over and squeezed Luc's knee. "It'll be okay." I turned to the room. "All in favor of Estrella? It was Ace's choice."

Everyone raised their hand. "Okay then. Estrella it is. Estrella Odette Lara, and Hope Billie Shae." I rubbed my belly and smiled. "They're good names. We should toast." I lifted my glass of seltzer. Luc magicked a glass of champagne into each of the guys hands.

"To Redemption." Luc tapped his beer to my glass. "To life."

We sipped our drinks in silence, but silence and Oz don't mix. "Can I ask you a question? Are all angels as douchey as Azriel, or did a bug just crawl up his ass? Do angels even have assholes? Where do they pee? Are their like heavenly public toilets? Or are you just smooth down there like…"

"Oz, for the sweet love of all that's holy, just stop." Valery smacked his forehead.

Luc smirked as he sipped his beer. "Which question would you like me to answer?"

Oz opened his mouth, but I interrupted. "Just the first, please. I'm not sure I'm ready for the answers to the rest."

Luc tapped his beer against his chin. "Azriel is a spectacular example of douche baggery, however, not all angels are like that."

"I can vouch for that. Michael seemed quite nice."

Luc's face whipped toward me. "Michael? The Archangel Michael? When did you see him?"

I shrugged and sipped my seltzer. "A couple of weeks or so ago. It was no big deal."

Now everyone was scowling at me. "What? It was like three minutes. It was hardly worth mentioning. He was just curious."

"Arcadia, angels do no get curious. Especially not Archangels. And especially not Michael. He cast me into hell for my curiosity."

I hardly call boning a bunch of cavewomen 'curiosity' Lucifer Morningstar, Ace said primly.

I cackled. *Oh, she's using your full name. Trouble in paradise?* I lived for these moments of payback. All that snarky commentary for years. Every snide comment, every disapproving comeback, paled when she was arguing with Lucifer like an old married wife. It was perfect.

WATCH YOURSELF, ARCADIA JONES.

I laughed out loud. "Don't be such a grump."

Eli sighed. "I really wish you guys wouldn't do that thing where you talk in your head. It's... disconcerting."

It finally got too much for Lux, and he came over, pulling me off the couch and into his arms, and sat me in his chair. He perched on the arm, his body poised and ready for a fight. I laid my hand on his arm, the muscles under my fingers tight. I gave him a little squeeze. Luc was not our enemy, had never been our enemy. Our enemy was time. And there was no beating that. There was no one to fight, except maybe Azriel the asshole.

"You never told us why Azriel is a dick."

Luc downed his glass of scotch, and another one appeared immediately. "Azriel, Acerezeal and I used to be friends. Maybe friends is too strong a word. Comrades perhaps? I was Ace and Azriel's squadron leader. I fell in love with her the first day I saw her. Even as an angel, she held this spark. This *something* that no other angel had, and it burned in a heart bigger than any I'd ever seen. That spark was passion. A completely unheard of emotion in angels. I wanted to spend time with her, so I raised her up the ranks to the same level as Azriel, the rank below mine as commander. He was not a fan, but it was hard to resist Ace's special *joie de vivre*, even though none of us could label the emotion.

"We became friends by proximity, and then confidantes. When I fell though, he changed. When Ace fell also, it pushed him into being even more...what is the phrase the humans use? Ah, by the book. I think that he thought the taint of our unholy thoughts coated him like a layer of filth that he just could not shed. That he had to be an extra douchey asshole angel that did everything perfectly and without question, or else he would fall too. And he was terrified. Another sensation that was unfelt by angels before."

"Before what?"

"Before I fell. Now they all know fear."

CHAPTER THIRTY-ONE

Lux drove me over to Brooklyn, and double parked outside a skinny little building with big plate glass windows. Ri was standing on the curb, with a huge smile on his face. Oh god, he looked handsome. The sun glinted off his olive skin, and his dark hair shone until it was almost blue.

"You know what, I'm pretty sure you guys must contribute a little to my heart troubles. Just look at him," I pseudo complained to Lux. Honestly, I was a little breathless.

He just rolled his eyes. "Damn pretty boy," he leaned over and kissed me goodbye.

Ri opened my door and helped me out, leading up onto the footpath.

"Have her home by six!" Lux yelled out the door.

"Or what?" Ri taunted back.

He gave Orion a menacing look and I couldn't help but laugh. Lux was not the boogeyman. I preferred him in my bed rather than under it.

Ri flipped him the finger and Lux was smiling as he pulled back into traffic. We turned and walked toward the restaurant door.

"Are you ready for this? This is gonna blow your mind."

"I'm ready!"

He pushed the door open and walked in first, guiding me in with a flourish of his arm. It was a sushi train. But...

"Is that a cake?"

"It's a dessert train! And also tapas. Dreams can come true."

I stared at the desserts and tapas going around the small track. They looked delicious.

"How'd you know I loved sushi trains?"

Ri helped me up onto one of the stools that ran around the train track and grabbed us down two plates of tapas. One had small deep fried balls of something, and the other was small pastries.

"I may have asked Clary about your fave restaurant. I was going to take you back, give you a little piece of the normalcy from your old life for a night. But when she told me you loved sushi trains, I knew this was the place."

Ri was right. I did crave the normalcy of my old life sometimes. Not that it was very interesting, and I loved the guys and the babies and wouldn't go back for the whole world, but sometimes it's just nice being a normal person doing normal things. Like talking to a hot guy as the tiny plates stacked up in front of you.

We talked about normal things, things you would talk about with a man on a date. It was a balm.

"How's the club?"

Ri stuck a third marinated mushroom into his mouth. Two quick chews and then he swallowed them almost whole. I resisted giving him a speech about good mastication. It could go nowhere good.

"The club is great. After the incident with you, I thoroughly vet every person who comes into the VIP area. Everyone goes on the waiting list. Somehow it's made the whole thing even more exclusive and popular. Go figure."

"And S&M night?"

He gave me a lustful look. "Still as popular as ever. I look forward to showing you myself. As it is, I spend that night doing my paperwork. Alone. Naked but alone."

"Why naked?"

He grimaced. "All the lust flowing around makes my skin tight and other things hard. It's just more comfortable if I'm not chafing against my clothes."

Respect filled my chest. I leaned over and put my head on his shoulder. "I love you, Ri. Soon I'm going to make love with you until neither of us can walk for a week."

He kissed me gently, but with tongue. That was Orion though. He didn't believe in pecks on the cheek. It was always maximum effort and his kisses always left me breathless.

I rubbed my belly. I probably shouldn't have had that third crab puff.

"Okay?"

"Yep, just full," I gave him a reassuring smile.

He pulled off two dessert plates. One had a mini key lime pie and the other was a type of brownie. "Too full for dessert?"

I gave him an affronted look! "Never!"

"I think the babies look like you." He pulled out the print out that Doctor Hamilton had given me of both the babies faces. He kept it in his wallet. The photo caught Hope mid yawn.

"They are smooshed into my amniotic fluid. They don't look like anyone yet. Unless you think I look like a smooshed potato?" I laughed. It felt good to laugh.

"The most beautiful smooshed face in the whole world," he kissed my temple.

A sharp pain bolted across my stomach and I grabbed at it. Ouch.

"Hey, what was that?"

My heart thudded. "I don't know."

Ace?

Silence. Panic trickled in.

Ace?

More silence and another shooting pain.

Something was wrong.

I didn't say anything but Ri was throwing down cash in the table and getting me to my feet. "I'm taking you home to see Eli."

Another sharp pain, and the world dimmed at the edges. "Something is wrong, Ri. Take me to the hospital.

Oz's health tracker started to flash on my wrist and

both mine and Ri's phones started going off as he pushed his way out of the restaurant.

The phones continued to buzz until Ri answered. "There's something wrong with Cady. Yeah, I'm taking her to the hospital. No, Val has the Jag. Yes. Yes. Ok." He hung up the phone.

"I need you to stand here," he said, and halted me right next to the door. Another sharp pain made me nearly double over.

"Fuck. Just hold on, okay?" He walked over to a guy just getting out of his car. He was so far away, I could only just pick up their conversation.

"Hey, I'm gonna borrow your car, okay? I'll leave it for you at Mount Sinai." The guy smiled shyly, his jaw slightly unhinged and he just nodded as he handed over his keys.

"Will you be there?" The guy cooed, and Ri stroked his cheek.

"Maybe. Thanks, man." So that was Lust at work. It was scary how easily it worked and how open to sugges-tion the guy was.

Ri hustled back over, and led me to the guy's car. I frantically willed my mind and body to stay as calm as possible, but inside I was freaking the fuck out. Silent tears streamed down my cheeks as Ri helped me into the car.

"It's going to be alright, Beautiful Girl. This is probably just those phantom contraction things. We'll be at the hospital in five minutes and everyone will be okay."

His voice was calm, but I could see the panic in his

eyes. I nodded, and he shut the door, half jumping the hood of the car to get to the drivers side quicker.

It was too soon.

IT ALL HAPPENED IN A BLUR. Ri carried me into the emergency room and I was rushed through. Before I knew it, there were six doctors, four medical students and a barrage of nurses standing around my bed. The rest of my seven hadn't arrived yet, though I had no doubt they'd be there and not even the Devil would stop them. Not that he would.

"We believe you've experienced a placental abruption. This is very serious for both you and the babies. This needs to be treated immediately, as the babies are not getting enough oxygen. I've booked a theater, and as soon as you are prepped, we will undergo an emergency c-section. The nurse will get you the appropriate forms to sign. We've contacted your specialists, and they will be on standby." I just nodded along. The words weren't connecting in my brain, but I would agree to anything that would give the babies a fighting chance.

"Will I be awake?"

"If you wish. You aren't hemorrhaging large quantities, so the anesthetist will be along asap to give you a spinal block and epidural. However, we may put you under general anesthesia at any point if we judge it necessary."

I nodded again. I wished Eli was here to tell me if we were doing the right thing. My intuition was saying yes, but what did I know?

Ace? I need you. Please be okay. I'd called her repeatedly, but no answer. A dark ball of dread in my gut formed at the thought she was gone forever, but I couldn't dwell on it. I would deliver the babies and then I would mourn my best friend.

The anesthetist left just as the Lux, Sam and Eli arrived. Eli looked determined, and Sam looked terrified. Lux looked... broken. He came over and put his head on my chest. I ran my fingers over the smooth stubble of his skull. I couldn't give him reassurances. I didn't have them in me.

An orderly in scrubs came to wheel me down to the operating room and there was no more time.

"Wait, wait. I need to say goodbye to the others." I reached for my guys. "We have to wait. Oz and Tolli and Valery. I need to see them first."

"I'm sorry, ma'am. You are booked down in theater." The guy looked apologetic, if kind of confused. The look of confusion increased when each of the guys came up and kissed me. A tear dropped down onto my cheek when Sam pressed his forehead to mine. "I will see you when you come out. We will hold our babies together."

The orderly cleared his throat and everyone moved back.

Lux reached out and touched my cheek. "You will come back to me."

I could only nod. A nurse, who looked a little like Clary - god I needed Clary right now - met us at the lift.

"Hi, I'm Rose. I'll be taking you down. Can I have your name and date of birth?"

I must have murmured the right thing, because I was down in theater before I knew it. The rest was a blur. I couldn't feel anything below my rib cage, except the arrhythmic thumping of my heart and lungs that couldn't draw enough air.

A bunch of specialists stood around me, all looking the same in their gowns and masks. Everything faded in and out, as the babies stopped moving.

"You have to hurry."

"It's okay, Arcadia." I recognized Doctor Hamilton's voice behind the mask and I calmed. "I'm making the incision now, and your babies will be in this world before you know it. Your only job is to stay calm."

I felt no pain. Pressure, tugging, but no pain. Then I heard the most beautiful sound in the world. A cry. A tiny mewl. And another. It was perfect. "Baby number one is perfect, Arcadia. Ten fingers. Ten toes."

More pressure, more tugging, and then silence. I was beginning to dread the silence. The nurses rushed around, one of the blue robed doctors taking Hope to another bed, working on her. Then another tiny cry. "That's two for two. Congratulations Mama. But your job isn't over yet," Doctor Hamilton said reassuringly.

Goodbye, Arcadia. The voice wasn't even a sound. It was a vibration I heard in my soul.

Ace? What do you mean goodbye? Ace?

I couldn't leave without saying goodbye. Silence, and I could hear her struggle. *This is the best thing I have ever done. I love you.*

I struggled but I couldn't move, though moving would have been useless. I couldn't grab hold of her. I couldn't take her hand and make her stay. I turned to yell at the person beside me to make her stay.

Rather obscurely, it was a man wearing a poncho that stood beside me. "Where's the faith?"

He was cute. Maybe a little older, but he wore his age well. Like George Clooney or Brad Pitt, but with more grey hair. A silver fox.

I was definitely dying. This was the weirdest death hallucination ever. "Shouldn't you be wearing scrubs?"

The man looked down at his poncho. It was blue and yellow in a repeating zig zag pattern. "This is freshly laundered. I got it from Tijuana."

"It's nice."

"Thank you, Arcadia. Someone said they saw the face of Jesus in it. I don't see the resemblance myself. The holy chicken nugget though, that was uncanny."

I nearly swallowed my tongue. "Are you Jesus?"

The man laughed. "God no. Or would it be Me no? I can never get the terminology right. I am the Father. God. Big G. The name you scream during climax." He laughed and I just blinked. This was the weirdest coma dream ever.

That was when I noticed no one else in the room was moving. Everyone was frozen in a moment.

"Oh fuck. I'm dead. You're here to take me to heaven. The guys. The guys are going to be so crushed. And the babies." Tears streamed down my cheeks.

"Hey, hold up. I don't personally collect the dead. I have angels for that. They are much more-"

"Biblical looking?"

God shrugged. That was weird. I had to stop referring to him as the G word. I was beginning to freak out, like my heart could beat out of my chest. "As you say. Call me whatever you like. It doesn't matter to me as much as everyone on earth seems to believe."

"Okay. The Big Guy. How's that sound?"

"Just fine, Arcadia. No, I'm not here for you. I am here for my child. Acerezeal." He snapped his fingers and a tearing sensation ripped through my chest. I screamed.

"Sorry about that. It's like ripping off a Band-Aid. It's better without forewarning." He snapped his fingers again, and Ace stood there before me. Solid, in her angelic body. Wings and all.

She was beautiful.

"Father?" She looked around the room, confused. "I ceased to be. I felt my consciousness stop. How?" She touched her naked body, wrapping her wings around herself and stroking the feathers. "My body. My wings. I'm me." Her eyes shot to mine, and then she leaned forward and wrapped me in a hug that crushed my bones.

"But why? Are all the sins redeemed?"

The Big Guy shook his head. "No, though Lucifer's Redeemer did a far better job than I anticipated. No, there is still one to be redeemed." He cupped Ace's cheek in his hand, and she leaned into the embrace, her body shuddering. "But Lucifer proved his point in a way that neither of us could have seen. She didn't just redeem those who had succumbed to the deadly sins. She redeemed one of my Fallen. A Fallen who willingly gave her life for two innocents. Despite the wishes of her beloved. That deserved a reward. You have earned back you body, Acerezeal, my favored child. Willful, but you have always held more love, more life, in your heart than the rest of my angels."

Ace fell to her knees and cried. Wracking sobs made her wings drag on the floor, their shade that of clouds in a summer storm. So beautiful.

"Thank you." She reached up and wrapped her fingers in mine. "And you." She pulled herself to her feet, and sucked in a deep breath. "Does this mean I am no longer Fallen? Am I welcome back in heaven?"

The Big Guy laughed. It was the most beautiful sound I had ever heard, even more beautiful than the Archangel Michael's, and again the tears were streaming down my cheeks.

"Would you want to come back?"

Ace shook her head. "No."

I wanted to slap her, but I couldn't raise my hands. Was she insane? How could say no?

The Big Guy just shrugged. "I didn't think so. Besides, you are fine where you are. You temper Lucifer's more impulsive side."

"Ace is the responsible one? Eesh." Ace threw me a dirty look, and it was exactly how I imagined it. She was exactly how I imagined her, right down to the long raven hair and the pale, milky skin that was way too exposed right now. "You should find some scrubs before someone sees you." I still wasn't convinced that this wasn't just a death hallucination.

God checked his nonexistent watch. "I should be

going. Time waits for no man." He threw me a smile.
"But then, I am no man."

"Wait!" Ace reached out and touched The Big Guy's
arm. "What about Arcadia? You can heal her right?"

The smile slid from his face, and I mourned its loss.
"Unfortunately no. She stepped outside of my plan as
soon as Lucifer placed your soul in hers. Arcadia's fate
rests solely on the shoulders of destiny now. Goodbye
Arcadia, I wish you the best of luck."

He was gone, and the world started moving again.
Pain gripped my chest, and I couldn't suck in any air.
The monitors were blaring and doctors were yelling.

"We're losing her!"

I tried to breathe enough air to call for Ace, but
there was none.

And then Azriel was there, leaning over me, his nose
inches from mine. "Balance is always restored, Arcadia
Jones." He clawed his hand and plunged it into my
chest.

Machines wailed in one long screech, but I could
barely hear it over Ace's screams. Azriel pulled out his
hand, clean despite just being in my chest, and in it held
the glowing light of my soul. He let it go and I watched
it drift toward the roof, briefly aware of the searing
agony, the ice cold emptiness in my chest, as the world
faded to blackness.

Ace was right. Having your soul torn out did hurt.

PART IV

CHAPTER THIRTY-TWO

ACE

I reached for my sword, then realized I was naked. No shirt, no pants and definitely no sword. I screamed in frustration as Azriel plunged his hand into Arcadia's chest and tore out her soul.

Fuck, fuck, fuck! I jumped toward him but my body was as weak as a fawn's from decades of stagnation.

"Lucifer!" I yelled, feeling a little ashamed that I had to call for my lover to take care of Azriel.

"Too late now, Acerezeal. It's over." His smug voice grated against my nerves. Weak or not, I stumbled toward him, keeping one eye on Arcadia's soul as it drifted upwards.

"You better get out of here before I gain back enough coordination to kick you where your balls should be!"

He just laughed, and I silently vowed revenge. He must have seen murder on my face, because he quit laughing.

"Lucifer!" I yelled again. "I'd go if I were you; he

isn't going to be happy that you snuffed his Redeemer." I let out a humorless laugh. "You know what, stay. I'd love to see him pummel the shit out of your smug angel face."

Azriel narrowed his eyes. "It's good to have you back, Acerezeal. I look forward to separating your body and your soul again, hopefully permanently this time."

I grinned as a knife came from behind him and pressed against his throat.

"Threaten her again, Azriel, and the only thing being separated will be your head from your body," Luc growled. My heart beat faster. I'd forgotten how sexy he was when he was threatening our enemies with decapitation.

Azriel disappeared in a flash, the coward. Luc just stared at me in awe. I wanted to run to him, wrap my arms around his body and feel his touch against my skin. But first...

"Quick, Arcadia's soul!" I pointed to the luminous soul getting closer to the roof.

Luc shot out a hand and whispered in Latin. Angels like me could do a lot of things, but manipulation of souls was strictly an Archangel thing. And despite his Fallen status, Luc had once been an Archangel.

He called it back to his hand, like a puppy to heel.

"Acerezeal, I cannot place this back in her damaged body. She will just die anyway." I took a moment to watch the humans work as they desperately tried to save Arcadia. I trusted that they would ensure she lived, but I needed to keep her soul safe until they fixed her physical form.

"Put her soul into my body. She shared her body with me for so many years, it's time I returned the favor."

Luc raised his eyebrows. "You want to put a human soul in your body?"

"Yes. Now let's do it before anything else goes wrong."

He leaned down and kissed me. "I have missed you, my love." I relished the feel of his lips on mine. I would never take his kisses for granted again. I would appreciate every touch, every embrace. "This might feel a little uncomfortable," he said as he jammed his hand at my chest and I felt my body's confusion as another soul settled beside mine. It was like a heart attack, or maybe a panic attack. Living with Arcadia had taught me what both of those sensations felt like. It would adapt. My body was angelic. I could carry Arcadia with me forever, if need be.

As Cady's soul settled in my body, the screeching of the human vitals machines stopped, and they stabilized her body.

Arcadia?

I could feel her confusion. *What's happening? Where am I?*

Ugh. I forgot the soul amnesia. We needed to kick start her memory ASAP because this whole thing was going to be way too hard to explain. I walked out of the operating theater, taking Luc's hand. His strong fingers threaded through mine, and I wanted to weep with joy. But fallen angels don't weep. Hell, angels don't weep at all.

Am I naked? Arcadia asked, outraged and a little embarrassed. She must have caught a glimpse of me in the glass windows.

Technically I'm naked. But don't worry. No one can see us unless I allow them too.

We made it to the waiting room, and there were Arcadia's Seven, looking like utter shit. Oz was sitting with his head in his hands, his eyes bloodshot red. Ri was beside him, worry and fear fighting for prominence on his face. Lux was standing in the corner, his face a hard mask to keep in the emotion. Sam kept running his hand through nonexistent hair as he paced back and forward. Valery was leaning against a wall, wiping tears on his sleeve. Tolliver was at the nurse's station demanding answers. And Eli looked... devastated. He looked as if his soul was being put through a meat mincer.

Oh. There was such pain in Arcadia's single, whispered word. *Oh, my guys. I'm so sorry.* A huge wave of sadness flowed through my body. *I remember. Azriel, that motherfucking asshole. Angel or not, I am going to shred him when I see him next. Wait until I tell Lux.*

"He'll have to get in line. Azriel was lucky I didn't have my sword."

Luc gave me a lopsided grin. He was so happy, and I was so torn. I was ecstatic to be back with him, always, but not at the cost of Arcadia's life. I wouldn't be truly happy until she was back in that weird poly lovefest she called a relationship.

What are we going to do? Arcadia asked, her voice suddenly small.

We're going to fix this, but first…

I uncloaked myself and so did Luc.

"Luc? What's going on?" Eli asked

"Who's the naked angel?" Ri joined in, though there wasn't anything remotely lascivious about the question.

"Arcadia?" Lux asked, but his face said he already knew.

Luc looked at me and I shrugged. "They'll take it better from you."

He shrugged out of his jacket and handed it to me. It had slots for my wings, and I put it on and zipped it up. It fell to my upper thighs, but covered all the important bits. It was still warm from Luc's body, and smelled like him. God, I'd missed his scent.

"You should explain, my love. You were there."

"My love? Ace?" Oz gaped at me, and I could feel Arcadia's desire to reach out and stroke his cheek.

"Yep, it's me. Acerezeal. I got my body back, though it was touch and go there for a second. The Father sends his regards by the way," I said to Luc.

"Arcadia?" Lux prompted again.

I grimaced. "It went badly. The babies are both fine, I imagine they'll both be in neonatal about now, but there were complications for Arcadia. She… died."

Nothing could have prepared me for the look of utter devastation on their faces. Each one. It was like a sucker punch to the heart.

"Azriel came, separated her soul from her body, and then Luc turned up and stopped Arcadia's ascent. We decided it was best if we placed her soul into my body until you," I looked at Eli, "can fix her body enough that she won't die as soon as it's returned."

Tolliver slumped down on the chair. "So she's there, with you now? She's the voice in your head?"

I gave him a small smile. "The irony isn't lost on me. But it's okay, we are used to sharing now."

Arcadia was beginning to cry. I didn't know a soul could cry. Wail yes, there were plenty of wailing souls in hell, but not cry.

I'm just a passenger. I didn't realize how frustrating this would be. I'm so sorry you had to do this for so many years, Ace. I miss them so much already. And my babies. I'll never get to hold my babies.

I firmed my jaw. *You will. I will make sure of it.* She deserved her happiness, and I was determined to help her get it. *Now, suck it up. I don't want to listen to you cry for a month.*

Arcadia let out a soft laugh. We needed to get used to this as the new normal, because shit was only going to get weirder.

"How will this work?" Eli asked, sinking down into the chair beside Tolliver.

"You work on getting her body better. I want her to be able to skip out of this hospital and never come back except to have Casanova's pretty babies." I poked a thumb towards Ri. "I'm going to find a way to get her soul from my body and back into her own without involving Azriel the Dickhole."

"Can't he do it?" Lux asked, his voice a combination of pain and promised retribution that made my skin prickle. The dude was gonna spiral without Arcadia.

"Luc can put a soul back into a body, otherwise deathbed deals with the Devil wouldn't be a thing. But he can't take one out. That is the strict purview of very few of our kind. Just the big three, and Azriel the Douche Canoe."

The big three?

"The big three are Michael, Raphael and Gabriel, in case you are wondering."

Maybe we can try Michael? He showed an interest before.

I looked at Luc. My sexy, short tempered lover. He was as beautiful as the day I first saw him, when his wings were still milky white and he hadn't yet fallen. He liked to pretend he was okay with his new role, but deep down being cast out still hurt. Especially being cast out by Michael, who he'd considered a friend. I'd considered him a friend.

Yeah, we'll probably keep a visit to Michael as a last resort.

Lux stood in front of me, towering over me even though I was back in my willowy 5'9 body and no longer in Arcadia's vertically challenged one.

Hey!

"I'm going with you," Lux said. It wasn't a request, or even a demand. It was a statement of fact.

"I'm sorry, but we are going places you cannot go. Well, places you would never return from," Luc said with something that almost sounded like compassion. From the Devil. Today was a strange day all round.

Lux let out a frustrated grunt between his teeth. "I need to do something."

I put my hands on his cheeks and did something I

hadn't done in centuries, since I fell. I sifted with another person.

I sifted him to the fourth floor of the hospital, into the neonatal care unit. I checked him over to make sure all his molecules came with him. Arms, legs, only two eyes. Okay, we were good. Apparently moving people through time and space was just like riding a bike.

In the nursery, in two humidicribs side by side, laid Arcadia's babies. Tiny, pink and defenseless.

"They need you. All of you."

Lux stared at the babies; Estrella was small but still bigger than Hope, who would have fit in one of Lux's massive hands.

"Do you know who's they are yet?"

I stared at him. "Does it matter?"

He shook his head, sadness dragging down the lines of his handsome face and for a second, every one of the two thousand years he'd lived was etched on his face.

"No. They are hers, and I will love and protect them with my life."

Arcadia was so quiet, but I could sense her awe of the babies. I wasn't going to lie, they were the most perfect creations I had ever seen.

I turned back to Lux to find him staring at me. Not at me, past me, as if he could see into my soul like an angel.

"You will come back to me, Arcadia Jones."

Tell him I love him.

"She says she loves you." We turned back to the babies. "I'll bring her back, I promise."

Committing their tiny faces to memory, I knew it

was time to go. I walked to the window and slid it open, spreading my wings wide.

"By the way, congratulate Oz on becoming a Papa for me, yeah?"

With that, I fell into gravity's calm embrace and for the first time in decades, I felt the wind beneath my wings.

Now that song was going to be stuck in my head. Damn you, Barbara.

CHAPTER THIRTY-THREE

"I thought I'd find you here," Luc's rough voice washed over me like a balm. I fought the wussy voice in my head that screamed, "hug him now!"

It must have been the other wussy voice in your head, because I didn't say any such thing, Arcadia said primly.

"I've always liked it up here. It has good harbor views. Plus, I'm a fan of extravagant gifts, you know that."

He sat beside me, atop the Statue of Liberty's crown, our feet dangling down.

Luc grinned. "Yes, the view of New York Harbor is pretty good from the middle of the water." He picked me up, and sat me across his lap, my wings spread out behind me. The hard knot that had sat in my gut for the last two decades, a twisted ball of anger and doubt and pain, finally relaxed as the heat of his body settled into mine. His scent wrapped around me and comforted my soul. I was back where I was supposed to be.

I ignored Arcadia's sniffling.

"What am I supposed to do here, Luc? I need ideas, a plan, anything. Do I go beg Azriel to put her back? Do I trust him to do that?"

Luc snorted. "I wouldn't trust him to reanimate a cat."

He made a good point. Azriel was a good angel but a shitty person. He'd deliver Arcadia's soul to the pearly gates himself if he got another opportunity.

I stood and ruffled my wings. It was still weird being back in my body. "There's only one thing to do."

"Have sex in Lady Liberty's torch of freedom?" Luc winked and grinned. I'd forgotten his grin was my kryptonite.

"Okay, two things." He leaned in to kiss me, and I dived into the kiss like a starving woman, which I was. Sure, watching Arcadia have sex with her guys was fun and all, but it wasn't the same as feeling Luc's mouth on mine.

Hey, we had a deal! No watching! Both Luc and I chuckled. Never make a deal with a fallen angel.

"I have no problem with you watching, Arcadia Jones."

Ugh, I'm fine thanks. We aren't all giant perverts.

He kissed me again, and then bit my lip hard. "Damn it, what was the second thing you had to do?" Luc hated not knowing things. It was his pet peeve.

"Go home," I said, a genuine smile splitting my face. How I'd missed the place.

Luc stroked the hair from my face with such tenderness that I wondered what the humans would think if they could see him now.

"Home it is, my love. Lady Liberty can wait." He grabbed my hand, and together we sifted.

HOME. The landing room in Luc's palace looked just the same.

That is a lot of white marble. The awe in Arcadia's voice made me smile. *This isn't how I imagined hell at all. I thought it would be more...*

Dark? Fiery? I suggested.

Stinky. Where's the sulphur smell? And is all that gilding real gold?

I looked around and tried to see the room from Cady's perspective. The milky white marble was struck through with only the palest grey marble, as close to the color of clouds as you could get. Every corner, every edge, and the entire domed ceiling was gilded. With real gold, so the whole room was lit with this luminance. It was as close as you could get to landing at the pearly gates, minus the choirs of heavenly song.

"Where are my Princes of Hell?" Luc shouted, and I grinned. "Princes?" He shouted again, so it echoed through the room.

The giant golden door opened, and a figure clad only in black camo pants walked out, rubbing sleep from his eyes. "Luc, dude, you know he hates it when you call us..." his words stuttered to a stop and his mouth swung open.

"Acerezeal?" He rubbed his eyes, almost comically, and whispered, "Ace?"

Holy shi... Cady whispered.

"Gusion!" I smiled as I ran to my old friend, and he wrapped me in his arms.

"Ace, it is really you. How? Luc said that all his Sins weren't redeemed yet. He was worried that the Redeemer wasn't going to make it." He pushed me away a little and his eyes ran an inventory of my limbs. "You look great!" Then he pulled me back into his arms again. "We've missed you so much, it hasn't been the same around here. Mostly because Luc has been a giant asshole for two whole decades." He squinted a little, as if he was looking at the sun. "Uh, Ace, do you know you have two souls right now?"

"I missed you too, Gus. It's a long story. Let me introduce you to Cady. Cady, this is Gusion, Angel of the Past, Present and Future."

Former Angel. It is nice to finally make your acquaintance, Arcadia Jones, Lucifer's Redeemer and Saviour of the Damned.

Uh, just call me Cady. It's nice to meet you too, Gus. You're very... um...

"She thinks you're hot, Gus," I finished for her. She wasn't wrong. Of all the Fallen, of which there were only three, including me but not including Luc, Gus was the most ethereal. He had long, golden hair that hung down to the center of his back, and a body that was a beautiful pale gold, rippling with muscles like every teenage girl's wet dream.

Gus looked down at his body, as if seeing it for the first time. "Hey, I guess I am." He grinned at me, a naughty grin that reminded me why we had all fallen in the first place.

"Where's Memphis?" I asked.

"I'm here, Acerezeal."

Memphis was inky darkness where Gusion was golden light, although Memphis's hair hung down his back also in a long black braid. His dark ebony skin meant the deep blue of his eyes were startling in their shining brilliance. Gusion and Memphis's visual differences only mirrored their personality differences.

I went to Memphis, wrapping my arms around his body although it remained stiff under my hands. That was just Memphis' way. He was stoic. He made Arcadia's Lux look like a CareBear.

"Let me introduce you to my, uh, passenger soul? Memphis, this is Arcadia."

Nice to meet you, Memphis.

"No one calls me Memphis except Acerezeal. My name is Mephistopheles."

The Mephistopheles? I thought you were a figment of some old poet's imagination.

"It suits me to be seen that way." His face was as scary as he could possibly be while with such beautiful lines, but it was enough to strike fear into most mortals. But my Arcadia wasn't a mere mortal

Okay. What kind of nickname is Memphis for a fallen angel anyway?

"A good one! Have you tried screaming out Mephistopheles during climax? I can tell you from experience that it seriously kills the mood. Now Memphis? The home of rock'n'roll? That's enough to make you wet just thinking about it."

I could feel Arcadia mulling over what I said. I hope she didn't short circuit something important.

So you and Memphis-

"Mephistopheles," the angel in question growled.

Sorry. You fallen angels are really touchy about your names. Anyway, so you and Mephistopheles, you know...

"Fuck?"

Uh yeah. And Luc is okay with that? she whispered, even though literally every person in this room could hear her no matter the volume of her mental projection.

"I am fine with the arrangement, Arcadia. Acerezeal's heart belongs to me, this I know for sure. But this is also Hell. We didn't all fall to spend eternity alone and as chaste as monks. We have already been judged and been found wanting. May as well make our banishment fun."

"Me too," Gusion added, grinning, his perfect straight teeth as blinding as the gilded marble floors.

Uh huh, Gus too? You never get to call me a hussy ever again, down here with your own little fallen angel harem, Cady crowed and I laughed.

"We should move from the landing room," Memphis grunted, and moved toward the double doors. We all followed behind.

Do all souls land here? Cady asked, though I wasn't sure if she was talking to me or the rest of the room. It was Gus that answered.

"Yes. Everyone who passes into Hell, or the underworld, must do so through this room. One way in, one way out, even for angel kind."

So people who say they saw a white light at the end of the tunnel, it doesn't mean they are going up top?

"Unlikely," Luc said, holding the door open for me. I

ran a finger down his abs. He still hadn't replaced his shirt, but no one was going to hear any objection from me. He looked incredibly sexy with his V leading down into tight leather pants.

A wave of sadness hit me, and I knew it wasn't my own. I sent a silent apology to my vagina and straightened my shoulders.

"Let's go to the billiards room. We need a plan. I need Arcadia to go back in her own body so I can have sex without her virginal judgement killing my orgasms."

I love you too, Ace.

We walked through Luc's palace, as huge and ostentatious as he could make it. The floor was gradually darkening marble, so by the time you've reached the large double doors that opened up to the courtyard, the floor was a pitch black onyx. That's when you realized you weren't in Kansas anymore, Dorothy.

Chandeliers hung from every ceiling, all the furnishings the finest money could buy. Not that money purchased any of this stuff. A lot of fine craftsman ended up in the pits of hell, and were more than willing to bargain for their skills for a moment's reprieve. You think they would have learned about making deals with the Devil, but some people just didn't learn.

The Billiards Room was the kind of room you'd find in a hunting lodge built by an eccentric, rich weirdo. Chesterfield lounges sat below huge canvases of unicorns mating. A teak bar sat in front of a bar shelf, packed with bottles of every shape and color. There was only one shelf because every liquor we owned was top shelf. Sitting on the bar was a six inch hula girl bobble head and the disembodied spirit of a bartender given semi-corporeality.

"'Sup Frank?" I said. He was only semi cognizant, kind of like a walking, talking Nespresso machine. He could fulfill your drink order, but couldn't give you life advice.

"Miss Acerezeal. The usual?"

"Thanks, Frank. Two umbrellas."

I sat down on the chesterfield, and relaxed back against the soft leather. It was nice to relax.

"I need to know if there is another way to get a soul back into a body without asking any of the big guys, or Azriel."

I looked Memphis, his high cheekbones pressing against his ebony skin. He was a scholar by nature, if anyone would know, it would be him.

"There is no other way, without the intervention of the Father himself," Memphis said, his deep voice lacking inflection but I knew him well enough that I could tell he regretted his answer.

I wasn't so easily deterred. They should know that by now.

"I don't accept that." I jutted out my chin and stared into his beautiful midnight blue eyes defiantly. Luc sat beside me, his hand wrapped around my thigh. "We will find a way, my love, but first you need to rest, adjust to your body again. Celebrate a little. Arcadia would not begrudge you a moment of happiness. She is not that kind of person."

My jaw flexed. He was right, she wouldn't. She was kind, and thoughtful, and had thought of my happiness at all times, even to the detriment of her own. I could do the same for her.

Arcadia let out an unflattering splutter. *Don't be an idiot. My problem isn't going to be an easy fix. It will all still be here tomorrow. Enjoy your redemption. Drink your cocktail, kiss your pretty boys-*

"Men. Pretty men," Gus interjected.

Arcadia sighed. *There's no such thing as a private conversation with angels about, is there? As I was saying, kiss your pretty men. Feel joy. I owe you everything. You deserve this moment of happiness.*

Mephistopheles huffed out a laugh. "You are going to regret your generosity later."

I reached over and punched him in the arm. "Gus is the fortune teller, asshole."

Despite myself, I could feel my face curve into a smile and happiness swell in my chest. Home. No one could have predicted that I would be just as happy in the bowels of hell with three fallen angels as I ever was in heaven among the heavenly choir and the pompous attitude of my fellow angels.

"I missed you guys so much."

Gus, who'd been sipping his moonshine at the bar, came over and squatted down, his spun gold hair falling over his bare shoulders. Fuck, I'd forgotten how radiantly magnetic he was. He kissed my forehead.

"We have more than missed you, Ace. We have been incomplete without you."

I ran my forefinger down the hard lines of his face. "I'm sure the demonesses have been soothing your pain."

He laughed and shrugged guiltily. I screwed up my nose. Ugh, demonesses. I hated those bitches, with their wailing, their stupidly big breasts and their grossly long talons.

I looked at Memphis. He rolled his eyes at Gusion, as he did a hundred times a day.

"You too?" I asked him, already knowing the answer. Memphis didn't mess around with the demonesses like Gus. Memphis didn't mess around with anyone, except me. Not out of loyalty, though I knew without a doubt that he had my back until the End of Days. Memphis had his own demons, but they were the demons of memories long past.

"No." He maintained his scary expression. He had a bad case of Resting Bitch Face. Luc batted Gus away from me.

"He can continue with the Demonesses for one more night, because I am not ready to share you yet." He pulled me onto his lap, turning me so we were facing each other. His hands slipped into the slits in his jacket, running up the bare skin of my back and under the arch where my wings met the muscles of my back. I moaned. That felt better than I remembered. "Tonight, my love, you are mine, and only mine."

And then he kissed me. His fingers wrapped in my hair as his mouth plundered mine, his tongue branding me as it tangled with my own.

"That's my cue to leave," Memphis muttered. "Come on Golden Boy, unless you wanna see how long it takes to grow back something important." He stopped at the door. "Good luck, Arcadia." There was a smirk in his voice, and I flipped him the bird over my shoulder, but I was smiling against Luc's lips.

I don't need luck. What I'm going to need is therapy.

In the same way that Arcadia had been doing to me for years, I could block her out. Only, I could do it a little more effectively. I could probably trap her soul so far down inside my own that she would float in blackness forever more, but I wouldn't tell her that. She would definitely freak if she knew that I had that much control. I let her have free rein. I wanted her to be comfortable.

"You are thinking far too hard, Acerezeal. Apparently, I am not doing my job if you are able to form coherent thought." With that, he flipped me over onto the couch, and put his arms either side rib cage. He unzipped his jacket, slowly revealing every inch of my flesh to his gaze. Achingly slowly.

"Fuck, I'd forgotten how beautiful you are. You steal my breath." His jacket was a little big on me, ending just at the top of my thighs, and when the cool air reached my soaked pussy, I sucked in a breath. Luc finished zipping and pushed the lapels apart, baring me to him. He inhaled deeply. "The scent of your desire, however, is forever etched into my memory. You are so wet for me." He ran his tongue across one nipple, then the other, before trailing his tongue down my stomach, dipping into my navel and then over the swell of my pubic bone. I bucked into his mouth, and his tongue dipped to my clit, striking it hard. I moaned. My body was electric.

Luc sat up and unzipped his pants, his cock

bouncing out as if he too was ready to greet an old friend.

I can't wait to tell Oz that Angels are definitely not smooth like Ken dolls down there. Arcadia let out a long, low whistle.

"I rescind my earlier offer, Arcadia Jones. You may not watch. Do not panic, I will undo this when we are finished." He waved a hand, and Cady went quiet.

"That was mean. She's going to freak," I said as I used my flight feathers to stroke down his back.

"I do not want to share you tonight, not even with your Redeemer." He snapped his fingers and the jeans that had clung so tightly to his thighs were gone. He had unlimited control in Hell. He could build a mansion of gold, so getting rid of his pants was child's play.

I forgot about talking as I took in his body, every hard line, lightly shadowed dip and sharp angle. The long gash that ran from his left shoulder down his torso to his left hip was a constant reminder of falling, and the searing edge of Michael's sword. I'd run my tongue along it many times over the centuries, and my mouth watered to do it again. But Luc had other ideas as he practically dove between my thighs, kissing my pussy with as much intensity, and tongue, as he'd just kissed my mouth. I writhed against him as his tongue stroked up and down my folds in long, hard strokes. He sucked my clit, then swirled his tongue around it, before giving it a careful nip. He did that over and over again until I was screaming his name so loudly that they could probably hear me in the Elysian Fields. I came in wave after wave of pleasure, and I'd barely finished my orgasm when he picked me up, and pulled me against his torso and then impaled me on his granite hard cock.

"Fuck, Luc!" I screamed as he stretched my pussy wide. I wrapped my legs around his waist, drawing him tight against me, so every little movement shot waves of pleasure through my body until I was on fire with electric heat. His hands on my hips, he pulled me up and down, moving in the rhythm as old as time itself, muttering in the angelic tongue. I couldn't even concentrate on what he was saying, but I knew it was probably an ode to me. It was probably a little sacrilegious to use the language during sex, but fuck it. We were already Fallen.

My orgasm crashed over me as Luc wrapped his onyx wings around me and caught my screams against his lips.

"I love you, I love you," I panted, a pledge and an ode.

Luc roared as he reached his own climax, thrusting deep into me, edging the pleasure with pain. We rode it out, and I collapsed against his body.

"It's better than I remember," I gasped out.

"It's exactly how I remember," he said as he kissed each of my cheeks and then my forehead. I snuggled into his arms, still wrapped in the blackness of his wings, and slept.

CHAPTER THIRTY-FOUR

Arcadia's red hot rage woke me. *Ten hours. I've been trapped in the abyss of nothingness for ten hours. Who has sex for ten-freakin'-hours?*

Whoops.

"Sorry, Cady. Trust me, it was better than watching me tongue Luc's balls. Well, for you anyway."

Ew.

I rolled out of bed, the one Luc and I shared, and slipped on a T-shirt from the walk in robe. The bed was massive. Arcadia and all seven of her guys could sleep in it, comfortably. Hell, maybe even me, Luc, Gus and Memphis could fit as well. Like one big happy orgy.

Um, nope! Never going to happen. I don't share.

I laughed as I brushed my teeth in the ensuite. Ensuite might be a bit of an understatement. It was larger than all the apartments Arcadia's lived in combined.

"Lucky for you, I share very well."

I walked along the stone floors that were beautifully

warm. The bowels of Hell; it was the most efficient underfloor heating ever.

I strolled into the kitchen to find everyone already there. Memphis was reading a book that's title was in Greek, and Gus was still drinking moonshine, though in consideration to the time of day he was mixing it with freshly squeezed orange juice. Luc was sitting at the head of the table, in his hand carved mahogany wing-back chair, reading a newspaper.

When I saw the last person in the room, I resisted the urge to groan.

"Gus, you didn't?" I whisper-yelled, and he had the brass balls to grin. I shook my head. "I thought you loved me?"

Unfortunately I hadn't been quiet enough, because the person cooking pancakes turned. I hated pancakes.

"Acerezeal! It's so good to have you back!" Bacciria gave me a huge fake smile, all teeth and big hair. And boobs. Bacciria was my least favourite demoness. She was practically my arch-nemesis.

"Baccy!" She curled her lip at the hated pet name. "It's good to be home and back in my own bed."

She continued to give me the snarly version of a smile. "I bet. I made you your favorite. Pancakes. I've been taking such good care of the guys while you've been away." Her voice was saccharine and I was about two seconds away from stuffing the pancakes somewhere a person shouldn't have baked goods.

I walked over to Gus and sat down on his lap, kissing his cheek. "Thanks, Baccy. I really appreciate you keeping them in such good, mmm-" I ran my finger down between Gus's pecs and over his abs, twirling my finger in the golden hairs just above his waist band. I waggled my eyebrows. "Health." Gus's body shook with contained laughter. Asshole.

"Tired of Lucifer already?" She wasn't even trying to keep up the sweet charade now. I sucked in a breath through my teeth.

Uh-oh, wrong zinger there, Baccy, Arcadia groaned. She got it. But unfortunately, Demonesses weren't known for their large intellects.

Luc stood, and spread his wings wide, their onyx hue casting the whole room in shadow. He appeared to grow and he became the imposing King of Hell that he was. Only fools forgot that he was scary as fuck, even when he was sipping juice and reading the sports pages.

"Bacciria, you forget yourself," his voice boomed, shaking the walls of the palace. "You dare speak of me in that manner? I am you Master, your creator! You do not speak to me or my consort with such disrespect."

Baccy fell to her knees and prostrated herself on the floor. "I'm sorry, I'm sorry, I'm sorry," she wailed over and over again.

Holy hell, I'm glad I'm not corporeal right now, because I would have wet myself. That's one scary mofo, Arcadia whispered. She had no idea. She'd only seen the warm, loving side of Luc. Even when he was angry at us, I was his beloved and she was his Redeemer, and we were never at risk of the full extent of his wrath. I had seen Luc when he was in full Devil mode. It wasn't a sight easily forgotten, unless you were a vapid demoness with more cup sizes than sense.

"Be gone from the palace. If you return, I will send you to the seventh circle for eternity."

Bacciria blanched and scurried out the door.

What happens in the seventh circle? Actually, don't tell me. I'll probably never sleep again. "They peel your skin off your flesh inch by inch, and then when the process is complete, they stitch it back on, let it heal and then peel it back off again. Over and over, for eternity," Memphis answered from the stove, where he was removing the burning pancake from the heat.

I'm going to throw up. I said I didn't want to know!

Memphis shrugged. "I always maintained that if the humans had a better understanding of what awaited them, they'd try harder to be good."

Gus scoffed. "Good. Bad. Those definitions are what led us all here in the first place. You need to let go of your notions of good and bad. Hell has its place. But we need to embrace the shades of grey and talk about it in terms of harm. To their fellow humans, to the world that they live on, to the other inhabitants of the earth-"

"Someone stop him before he devolves further into his rant. We are all here because we agree with you, remember?" I said, hugging is beautiful blonde head against my chest. "We all fell because we had questions.

I don't know. I liked his rant. I appreciate the shades of grey. All fifty of them, Arcadia laughed and I chuckled along with her, though the guys just looked confused.

I kissed the cute little frown lines on Gusion's other-wise ageless face. "I've missed your passion, Gus. And your beautiful face."

Gus dipped me backwards and kissed me like the

star he was, before nibbling my neck until I giggled. Legit giggled like a freshman in a sorority. I'd spent way too much time in the earthly realm watching teen rom-coms with Arcadia. I looked over at Luc, but he was back to sipping his coffee and reading the Algerian news. I waggled my eyebrows and he winked.

He didn't banish Bacciria because her statement hit too close to the truth; the guy knew he had all the moves that make me go boom. He banished her because she disrespected us all. We were angels, Fallen or not. Gusion continued kissing down my neck to my collarbone.

"Uh-uh, I've been distracted by sex once, now back to my problem."

Gus sighed and sat me back up straight. "This is why I appreciate the demonesses. They are always clamoring to climb onto my angelic staff."

I held a finger up to his lips. "Ew. Just ew."

I stood and poured myself some juice. "Are there no other deities who have soul manipulation? What about the Norns?"

Luc shook his head. "Decide a soul's fate, but can't move them around."

"There's gotta be someone? Another angel or a human shaman? The disembodied soul of Nicolas Tesla must be hanging around here somewhere?"

"Tesla is out on the Elysian Fields. You know how the Greeks loved their men of science. But I do not think he could help you anyway," Luc argued.

I sat on his lap and sipped my juice. "You know who could help?" I stroked his dark hair.

He flicked his eyes to me and unconsciously rubbed the scar on his chest. "Not Michael," he grunted and went back to his paper. "Try Raphael. Or even Gabriel. But I will not be beholden to Michael."

Arcadia wisely knew to stay quiet, despite the burning need she had to argue. I felt her frustration, but apparently I didn't hide it as well because Memphis jumped in to help.

"I'd try Raphael first. He's always been a bit of a softy for a good sob story. And he had a soft spot for you in particular. He might be able to do it, and if not, he might know who does."

I kissed Luc's cheek, and then bit his earlobe hard.

"Ow!" He rubbed his ear as I stood, wandering over to Memphis, but not before Luc swatted my ass with the back of his fingers. "You shouldn't bite, my love. You never know where I will bite back."

I threw him a saucy wink. "Who says I wouldn't like it?" I purred. I stood in front of Memphis. "I'm going to go find Raphael. Do you know where he is?" Memphis nodded. "Wanna come with?"

Indecision ran across his face. He'd always been a bit of a hellbody, loathe to leave the palace. "Come on, it'll be fun. I'm pretty sure he'll be in Afghanistan or somewhere equally as bloody. When was the last time you went to a conflict zone? Maybe we can help save a few guys while we're there. Perhaps even ensure a few of the baddies get an express pass to hell. Do not pass go, do not collect two million dollars. What do you say?"

"He's in Syria," Memphis said as he pushed off the

bench and headed toward the doorway. I followed behind him, blowing Luc a kiss and winking at Gus.

It'd been a long time since I'd travelled with Memphis, and I was kind of looking forward to it. But first we had a stop to make.

HOW ARE they so big already? Arcadia's melancholy musing broke my heart.

Time moves differently in the underworld. It's hard to predict. If Luc and the Father are opposite sides of a chess match, then time would be the board. It plays by its own rules. Next time we come up, it might only be minutes from this moment. I'm sorry. If I'd known, I would have come back earlier.

Two weeks had passed topside since I'd returned home. The babies had almost doubled in size, and although they were still in the neonatal unit, they were happy and healthy. We stood invisible in the corner of their room, a lumpy armchair in the corner holding a snoozing Valery. A nurse was helping Oz hold Estrella.

"Skin contact helps build a bond. Perhaps if you remove your shirt, I can place the baby on your chest," the nurse said hopefully. I resisted the urge to laugh. I was invisible, but not silent. Arcadia was fuming.

I died two weeks ago, and already people are trying to crack onto my guys? Do people have no shame?

Her outrage was beginning to color my own feelings. I moved into an empty hallway and dropped my invisibility, well except for the wings. I made sure I looked like a bombshell.

Memphis appeared beside me, looking like a sexy

vision in tailored black pants and a crisp white button down open to the second button.

We walked into the room, and the nurse nearly swallowed her tongue. I didn't know if the cause was me or Memphis, but it was the reaction we wanted.

Oz stood, baby Estrella still clutched gently to his naked chest. "Ace!" He turned to the nurse. "Could you just give us a minute? Thanks." His beard was looking scraggy, there were deep bags under his eyes, and his man bun was slipping to the left.

But he still looks damn good, Arcadia murmured.

"Valery! Ace is back. Is Arcadia okay? Have you made any progress? Eli hasn't left his office in a week and I'm pretty sure more than one cardiothoracic surgeon has put out a restraining order on him, but we are getting there." It all tumbled out at once, but I only half listened as Arcadia and I were both transfixed by the tiny little human pressed sleepily against his chest. Oz dropped his eyes to where we were looking.

"Sit. You can hold her. I'm not very good at passing her around. I'm still convinced that I'll drop her or break her or something. It's even worse with Hope. My finger is literally bigger than her little legs."

I sat, because what else could I do? I wasn't good at this, but the urge to hold them poured from my body. Arcadia's longing was consuming me, and quite frankly it was scaring me. But her need for the babies, for her Seven, was an overwhelming force. And when Oz placed the baby into my arms, I could feel Arcadia's soul pushing against mine, battering futilely to take control, so she would be the one who could stroke the down soft fluff of Estrella's head. So she could wrap her arms around Oz, and Val, who was fixing me with a bright eyed stare full of hope and longing.

I inhaled deeply. That new baby scent still lingered.

"Ace, why is a Prince of Hell standing in the same room as my daughters?"

I hadn't heard Lux come in, he moved with eerie silence, and he stood in a fighter's stance behind Memphis, ready to attack a possible threat.

Memphis whirled, very few could sneak up on the naturally cagey angel, and he pinned Lux with a cold stare.

"Come on Lux, you know he hates that." I resisted the urge to laugh. That would not defuse the situation.

"Lux."

"Mephistopheles."

They had a macho scary stare off, and I went back to the baby. Her eyes had closed as she listened to the steady thrum of my heart.

My sweet baby, Arcadia cooed, and the baby blinked, her eyes shifting slowly around as if she could hear her mother's voice. *My little warrior. Mommy loves you, and she'll get to hold you soon.* Estrella's little face scrunched, and if she hadn't been so very young, I'd say she looked confused. In reality, she probably had wind.

Memphis, who could hear Arcadia's soft words, turned to look at us. He walked to the other humidicrib, and turned to look at Lux.

"May I hold the baby?"

Lux looked like he was going to say no, pinning him

with a deadly look that promised severe pain if he so much as made her cry, but eventually nodded.

Memphis reached in and picked up Hope, her whole body fitting into one of his large hands. She smacked her lips and then opened her eyes. She looked up at Memphis, and stared him directly in the eyes, as if she could see into his soul.

Memphis looked like he'd been slapped as he just stared back.

"This is the first time she has opened her eyes," Val whispered, careful not to break the moment.

Memphis was shaking his head. "It is not possible. They are not Nephilim, nor Angel, yet they aren't entirely human either. Their souls have been shaped by the divine and it's left them something other. Something... beautiful." I'd never heard Memphis sound so awed. So at a loss for answers.

"They're special; I knew it from the moment their souls took root." I kissed Estrella's head. "I think they can hear the voices of other souls. Estrella could hear her mother just now, I know it. She knew that there was another voice in the room."

Memphis raised the baby closer to his face, his hands strong and sure, though Lux took a step closer.

"Be still, Lux. I swear on my immortal soul that I will not harm this child or her sister, as long as I am a part of the fabric of existence."

"You know, they've racked up a lot of blood oaths from a lot of powerful people in their short lives. Luc should be worried about being overthrown by the time they are five," I chuckled, although no one else was laughing.

Do you think that Lucifer will see them as a threat? Arcadia sounded legitimately worried.

"Seriously guys? That is one Big Bad you don't have to worry about. Cady gave them their beautiful humanity, and Oz gave them that strawberry fuzz sprouting on their heads, but their angelic traits are all me. As much as we have skirted around the topic, these babies are as much mine as they are yours. Part of my life force shaped their own. And Luc, for all his faults, loves me with a passion that burned through the Heavens. He will love these two because they are an extension of me. In Lucifer, they have the protection of the Devil himself. No one could ask for more than that."

Lux nodded, and Memphis was still transfixed by Hope.

Ask them how the rest of the guys are coping?

I relayed Arcadia's message.

Valery shrugged. "They are surviving. Barely. We take turns at being here with the *bebes*, and one of us is usually with Arcadia. We take it in shifts, though Eli does not rest. As Oz said, he is searching constantly for a foolproof way to mend her body quickly. Tolliver has pulled every string money can buy to get Cady to the top of the transplant list. They have started her on radiation therapy, but the cancer has spread throughout her body and it makes it difficult. But Eli will find a solution. Sam is keeping everything else afloat. Ri is taking the whole thing the worst. He blames himself for her death. Half death, whatever we are calling it. He can hardly look at the *bebes*, just sits at her bedside and mourns, despite our assurances that she will return to us." He sounded so stubbornly resolute that it was tough not to believe him.

My poor Ri. He is always so eager to take the blame for every wrong that happens in my life, and he has the bad luck to be there every time things go to shit.

"One problem at a time. We will soothe Orion's troubled feelings next time we are in town. Right now, we need to see an Angel about a soul."

Oz reached out and carefully removed Estrella from my arms. The baby let out a small, desolate cry that threatened to crack my black little heart wide open.

I will be back, Little One. Be good for your daddies. Ace, I want to hold Hope, even just for a moment.

"Of course," I answered Arcadia, and Oz gave me a startled look.

"She's really in there then?"

I nodded.

"God, I just wish I could hold her, or hear her for myself. It's killing me," his voice cracked and I couldn't help but reach up and stroke his cheek. It may have been Arcadia's impulse, or mine, but I wasn't sure.

"I'm going to do everything in my power to make sure you can do both of those things. I'm on my way to see Raphael now. By this time tomorrow, we may have a solution." I walked over and held my hands out to Memphis, who was still entranced by the tiny life in his hands. He whispered to her in the Angelic tongue, and she gurgled happily. He passed her over with confidence, and I took her awkwardly. She was so tiny and delicate. It was hard not to treat her like spun glass.

She is just perfect.

She was, with her tiny rosebud mouth and her tiny little nose, and her-

Ugh. I shook myself out of the mush spiral. Hope's eyes seemed knowing. Older than her sisters, as if she were an old soul.

"We should go," I whispered, though I could sit here and catalogue Hope's tiny features all day. I placed her back in her humidicrib. Lux stood beside me as we looked down at the baby.

"Will Raphael help?"

I wanted to lie to him and tell him it was a sure thing, but he wouldn't appreciate empty platitudes designed to make him feel better.

"Maybe. It is in his nature to heal the broken."

I was secretly worried that we may be too broken to repair, but I didn't say that out loud. Words spoken had power.

ALEPPO, Syria.

I'd been here several decades before Arcadia had even been born, and even then it had been a city that seemed to tremble on a knife edge. Now it was a ruined shell of humanity, a nightmare of rubble and smoke. Raphael would be here. He was drawn to the places of unimaginable suffering, where the weary had rightly lost their faith.

I had no idea… I mean, I knew, I'd seen the passing news

coverage, but this. I had no idea… she trailed off, and I didn't press her. It was a lot to take in, but I had seen wars. All the Wars of Man since the beginning of time, and the Wars of Heaven and Hell. Not even Luc had a hand in this mess, though. Sure, in the beginning, he'd gotten markers against souls on both sides, but this giant clusterfuck was beyond the dealings of Heaven or Hell. This was strictly the purview of man and their failings.

Memphis shook his head. "There is violence in the air. Something is about to happen." We were both cloaked, our wings held above the ash and dust that littered the ground. I could sense the violent intent in the air. I tilted my head. Air strike.

I looked toward the market across the street, where people still managed to live despite the constant threat of death and destruction.

"I'll get the people, you get the missile."

Memphis nodded, and lifted into the air. You couldn't see anything more than his huge midnight wings as he pushed the missile off course as if it were an annoying insect rather than a piece of equipment that could kill dozens of people. It exploded in the air, shrapnel falling down over the heads of the people in the market. I spread my own wings wide and caught the main flurry of falling steel. I'd miss a little, but a few cuts and bruises were better than death. I hissed against the pain of the debris hitting my wings, but it would all heal instantly.

I stood and shook out my wings as the crowd stared up at the sky. I could hear murmurings of misfiring missiles, and a couple of people praising their deity.

If you guys can stop the missiles, protect the humans, then why doesn't The Big Guy send down more angels to help these people? Arcadia, with her warm, empathetic soul sounded outraged. I understood her rage all too well.

"It is not the purview of heaven to interfere in the quarrels of men, or their results. As Azriel likes to say, balance must be maintained," Memphis spat Azriel's name.

If you interfere in the workings of the world, outside the preordained, you doubt the Father's plans and you fall. It's a small club so far. You've met all four of us. There's not enough of us to make a difference in any war. We'll do what we can, but while we aren't human, we aren't robots either. We would go mad, or become the heartless demons that Humans believe us to be. Gusion is especially sensitive to the needless death and destruction in the world around him. Each death he'd witness, he would also witness the life the person would have had, had they not been a victim of the war in which they died, I explained to Arcadia privately. Memphis had his own reasons for not crusading for the innocents in every war the humans cooked up, and they weren't my reasons to share.

"Let's find a field hospital, that's where Raphael will be," I said, walking past the oblivious humans. Memphis stopped near a child, no more than two, clutched to the shoulder of his mother, and kissed the top of his head. The baby looked around, and then met Memphis's eyes. He gave Memphis the warmest smile, and my heart swelled. I was getting clucky or something. That baby would probably be another tiny shroud wrapped corpse before this was over, but hopefully the kiss of an angel, fallen or not, would help ward off destiny. I kissed his tiny, hollow cheek. Two kisses were better than one.

We walked along the remnants of an avenue toward the outer edge of the city. I could sense Raphael's light, the heavenly beacon still calling me despite my status. Arcadia was quiet, shell shocked.

Memphis looked... worried. "What's wrong?"

He just grunted and pointed to a squat white building. One wall had a blown out hole in it. "He's there."

I reached out and grabbed his arm, halting him.

"What's wrong?"

"I haven't seen Raphael since we fell. His was the last face I saw before we landed in Hell," he mumbled.

"You told me yourself that Raphael is a softie. There's no animosity in his heart."

We stepped into the building, and for all intents it looked abandoned, nothing but a shell with hints at its previous occupants. A cross still hung on the wall. A child's stuff toy lay dirty and forgotten in a corner. But in the dimness of the corner, faint light glowed between the floorboards.

"Down," I mouthed, and looked around for some kind of latch or finger hold to lift the boards. Beneath a roughhewn piece of concrete was a single knothole, and Memphis reached past me to lift the large square of boards that opened to reveal stairs. We could hear voices, and we followed the stairs down to a large open room, with several kerosene lanterns burning and an old wooden table placed in the center. The smell of blood, desperation and hopelessness hit my nose. I lived in hell, I knew the scent of death well. This was the most rudimentary of field hospitals. A last ditch stop before you left the mortal plane forever. A tall man, with nondescript features and a blood soaked button up shirt, was operating on a child. The lower half of the boy's leg was a mess of torn muscle and shattered bone. The kid was thankfully out of it.

"Acerezeal. Michael said you'd probably drop by. Come, I need you to hold these." He waved the handle of a metal clamp at me." He hadn't looked up from his task. I took the clamp which was holding the kid's femoral artery shut. I noticed another boy in the corner, probably not much older than the boy on the table, but he was also covered in blood. Beneath the drying blood though, the boys naturally olive skin was a deathly grey cast.

"Is he okay?"

Raphael gave a humorless laugh. "No one is okay here, Acerezeal. But physically he is unharmed. He pulled Adnan from the rubble and carried him here. His parents are dead, as well as two of his siblings." Finally, Raphael looked at me, and I saw his clear green eyes filled with despair. His eyes flicked to Memphis and he finally smiled. "Mephistopheles. It heals my heart to see you looking so well. Please, soothe Nazir. It would be best if he didn't see me do this procedure on his brother. He has seen enough horror for one day."

Arcadia's gentle sobs became white noise in the back of my mind as I went to work with Raphael, his fingers deft as he pieced the boy back together.

Memphis waved a hand over Nazir's dark head, and the boy fell into a deep slumber. Memphis put him in a pallet in the corner, wrapping him in a heavy woven blanket.

"It is the third day of bombing in the city. Soon there will be nothing left to claim in victory. They will be claiming a country of corpses." There was a thread of steel in Raphael's voice, one that I'd never heard before, even during the angelic wars.

"Do you want us to stay? We could help," I whispered, though I didn't know why. The only people who could hear us were both out of it for the foreseeable future.

Raphael was silent as he used the bone saw to cut away the kids mangled leg just below the knee. We worked quickly to seal off the blood vessels and nerves and sealing the wound with two flaps of skin.

When it was over, Raphael wrapped the leg in dressings, but the kid still looked pale. Blood was being transfused, so he wasn't that deathly white, but he wasn't far off.

"You didn't use any angelic healing," I said, trying, and probably failing, to keep the accusatory tone from my voice.

"No. I'm not meant to be here, in an official capacity that is," he said as he stripped off his blood-stained shirt and threw it in a pile in the corner. He slumped down on a wooden chair near the head of the impromptu operating table. "It's all part of the plan. But it means I can only work with human medical advancements in a rather rudimentary setting. Still, I save as many as I can." He closed his eyes against remembered horrors. "Make your request, Acerezeal. I need a nap."

I knelt at his feet. "We need you to put Arcadia's soul back into her body. She doesn't deserve her fate."

He stroked the hair from my forehead, so he could look into my eyes. "She would live a few more decades at most. With you, she could live for eternity. Is it so necessary to put her back in a failing body?" I nodded vehemently. He stroked a finger down his angular jaw. "Would you have me put Arcadia's soul back at the expense of your own?"

"Yes."

No! Arcadia shouted vehemently.

Raphael smiled. "Michael was right. Your time with Arcadia did redeem you. I thought the Father must have been mistaken. But then, the Father does not make mistakes."

Memphis huffed. "Can you really mean that, with this going on around you?" He indicated the two sleeping boys and the sounds of gunfire and missile blasts in the background.

The smile slipped from Raphael's face. "I do mean that. At times, I don't understand it, but there is a plan. I do what I can, and I must be okay with that." He turned back to me. "I regret that that is also my answer. The Father has made it clear that the fate of your Arcadia is out of our hands. I'm sorry, truly." He seemed genuinely remorseful, and that was the only thing that kept a cap on the simmering rage I felt in my gut. I knew the feeling of helplessness when your hands were tied.

What will happen to the boys? Arcadia asked.

Raphael smiled. "Michael was right about you too, Arcadia Jones." He shook his head. "The boys have no family left. Adnan is only four, Nazir is twelve. They are two of many Syrian orphans that will be cared for by international aid foundations."

I could feel Arcadia's refusal at that sentiment. The boys would not be one in a multitude of orphans, not if she had anything to do about it.

Can Adnan be moved? Teleported or phased or whatever it is you guys do, back to the US? The guys will care for them, Eli will make sure Adnan gets the proper aftercare.

Raphael smiled. "I hope Acerezeal is successful in the quest to return you to your body. The world needs more of you. I will arrange it, the proper legal way. If you are sure?"

He needn't have asked. The Seven would do anything for her, and despite their gruff ways, they were softies too. Except Oz. He didn't even try to hide his gooey center. They'd love the boys and help them heal.

I had my own healing to do first. "If you can't help us, do you know of any way we can get Arcadia back to where she belongs?"

Raphael was silent for a long moment, and the noise momentarily quieted. It felt like Aleppo was holding its breath, waiting for the answer too.

"There are rumors of rituals that can temporarily move a soul from one body to another, but I do not know of anything permanent. The Father can do it of course, as can Michael. Gabriel will not, he is even more steadfast to God's word than I am. He disapproves of my actions here." A tiny quirk of his brow said volumes about Raphael's thoughts on that. "Uriel might be able to, but he would not do so easily."

I rolled my eyes. Uriel was an asshole. He was like Azriel, but worse. He'd been promoted when Lucifer fell, and he had a chip on his shoulder about being the booby prize ever since.

"You know I can't go to Michael."

Raphael nodded sadly. I could tell the rift in angelkind hurt the Archangel, but it was what it was. The universe needed balance. It needed the believers and the non-believers. It needs Angels and Demons. Those that follow and those that question.

"Thanks, Raphael. If you need help with any of this," I waved a hand around the room, with its over-powering stench of blood and antiseptic, "you only have to ask. We will come, won't we Memphis?" I looked at my compatriot, this dark demon of German folklore, who was staring at two small orphans and bubbling with contained rage at the fate that befell them because of greed for power. I knew that's what he was thinking, because that consuming need for vengeance burned in me too.

"Of course."

"The irony of our circumstances is not lost on me, Acerezeal. The people of this city pray daily, but it is the devils who offer to save them. Thank you for your offer, I will keep it in mind, but for now this is my burden to bear." He stood and began wiping down the table.

Memphis and I took our leave, waiting until we were in the bombed out building above to sift back to the landing room in Hell.

CHAPTER THIRTY-FIVE

I needed a nap. I needed to decompress from the turmoil of Raphael's chop shop hospital, preferably in the arms of someone who loved me.

Unfortunately, Luc was off rubbing shoulders with the world's superpowers at the U.N. Summit. I walked into the living room, which was kind of an ironic name for any room in Hell, and flopped down onto an overstuffed couch with a pale blue floral pattern that was completely out of place in this realm. It made me laugh, but damn it was comfy.

Gusion walked in carrying a bundle of herbs that stunk.

"I would like to speak to Arcadia, if she's receiving?" He asked like a nineteenth century gentleman.

Hi Gus, what's up?

"I was looking into your, err predicament, and while I can't find a way to put your soul back in its rightful body, I did find a way for you to spirit walk into someone else's dreams. I found it in a text I received from the wise woman of a tribe of Pictish warriors that ceased to exist long before civilization advanced enough to stop believing in magic."

I loved Gusion. Sometimes you were fooled by his good looks, his charming manner or his manwhore ways, but underneath that was a scholar with a genuine compassion for the plight of man.

That would be so amazing. It's just, I need them, you know? Would Ace be there? No offense Ace, but I'd like to have sex once in my life without you waiting in the wings, filling out scorecards.

Gusion laughed and I winked. I only ever scored them once or twice. Spoilsport.

"Unfortunately, Ace is the link to keeping your spirit on the earthly plane. She goes where you go by necessity, but she is more of a tether than an active participant."

Arcadia sighed dramatically, but I could feel her excitement bubbling inside me. *I can live with that. When can we do this?*

Gus waved around his bundle of greenery like a scepter. "Now, if you'd like?"

Arcadia let out a squeal of delight and I winced. That was not a pleasant noise inside someone else's head. "I think she would like that."

Gus sat next to me, and I swung around so I could lay my head on his thighs. He ran his fingers through my ebony locks, and I resisted the urge to purr.

"Stop making that noise, I have to concentrate," he mock chided. "Otherwise I might turn you into a goat rather than sending Arcadia's spirit anywhere." He grabbed his bundle of herbs, and I noticed golden string tying the bundle at each end. I could smell sage and rosemary, but couldn't identify some of the more pungent scents. One smelled like the river Styx. It wasn't pleasant. He snapped the bundle in half with ease, even though it was probably as thick as my wrist. He wrote an unrecognizable rune on my forehead, and I screwed up my nose as the scents got stronger. Arcadia better appreciate this. Gusion chanted in a dead language that I couldn't decipher, and then I was being tugged out of my body and through the spirit realm at breakneck speed. In a fraction of an instant, we were standing in Eli's bedroom, staring down at his sleeping form.

"Ace?" Cady whispered, and I looked at her. She was whole and in beautiful Technicolor, but still a little off, as dreams have a tendency to be.

"I'm here."

"I can't see you. Or feel you. It's like you're gone."

Huh. This must be what Gus meant about me being a spectator.

"I'm definitely here. Don't worry, I'll just hang outside the door until you're done. Have fun."

Arcadia smiled radiantly. "I will."

I walked toward the doorway and stopped. Not because I wanted to, but because I was physically unable to leave the room. Dammit. Gus was being literal when he said we were tethered.

I went and stood in the corner, between Eli's dresser and the wall. If they couldn't see me, I could at least give them the illusion of privacy. Arcadia climbed into bed with Eli, wrapping her body around his until she resembled a naked jetpack.

"Eli." She ran her fingers down his bicep. "Eli."

Eli rolled over and wrapped his arms around her waist, snuggling his face into the crook of her neck, still sound asleep. Then his eyes slowly opened.

"Arcadia?" He blinked rapidly. "How are you here?" He pulled back so he could see her, every tiny line, and every freckle.

"I'm not really here. Gus sent me into your dreams."

"Gusion? The Prince of Hell?"

Arcadia nodded. "They don't really like being called that, you know."

Back in my hidden corner, I held in a laugh.

Eli reached out and touched her face, his fingers tracing the curve of her cheek. Then he reached out with the other hand and dragged her close to his body, tucking her head beneath his chin. "I thought I'd never get to hold you like this again."

She kissed the hollow of his throat, her hands rubbing soothing circles on his back.

"I've been trying-" Eli started but Arcadia hushed him.

"I know. I know you are doing everything you can. That's not why I'm here. I want you to make love to me, like it might be the last time."

Eli shook his head in denial. "It won't be." His voice was firm, but Cady was gently shaking her head too.

"I know. But let's just savor it anyway, okay?" She tilted her head back for a kiss, and Eli's mouth covered hers with a ferocity that held too much desperation. His hands roamed everywhere, tearing off her imaginary clothes, until there wasn't an inch of her skin that he hadn't stroked.

I was going to give him a ten for enthusiasm that was for sure. I felt bad, voyeuristically staring at them. I turned and faced the corner. I could probably give them that much privacy.

"You promised to tie me up, remember?" Arcadia's husky voice reached my ears.

"I did indeed, Miss Jones."

Well. That changed things. Privacy be damned, I wasn't about to miss Fifty Shades of Doc McBuffins.

I turned around in time to see a length of silk rope appear from thin air. Looks like they were embracing the dream realm.

If only I could magically conjure up some popcorn.

He tied her hands together with the ease of a sailor and secured her to the headboard. Her feet were spread and secured to the end of the bed. I was glad I was off to the side. As much as I was enjoying this, I didn't want to see what she had for breakfast.

Then I watched the good doctor get to work. He slowly teased her body, a rough bite here, a tender whisper of a kiss there, working down her body until she was writhing as he reached the junction of her thighs. Then he stopped, and moved toward the base of the bed. Arcadia whimpered with need.

"I am yours, Miss Jones. Are you mine?"

"Yes." He knelt back on the bed. A finger reached out and circled her clit.

"Only mine?" She hesitated, and he withdrew his fingers.

"Eli…"

Arcadia seemed to be struggling to form coherent sentences.

"In this room, Miss Jones, in this bed, you are all mine. Outside, I can share you with the rest of the world. But here, I am your master, and you are my everything."

He leaned forward and gave her pussy a long, slow lick.

Dirty tactics. I liked it.

"Say it, Miss Jones."

"I'm yours, Eli. Only yours."

"Perfect," his murmur was content, as he slid up her body, and took a nipple in his mouth. He sucked hard as he thrust into her body. She screamed his name.

Then there were no more words, just the soundtrack to vigorous sex. Hmm maybe an eight for technique. But then I'm a little biased. Once you go Luc, you never go... err back? I looked at the ceiling, at Eli's thrusting ass, pushed his change off the dresser just to see if he'd notice and basically killed time until Arcadia was done. But then Eli stopped. Oooh, this was about to get good.

She was whimpering, pulling against the ropes. "You don't get to come, Miss Jones, until I say you can." Acadia frowned grumpily. How adorable. She was still lifting her hips, grinding against Eli trying to change his mind, or at least get his dick to overrule him. Given the way he was sucking in air, it was a good tactic. "Be still, Miss Jones, or I will punish you." But Acadia, bless her heart, would never make a good submissive. She kept straining and grinding until Eli let out a moan. He moved back and untied her feet. "I warned you," he growled, as he flipped her over and dragged her onto her knees. He positioned himself behind her, rubbing his cock over her slit. She let out a long happy moan and then SLAP! Eli's hand connected with her ass as he slid inside her in one hard thrust. He pumped in and out hard, and I was glad we were in the dream plane because the noise of her happy screams would have woken the dead, and even they would be aroused. He slapped her other cheek hard as he came on his own growled yell.

They lay beside each other panting, two glowing handprints like brands on Acadia's ass and I decided I could really use a cigarette. Even though smoking was bad, mmkay.

An uncomfortable tug began to pull at my chest, a little like indigestion, but as this was a dream, it was probably more mystical than my lunchtime burrito.

Our time was up.

I passed on whisper soft feet back to the door and rattled the knob like I was just returning from the hall.

"Arcadia."

She sighed and rolled into Eli's arms.

"I have to go. Tell everyone that I love them. Kiss the babies for me." She kissed him gently, and his eyes were wet. Despite his words, deep down he thought this was it. This would be the last chance he'd get to hold her.

We were drifting out the door, into the swirling nothingness beyond Eli's room. "Oh I forgot, Raphael will be bring-"

We were sucked out of the dream realm with a snap.

My head was on Gus's lap, and he was stroking the silky lengths of my hair rhythmically.

Eli is going to get a surprise when Raphael shows up with the boys, if he hasn't already.

I was resisting the urge to purr like a cat in heat as Gusion's nails scraped gently on my skull with each pass. Mmm.

"Memphis told me what you did for the children of Aleppo. You've changed the course of their lives."

Is that a platitude or a prediction from the Angel of the Past, Present and Future?

Gus chuckled deeply. I always thought his laugh was the most marvelous thing. It was like the rumble of thunder in an electric storm. It made you feel alive.

"A bit of both, Arcadia Jones." He leaned down and kissed me with reverence. "I've enjoyed the ability to stare at your beauty for a few hours. I'd forgotten how magnificent the curves of your face are."

I punched him in the shoulder. "Save the lines for the demonesses, you suave bastard. I just think you watching me sleep is creepy." I batted my lashes at him with faux coyness. "Although, I will take another kiss."

He leaned down and kissed me again, this time with more passion and way more tongue. This was why Gusion fell. No angel should know how to kiss like that.

A throat cleared in the doorway.

"I came to see how your meeting with Raphael went. As you still possess Arcadia's soul in your body and you are currently, as the humans would put it, sucking face with Gusion, I am going to assume it didn't go well." I shrugged and Luc shook his head bemusedly.

"Also, I've had a message from Lux. Apparently Raphael dropped off two small children from a war torn country this afternoon. I assured him that it had nothing to do with me. Does anyone want to explain?"

Uh oh. Busted. Why does this feel like I've been summoned by the Principal?

"Reminds me of this time when Luc bent me over his desk and caned me like a naughty schoolgirl."

Arcadia made a disgusted noise. *All that tells me is that A) you've never been to high school and B) you and Luc watch way too much porn and C) I am going to need a butt load of therapy after this.*

"Ha, butt load. That reminds me of a time when-"

Argh enough! Lucifer, did Lux seem mad?

Luc was barely containing his mirth. He relished making people uncomfortable. He liked it even better when his sexual exploits were the cause of people's uncomfortableness.

"Confused, yes. Mad, no. From when I gathered, Eli had a visit to the dream realm last night and he knew to expect Raphael, but not the reason why." He came over and stroked my face, but didn't try to move me from Gusion's lap. If there was a man more confident in his own appeal, I had yet to meet him. Maybe one of the Greeks, those guys literally had a god who liked to stare at his own reflection.

"Cady is a bleeding heart. She couldn't leave the boys to the subpar medical treatment of a country in turmoil."

Luc smiled. "Careful, my love, or we'll get confused

about which soul is the angelic one come time to divest you of your extra soul."

I rolled my eyes, but maybe Luc was right. My battered old soul would not have thought twice about those boys, beyond saving their lives from the immediate threat. As angels, we become immune to the daily suffering of the individual.

Unlikely. Her heart is bigger than any of you give her credit for, Arcadia argued. Bless her. I was going to miss her.

Luc nodded his head in acquiescence. "Touché, Arcadia Jones." His eyes focused back on my face. "So Raphael was a bust."

I nodded. "Yes. He suggested that Gabriel would be a dead end also. He is all about The Word, that one."

Luc scratched the dark stubble on his jaw. "That leaves Uriel."

"Or Michael," Gusion added, with an obvious lack of care for his physical wellbeing. Fortunately, Luc just ignored him.

"Uriel is in Kentucky."

In the States? Arcadia seemed shocked that an Archangel would be hanging out in Kentucky.

Luc rolled his eyes at her question. "Well, there's no Kentucky in Mongolia, so yes."

Gusion smiled and clapped his hands together once.

"Looks like we are going to Louisville. I'll get my suit!"

CHAPTER THIRTY-SIX

I *can't be the only one who thinks it's weird for an Archangel to hang out at the race track, right?*

People milled around, talking loudly, drinks in their hands and hats a mile wide on their heads. The cacophony almost drowned out the sound of Arcadia in my head.

"It's a den of mortal sin, really. Liars, fornicators, those who have eaten shellfish. Besides, Uriel is…"

"A dick?" Gus so helpfully supplied.

I nodded. That seemed right. Though I did like the excuse to wear my very favorite red silk sheath dress for the first time in two decades. It's true what they say. Chanel never goes out of fashion. I looked like sex wrapped up in a pretty package in this dress, at least that's what Luc whispered in my ear as he kissed me goodbye. By the way the human punters were ogling me, he was probably right. Or maybe it was Gusion, in his perfectly tailored grey morning suit, a matching blood red carnation. His long hair was braided into hundreds of tiny strands and then piled into a man bun on top of his head. He looked hot. Women literally stopped and stared as he walked past, some men too. Hell, if there's been a conveniently shadowy nook, I would have fucked him in an instant. Between us we probably made a few humans question their sexual orientation.

We are on a bit of a time crunch, you know, so if you could stop making fuck me eyes at Gusion, that'd be great.

I realized she could see me in the reflection from the plate glass windows. I poked my tongue out at my reflection and she chuckled.

"Uriel will be in the VIP tent." I knew it for a certainty. Always with the illusions of grandeur, that one.

We threaded our way through the Derby crowd, which was in the thousands. Security didn't even try to stop us as we walked into the roped off VIP tent of some corporation or another. Given the amber liquid being served by snappily dressed men in penguin suits, probably one of the whiskey companies. I spotted Uriel immediately. He wasn't even trying to shield himself. He had flaming red hair, in a shade that was not found in human hair naturally, but might come out of a bottle. His skin was alabaster pale, similar to Gus and my own. Actually, we could all be part of a matching set. Similar, but different. His eyes went straight to mine, and his lip rose in a sneer.

Ugh.

I resisted the urge to turn around and go home. Arcadia needed me to exhaust all avenues, even if the avenue ended in a giant dildo factory like Uriel.

"Ah, if it isn't the B Team. To what do I owe the displeasure of this visit?"

I rolled my eyes. "The Father sent us to see if we can't remove the giant stick from your ass, but I'm pretty sure not even the big guy himself could do that."

Fiery brows lowered. "This isn't the way to garner my aid, Acerezeal. I'd definitely prefer you to beg, I think." His face twisted in a smile. I wanted to punch it.

Screw this. I'll stay with you for eternity before begging this jackass for anything. Let's go, Ace.

I wanted to do as she said, but if I was honest, I would beg if it meant that she got back to where she belonged. But I had a feeling that Uriel was just fucking with us.

"Ah, Luc's Redeemer. You are as disrespectful as Azriel described."

I miss being able to flip the bird.

"Will you help us, Uriel? Without the posturing and grandstanding and the jostling for who has the bigger dick. Just give it to me straight. Will you help?"

Uriel pretended to ponder. "Let me think about it. Hmm. No. I wouldn't lift a finger to help you traitors to the creator, even if you were on hellfire."

Gus scoffed. "What he means is he can't do it. He thinks we are the B Team, but he is Luc's poor substitute. A booby prize. The runner up in the Miss America contest."

Red tinged Uriel's cheeks. "And what of you,

Gusion? What were you? You were just some cheap angel who fell for a daughter of man but was too useless to save her when the time came. You couldn't save her, or her tribe, and now her people are completely forgotten. You won't be able to help this daughter of man either, Gusion. Because you are useless. You were useless as an angel, and now you are useless as a Fallen. You are a waste of celestial power."

Gusion's face blanched. Oh, that was too far. No one, not even Michael himself, got to speak to my loved ones that way. I pulled back my fist and felt a painful satisfaction as my knuckles cracked into his face. Sure, it would heal almost instantly, but I'll have made my point. Plus, he couldn't hit me back. It was against the rules, really. But luckily, I no longer played by the rules.

The Big Guy would be so disappointed in you right now, Uriel. I've only met him once, but even I know he wouldn't condone your words.

True that!

I turned my back on Uriel, and on Arcadia's last chance at getting her soul back where it belonged.

"I'm sorry," Gusion murmured when we'd left the VIP areas, more subdued than I'd seen him in years.

Not your fault, Gus. It'll be okay.

But I heard her voice break, I felt her pain. It wasn't alright. She needed her guys right now, even if she couldn't be with them. The babies would make Gus feel better too. And if I was honest, I needed them as well. I took his hands and we sifted to SoHo.

· · ·

LUC MUST HAVE SENSED SOMETHING, because he was there when we arrived outside the doors to the Sevens apartment building. He was leaning against the wall, his tight, dark jeans doing little to hide the fact he had Mount Dickerest in his pants. He did that slow, judging appraisal thing he does when he's analyzing a situation, or weighing up a soul.

"Uriel said no?"

I nodded, and entwined my fingers in his as we walked into the apartment. Arcadia was eager to see her men. And her babies. I hustled my guys into the lift and pressed the button to Oz's floor. Call it a hunch.

We knocked on the door, polite like, as if it wasn't as easy as breathing for us to just appear in any room in this apartment. Ri opened it, his face drawn and haggard, white colored spit up staining his black shirt.

His eyes lit up when he saw me. "Ace! Do you have good news?"

Ah shit. Maybe this wasn't such a good idea. Now I felt guilty on all fronts.

I just shook my head sadly. As Orion's face fell, the combination of everyone's sadness, Ri's, Arcadia's and my own, threatened to sink me. Luc and Gus both placed a hand on my back, Gusion on the curve of my spine and Luc's just above the slope of my ass. I felt their love, and their resilience through their touch, and it bolstered me.

Hug him for me. He needs it, Arcadia said softly. We all did. I stepped out of the grasp of my guys, and wrapped my arm around one of Arcadia's Sins. The tension in his body thrummed against my angelic senses, and his pain, his guilt, was overwhelming. So I did something that I hadn't done in years. Long before I lost my body, not since I fell. I sent some of my angelic light into his body to soothe him.

"She wants to be here," I whispered in his ear. He nodded and pulled back. His face held less strain, but I couldn't chase away all the sadness.

"Come on in. The babies came home yesterday. We are adjusting." He pointed to the spit covered shirt. "Plus, Eli has been gone all day with your little surprise delivery."

"Don't blame me. It was all your Lady Loves idea." I followed behind him as he walked into the apartment. He gave Luc and Gus a cursory glance.

How can they be home already? It was a rhetorical question. We could both felt time slipping through our fingers. Both babies were asleep in the one cot, and I reached out to trace a line down Hope's tiny cheek. Her eyes fluttered open and she stared into my eyes, deep down into my soul. To her mother.

Hello, my Sweet One, Arcadia cooed. Her tiny pink lips formed an O, and she gurgled softly, like she didn't want to wake her sister.

"Memphis was correct, they are something special," Luc said from behind me. Hope's face changed, turning into a frown as she tried to discern where the voice came from. Luc stepped forward to peer into the cot. Hope stared at the Devil with a concentration that belied her twenty-one day old age. She should be asleep, or eating, or pooping, but instead she was taking the measure of Lucifer's soul.

She'd managed to unswaddle a single arm, and she reached toward Luc. He reached into the cot, and Hope wrapped her tiny hand, no bigger than Luc's thumbnail, around his finger.

Luc laughed with delight. Such a pure happy sound, something I hadn't heard from him in centuries. Sure, we laughed a lot, but there was always a dark undertone of bitterness or sarcasm. This was just pure joy.

"I am so happy to meet you too, Little Hope," he whispered softly.

Is the baby talking to him? Arcadia sounded equal parts aghast and jealous.

Luc just raised an eyebrow. "Of course not. She is an infant, she does not have language yet. But she sent me a wave of happiness, and I took that to mean she likes me."

Hope's eyes fluttered closed, and we crept out of the nursery.

Where's everyone else?

I repeated Arcadia's question out loud to Ri.

"Not here, thank god. If Lux had seen Luc reach into the cot, he would have lost his shit. The guy has gone into super watchdog mode since the babies came home yesterday. He's like Robocop or something." He flopped down on the couch, putting his head back on the headrest and closing his eyes. "Eli, Tolliver and Sam have taken the boys to get checked out. Nazir looks fine, but hasn't said a word since he arrived. Adnan is pretty perky for a kid that just had his leg blown off. Eli said that Raphael did a good job given the circumstances of the surgery. It's healing nicely, and the kid is already a superstar on crutches, considering that it's been only a couple of days. Lux is at your bedside. Valery is at work. Oz has gone to get groceries. And they left me to babysit. The most unqualified one."

I shrugged. "They were both asleep and breathing when we got here, I'm pretty sure that makes you qualified. Congratulations Daddy-o."

Ri looked like he'd been electrocuted. "What?" I asked, looking at my hands just in case I'd developed the ability to shoot lightning bolts from them. It was possible. Stranger things have happened this week alone.

His brow wrinkled. "It didn't occur to me that I kinda am. I mean, not biologically of course, but I'm kinda their dad. It just seems so unreal without Cady, you know? Like I couldn't be their dad unless she was here, tying us all together. We all know Oz is biologically their father, but I can be their dad too."

I resisted the urge to smack my forehead and say, "duh". I was saved by an unholy caterwauling cry from the bedroom. Instinctively, I ran into the babies' room, ready to slay any threat, my sword already in my hand. Luc swaggered in behind me at a leisurely pace. There was no threat, unless the threat of a hungry belly counted.

Estrella was awake, her little face scrunched mid-cry as she looked around at the strangers in the room. Then she looked at my sword, fascinated. I put it away, making it invisible at my side again. Her face scrunched back up and she howled the most awful noise I'd ever heard, way worse than the wailing of the demonesses.

Panicking, I drew my sword again, and she stopped. Huh.

Gusion was laughing his ass off. "Arcadia is going to have some serious problems with that one." Luc was laughing too as he made a tiny stuffed sword appear from nowhere. It looked like mine, but baby safe. Estrella took the sword in her tiny hands, admiring it. The she put the end in her mouth and gummed it.

"We'll have a talk about sword safety when you're older. Rule one though, don't eat your sword."

I made my own weapon disappear again, and this time there was no high pitched yowl.

Hope just looked on, unaffected by her sister's theatrics.

Gusion came over, and reached down to touch Hope's head. I held my breath, as did Arcadia. I didn't know if his power would work on the babies, being the strange mix of human and angel that they were, but I was nervous all the same.

Gusion's face folded into a frown. He reached across and placed the other hand on Estrella's head. And then he laughed. A loud, booming, joyful laugh.

He looked at me, a smile wide on his face. "We are all in so much trouble. These two will be a handful. But I see them living long, happy lives filled with adventure. Estrella especially will give you a few grey hairs. Hope…" He bit his lip, looking off into the distance. "Hope will change things for us. She will tread roads that no human has. She'll change the status quo."

I stared down at my tiny Hope, no bigger than my forearm.

I'm not sure if Gusion's premonitions make me feel better or worse, Arcadia whispered.

I didn't either. Part of me wanted the babies to grow up and live nice, boring lives with a husband and two kids and a career they liked. But I guess I'd doomed them to a life of the extraordinary.

CHAPTER THIRTY-SEVEN

W e hung around until all of Arcadia's Seven returned home. I hadn't seen them all in the same room since I told them that she was dead. At Arcadia's request, I hugged each and every one of them. They all looked haggard. Like attractive zombies. I guess redemption, and the inevitable human frailty that came with it, had its downsides.

Eli, Sam and Tolli arrived home with the two little boys. Orion had been right about them. Adnan, the littlest one, raced around on crutches speaking too fast in his native language and bumping into things. He didn't look like the kid on death's door literally days ago. He also didn't speak a scrap of English, but the guys made do with an elaborate game of charades.

"Mac'n'cheese!" he yelled. I lied. He spoke one word of English. I sat on the couch between Luc and Gus, holding Hope in my arms.

The rest of the guys say across from me except Valery, who was making the aforementioned Mac.

"So that's it? We are out of options?" Tolliver asked, his tone angry.

"Essentially yes." I was prepared for their wrath. This was my fault.

We've tried. They know that.

"That's unacceptable," Lux growled. "It is unacceptable that she will never hold her children, or those who love her ever again. There must be another way."

Arcadia sniffled in my mind.

"What happens now?" Eli asked. He was the only one who didn't look like he'd run a marathon, because he wasn't yet redeemed.

"Her soul stays with me until her body dies. When that connection is lost, she will ascend to heaven."

I don't want to go to heaven with the likes of Uriel and Azriel. I'd rather stay with you guys.

Luc scoffed. "You know not what you say. You aren't a Fallen. You wouldn't be in the palace."

"Why couldn't she be?" I asked. "You are the Lord of Hell. She can go wherever you send her. She's as sin free as you can get in the age of Tinder and Hedge Funds."

Luc gave me a disapproving glance and I resisted the urge to kiss the look from his face. "That is not the agreement. It is not how the division of souls works."

I looked toward the corner where Nazir watched me intently. I had a feeling he remembered me from that room, and although he hadn't spoken to me yet, I was interested to see how much he comprehended about what went on down in that blood soaked room.

I stood and walked over to the boy. He watched me

with dark eyes that were older than they had any right to be.

"Hey, Nazir."

The boy just slow blinked.

"Do you remember me?" A nod. "Are you afraid of me?"

He paused this time, thinking hard. None of that childish bravery that demanded everyone knew he wasn't scared of anything. He'd known real fear. Finally, he shook his head.

"That's good. You have no need to be scared of me. Do you know what we are?"

This time his long lashes lowered as he frowned. "Angels," he whispered.

Hmm, well kinda. I wouldn't overwhelm him with the semantics. "I was once. But I will never hurt you, and these guys," I pointed at the men around the room, "they will care for you and Adnan, and love you if you let them, as long as you need them, or forever. Whichever comes first. Do you understand?" Another nod and I gave him a smile. "Do you want to see my wings?" He cast a look at Luc, who had a kind of scary aura, even when he was trying to be as nonthreatening as possible. "Don't worry about him. He's a big pussy cat." I threw Luc a saucy grin and his raised eyebrow promised retribution. "Okay, ready?"

I spread my soft grey wings wide in the room, thankful for the open plan of the apartment. Nazir's eyes lit up and he reached out to touch them before stopping himself. "You can touch," I smiled as Adnan barreled toward me from where he was playing with

Oz's LEGO in the corner. He was going so fast that he tripped on his crutches and I had to catch him with my left wing, curling it gently around his body to cushion his fall.

"Look, Naz, an angel. Her wings are so soft and she's so pretty. Do you think she'd let me have a feather? Eli said when I get my new leg I'll be able to run like the wind. Do you think he could get me wings too?" I laughed, and realized I'd switched my speaking to Arabic.

"I'm not sure if you'll be able to have wings, but there are plenty of other ways to fly."

"Even with one leg?"

"There is nothing you can't do, even with one leg," I replied.

The boys stroked my feathers a bit more, and then Adnan looked at Luc and Gus. "Are they angels too?"

I nodded. "They were once."

"The big one is scary." The kid had good instincts.

"Yeah he is, but he shouldn't be scary to you. You're a good kid, you have nothing to fear."

Adnan took me at my word and raced his way over to Luc and Gus.

"Can I see your wings?"

"No," Luc said, and I sent him my best 'do it if you ever want to get laid again' look. "Fine."

He stood and spread his onyx wings as wide as the room allowed. His wingspan was bigger than mine, given his status. Not even Adnan dared to touch them, which confirmed he had good survival instincts. Luc tucked them away again and sat back down.

Gusion was more than happy to spread his wings, because he was a show off and they were truly beautiful. White with threads of gold, they shimmered in the sunshine. The colored wings were something we got when we fell. Normal angels have pure white wings. Archangels have white wings with silvery flight feathers. Even after all this time we hadn't been able to ascertain why we all got the colors we did.

Gusion plucked out a silver feather. "You will both grow to be good men. Do not be afraid to feel. Your loved ones would want you to be happy again." He directed this at Nazir, whose eyes welled up before he blinked rapidly. He didn't acknowledge Gusion's words, and I could only hope they both took them to heart.

They need a mother. Arcadia was right, but I was in no position to be a mother figure.

"Where's Clary?" I asked.

"She went home for a funeral. Great Uncle Seamus died last week. She thought it would be okay while the babies were still in hospital to see her family and tell them about Arcadia as well. Apparently they are quite fond of her. She should be back tomorrow, now the babies have been released and Seamus is in the ground," Oz said.

Aw not Uncle Seamus. He was such a nice old man.

Luc scoffed again. "Guess it depends on your definition of nice. He was an enforcer for the Mulligans for decades. The true miracle is that he lived to 85."

He was nice to me, anyway. He used to tell me stories about growing up in Ireland and all their folk stories.

"There is good and bad in everyone, Arcadia Jones. Even in you."

Balance, as Azriel so aptly put it, was the center of all things and must be maintained.

"Can we get back on topic?" Sam asked.

Seriously, he even makes scruffy look good. Like some kind of Nordic Lumberjack. I'd give anything to kiss him again.

"Me too. I mean, for you to kiss him again. Even scruffy, he's still too pretty for me."

Sam looked confused and Arcadia laughed. He shook his head. "What do we do about getting Arcadia home?"

I shrugged. "I've exhausted all my options."

I looked at Lucifer, my one true love in this world, the other half of my soul, and gave him the stink eye. Gusion stared at him too, until he sighed.

"There is one more option, but just know I hate you all." He stood, his demeanor getting icier by the second. "I'll go and see Michael myself."

I handed the baby to Gusion. He wasn't going anywhere without me. With a clap of thunder that scared the kids and woke the babies, we left.

He always had to make a dramatic exit.

ONE OF THE perks of being an Archangel is that they always knew where the others were. They knew where all of angelkind were. Where they gathered, if they were injured, all of these things flooded the Archangel's psyche every day. They weren't quite as omniscient as the Father, but close. It was no wonder they were all a little kooky in my opinion. Luc was no exception, but luckily he let his freak flag fly. It was the ones that were buttoned down that were the problem.

Michael was in his Cathedral. Luc and I stood on the steps, unable to go past the heavy wooden doors, or even look through the beautifully rendered stain glass windows. We could not step foot on the hallowed ground.

"Michael knows we are here," Luc muttered under his breath.

"Of course, old friend. I always know when you leave your domain and come to earth." A voice said from behind us.

I saw Luc tense, resisting the urge to whip around. Instead he turned with slow deliberateness, as if Michael was no threat to us. Well, he wasn't, not anymore, but the large scar on his chest said that he hadn't always been this harmless.

Luc met his eyes.

"Michael."

"Lucifer Morningstar. I have missed you." Michael had no artifice on his face. He looked like the pleasant man Cady had met at the Lego store. "Acerezeal. You are a sight for sore eyes. Come," he beckoned me closer. I went. You didn't turn down Michael's requests, no matter how congenial he seemed. He cupped both my cheeks, his face shining with genuine happiness. "Ah, Arcadia is here too," he said, looking past me.

It is nice to see you again, sir.

"Psh. Michael, if you please." He looked toward

Lucifer. "Shall we sit?" He indicated a park bench under an old oak tree.

We followed behind the Archangel, and you could see the warrior in his stance. In the corded muscles of his back, in the way he held his wings poised. The way he accommodated for the Sword of Heaven at his side. He radiated power. We sat down on the bench, and I perched on the fence a few feet away.

"They all refused your request then?"

Lucifer nodded. "Despite her worthiness, none were willing to defy God's word."

Michael nodded sadly. "I did not think they would. Though I wondered if perhaps Raphael would. He is going through a period of doubt, as we all do from time to time, though he never voices this. It would break the Father's heart to have another of his Archangels fall. He still laments your loss, daily."

Luc gave a non-committal grunt.

I went and knelt at Michael's knee. A sign of respect that we afforded all Archangels. I still knelt at Luc's knee, but usually he wasn't wearing pants and my mouth was busy.

Seriously? You are thinking about that now? Givin-

I interrupted her. *Everyone can hear your thoughts. Zip it.*

Both Luc and Michael looked amused. I can only imagine what they thought she was about to say. I looked at Michael, and then bowed my head in reverence.

"Archangel. Would you consider righting this wrong? She does not belong in the body of an angel, but she does not deserve for her life to be cut short either. Please," I begged. I wasn't above begging anymore.

Michael looked to Lucifer, although he put a finger beneath my chin to lift my face. "Stand, Acerezeal. Lucifer. Do you request this also?"

Luc nodded. "There is little I wouldn't do for Acerezeal, as you know."

Michael's lips twisted into a smile. "Indeed."

Luc was unapologetic. "And I feel that Arcadia has been caught up in something she had no control over. Her fate was not preordained, it has no use in the Wheel of Fate. She needs to be returned to live out her life."

Michael looked out into the distance. It was a perfect day. The sun was shining, and everything seemed to be teeming with life. I watched his face as he contemplated. Then he shrugged. "Okay."

He punched a fist toward my chest. The pain was incredible as Arcadia's soul was torn from my body.

ACE!

Then Arcadia was gone. I stood, looking around to see if her soul was ascending, but it was gone. She was just gone.

"What did you do!"

Michael shook his head sadly. "What you asked. I put her soul back in her body. Her fate is once again up to human medicine. But if she dies, there is no last minute deals with the Devil this time. She dies, she goes straight to heaven. I will not be tested again." His face turned from serene to scary.

Scary Michael was just as terrifying as Lucifer on a bad day. No one wanted that shit.

Still, Arcadia was back in her body. I threw myself in Michael's arms. "Thank you. I know that this was a more difficult decision than you let on," I whispered in his ear.

He squeezed me back. "I owed her one for returning you to the light, even if you chose to stay down in that cesspool of sin with Lucifer." He was smiling, and there was no malice in his words. He was...teasing me? Today was a weird ass day all around.

Luc stood, moving towards us. "I owe you one, Michael."

Michael appraised him much in the same way Luc appraised others. "Yes. I may collect one day. But then, maybe not. It is not good to make deals with the Devil, no?"

They shook hands as I bounced on my toes. I needed to see if Michael was telling the truth. Not that I thought he was lying, but I needed to see it for myself.

Michael laughed. "I know, I know. Off you go now. Tell Arcadia I shall be by to see her sometime. Maybe I'll bring her flowers. That's the human gesture, isn't it?"

I laughed and waved as I sifted to the hospital.

Some of my good humor seeped away when I got to the hospital and saw her lying there in the hospital bed. She still looked grey and small against the white sheets, as close to death as you could get while still making the heart monitor beep. All her hair had fallen out and she had tubes and cables hooked up to nearly every part of her body.

Eli was at her bedside, his hand wrapped in hers.

"Eli." He turned at the sound of my voice. "I did it."

He stood, the hard plastic chair scraping against the linoleum floor. "She's back in there?"

I strode forward, putting my hands on her head. She was in a hazy dream land, her consciousness not as alert as it had been inside me. She was comatose, but her soul was in her body.

"Yes. She's in there. We did it."

Eli's smile slipped. "You did it. I've failed."

That was when I noticed his red rimmed eyes.

"What's wrong?"

"She's dying."

CHAPTER THIRTY-EIGHT

"Well, duh. She's been dying most of her life. You are meant to be fixing her," I tried to keep the sarcasm out of my voice, but failed. It was weird not having Arcadia there, in my head, chastising me for my harsh words, or trying to get me to soothe Eli's obviously wounded heart.

"I can't find her a heart. Oz insisted that she would hate getting one from the black market, and no matter who we bribe, we can't get her to the top of the list. She has an uncommon blood type which is making it hard to match her. The cancer is responding too slowly to the chemo and it's going to come down to taking the risk on whether her body can take it if we operate too early or with a make-up heart. A gamble. The life of my love rests on a gamble. Too soon and she dies. Too late and she dies. I just can't."

Dude was spiraling. I didn't know what to do. WWAD? What would Arcadia do? I was probably going to hell for that one.

Whoops, too late.

"You will do it. You have to. I will help. Clary will help. The guys will help. You aren't in this alone." Ergh. Probably not quite as empathetic as I should be. "You need to go home. Take a break. Have a shower, because you smell like old feet. Then we'll make a plan. I'll stay here with her so she isn't alone."

I didn't want to tell him that I was feeling a little weird without her. We'd been two halves of a whole for so long. He nodded and left, and I moved his chair back towards the bed. I touched her head, now devoid of hair, and ran my thumb over her temple. I wanted to rely on modern medicine, on Eli's medical knowledge and Tolliver's money. I wanted to have faith. But I didn't. I closed my eyes and laid my head on the edge of her bed.

"I'm sorry," I mumbled against her shoulder. "This is all my fault. If it hadn't been for me and my big mouth, my inability to follow any rules, you wouldn't be in this position. Sure, you might have been a bank teller with a drinking problem, but your life and death would have been of your own making."

I sighed and let my thoughts roll around and around in my head until I fell asleep. That was how Memphis found me. Sleeping alone for the first time in twenty years.

I WOKE UP IN HEAVEN. Well, it was actually hell, but I was surrounded by the naked bodies of three extremely attractive fallen angels, and if that wasn't heaven, what was?

We were in Luc's bed, and the man himself was acting as my pillow. Somehow Gusion was asleep on my thigh, my other leg thrown over his ribs. He was literally five inches from giving me a very good morning.

Memphis was next to me, his hand on my hip. When I looked up into his face, I realized he was awake too.

"Hey," I whispered, and it came out rougher, sexier, than I'd intended.

"Good morning, Acerezeal." With his eyes hooded like that, his hair all tousled, he looked delicious.

"Did you bring me home?"

He nodded. I moved my head off of Luc's and scooted closer to Memphis. I pressed myself closer to him, my chest against his. "Thank you."

He shrugged, then kissed me. It was so unlike him that I was momentarily shocked. I mean, we'd had sex numerous times before, but I always initiated. Always made the first move. It made me wonder what had changed.

"I'll always bring you home, Acerezeal." His deep voice was weird, and I pulled back a little to take in his face.

"What's going on right now? Have you been body snatched or something?" Seriously, I was confused.

A small smile curved his lips.

Yep, it was official. He was possessed. I leaned back and jabbed Luc in the ribs.

"Wake up, there's something wrong with Memphis."

Luc opened one eye. He looked between us both and closed it again.

"He looks fine to me, my love. Call me if he starts bleeding from the ears."

Memphis's body began to shake as he held in a laugh. A fucking laugh.

"Seriously, Luc. He's laughing now. And smiling. Gus wake up, there's something wrong with Memphis."

I jiggled my leg and Gus sat up. His abs flexed and light blonde hair pointed its way down to his morning wood. I almost swallowed my tongue, but then Memphis laughed out loud again and brought me back to my point.

I pointed at him. "See!"

Luc opened both eyes and stared at Memphis. Then he closed them again and sighed. "He's just happy, Ace. Go back to sleep."

My mouth swung open. "When is Memphis anything but dark and brooding? Have I missed something?"

Gus climbed up my body, bracketing me with his arms. He leaned down, his body pressing into mine, his nose pressed against my nose.

"Everything has changed, Ace. It's a brave, new world. You'll see."

Then he kissed me, and I momentarily forgot about how strange they were all acting as I pulled his body close to mine, raising my hips to grind against the hardness of his cock.

"Wet already? We've only just started." He made a mock disapproving sound as he headed down my body toward the V of my thighs. I looked at Luc and he was watching on with a hot look in his eyes.

As Gus buried his face between my thighs, Memphis leaned over me, catching my gasps with long, hot kisses. His hand reached up and ran along my ribs, moving over to cup my breast. He bent down and sucked my captured nipple into his mouth, and I bucked against the sensation of their mouths working in unison.

Gus's tongue swirled and flicked, teasing my clit until I was soaking his face with my juices. Memphis moved on to my other breast, and I wrapped my fingers in his long dark hair to hold on for dear life.

I threw a desperate look at Luc as my orgasm built. "Please."

He leaned over, kissing me then biting me firmly on my lower lip. "You're going to come all over Gusion's face aren't you, my love?"

His words pushed me over the edge, and my body was helpless to resist fulfilling his words. I came on a banshee scream, but they weren't done yet.

Luc reached out and dragged me onto his body, not giving me time to adjust before he was sliding his cock into me, filling me. I moaned his name as he held my hips, thrusting hard and shooting waves of pleasure all over my body as I rode him.

I looked over my shoulder as someone settled behind me. Gusion dipped his fingers in my wetness, than ran it up to circle my ass. He slid a finger inside and I let out a guttural moan of pleasure. He slid it in and out in time with Luc's thrusts, stretching me until he could replace his finger with his cock. Luc stopped, his control absolute, as Gus slid in inch by inch, until I was completely filled by the two of them. Luc held me still, even after my arms collapsed, as they moved in synchronization. One in, one out. In, out, in, out until I lost all sense of reason and orgasms crashed into me one after another. I screamed their names, clenching hard until Gus let out his own guttural yell, coming on hot, hard thrusts.

He collapsed to the side as Luc continued to pound me, his movements getting uncoordinated as he got closer to his own ending. Finally, he slammed my hips down, burying himself deep inside me, growling my name over and over as he came.

I collapsed on his chest, breathing heavily. But there was no rest for the wicked. Memphis lifted me gently off of Luc chest, and placed me back on the bed.

I stared up into his heated dark eyes. "I'm not sure I can go again," I whimpered pathetically.

He brushed my hair back from my sweat covered forehead. "I know you can."

He kissed my mouth softly, then on both cheeks, down my neck and across my collar bones. He kissed every inch of me with soft reverence, like he was memorizing the sensation of my skin, cataloguing my responses.

I mewled when he reached my breasts, kissing and sucking them with tenderness. His hand traced over my hip, the curve of my stomach, dipped into my navel.

"Are you ready for me, Acerezeal?"

I nodded as he settled between my thighs, placing one of my legs over his shoulder. Then he slid home in one controlled, firm thrust. Then another.

That had always been Memphis's way. Slow, deliber-
ate, and ridiculously thorough until you were a
screaming mess and he was an instrument of pleasure.
Each stroke hit my g-spot every single time, and I was
clawing at his arms trying to keep myself anchored, so I
didn't shatter and blow away on the next orgasm.

"Memphis!" My yell echoed around Luc's bed
chamber as I came again, but still, Memphis wasn't
finished. He hooked my other leg over his shoulder,
settling into me deeper and hitting spots that made my
eyes roll back in my head and my moans turn in to feral
noises. "Oh fuck, oh fuck, I'm going to come again," I
panted, and Memphis upped his pace.

"Come with me," he growled, his movements getting
faster and faster. My pussy clenched around him as I
held back my orgasm, waiting for his word.

"Now," he grunted and I let myself slip over the
edge, wave after wave of pleasure kicking my ass.

I was wrung out.

Gus got me a drink of water and a washcloth,
cleaning up the combined fluids running down my
thighs. I raised my eyebrows in thanks and he blew me a
kiss. I couldn't do words right at the minute.

Silently, we all laid back down in bed, and dozed off
into a satisfied sleep.

Something was different, I just didn't know what.

CHAPTER THIRTY-NINE

The second time I woke in a bed surrounded by sexy fallen angels, I refused to be tempted by hot bodies and hard cocks. I had shit to do, and being down here in hell with its wobbly laws of time wasn't going to help.

I stretched, rubbing my butt against someone's groin and petted the abs of whoever I was curled around. Given the blonde hair, probably Gusion.

I sat up and crawled out of bed on my hands and knees.

"I can see you have somewhere to be, but you should be careful of waving such a delectable ass in my face. I might just lock you away in my dungeon and have my way with you whenever I please," Luc murmured huskily.

I blew him a kiss from the end of the bed. "I've been to your dungeon, lover, and I can't wait to go again."

I looked at my imaginary watch. Probably time to hustle. With one last blown kiss, I had the world's quickest shower and headed up top, straight to Arcadia's hospital bed.

It was weird without her. No one was in her hospital room, which was odd. Then I realized it was 4:20am. I shouldn't be here either. But I didn't want to leave.

Memphis sifted in behind me, and he came up and wrapped an arm around my shoulders. He didn't give me meaningless platitudes about how it would all be fine. I loved that about him.

I rested my head against his shoulder. "What's going on with you?"

I hadn't forgotten his weird behavior.

"Gusion had a premonition for me."

I was so shocked I pulled away. "What? Gus doesn't have premonitions about other angelkind."

He shrugged. "He seemed pretty certain."

"What was the premonition?" I was desperate to know. If Gusion could make correct predictions about other angels, then it really would change everything.

"He said I would know a love as deep as my love for…" he went silent and I squeezed his forearm. We didn't talk about her. The reason he fell. The reason he is now the man he is.

"Anyway, he said I'd know that kind of love again. And I'm ready for that. But I wanted to feel you one last time. To make you happy one last time, before I waited for the person I will love."

My heart felt a little bruised, but happy too. What an oxymoron. Or maybe I was just a moron. But I loved Memphis. Not the way I loved Luc, but more than you would love a friend. A love that comes with knowing someone intimately.

"She better be worthy of you, otherwise I'm going to kick her ass. And it better not be Baccy!"

Memphis laughed, and even though it was just a premonition of a possibility, I was happy for him.

I looked back at Arcadia and horror dawned on me. "It's not Arcadia, is it?"

Memphis laughed. "Gusion didn't say. But I do not think it is Arcadia."

I let out a sigh of relief. "Thank goodness, because I'm pretty sure her snatch is at max capacity."

Plus she might not survive. That would be doubly heartbreaking. I didn't need another of Arcadia's lovers looking at me with accusing eyes.

The door to Arcadia's room opened and a huge bunch of flowers walked into the room. Seriously, it must have been three feet wide. The flowers walked to the nightstand, revealing Clary, who jumped two feet in the air when she saw us.

"Who are you?" she snarled, going into full honey badger mode, putting herself between us and the bed. I loved Clary. Both Memphis and I must have both topped her by a foot, and Memphis was scary as fuck, but she was still ready to take us on singlehandedly.

It occurred to me that we had never met in person. "I'm Ace. This is Mephistopheles."

"Ace? As in Cady's Ace?" I nodded and flashed my wings for a second.

"And this is the Mephistopheles?" He nodded. "Huh. That never gets less weird."

I laughed. She was the shiz. "Sorry to hear about Uncle Seamus. He was one of my favorites."

"Because he boozed, cracked skulls and woman-ized?" she asked, arching an eyebrow primly.

"Pretty much. He had the best stories."

Clary opened her mouth to reply, then hesitated. "Is Uncle Seamus…?" She pointed toward the floor.

"In the gift shop?" She scowled and I laughed. "He is almost definitely in Hell. Trust me when I say that's as much as you wanna know."

She went over to Arcadia and settled her in the bed, her gentle yet firm grasp repositioning Arcadia to prevent sores, fluffing pillows and making her as comfortable as possible.

I watched on as Clary fussed over her best friend. They were both such great examples of the capacity humanity had for good.

"Eli told me you managed to get her soul restored. It's how it should be." She sat down on the hard plastic chair as if she were defeated. Perhaps she was.

"You talk as if she isn't going to recover." I sounded more accusing than I intended.

She heaved a sigh. "I've seen a lot of death. I some-times feel like I'm part Banshee. I can smell it. She's gonna die if something big doesn't happen soon." She wrapped her fingers in Arcadia's and I could see her facade cracking. She would hate crying in front of strangers, I knew that much from my years as her pseudo-bestie. I reached over and squeezed her shoulder.

"Don't lose faith yet, Clary Mulligan. We have a lot of fight left in us; me, you and Arcadia."

With that, I left her to her grief.

We sifted to the apartment to find it in chaos. There were babies crying, Adnan was howling hysterically and Nazir was standing over him, teeth bared. It was barely seven a.m.

"What the hell…?"

Lux was trying to get Nazir out of the way, as Eli attempted to get to the crying Adnan. Oz held Estrella, rocking, and was using the other hand to soothe Hope.

"Enough!" I boomed, taking a page out of Luc's books. The room went still, even the babies stopped crying, for about two seconds. Memphis went over and picked up Hope, and the baby instantly calmed. Once her sister stopped crying, Estrella settled in Oz's arms. I strode over to the other occupants in the room.

"What's going on?" I asked in a calm voice.

Eli stood beside me, his voice just as neutral. "Adnan tripped on his crutches and opened the wound slightly on his leg. Nazir saw the blood and is having a moment of PTSD and won't let us near him. I don't have any sedation here, and I don't want to manhandle the boy."

I nodded. I took in the wide-eyed feral look in Nazir's eyes. He wasn't in an apartment in SoHo. He was somewhere much worse.

I pushed some of my angelic light toward him. "Be still, Nazir. Eli is going to fix Adnan." I reached out and touched his head, and his body slumped on contact. Lights out. Lux caught the boy before he hit the ground. He picked him up as if he weighed nothing and cradled the boy with gentleness that belied his rough exterior. I noted the bite marks and crescent gouges in his arms. He walked down the hall to the boy's bedroom.

Adnan was still sobbing, but it was probably more from fear than pain.

"Hey now, tough guy. It's okay." Eli lifted him up and set him on the bench. "It's not too bad at all. We'll just put some stickers on it and cover it back up."

Eli went to work, and I stroked Adnan's dark hair. Poor little guy. Eventually, he nodded off to sleep too. "Whoops. Must have still had a little juice in the tank," I said, as he listed to the side. Eli caught him up and walked him down the hall on silent feet. The boys shared the second bedroom.

A minute later he crept back down the hall and flopped onto the couch. "Who's with Arcadia?"

Lux handed him a beer, then gave one to Oz and Memphis. "Clary's there. Just got back from Boston." He offered one to me. "It's not even eight in the morning." Lux raised an eyebrow. He made an excellent point. I took the beer.

"Where's everyone else?" I asked. We all needed to talk.

"Ri is at the bar, Valery has gone to chase down some weird medicinal herb that he is sure will cure her cancer according to the Internet, but Eli will veto immediately. Sam and Tolliver are hiring a management team to take care of the foundation while we figure this whole thing out," Oz said, sucking down half his beer in one gulp.

Lux's phone rang. I didn't need angelic hearing to pick up Clary's frantic words.

"She's crashing!"

I'D NEVER SIFTED with three humans before, but we had no time to waste. Memphis offered to stay with the kids, and it was a testament to Lux's fear that he didn't even protest.

I sifted us into a supply closet, and the effort made my knees buckle. Lux and Eli were out the door in a flash, but Oz bent down and hoisted me to my feet, a hand around my ribs keeping me on my feet as we ran towards Arcadia's room. The doctor was there with the crash cart, trying to shock her heart back to life, the eerie whine of her machine threatening to break my world apart.

"Clear!"

The thumping pulse of electricity hitting her chest rocked me. But it was followed by the modulated beeping of her heartbeat on the monitor.

I released the breath I was holding. And Oz. I hadn't realized I was clutching his forearm like a lifeline. It was a wonder I didn't snap his arm.

The doctor spoke in a low voice to the nurses, before turning toward our fragile little group. He placed a hand on Eli's shoulder. "It's too late, my friend. There is no time left to wait for a viable organ."

Lux growled a low, ominous sound. "She can have mine."

Eli shook his head. "It doesn't work like that. Besides I had us all tested. None of us would be a match."

The doctor had on his warm compassionate mask. "It's time to say goodbye."

With that, he left us alone with Arcadia. Clary went back over, and straightened her skewed gown, placed a pillow back under her head.

Eli walked over and laid his head on her chest. And cried. He cried until his body shook with the force of his sobs.

"I'm sorry, I'm sorry, I'm sorry," he just repeated it over and over. "I wasn't enough. I couldn't save you, no matter what I did, and I'm sorry. I couldn't believe that there wasn't something I couldn't do, that your death was preordained. My fucking pride wouldn't let me believe that and now I failed you and I'm so fucking sorry." The force of his pain tore at my skin, at my soul.

Lux sat in the chair and covered his face with his hands, letting out a feral sound of pain that was only partly muffled by his palm.

Clary was surprisingly calm. She moved to Oz and took the big man in her arms, stroking his back as he cried silent tears of pain.

I was numb. Battered by their pain, I knew this wouldn't be the end for Arcadia and I. We would see each other again. But I still mourned the life she could have had.

"Please, please," Eli was beginning to sound more desperate, and I was glad that I didn't have Arcadia's soul with me right now. She'd be ruined seeing these three in that sort of pain and unable to soothe them.

The door opened and closed, and I ignored the sounds of nurses fussing around. I couldn't drag my eyes away from tragedy playing out before me.

Another nurse slammed into the room, the sound of the door hitting the wall making me jump and whirl around to look at her, my irrational anger flaring to life. We wanted to mourn in peace, how hard was it to give us just one moment?

The newcomers cheeks were flushed red and she was out of breath. "A heart has just become available, right in this hospital. We have to get her to theater now." She stopped what she was doing and just blinked at us, wide eyed. "It's a miracle."

I raced out into the hall, and watched a man wrapped in the world's ugliest poncho walking down the hall, completely unseen by the humans around him. He raised a hand in greeting, but he never turned around and met my eye.

My smile threatened to crack my face in two.

CHAPTER FORTY

"Would you please take it easy," Sam chastised as he took the basket from Arcadia's hands.

"Nope," she said, rising up on her toes to kiss her Viking.

I puked a little in my mouth at the sweetness. Cady looked at me and laughed. "The expression on your face is priceless. It's not that bad."

I toed the corner of the picnic rug until it was straight.

"It's not that bad, maybe once or twice, but seriously you lot totally overkill it with the public displays of affection. It's so sweet it's giving me cavities."

Arcadia snorted. "Says the person who had sex in the middle of the town square in an Italian village. I shudder to think where else you have gotten it on in the public eye."

She eased down on the ground, and I passed her Estrella. It had been two months since her surgery aka the longest seventeen hours in history aka my new version of hell. But she lived.

I don't know if it was Eli ditching his pride and begging that changed the Big Guy's mind, or if it was the fact that he was the last redemption, or if the Father was just having a good day. I didn't care. The important thing was that she lived.

A month after she came home from hospital, they decided to move from SoHo to a massive estate outside of Boston. The rural lifestyle wasn't as fun as New York in my opinion, but hey, if this was what made them happy, so be it. And it was closer to Clary and all those crazy Mulligans. Besides, the kids probably needed a yard.

I watched Adnan race around the yard on his new prosthetic. It was state of the art, of course, and the kid adapted to it since day one. He was being chased around the yard by Nazir and his therapy dog, Muffin. When Tolliver had suggested a PTSD support animal, I'd been all for a support chicken. But apparently a Labrador was a better fit for a twelve year old boy. I'd only pouted for a week.

I looked over and caught Arcadia staring at me. Again. "What?"

"I just can't get used to you sitting beside me. Speaking out loud. Sometimes in the middle of the night, I wake up to tell you about this really weird dream I had and I'm halfway through explaining when I realize you aren't in my head anymore." She smiled, but it was tinged with sadness. I knew the feeling; it had been a little like losing a limb there for a while. I looked at Adnan. Probably the wrong turn of phrase.

But I wasn't going to tell Cady that. "Toughen up. It's not that bad."

She laughed. "It has been nice having sex without the peanut gallery, though."

I wanted my eyebrows. "I've seen all your guys naked. There ain't any peanuts in those galleries."

Tolliver came over, Hope in his arms. He passed her to me and sat down behind Arcadia, his whole big body wrapped around hers. Ugh, more PDA's.

"Is Luc coming?" he asked, and I shrugged.

"I think so. A coup broke out in one of those tiny Middle Eastern countries so he's pretty busy, but he said he'd pop in. Gus and Memphis should be here soon though."

Oz walked over to us too, carrying a cooler. He handed me a beer. "Like this party wasn't a big enough sausage fest." He clinked his bottle to mine and sat on the cooler. It groaned a little ominously.

Arcadia and the guys were having a housewarming potluck. I was just here to see the fireworks when the strict Roman Catholic Mulligans realized that Arcadia was a partner to all seven of the guys.

Arcadia was staring again.

"I love you, Acerezeal, you know that right? Even though we are two people now, you are still a part of me."

I turned away from her earnest face and nodded, blinking rapidly because I had an eyelash or a twig or something in my eye.

"You too," I squeezed out. Apparently near death experiences made people prone to throwing deep and meaningful things out there in normal conversations.

Oz slapped me on the back. "Luc's here. Saved by the Devil."

I watched Luc stop and talk to the boys halfway across the lawn. He made a football appear in his hand and the kids whooped with joy and the dog barked happily. That ball was gonna last two seconds if Muffin got hold of it.

"You know what I think has been the most romantic thing about this whole experience?" Arcadia asked, and apparently it was rhetorical because she just barreled along anyway. "This whole thing, from start to finish, has been your love story, Ace. Your happily ever after. A fairytale about how far a man would go for the woman he loves. It's beautiful," her eyes misted up and I resisted the urge to roll mine. No more Nicholas Sparks books for her. I was putting a blanket ban on it.

I'd never admit it to her, but she was right. Through all the pain, the arduous journey to get the guys redeemed and then to save Arcadia, Luc's love for me was a force in the background, unwavering in its intensity. I laid Hope on the picnic rug and stood, walking toward my heart. He met me halfway.

"Good afternoon, my love. You look beautiful, as always."

I turned my face up for a kiss and he was all too glad to supply me with a one that made my toes curl.

"I love you, Luc."

"I know, Acerezeal. I love you too, with a force strong enough to tear the heavens apart."

Sheer happiness, finally, made my face stretch wide in a smile.

My smile turned mischievous though, when Grand-mammy Mulligan, eighty year old Matriarch and all around Irish Catholic badass, arrived and was mentally doing a headcount of the ratio of men to women. This was gonna be good.

Let the fireworks begin.

EPILOGUE

21 YEARS LATER

I t wasn't often that I got to mix work and pleasure, but today was one of those days. I stood in the back of the large auditorium, invisible to the world leaders that filled its seats, but not to the woman on stage. She saw me all too well, and her smile lit up my heart like a Christmas tree. She looked beautiful on the stage, her deep red hair ethereal under the lights pointing at the lectern. Hope. That tiny baby had turned into this beautiful, strong, intelligent woman, and I couldn't be more proud.

I gave her a thumbs up as she began to speak.

"Ladies and gentlemen, esteemed leaders of the world, I thank you for inviting me to speak at the World Humanitarian Summit. I know that you wished for my father to speak here tonight, but unfortunately they are caught up in Hurricane Katherine in Polynesia, where they have been building clinics and schools in the poorer island nations. But as the director of the NRH foundation for the United States, I can assure you I am more than qualified to speak in his place.

"As many of you know, NRH started as seven people with an idealistic idea to use their wealth to better the lives of others by dressing as ninjas. Hence the Ninja Robin Hood name." There was a muted laugh from around the room. "Since then, NRH has spread across the globe, teams of people working on the ground to better the services and facilities available to all. My parents were the first team on the ground, and they will continue to do so until they can do no more. Luckily, between them all, they make quite the team." There was another small chuckle from those who knew the story, who'd read the tabloids that 'exposed' them as a polyamorous group. Hope continued.

"Our mission is to globally raise the level of health-care and education to a standardized level, so everyone can have an equal opportunity to survive and thrive. And whilst we are doing that on the ground, we also want to do that on a much larger scale. We want to eradicate viral diseases that can cripple whole countries. The pharma-ceutical wing of NRH has purchased half a dozen patents to crippling diseases such as the vaccines for aids, hepatitis and the omega virus. We have also purchased the patents for the new cancer cure for twenty-seven billion dollars and intend to distribute it at cost price plus 1%. Our working model is that if it pays itself off before the patent lapses, which is unlikely, we will make the patent public for free use by other companies. We do not want to make money, we want to eradicate needless deaths."

Hope continued, and I dragged my eyes away as I felt a presence beside me. I almost started when I realized it was Michael. I nodded my head in respect. "Archangel. What brings you here?"

He smiled at me, in that beatific way, but his eyes stayed on the stage. "She speaks beautifully, does she not?"

I nodded warily. Michael laughed. "Don't look so worried, Acerezeal. I am just touching base? That's the human phrase, no?"

I nodded again. "How are they doing? Your Arcadia and her redeemed Sins?"

"They are well, bettering humanity as Hope said. Banging like monkeys in their down time. Seriously, if they don't cut it out, one of them will have a heart attack."

Michael frowned at me disapprovingly, but he couldn't hide the shine of amusement in his eyes.

"I am glad it all worked out in the end. There has been too much animosity through the ages and it has led to attitudes like Uriel and Azriel's, though I think Azriel may be tested soon." He looked back at the stage, and I didn't blame him. Hope looked magnetic. Michael continued. "Lucifer, for all his faults, fell because he cared too much not to question the Father. There is so much heart in him, more than he gives himself credit for. But there's a faction that believe in following the Father's word to the letter, and then twist it to go down the path of near cruelty," Michael sighed.

"Uriel is an asshole," I agreed. Being the top Archangel had to suck. "You'll bring him to heel,

Archangel. Without more of us falling. Though, if they do fall, I promise that Lucifer will squash the cruelty right out of them. Fire meeting fire, and all that."

We watched the crowd, their attention transfixed on the stage also. Hope definitely had a little extra oomph that wasn't entirely human. Her eyes glanced our way and she startled slightly at the sight of Michael. He smiled and gave her a wave and she raised her hand back, before continuing her speech, the consummate professional.

"I fear she'll be tested too, soon enough," he murmured. "And the other twin? Estrella?"

"She joined the Boston Police Department," I smiled, still remembering the Mulligans horror that she was going to become a cop. Hilarious.

"Aiding humanity too," Michael nodded. He placed a hand on my shoulder. "You did a good thing all those years ago."

"I know."

As the rapturous applause echoed at the end of Hope's speech, I realized that Gusion had been right all those years ago. They had changed everything. They'd certainly changed me.

CONTINUE ON FOR A SNEAK
PREVIEW OF THE UNREPENTANT

HELL'S REDEMPTION BOOK 2

ACKNOWLEDGMENTS

This book has spanned so many different facets of my author journey, it's hard to know who to thank first. Actually, it isn't that hard. Thank you to my mother, who has unwaveringly supported me through my journey as an author with good humour and patience. It hasn't always been easy. Thank you for not laughing when I said I wanted to be a writer, for reading every novel, and never mentioning the smutty bits. I appreciate you more than you can imagine.

Secondly, I'd like to thank Kitty, who has been so very supportive and an amazing writing buddy for so many years. I gave her the first part of this book in chapter increments, and her demands for more are what kept me going. I'd also like to thank Vicky, who has gently chastised me about my social media presence and marketing, who beta read and devoured all my novels, and who has been such a great support.

I'd like to thank the readers who reached out of their own accord and somehow became integral to my journey as a Reverse Harem writer. Author Kelly A. Walker (seriously, she is amazing, check her out) who started shouting loud and proud about The Redeemable when it was first released, recommending it to anyone who would listen. She still does this and I owe her such a great debt of gratitude.

Later in the game, I was social media stalked by an amazing woman named Tash, who became a great friend and a wonderful support. She couldn't help me enough, and loves my characters as much as I do! Her cover work is amazing and I cannot recommend her business, DAZED Designs enough. I also want to thank Tegan, who kind of got hijacked into being a beta reader, but became a friend. She is the cool rationality to my craziness, and gives great advice. Plus her meme game is on-point!

Lastly, I want to thank the readers, those of you who mention The Redeemable on FB posts, who leave reviews, who reach out to tell me that they loved the series. You guys are the best. Without you, I would have quit years ago. Never underestimate how important you are to each and every indie writer. THANK YOU!

ABOUT THE AUTHOR

Grace McGinty is eclectic. She has worked as a chocolatier, a librarian, a forensic accountant and finally a writer. Like her professional career, the genres she writes are also eclectic. She writes romance, reverse harem romance, fantasy, contemporary young adult and new adult books.

She lives in rural Australia with her crazy family, an entire menagerie of pets, and will one day be crushed by her giant piles of books that litter every room.

The story of Arcadia and her Sins might be over, but Hope and Estrella's stories are just beginning. Continue on to read the first chapter in Estrella's novel, *The Unrepentant*.

THE UNREPENTANT

CHAPTER ONE

Estrella

The force of Hope's scream in my head knocked my legs out from under me. My 'World's #1 Cop' mug slipped from my hands and fell to the ground, shattering. My head cracked against the old linoleum floors, and the world went grey.

Hope! I screamed back, but all I got was complete silence. I mentally scrambled around for my bond with my twin, but although I could feel she was still alive, I was getting nothing back. I jumped to my feet, slipping into the supply closet at the back of the precinct, thankful that no one else had arrived this early. Being an overachiever had its perks.

Luc! I shouted. *Luc, I need you! I'm at work, supply closet in the back of the building near my desk, fourth door on the right.* I could feel my call connect with Luc, and an instant later, the door to the supply closet was yanked open by no one; at least that's how it would appear to normal humans. But I was not normal. I saw the two huge Fallen Angels that stood there. One was Lucifer, Lord of Hell, and the other was one of the Princes of Hell, Mephistopheles. They jammed their way into the supply closet with me, and I was soon crushed in by a solid wall of muscle and massive wings.

"What is wrong, Estrella?" Luc's voice held a sense of urgency.

"Something is wrong with Hope. She screamed and our connection went dead." Luc's body tensed against mine.

"Last location?"

"UN offices in Geneva." Luc grabbed my arm and we sifted, and that rollercoaster feeling swirled up in my guts like always.

Sifting was like teleporting, but with a greater chance that all your parts won't mesh back together properly at the end. It was the worst and left me incapacitated for about ten seconds after we landed. Didn't sound like much time, but I'd learned even seconds counted.

We landed on the footpath beside the conference center, and I sucked in a gasp, cold dread settling over my body. Hope's bodyguard, JJ, lay dead on the pavement, two shots in his chest and one between his eyes. He'd been professionally executed. I scrambled for my connection to Hope again, but it was still blank. My fear threatened to choke me.

Luc looked down at me. "Be calm. You would know if she were dead." I nodded stiffly and tried to slip back into cop mode. I looked at the scene with cool professionalism.

JJ's gun was still holstered, which told me that it was a surprise attack. Hope's tote bag lay beside him, contents spread across the ground, as well as her purse and the latest model cellphone. She was a bit of a tech geek, not that she would admit it. The fact that it was all still here told me that it hadn't been a random act of violence. As if JJ's wounds hadn't been enough. The fact the stuff was still here and the place wasn't crawling with cops told me that it hadn't happened that long ago. Skid marks led away from curb.

"Luc," Memphis called. I turned to where he stood beside a small row of box hedges. I looked over, holding my breath, prepared for it to be Hope's dead body despite Luc's confidence that she was alive.

I felt like an asshole when I was overcome with relief that the bodies of two valet's lay crumpled there, like discarded trash blown into the shrub.

"They masqueraded as valets," I whispered to myself, though Luc was nodding in agreement.

I pulled my phone from my pocket, scanning through my messages to the group chat we had with our parents. Hope had sent a picture of her rental Prius to taunt Tolliver. He hated her Prius at home, and she loved to tease him about his car snobbery. I clicked #3 on my speed dial but there was no answer. Dammit. Stupid Hurricane. I needed my Dad right now. I called #4 on my speed dial instead. It answered on the second ring.

"Charlie speaking," a bored voice said on the other line.

"Charlie, it's me. I need your help. I need you to track Hope's rental Prius, license plate number VK-96-KT. It should have a LoJack. She's been taken." I cursed myself when my voice wavered, but Charlie wouldn't care.

"Fuck. Fuck. Hang on, Rella." I could hear his fingers flying across his keyboard. Charlie was a Mulligan, of the Mulligan mob, and he was their resident tech expert. Everything he knew though, he learned from Oz, my dad. Mom was not amused when she found out, though the Mulligan's had been over the moon. "It's on a stretch of road about three miles away; sending you the coordinates now. Looks like it's been dumped." He hesitated. "Rella, can you, you know?"

We'd grown up with Charlie. He knew Hope and I had a bond; that we could communicate telepathically and feel the twin bond no matter where we were in the world. It defied explanation, but it was hard to hide as a kid.

"She's not dead, Charlie. I can't reach her, but she's not dead." With that I hung up. I showed Luc the coordinates, and he sifted us there. My heart pounded as we walked toward the car. I knew how Schrödinger's cat felt now. If I didn't look in there, I could hold onto the belief that she may still be alive. Luc strode ahead and looked into the backseat. He pulled open the boot using brute force.

"She's not here." I let out the breath that was burning my lungs. I looked through the car, careful to not touch anything for the lab guys. Did Geneva have lab guys? Fuck it, I didn't care. There was blood on the backseat, and my heart lurched. She was injured, but I knew that. She'd have to be unconscious for me not to be able to feel her.

"You guys getting anything?" The Fallen had abilities, especially Luc. I didn't know what they were really, other than being piss-your-pants scary. Memphis looked at me, his eyes swirling with anger.

"They left an imprint of evil. Death. Bloodlust."

"Can you tell where they were going?" Memphis shook his head, and Luc just stared at the car intently. Any more intently and the Prius would set on fire.

"Nothing," Luc growled out.

I looked at my watch. Thirty-seven minutes from her abduction. The golden hour was winding up fast, and we had nothing.

Wake up, Hope. Goddammit, wake the fuck up! I shouted down our link. I yelled it over and over, until I felt her stutter awake. And then I let out a scream and fell to my knees. She was in so much pain. Luc was beside me, dragging me to my feet.

"North, about five miles. Warehouse." I sent him a mental image. Luc's face got even scarier, and he sifted us to the location that only I could feel.

Three sifts in quick succession had left me disorientated, and I barely held my feet and my lunch when we landed

"Azriel, no!" Memphis yelled, and I spun, my vision whirling with me like I was drunk. I saw an angel sift out of the room, taking all my oxygen with him.

Hope was chained to a pipe, her body naked and severely beaten. She made a wracking, gasping noise, and blood pooled on her lips. I moved inhumanly fast to her side. I whispered reassurances, though I didn't comprehend what was coming out of my mouth. I tugged at her chains, but then Luc was there, pulling them apart like string, and Memphis was catching her frail body in his arms as if she were made of the finest porcelain. Then Memphis disappeared. "What the fuck? Luc, where did they go? She needs a hospital!" Luc looked pissed, but he managed to mutter. "Memphis will not let her die. Let's go see if there's anyone here that knows death stalks them."

I followed behind him as he strode out of the basement, and up into the main room of what appeared to be mechanic workshop. A man leaned against the wall beside the door, and all the color left his face as he took in the Devil.

"Who are you?" Luc roared, and the guy legit pissed himself. I got it. I was tempted to do the same, lucky I did my Kegels. "Answer me!"

"Paul-l-o Varucci," the guy stuttered out.

"Why did you take the girl?"

"I didn't." Tears were beginning to stream down his face.

"Do not lie to me." Luc's voice went whisper soft, and it was even scarier than his yell.

"I just get paid to guard the door," the man cried, as blood began to trickle from his ears. "By the Estonians." The last word was a whisper.

Luc leaned forward, putting his hands on both sides

of the guy's head, and it looked almost loving. He leaned real close, and I thought he might give him the kiss of Judas. Instead he whispered, "You will know no rest in my domain," and ripped the man's head from his shoulders.

I struggled to stop myself from throwing up, but I didn't want to leave any evidence that I'd been at the crime scene. It was a close-run thing though.

Luc cocked his head. "There's no one else here. Let's go."

He wrapped an arm around my waist, and I stared up at him. "I'm going to kill them all, you know."

He nodded, and there was a glint in his eye that may have been pride. He sifted us one more time, and I clung to his shirt until my land legs came back. Then I gaped. I stood in the presence of an Archangel. I couldn't be sure which one, but there was no doubt in my mind *what* he was. Luc smiled and wrapped his arms around the Archangel. "Hello, old friend."

I was more shocked by Luc hugging someone than I was about him ripping the head of that guy. I was so mesmerized by the brilliant light coming from the Archangel that I missed all the conversation, unable to drag my eyes from his face.

Memphis handed Hope to Luc, and Hope looked less like death. They sifted away, and I looked back at the Archangel. He smiled at me, and cupped a hand around my temple, his warmth flooding my mind.

"Don't let it consume you, sweet one," he said, and I resisted the urge to turn my face into his hand. I couldn't make my tongue work, and Memphis just rolled his eyes and sifted us away, the Archangel's laughter trailing us.

We were back in Hope's Manhattan apartment, and she connected with me straight away.

I could read Raphael.

I jolted with shock. So that was who the Archangel was. Still, I gave her the same warning I always did. Keep it quiet, don't tell anyone. It was more important than ever now. Her empath abilities were our lifelong secret, though I suspected everyone knew, and kept it a very close secret. We never spoke about it. It was too much of a threat.

After Luc laid her on the bed, I wrapped the sheet around her and then I laid down beside her, wrapping my body around her small broken one.

I'm okay now, she whispered in my mind. I let the tension leave my body. When Mom and Eli turned up with Ace, I knew that it would all be okay.

But I knew what I had to do.

Get it here: www.books2read.com/Unrepentant